Quintin Jardine was born once upon a time in the West – of Scotland rather than America, but still he grew to manhood as a massive Sergio Leone fan. On the way there he was educated, against his will, in Glasgow, where he ditched a token attempt to study law for more interesting careers in journalism, government propaganda, and political spin-doctoring. After a close call with the Brighton Bomb in 1984, he moved into the even riskier world of media relations consultancy, before realising that all along he had been training to become a crime writer. Now, more than forty novels later, he never looks back.

Along the way he has created/acquired an extended family in Scotland and Spain. Everything he does is for them. He can be tracked down through his website: www.quintinjardine.com.

Praise for Quintin Jardine:

'Well constructed, fast-paced, Jardine's narrative has many an ingenious twist and turn' *Observer*

'A triumph. I am first in the queue for the next one' *Scotland on Sunday*

'The perfect mix for a highly charged, fast-moving crime thriller' *The Herald*

'Remarkably assured, raw-boned, a *tour de force*' *New York Times*

'"Revenge is a dish best eaten cold," as the old proverb goes. Jardine's dish is chilled to perfection with just the right touch of bitterness' *Globe and Mail*

'[Quintin Jardine] sells more crime fiction in Scotland than John Grisham and people queue around the block to buy his latest book' *The Australian*

'Very engaging as well as ingenious, and the unravelling of the mystery is excellently done' Allan Massie, *Scotsman*

'There is a whole world here, the tense narratives all come to the boil at the same time in a spectacular climax' *Shots* magazine

'Engrossing, believable characters . . . captures Edinburgh beautifully . . It all adds up to a very good read' *Edinburgh Evening News*

Quintin Jardine

LAST RESORT

headline

First published in 2015 by
HEADLINE PUBLISHING GROUP

First published in paperback in 2016 by
HEADLINE PUBLISHING GROUP

1

Cataloguing in Publication Data is available from the British Library

ISBN 978 1 4722 0564 3

Typeset in Electra by Avon DataSet Ltd, Bidford-on-Avon, Warwickshire

Printed in the UK by CPI Group (UK) Ltd, Croydon, CR0 4YY

HEADLINE PUBLISHING GROUP
An Hachette UK Company
Carmelite House
50 Victoria Embankment
London EC4Y 0DZ

www.headline.co.uk
www.hachette.co.uk

This one's for Martin Fletcher, who keeps Skinner honest.
Cheers, mate.

One

When the call came, the one that put me back in place as a functioning human being, I was, not to put too fine a point on it, really screwed up inside my head.

I had begun a year that seemed to be full of promise, but if I'd been granted foresight of what most of those promises actually were, I'd probably have stayed in bed on the first of January and waited out the next twelve months.

I'd have been on my own, though; even then I should have been able to spot the fault lines in my unstable marriage to Aileen de Marco.

When our relationship became public knowledge, a smart-arse broadsheet journalist wrote a flowery piece about the attraction of unlike poles, the policeman and the politician, the authoritarian (me) and the libertarian (her), and topped the allegorical nonsense off by labelling us 'Scotland's most magnetic couple'.

I fell for some of that for a while, until the day when I realised that it was the diametric opposite of the truth. Aileen and I were both leaders in our chosen professions and we were both (although I'd have denied it) ambitious. However, she was as authoritarian as me, and neither of us had any trace of compromise in our nature.

1

When we found ourselves on a collision course over the future of the Scottish police service, and its implications for my personal position, with Aileen determined to ensure that her side of the argument came out on top, and having the power to make that happen . . . well, to complete that journo's analogy, the like poles that, in reality, we had been all along, repelled each other, as they always do.

Everything fell apart after that, very quickly indeed; not only my marriage, but my job, my career, my vision of the future; they were all cut from under me.

The one saving grace . . . and that's something of a pun, given her family name . . . was the return of Sarah, the wife I should never have left in the first place, and the cautious rebuilding of our relationship. She and I have only two things in common: we love each other and we love our kids. She's good for me and I know now that I was lost in the time we were apart.

When disaster followed disaster in my life, and everything reached its grim conclusion, it was only Sarah who kept me on the rails. I'd have sat brooding indefinitely in the house, over the offer of an unspecified role at an unspecified rank, or giving my lawyer a hard time as he tried to sort out the alternative, the terms of my departure from the police service. Indeed that's what I did for a few weeks until she had enough of it.

'Bob,' she said, plucking what would have been my fourth Corona of that Saturday evening if she'd let me uncap the bottle, 'this will not do. I know how shitty the last few months have been, but not even you can undo an Act of Parliament.

'I know you're having difficulty with the fact that you're not Chief Constable Skinner any more, but it is not the worst thing that's ever happened.

'You've given thirty years of public service. Now it's somebody else's turn to catch the bad guys, to clear up after the pubs close, and to keep the traffic flowing smoothly, and those people are more than capable, since your generation has trained most of them. There was a police force before you and there will still be one without you, if you decide to go completely. What you have to work out is what you might be without it.'

I felt the corners of my mouth turn down as I watched her put the beer back in the fridge. 'I might be nothing,' I countered, mournfully. 'Being a policeman might be the only shot I had in my locker.'

'Rubbish!' she laughed. 'You've already been offered three non-executive directorships.'

'I don't do non-executive anything, love. You know that.'

'Then you could write.'

'About what?'

'Your career.'

'I'd have to leave too much out. A lot of my files are closed.'

'You could try fiction,' she suggested. 'You could jump on the Tartan Noir bandwagon.'

'Christ,' I complained, 'can't we find a word in our own language to describe a Scottish institution, rather than nicking one from the bloody French?

'If I did that, love,' I pointed out, '. . . although I doubt that I have the talent . . . everyone would be convinced that it was all Skinner's Casebook thinly disguised. There could be all sorts of legal problems . . . and besides, I don't have the patience.'

'Then you could teach.' She pointed an authoritative figure at me. 'I'll bet that if you put the word out that you fancied a university chair, you'd have half a dozen offers.'

'It's easy for you to say that, my dear,' I countered. 'You're a consultant forensic pathologist; you can do your job and teach it at the same time. Mine wasn't like that. What would my lectures be about? Police procedure? Criminal investigation?

'Sure I could do that stuff, but what I couldn't teach, probably couldn't even explain, is the instinct that separates an efficient officer from an exceptional one; the reason why one patrol officer in twenty will know when it's time to kick a door in, then finds a sick old person or an abused child behind it, or why only a single detective in a squad might be able to look at all the known facts of a case, understand logically what must be hiding behind them, and then back his own judgement. I wouldn't be interested in turning out clone cops, only risk-takers.'

She smiled, challenging. 'Well?'

'There would be no market for them. Risk only works when it's rewarded.'

'It worked for you.'

'God knows how.' I heard myself chuckle. 'When I think of some of the chances I took . . .'

'Then take another.'

'How?'

She took a few moments to frame her reply. 'Get the hell out of here for a while. The longer you sit around here sulking, the likelier it is that you'll wind up as a middle-aged house husband with a shrinking golf handicap and an expanding waistline.

'Already you're drinking more beer than you should, and your coffee addiction's come back. Is that what you want from the rest of your life?'

'Probably not,' I conceded, 'although I like the bit about the golf handicap.'

'You can play golf anywhere, and you need to do it somewhere else for a while. It's less than a month to Christmas; take yourself off to the Spanish house for some of that time. You'll be able to look at the future more objectively out there.'

'I'm needed here,' I protested. 'My kids need me . . . all of them.'

'They can do without you for a couple of weeks . . . they've had to in the past. Go away, Bob, and look forward, not back.

'You're in a great position. With the pension you'll have kicking in if you decide to leave the force, you'll be financially fireproof for life. The world's the shellfish of your choice, since I know you don't like oysters. Go: work it out.'

Two

These days I have a simple rule: what Sarah wants, Sarah gets. Two days later, on the following Monday, I was on a flight to Barcelona, with a one-way ticket.

I hadn't expected to be heading back to L'Escala so soon; my last trip to my Spanish hometown had ended calamitously, and that bad memory was still burned into my brain.

The flight touched down late in the evening, so I spent the night in a hotel above Estacio Sants, the main railway station in Barcelona, and took a train north after breakfast.

The house was cold when I arrived on Tuesday morning, just before midday. Anyone who believes that the north of Spain enjoys a year-long summer has never been there in the winter. My priority task was firing up the heating; that done, I unpacked, and then made the place habitable by moving the garden furniture out of the living room. By the time everything was as I wanted it, I was experiencing lunchtime symptoms, so I left a message on Sarah's phone to let her know that I'd got there okay, and strolled down into the old town, the heart of L'Escala.

Although I've had a home there for all of twenty years, I had never visited Spain in early December. I'd expected the place to be quiet, with half the cafes and restaurants closed for holidays or maintenance, so I was surprised by the buzz around the little beach.

The tourists were gone, but the expatriate population was out in numbers. The languages that caught my ear as I sat at a pavement table in one of the few bars that caught the watery early afternoon sun were mainly English and French. If it hadn't been for a trio of Spanish business people . . . the two guys in the group were wearing ties, and that's a real giveaway . . . I might have been the youngest person there.

As I leaned back in my chair and looked across the bay, watching the waves lapping against the rock they call El Cargol, the snail, I was seized by the curious notion . . . erroneously, as I was to discover very soon . . . that I was an unseen observer of my surroundings, encased in an invisibility bubble.

It didn't take me long to rationalise the feeling: I was in the midst of a crowd of people and nobody, not one person, recognised me.

I've never regarded myself as a celebrity, but in recent years I've been forced to recognise that as a chief constable I was a public figure. Even before that, when I was involved in hands-on criminal investigation, my image featured regularly on television and in the press. I was used to heads turning when I walked into a room, and to registering the expressions of people as they clocked me. (You can tell a lot from that first glance.)

I smiled as I ordered a beer, a couple of tapas, and a long *flauta* sandwich. As the waiter departed, I logged my iPhone on to the house wi-fi, and checked my emails. Apart from my daily newspapers, I had three. One was from Gullane Golf Club, setting out its programme for Christmas and New Year, the second was from Mitchell Laidlaw, my lawyer, and the third was from Neil McIlhenney, on his personal account rather than his Metropolitan Police address.

I opened that first, and read. *'Thanks for the good wishes,'* he began. I'd left him a voice message the day before congratulating him on his promotion to Commander.

It's bloody ridiculous that I'm still climbing the ladder while you might be jumping off it, given that I'd probably never have made it past DS if not for you. Good luck to Andy as the first head of Police Scotland, and to Maggie as his deputy, but we're all sorry that you might not be there. If you fancy a complete change of scene, there are whispers of an assistant commissioner vacancy down here, one that would suit you down to the ground.

I smiled as I closed the message. Those whispers had reached my ears, straight from the mouth of the Met Commissioner herself, who'd called me to sound me out. I declined as politely as I could; a few years ago I was encouraged to apply for the job that she holds now, but a London move has never held any interest for me.

Neil was right. A large part of me did indeed want to jump off that damned ladder, for a whole raft of reasons, some professional, others personal; the latter included one that had made me judge my position to be untenable. Better to leave it to the next generation, I'd been thinking, even if launching myself into the unknown was a daunting prospect.

I was a cop in limbo; officially I was still on the strength, but the force that I'd led had disappeared in the creation of the new unified service. I was on sabbatical; the PR people had said that the Police Authority was looking at possible roles for me in the new service.

That was true, but its chief executive had come up with nothing of any interest to me. I had made noises about wanting out, but the authority was reluctant to negotiate a severance package, and I was equally reluctant to go down the tribunal route. Also I was unsure.

From my first day in the service, there had been certainty in my professional life. If I did cut the cord, irrevocably, that would be gone; deep in my heart I wasn't sure I could cope without it.

I knew that was what Mitchell Laidlaw's email would be about, another offer of a sinecure job . . . the last one had been head of strategic planning, whatever the hell that means, and I'd laughed it out of court. I was about to open the message when my phone sang its song, letting me off the hook for the moment.

I glanced at the caller's number, but it told me nothing. However I did recognise it as a Spanish mobile, by its format. I frowned; that was a puzzle. Nobody had known I was heading for L'Escala and there had been no time for word of my arrival to have spread around my few friends in the town. I came close to deciding it was a marketing cold call and hitting the red spot, but my curiosity overcame me. I took the call, answering with my usual simple grunt of, 'Yes?'

'Bob?'

The voice in my ear was deep and mellow and although it had been a while since I'd heard it, I recognised it at once. 'Xavi,' I exclaimed.

'The same,' the caller agreed. 'How are you?'

'Personally, I'm okay,' I replied. 'Professionally, I'm fucked.'

Xavier Aislado has been a friend of mine for around twenty-five years. For the first few of those, ours was a business relationship . . . Xavi the journalist, Bob the cop, it had to be that way . . . but somewhere along the line we'd come to be friends.

He was born in Edinburgh, into a family of refugees from the Spanish Civil War; they had done well in business, and the young Xavi had never wanted for anything, other than the love of his parents.

After a brief career as a pro footballer was cut short by injury, he found a job on a tired, rickety old Scottish broadsheet called the *Saltire*. He proved himself to be a natural journalist, and breathed new life into the place. It's no exaggeration to say that he was almost entirely responsible for turning it into one of Scotland's leading newspapers.

Eventually, his input was more than simply editorial. When the title fell into the hands of a business scoundrel whose mismanagement and crookedness brought it perilously close to liquidation, Xavi engineered its purchase by a media group that his half-brother Joe had founded on his return to Spain after Franco's death.

While Xavi's professional life was outstanding, his private life was an even bigger disaster than mine. After his marriage ended in a horrible bereavement that would have broken most men, he focused for years on nothing but work. He withdrew from the few friends he had, me included; any contact we had was by telephone, never face to face.

His isolation from social Edinburgh did the *Saltire* no harm, it must be said. He was able to devote his entire life to being its managing editor, driving it on until it had left all its rivals in its wake.

Its circulation continued to climb as those of other papers fell, so it came as a surprise when, without a word of warning, Xavi removed himself from our midst and joined Joe on his estate in the hills above Girona, leaving his life's work in the hands of June Crampsey, his sister from his mother's second marriage.

I couldn't remember when last I'd seen him, but I doubt that it was this century.

'How did you get this number?' I asked him. (It's known only by my inner circle of friends and family.)

'Why?' he chuckled. 'Is it on the state secret list?'

'Of course not. I'm just curious, that's all.'

'Don't worry, I'll forget it.'

'Don't be daft,' I told him. 'Add it to your contacts.'

'Thank you,' he said. 'As it happens, your daughter shared it with me. None of your old colleagues were forthcoming, so I called your Alex. June told me where I could find her. You must have spoken kindly of me, for she passed it on, once she'd satisfied herself of my bona fides, by confirming with June that I was who I said I was.'

'Did she tell you where I was?'

'That she did not share,' he admitted.

'I wouldn't have minded that either,' I said, pausing as lunch arrived at my table. 'So, my friend, good as it is to hear from you after all this time, you'll understand me wondering why you're calling me.'

'I've been following your story,' he replied, 'trying to work out why you seem to have walked out on your career, just as it was about to reach its zenith.'

'You're not being a journo, are you, Xavi?' I asked. I'd never made a public statement about my decision not to compete for the post of chief constable of the new nationwide Police Scotland force.

'Of course not, I'm just a curious and concerned friend.'

'In that case, if you look at your own paper's back issues you'll find that I made it pretty clear a few months ago that I thought the politicians had got it wrong over police unification.'

'I don't have to look up anything,' he said. 'I remember the piece you gave us. And then your marriage broke up, and everyone, me included, thought that your then wife's being on the other side of the argument had everything to do with that.'

'Not everything; there were other reasons. "Argument" is the wrong word, though. I wasn't for debating the issue with anyone; the interview I did with your June was a statement of my beliefs. Aileen knew what those were all along. She ignored me, and thought I'd have to fall in line when the change was forced through.'

'So did I. I always thought you were a pragmatist, and that once the decision was made you'd live with it.'

'Like I said . . .'

'Yes, there were other reasons,' he said, 'just as there's another reason for this call. I'd like to consult you.'

'Consult me?' I laughed. 'Do you think I'm Sherlock fucking Holmes?'

He chuckled in return. 'Nothing would surprise me about you. But I mean it, Bob. I have a situation and I need advice.'

'What kind of situation?'

'I can't say over the phone. It would have to be in person.'

'Where?'

'Anywhere you like. I'll come to Scotland if I have to.'

When he said that, I understood that it was serious. I knew from June Crampsey that Xavi had never been back to Edinburgh since the day he left his office in the *Saltire* building for the last time.

'You don't.' I held my phone up in the air for a few seconds then put it back to my ear. 'What did you hear?' I asked.

'Seagulls,' he replied, 'and someone speaking French, too loudly, in a Belgian accent. Does that mean you're not in Scotland?'

'I'm in L'Escala, chum. I got here less than two hours ago. At this moment I'm watching my *patatas bravas* cool down and the head disappear from my beer.'

'Then I'll come to you . . . if you're willing to talk to me, that is.'

'I am, but you can host me. Sarah says I need a complete change of scene, and I've never been to your place.'

'Great,' he exclaimed. 'When can you make it? I'll send a car to pick you up. Hell, listen to me! I'll come to fetch you myself.'

'There's no need for that,' I told him. 'I'll be on the road as soon as I've finished lunch; give me your address and I'll programme my satnav.'

'That's excellent, Bob. Bring an overnight bag; the very least I can do is put you up and give you a decent dinner.'

As we ended the call, I found myself buzzing and, to my surprise, grateful for Xavi's interruption, and his invitation. I'd only been in the house on the hill for a few minutes, but that was long enough for me to realise that the place was full of ghosts.

Three

As I paid my bill, a layer of cloud covered the sun, knocking the temperature down by about five degrees centigrade. It looked as if it wasn't about to go anywhere in a hurry, and I began to regret my casual decision to come out without a jacket.

I told the waiter not to bother about the change and stood up, keen to be on my way, but I hadn't gone ten paces before the corner of my eye caught a strange movement.

I stopped and looked around, over my shoulder. There was another cafe next to mine; it wasn't nearly as popular, with only two tables occupied. A young woman sat alone at one of them; she was holding a small Nikon pocket camera, and had a sheepish expression on her face.

'I thought it was you, Mr Skinner,' she said, in an accent that was almost as Scottish as mine, then snapped off another image as I frowned down at her. So much for my notion of anonymity.

'Okay,' I said, 'now you know for sure. I'm sorry I can't spend some time with a fellow Scot, Ms . . .'

'McDaniels; Carrie McDaniels.'

'. . . but I have to be somewhere.'

'That's too bad,' she replied. 'I didn't expect to find many

14

Scots here, in L'Escala.' She raised the camera and clicked again. 'Especially not one as famous as you.'

I felt my hackles rise and took a couple of paces towards her. 'Look, stop doing that,' I told her.

She frowned. 'Why?' she challenged. 'It's a free country. What are you going to do about it?'

I snatched the camera from her hand, flicked open the cover in its base and ejected the SD card.

Sudden anger flared in her eyes. 'Hey,' she yelled, 'you can't do that!'

I laughed as I laid the Nikon down in front of her. 'It's bloody obvious that I can,' I said, slipping my images into a trouser pocket.

As I did so I was aware of movement at the other occupied table. The two guys who had been sitting there were on their feet and heading towards me. One of them was holding a beer bottle, and his mate was reaching into his jacket.

Señor San Miguel reached me first, brandishing what he thought was his weapon. I jabbed two stiff fingers into his eyes, hard: welcome to the world of pain, chum. The other one had a flick-knife and looked ready to open it. Unfortunately for him he was left-handed, which meant that I didn't have to reach across him to grab his wrist and twist his arm, spinning him round and putting him in the 'come along' hold beloved of cops everywhere, then slamming his face into Carrie's tabletop.

'You just pulled a knife on me, son,' I murmured, then took weeks of frustration out on him with a short, sharp wrench that separated his shoulder and produced a satisfying scream. I took the blade from him, pocketed it and turned to have a further discussion with the first attacker, but he had recovered enough vision to spot the road out of town and was heading for it as fast as his legs could carry him.

15

A guy in a waiter's tunic was standing in the doorway, with a look on his face that contrived to be both fearful and quizzical at the same time. I caught his eye, shook my head, and called out, 'It's nothing. No problem.'

I glanced at the cafe where I'd eaten. Not unnaturally, the action next door had attracted attention. I frowned at them, collectively, and they went back to their beer and tapas.

Heavy Number Two was back in a chair, bleeding from the nose and moaning, holding on to his misshapen shoulder. He was dark-haired and brown-skinned, Moroccan, probably. 'You speak English?' I asked him.

He nodded, without looking at me.

'Okay, then understand this. If you go to the clinic along in Riells, they'll fix that for you. I don't have time to get involved with the police, but if I ever see you again, or your pal, I will hurt you far worse than the local medics can deal with. Go, now.'

He did as he'd been told, leaving me alone with Carrie. She was a lot less confident than she had been before. I sat at her table and took a closer look at her than I had before. I guessed that she was much closer to thirty than twenty. Although her hair was fair, it wasn't sun-bleached, and she was pale-skinned; two signs of someone who hadn't been in Spain for very long.

'You smell of two things, my dear,' I told her, over-confidently, 'duty-free perfume and journalist. Why are you here, and why the hell did you think you needed to hire those two clowns as protection?'

'They were supposed to be my interpreters,' she replied. 'My Spanish is non-existent. I met them in a bar last night; I only got here yesterday,' she added, in explanation. 'It was a weird wee place, but British-owned. The owner was friendly enough, so I told him I needed somebody to translate for me while I'm here.

Tony and Julio . . . that's those two . . . were drinking in there. They heard me, and they volunteered. That's to say, for a hundred euros a day each, they volunteered.'

'Did they indeed?' I laughed. 'I'll tell you one thing. However good their Spanish may be, their Arabic will be better.'

'But they've got Spanish names,' she protested.

'Not on their ID cards, they don't; you can be sure of that. Now, answer my other question. What are you up to?'

'I'm doing a travel piece for my paper,' she volunteered.

'That paper being . . . ?'

'Actually, it's an airline flight mag: it's a Belgian tour company called FlemAir.'

'You speak Flemish?'

'I write in English and they translate.'

'Well, Caroline,' I began.

'It's not Caroline,' she retorted, 'just Carrie.'

'Well, Carrie,' I continued, 'good luck to you, but don't go snapping any more strangers.'

'Fuck off!' she murmured. 'But give me my memory card back first,' she added.

I smiled at her pouting lip. 'No chance, lass. Put it down to experience, or on your expenses as my fee for saving you from those clowns. Sooner rather than later, you'd have been in bad trouble with them.'

I felt her eyes boring into me as I walked away, but I didn't look back. My unexpected exercise had made me forget about the gathering chill, but it reasserted itself pretty quickly and so I quickened my pace, to counteract it.

As I crested the hill called Puig Pedro, where my house is located, I took out my phone and scrolled though my stored numbers. Still on the march, I chose one and called it.

'DS Haddock,' a young voice announced, after two rings.

'Sauce,' I said. 'It's Bob Skinner. Are you free to speak?'

'Yes, sir, I'm clear. This is a surprise.'

'I'm sure it is. For me too in a way; it isn't a call I'd planned to make but I need some help, using channels that aren't open to me at the moment.'

'Then fire away, Chief.'

Young Harold Haddock, Sauce being his inevitable nickname, is one of my protégés, although Maggie Steele, my successor as chief constable in Edinburgh, has equal claim to him, having spotted his potential when he was a young PC in her nick. He's rewarded our faith in him by flourishing in the service and making detective sergeant as fast as I did.

He did have one close encounter with disaster in his climb up the ladder. He found himself a girlfriend named Cheeky McCullough, and fell head over heels in love. Unsurprisingly, her forename isn't how she was baptised. She was named Cameron, after her grandfather, a truth she wasn't keen to share with Sauce when they met.

That was understandable given that Grandpa's businesses, along with property, commercial and residential construction, and leisure, are said to include every criminal activity known to man, although he's never been convicted of anything. His closest calls were a murder charge, in which the crucial witnesses all vanished on the day of the trial, and a potential drugs prosecution that folded when the stuff vanished from a secure police store.

When Sauce found out, it almost broke the relationship, but it turned out to be stronger than that.

I could have called several other people looking for a favour, but I'd chosen Sauce because I knew he'd get it done with least fuss, and probably quickest. There was also the fact that he owed me one. Another chief constable might have forced him out of the service because of Cheeky, but I decided that he was too good to lose, and let him stay.

'I need a couple of things checked,' I said. 'First, is there a Belgian travel company called FlemAir? Second, if there is, has it commissioned a Scottish journalist named Carrie McDaniels to do a piece on Spain for its flight mag? Third, if there isn't, or there is and it hasn't, is there such a person and if so what's her story?'

'Can do, sir. What can you tell me about her?'

'Very little; she has fair hair, she's aged somewhere between twenty-five, if she doesn't look after herself, and thirty-two if she does. Carrie's her given name, not a shortened form, and she seems to be a Ms, not a Mrs. Likely she'll have been on a flight to Barcelona or possibly Girona within the last forty-eight hours.'

'Got all that,' Sauce confirmed. 'Are you going to tell me why you need this . . . just in case anyone asks?'

'I'm not even sure I do need it,' I confessed. 'The lady just crossed me, and I'd like to check that she is what she says.'

'And do you think she is?'

'Not for a second, lad. That might well be her name, but I'm doubtful about the rest.'

'Do I need to do anything else,' he asked, 'other than just check on her?'

'I don't think so. I've given her a talking-to, and that may be enough. Hopefully she'll get the message that I don't like being accosted, especially not by journos. When I deal with them, it's on my terms.'

'How do I get back to you, sir?' he asked. 'If she's in Spain . . .'

'Then obviously so am I,' I said. 'Just call this number.'

'It came up as withheld.'

'Of course, sorry.' Although Sauce was on my contact list, I wasn't on his. I recited it, from memory. 'I appreciate this,' I told him.

'Don't mention it.' I heard him chuckle. 'It feels bloody weird, though, you calling me on the quiet.'

'Hey, son,' I murmured, just as I arrived at my front gate, 'how do you think it feels for me?'

I ended the call, then went inside. The house was appreciably warmer than before, but it was more than creature comfort that lifted my spirits. Somehow, my call from Xavi, and my peculiar encounter just afterwards, had yanked me out of the torpor in which I had been languishing. I was beginning to feel myself again.

I went upstairs to pack a change of clothes for my overnight visit. As I did, I remembered Carrie's SD card. I took it from my pocket and held it between my fingers, ready to crush it. I would have done too, had my cop's curiosity not kicked in. Instead I went through to my small study and switched on my computer. When it had booted up I fed the storage device into the appropriate slot and then clicked on its icon to open it.

The card wasn't a new one; lines of thumbnail images filled the screen. I took my reading specs . . . I detest them, but I gave into the need for them around my fiftieth birthday . . . from the breast pocket of my shirt so that I could study them more closely.

The first three images showed the inside of a house; a young person's place, I guessed from the furniture, which was modern . . . IKEA or something very similar, from the open-plan layout, and from the clothing that was scattered on the back of a couch; a young woman's place, for all of the garments were feminine. I clicked on another and saw French doors with something beyond.

A few photos later, and I knew that they had been taken in a flat, in a modern block, with a small, enclosed terrace, from which the photographer, Carrie for certain, as she'd managed to catch an image of herself in a mirror, had taken some outside shots.

Some were panoramic, some were close-ups as if she had been testing the zoom capabilities of the camera, but all of them gave away her location. In each of them, there was the unmistakable shape of the one-time royal yacht, *Britannia*, in her permanent mooring beside the Ocean Terminal centre in Leith, Edinburgh's port.

'That's handy,' I murmured. 'Now I know where you live, Ms McDaniels, if needs be.'

I could have scrolled straight to the end to find and delete my own mugshots, but I was curious so I went on slowly. As the pictures progressed it was obvious that Carrie had been learning how to use the camera properly, as they became more skilled, sharper and better composed.

All of the early images were of places, street scenes in Edinburgh, a series in the Royal Botanical Gardens, which were actually pretty damn good, and crowds of shoppers in a covered mall that I recognised as Cameron Toll, not far from the new Royal Infirmary.

The naked man took me by surprise, as he had been taken also, from the expression on his face. He was on a beach, and she had caught him changing into swim trunks, behind a windbreak that would have given him a degree of privacy had she not been on the same side. She had caught him with his right foot in mid-air, toes pointing towards the costume that he held in both hands, leaning forward yet looking sideways, mouth open, half-smiling as he looked at her, showing bright eyes and perfect teeth.

Five more shots followed, catching him in the act of over-balancing and falling over, laughing as he rolled in the sand, then struggling into his garment as he sat there. The last was a normal pose, a more controlled grin half-turned towards the camera: close cropped dark hair, thick straight eyebrows, good muscle definition, perfect teeth, age thirty-something, maybe. He reminded me of someone; I studied him for a few moments then decided that he looked like the actor, Dominic West, and moved on.

The next few photographs were of Carrie herself. The man had pinched the camera and paid her back in kind, catching her sleeping on a beach towel, mouth open slightly, topless, then in a couple more as she woke, startled possibly by the click of the camera. She was comfortable with him, that was for sure.

I paused and checked the time on the top corner of the screen. I knew I should be going, for I couldn't be sure how long it would take me to find Xavi's place, but I pressed on, and into a surprise.

The next sequence of photographs showed the beach. I knew it very well: I live just above it. There were a few zoomed images across the Forth of the coastal villages that I knew to be Elie and Earlsferry, but the rest looked inland, up towards Gullane Hill, and at the properties there.

But not all of the properties: they were concentrated on one specific house; quite a few of them were close-ups. It was a modern two-storey building, set on quite a big plot. Overlooking the beach there was a bay-windowed structure that some might call a conservatory. But I don't; I call it the 'garden room'.

Yes, it was my house.

The last photograph had been taken at what must have been the camera's maximum zoom; there were two people in the room, a man and a woman. They were standing, and while Carrie had been too far away for either to be facially recognisable, I knew for sure from her body shape that one was Aileen, my ex-wife now, but not then, not on 5 May, the date on the image.

I was pretty certain, too, that I could put a name to the bloke, from his slim build, his height in relation to her, because they were standing pretty close, and from his distinctive head of hair. A pound to a pinch of pig-shit, he was Joey Morocco, the actor she'd been caught with, post flagrante, one might say, by a tabloid newspaper.

I hadn't really given a toss when it all came out, for we'd been history by then, but on 5 May we hadn't been. The gloss might have worn off, but we were still Mr and Mrs, and she had had him, literally for sure, in our house, in my house. A quick memory trawl reminded me that there had been a chief police officers' conference in Durham that weekend.

I'd gone easy on Joey until then, but I've made a mental note to have a private word with him next time our paths cross, as I'll make sure they do.

I was so angered by that discovery that its main import almost passed me by. Carrie McDaniels had photographed my house, seven months before our meeting in L'Escala that afternoon.

Yes, it was possible that she had been doing no more than taking away-day snapshots with her clever new camera. It is also possible that Motherwell Football Club will win the Champions' League in eighteen months or so, but you will not find me betting a single euro-cent on either of those outcomes.

Suddenly, my interest in Carrie's card sharpened. *If she's done it in Scotland*, I thought . . .

I scrolled down, fast, to the final images. There I was, taken unawares in the first, then growing more annoyed in the other two. But what had she been doing before that?

The answer was, she'd been taking surreptitious shots of me as I looked across the bay, lunched, and talked to Xavi on my mobile. I went a little further back. Clearly, her two guides had been taking her around the town. They'd shown her Plaça Catalunya (where the football ground used to be if you've known L'Escala that long), they'd shown her the church, they'd shown her a restaurant called La Clota, all closed up for the winter, and surprise, surprise, they'd shown her Puig Pedro, and the street where I live.

They'd even taken her along the cami that goes to St Marti d'Empuries, and up the walkway, from which she'd been able to take a fine shot of the front of my house.

Those who know me a little say that I'm quick to anger. Those who know me well could tell them that's simply me blowing off steam, and that when I get really angry it happens slowly, and builds up inside me, with very few warning signs. That's how it was as I looked at those images.

I did a trick with the computer that boosted the size of the thumbnails, so that I could make out more detail without having to look at them individually, and went back through the catalogue as swiftly as I could without missing anything.

It seemed that I'd been Carrie McDaniels' favourite subject. At least one-third of her photo files were of me. She had me in uniform and in civvies, in Glasgow, in Edinburgh. She had me off duty, walking the course at a golf championship, and heading for the Mallard Hotel bar with Sarah on a Friday evening in late September.

She even had me on the beach with my kids, carrying Seonaid on my shoulders while Mark and James Andrew worked on a sand sculpture of a car. Each child was photographed too, separately.

That was the point at which my quiet anger turned into fury and I roared at the screen in frustration.

'Thank Christ I took that fucking card!' I shouted. The words were barely out before I realised that all the images, other than the most recent, would have been backed up, on at least one device.

I'd never in my life felt vulnerable before, but I did then. I'm used to being fair game, but not my children, not them, never. On my patch, even in my strange emeritus situation, Carrie's feet would not have touched the ground on the way to the nearest police holding cell; I'd have thought about charges later.

But I wasn't on my patch, was I, and she hadn't done enough in Spain for me to set the Mossos d'Esquadra on her.

Instead I did something worse. I called Sauce again. He was tied up with an interview, but as soon as he was clear he rang me back.

'Things have gone up a couple of notches,' I told him. 'Check out the Belgian thing, yes, but I'm pretty sure you'll find it's bullshit. I'm going to email you a couple of images, a man and a woman. She's Carrie McDaniels, but I don't know who the fuck he is. He may be no more than a boyfriend, but I'd like him identified anyway. There's no need to keep this to yourself; if you need help from up the ladder, ask for it.'

'Will do, Chief,' he said, briskly, 'but if I have to ask my gaffer, he'll want to know what this is about.'

'I'd like to know that myself, son,' I replied. 'All I can tell you for now is, it appears that I'm being stalked.'

Four

I put the beast back in his cage before he had a chance to send me out to find Ms Carrie McDaniels and put the fear of several serious deities into her. Instead I loaded my bag into my car and headed off to find Xavi's place, hoping that I might still get there in daylight.

As it transpired it was a close-run thing. My Spanish car is a Suzuki four by four . . . some of the minor roads there can be very bumpy and it pays to have a vehicle with its arse well clear of the ground . . . but it hadn't come with built-in satnav, so I had to use the app on my phone. Post codes in Spain only take you to a town or district, and my destination was rural. The upshot was that I had to phone my host from a crossroads for final directions.

I followed Xavi's instructions and found myself in a broad flat valley, surrounded by towering hilly forests, a few kilometres past a tiny place called Constantins. I looked out for a sign that read 'Casa Forestals', and took a right turn when I found it.

The gate at the end of the one-way road that led to the *masia* had been opened for me; I drove through and on to a long driveway that was smoother and better shod than the trunk road from Girona. At its end, it widened and turned back on itself in a circle, with a single oak tree in a green island in its centre, and with the great stone house beyond.

I parked my humble vehicle in a space between two white Range Rovers, one of them the new coupé version, and just beyond, a Mercedes S-class saloon. It had an old-style Spanish number plate, and was on its way to becoming a classic.

Xavi was standing in the doorway; he saw me admire it. 'That's Joe's,' he said. 'Ever since he moved out here he's always had a Merc. He really loves that one; says it'll be his last. These days his main exercise consists of polishing it.'

He walked towards me, hand outstretched, towering over me . . . I don't think I mentioned that he's six feet eight inches tall, or that he was a goalkeeper in his football days. 'Thanks for coming, Bob. It's good to see you. You're looking well.'

He was being kind, for I've looked better than I did then, but when I replied, 'So are you,' I wasn't kidding.

He's only a couple of years my junior, but he looked at least ten years younger. His handshake was politely firm, but I suspected he would only need a nutcracker if he chose to use one. The complexion that I remembered being greyish even before his solitary days in Edinburgh was bronzed, even though it was winter, and he seemed to have lost a few wrinkles rather than gaining any. His thick hair was flecked with a only a few grey strands, whereas I haven't found any dark on my comb for at least five years.

'Come in,' he said, 'and meet the family.'

I followed him through the double entrance door into a big, high-ceilinged hall, with a marble floor. It was lit by a wrought-iron chandelier that had probably held candles when put in place but had been adapted to accommodate electric replicas.

He saw me glancing at it and chuckled, softly. 'Hideous, isn't it? Joe loves it, though, so it'll last as long as he does.'

'Which will be longer than you imagine, lad.'

The retort came from a doorway to our left, from an old man in black trousers, a checked cotton shirt that was predominately red in colour, and sheepskin slippers. His hair was silver and facially he looked more like a walnut than anyone I'd ever seen. He could have been any old bloke in any town square in any Catalan village, apart from the fact that very few of those are multimillionaires.

'Mr Skinner,' he exclaimed, coming towards us, 'I've heard and read a lot about you over the years. It's a pleasure to meet you at last.' There was a faint similarity to Xavi in his accent, but most of the Edinburgh influence had been worn away by decades in Spain.

'Likewise, Mr Aislado,' I replied.

He smiled. 'Joe, please. My birth name is Josep-Maria, but that never saw the light of day in Scotland. I only use it here in business, or rather I did, when I was involved.'

'Don't believe a word of that,' Xavi snorted. 'Joe founded InterMedia, and he's still its chairman. I might be the managing director, but there isn't a major decision I take that I don't talk through with him first. I do the travelling around Spain, when it's necessary, but he does the thinking.'

I was surprised at the warmth between the two of them, but I wasn't about to say so. Joe was in his eighties, and Xavi had lived the first thirty years of his life thinking that he was his son, not his half-brother. That was their family history, and it was not going to be disturbed by any questions from me.

The company they ran between them had grown from Joe's purchase of a daily newspaper called *GironaDia*, after he sold up in Scotland and took his mother back to the land they had left during the Spanish Civil War, when he'd been a baby.

It had been doing its first few circles around the plughole at the time, but he had kept it alive by cutting out the dead wood and easing the old Franco loyalists through the revolving door. It had gone on to prosper and in time it had become the cornerstone of the biggest media group on the Iberian peninsula, with interests in radio and television, as well as newspapers.

Having greeted me, Joe went back to what Xavi told me were his own quarters within the great house. 'He's always lived there since he bought this place, over thirty years ago. Grandma Paloma, his mother, ran the house but she insisted that each of them should have their own space. The rooms on the ground floor are all he ever wanted. They have their own entrance, which was handy for him, when he and Carmen were a secret.'

'Carmen?'

'Carmen Mali Sans. Joe's . . . partner, I suppose we call her nowadays. Her dad was the gardener here and her mother helped in the house. Carmen lived with them, but she supported herself by painting. I don't mean houses either; she's a portrait painter, and an eminent one at that. You'll see her work through here.'

He opened a door and we stepped from the hall into a great drawing room; an interior designer had been given free rein on it at some time in its history, and that person had been a big rococo fan. The walls and ceiling were decorated with plaster sweeps and flourishes, everywhere, and on the wall facing the fireplace there was an ornate mirror that was worthy of a palace.

Above that great hearth there was a portrait; I looked at it and gasped, involuntarily. The subject was a tall, majestic woman, dressed in black, with long white hair; the work was life-size, and she might have been in the room with us. I knew without having to ask that she was Grandma Paloma.

On each side of her, another painting hung. When I looked at the one on the right, my eyes widened. It depicted a young woman; she was blonde and naked . . . and familiar to me. 'Is that . . .' I began.

Xavi nodded.

The subject was his first wife, Grace. I knew because I'd met her, when my old gaffer, DCS Alf Stein, and I went to interview her in Xavi's flat in Edinburgh, after her parents had been murdered. Many things happened after that, leading up to a sad ending in which I played a small part. I was surprised to see her likeness there, and my expression must have said as much.

'I'd take it down,' he said, 'but Sheila won't let me. She says that since you can't erase your past from your memory, you should live with it around you.'

'And to be honest,' another voice cut in, 'it keeps me on my toes as well.'

He turned to face the woman who had spoken, as she came into the room through a side door, stretching out a hand to her as she walked across to join us. 'And this is Sheila, whom you have never met.'

'No,' I agreed, 'but I've heard of you,' I told her, nodding as I met her gaze, and her smile, 'from June Crampsey. In my line of work, I have to know the editor of the *Saltire*, and every other paper in Scotland.'

Xavi's second wife was nothing like Grace in appearance, but just as attractive, dark where she had been blonde. She was the subject of the third portrait, from which serenity shone.

'So it still is your line of work, Bob,' he exclaimed. 'The

whole of Scotland thinks you're finished with it; my sister certainly does, I know that.' Before I could respond he carried on. 'Hey, come on, I have no manners. Drop your bag and sit down. Would you like a drink? You must have had a fair old drive from L'Escala.'

'It's not all that far,' I replied, 'but any excuse for a drink is a good excuse, as they say.'

'What do you fancy?' he asked. 'You name it.'

'I'll have what you're having.'

He grinned. 'In that case, it'll be cava.'

They're big on cava in Catalunya; it's the local fizz. They used to call it Spanish champagne, until the protectionist French put a stop to that, forcing the producers to create a new identity. They've never looked back since.

Xavi left the room, through the door that Sheila had used, leaving the two of us together.

'June's told us a lot about you too,' she said, as we sat facing the massive hearth, in which a log fire was burning. 'Xavi speaks to her often, on Facetime, and sometimes I'm there. I gather you've been very helpful to her over the years.'

'I hope I've been helpful to all the editors,' I countered. 'Well, maybe not all of them; most of the Scottish outlets have been fair to me over the years, but there have been one or two that have stepped over the line.'

'Where's your line drawn?'

'Between my professional and private lives; the second is off limits.'

'Mmm,' she murmured. 'Xavi will sympathise with you there. When he and I met up again . . .' She paused. 'You know we met twice, sort of? Briefly, when we were in our teens, then later, after we'd both been through the mill.'

She glanced up at the portrait of Grace. I nodded. 'So I understand,' I replied.

'The second time around, Xavi was really withdrawn. He spent nearly all of his life running the *Saltire*, and cut himself off from everything else. His day consisted of cycling to the office, via the gym at his health club, then cycling home again, usually around midnight. He never accepted business or social invitations, not ever. If he hadn't come into the minor injuries clinic after he fell off his bike and buggered his knee, we might never have met up again, and he might still be doing that.'

'But he did,' I said, 'and all's well.'

'Yes, but he didn't become any less private, not even after Paloma was born.'

'How old is your daughter now?' I asked.

'She's twelve. She'll be here soon, in fact; my son Ben's gone to pick her up from school, in Girona. He's here with us just now. He's as fond of his half-sister as Xavi is of his. He should visit her more often.'

'He doesn't live in Spain, then?'

'No, he's in Scotland, still; he's never been tempted to move here. He works as a bookseller, or rather he did, until his company folded a couple of months ago.'

I'd noticed the collapse of a book chain earlier in the year, but hadn't focused on it, having my own worries at the time.

'It's the impact of eBooks,' Sheila continued. 'It's happening to newspaper sales too. Everything that you and I grew up with, Mr Skinner, it's all changing.'

'Tell me about it,' I grunted, with what was meant to be a smile but probably came across as a grimace. 'It's not just in the media that things are being stood on their head. We're in the middle of a social revolution, and it's having a greater effect than any other period of major change in our history, because it's all happening so fast.'

'The social revolution: I like that, Bob. I may suggest to our editors that they focus on that phrase from now on.' Xavi had re-joined us, carrying a tray with three glasses and a bottle of Freixenet Elyssia. 'Are you a one-man resistance movement?'

'Hell no!' I retorted. 'I'm for everything that improves people's lives. In my book man's three greatest inventions have been the wheel, the condom and the Internet.'

'I know some old guys here who have no time for two of those, and would get by without the third if they could.' He popped the cava and filled the three glasses. 'But you have limits?' he continued, as he finished and handed them round.

'Yes, I do. I'm not against change, as long as it's for the better. I'm not against cost saving either, as long as there are benefits. It's okay to fix things, even if they ain't broke, as long as you don't make them worse. For example . . .'

'The new Scottish police service?'

'A prime example,' I agreed.

'Why?' Sheila asked. 'We have a National Health Service, so why not a national police force?'

'We've had an NHS for over sixty years, and we still haven't got it right,' I pointed out, 'not the management of it, at any rate. Very few things in this life are black and white; every large community has its own culture and its own problems. In policing these have to be handled sensitively, and sometimes with a large dose of common sense. To do that properly, the decision-makers have to understand the issues involved. They also have to work with the local authorities, the councils.'

I smiled, seeing an imaginary soapbox in the middle of the room, and realising that I was in danger of stepping on to it.

'Ach, don't get me started. Police Scotland's a done deal, and there's nothing more to be said about it.'

'So that's why you pulled your application form,' Xavi murmured.

'Who said I ever submitted it?'

'My newspaper, the *Saltire*; it said so, based on information from good sources, and so did most of the other Scottish titles. My sister even ran an editorial about it, criticising you for going off in a huff.'

'That's June's view,' I retorted. 'I wasn't about to get into an argument with her about it.'

'Are you saying she was wrong?'

'Of course I am; she should have talked to me before she published. It wasn't that easy a call for me. I might have gone ahead with my application, but something else got in the way.' As I sipped the excellent cava, a small wave of suspicion rippled through my mind. 'Hey,' I said, 'is that why I'm here? Is this really an interview? Am I being recorded?'

I'd never seen the big man look remotely angry, not even in terrible circumstances, but he did then. His eyebrows came together hard as he frowned. 'Do you really think I would do that?' he boomed. 'Invite you to my home just to pump you for information? Jesus, Bob . . .'

I realised that he was hurt, as well as annoyed; guilt blew away my doubts. 'I'm sorry, man,' I exclaimed. 'Of course I don't think such a thing. I've been a bit paranoid these last few months, that's all.'

He tipped his glass in my direction. 'Apology accepted. Let's change the subject.'

I'd have been glad to but in the circumstances I felt that a gesture was in order. 'No,' I said. 'It's time I shared this with someone else, as well as Sarah and Alex. But within this room, okay?'

'Of course,' Xavi agreed, 'but I wasn't asking, really.'

'I know you weren't, but I'm going to tell you. Do you remember, a few weeks ago, a case coming to the High Court in Edinburgh, in which a young man named Ignacio Centelleos pleaded guilty to the culpable homicide of his grandmother, a woman called Bella Watson, and to perverting the course of justice by dumping her body in the River Forth?'

'The Cramond Island Woman story? Of course I do, it was big news. As I recall, the Crown accepted his story that Granny . . . whom he'd never met before . . . had gone berserk and tried to kill his mother with a cleaver. What did he get? Two years?'

'Four, but half of it was suspended. Lord Nelson was the judge,' I added.

'Yes, that's right. June wrote an editorial on that too, congratulating him on the fairness of his sentence. What about it?'

'There's something the court wasn't told. Ignacio is my son.'

Beside me, Sheila gasped, but Xavi's expression didn't change, not by as little as a twitching eyebrow.

'I didn't know about him,' I continued. 'I had a one-night stand with his mother, going on for twenty years ago. She left Edinburgh very shortly after that, because of family problems . . .'

'The same problems that led Granny to go for her with a chopper?' Xavi murmured.

I nodded. 'Do some research on Bella Watson's history and you'll understand. Anyway, Mia . . . that's Ignacio's mother's name . . . ran off to Spain, and I didn't hear from her again until a few months ago. That's when I found out; by that time all the bad stuff had happened.' I sipped some more cava and stared into the glass. 'Quite some mess, eh?'

'He's definitely your son?' Sheila blurted out, then winced. 'Sorry, that was . . .'

I forced a smile to put her at ease. 'That was a natural question. Yes, he is. Our DNA says so, beyond doubt. There's a resemblance, too . . . although it might not dawn on you straight away, not unless you'd known me when I was his age.'

'Who knows about it?' Xavi asked.

'Sarah, my partner, she knows. So does Alexis, my daughter; she's a lawyer and she organised Ignacio's defence team. The detectives who worked the Bella homicide found out during the investigation. They kept it tight, so only a couple of their senior officers are in the loop. They're all good friends of mine, so nothing will leak.'

'How about the scientists who found the DNA match?'

I glanced at Sheila, who put the question. 'They're tight too. Their boss and I go way back . . . plus, I'd know where to find them if anyone did tip off the media.'

I paused, but only for a second or two. 'Be clear on this,' I said. 'I am not ashamed of the boy. If you're wondering why I didn't speak up for him in court, or haven't acknowledged him publicly, I can tell you that has nothing to do with what people might think of me. In fact it's the opposite.'

'I think I know what you mean,' Sheila murmured. 'You're protecting him.'

'Exactly,' I declared. 'The day he's released from Polmont Young Offenders' Institution, in a little more than a year from now, I'll be waiting there for him. But while he's in prison, if it was known that he's my son, he'd have a target on his back.'

Xavi nodded agreement. 'True. Does that mean you won't visit him while he's in there?'

'I'm afraid so. But Alex will; she's on record as his solicitor, so that won't raise any eyebrows.'

'How did she take it when you told her?'

'She was in her early teens when Mia was around. Even then she was old enough to know that I was attracted to her, so that took some of the surprise out of it. She's very protective of her other siblings even though they're children and she's hit the thirty mark, and she liked Ignacio when she met him, so she's fine.'

'And Sarah?' Sheila asked. 'What about her?'

I shrugged. 'Ignacio comes from the time before her, just like Alex does. As she was very quick to remind me, she and I have been through worse than the arrival of a surprise love child.'

'What will he do when he's released?'

'He'll be going to university, Sheila,' I told her, 'if I have anything to do with it. He's a clever lad, a brilliant chemist . . . a talent that he hasn't always put to the best use. Alex will be talking to him about that.'

'Will his mother have a view on it? Or has she gone back to Spain?'

I grinned. 'Mia's outlived her welcome in this country. She's gone back to her old career, as a radio presenter. She's done a couple of stand-ins on Radio Scotland and they've helped her pick up a twelve-month contract with an independent station in Dundee.'

Xavi registered surprise. 'She's managed that, even with all the adverse publicity about her mother's death?'

'She's never used her family name professionally. She calls herself Mia Sparkles; Bella's maiden name was Spreckley; it springs from that.'

'I see.' His eyes met mine. 'That's quite a story, Bob, but I've

37

heard nothing that would stop you from being a police officer. So why is your future in doubt? I know via June that the new Police Scotland chief executive is looking at a role for you.'

'The doubts are in my head, Xavi. That's why I'm in L'Escala: to sort them out. But it's not why I'm here now, is it? You said you wanted my advice on a "situation"; your word. So, what's up?'

My host rose from his chair, and refilled his wife's glass and mine. 'I believe that someone is attacking our business,' he said, abruptly, as he resumed his seat.

'How?' I asked. 'Are your shares under pressure? Is someone lining up a hostile takeover bid?'

'Our shares aren't traded. The group's still in our hands, Joe's and mine . . . and Sheila's, of course. We've had bids over the years, from some global media players, but we've refused them all, politely. I'm very proud of what Joe's achieved since he took over the old newspaper back in the seventies, and pleased with my own contribution since I got involved. We like what we do, Bob, and we have no wish to stop doing it.'

'But someone else wants you to?'

'That's how it seems.'

'Explain,' I said.

'Our success over the years has been based on two things: the quality of our journalism, and our ability to anticipate change. When regional radio began to expand, we were first there; today you'll find the InterMedia brand all over the country.' He smiled. 'Only InterMedia, note; we dropped "Girona" from our corporate identity several years ago. We Catalans aren't universally loved in the rest of Spain.'

'So I've heard.'

'But we've prospered in spite of it,' he continued. 'When the

Internet arrived, we were the first company in Europe to realise its potential, and to exploit it. Every one of our newspapers has an online edition, with a total readership that's now greater than the print versions, and significantly more profitable. Our larger radio stations were used as the basis for new television channels as soon as digital broadcasting arrived.'

'That's very impressive,' I told him, sincerely. 'How did you achieve it?'

'We did it through the skills of a very exceptional young man. His name is Hector Sureda Roca. He's the son of our editorial director Pilar Roca and her husband, Simon Sureda. Simon is the finest journalist I know. When I met him, he changed my life. After listening to him I knew that there could only be one profession for me. Before I ever went to work for the *Saltire*, he was my mentor.' He smiled, his mind back in his past for a few moments.

'Hector inherited all of his parents' journalistic instincts and skills,' he continued, 'and added to them through his under-standing of the new world in which we're operating. He was very young when we gave him his head, but it was no risk, because he's a genius.' He drew a deep breath into his massive chest. 'And now he's disappeared.'

'Disappeared?' I repeated.

'Without trace, four days ago. He left home for the office last Friday morning, at eight o'clock as usual, but he never arrived. He hasn't been seen since, or heard from.'

'Could he have jumped ship?' I asked.

'What do you mean?'

'Could he have gone to work for someone else?'

'Not a chance,' Xavi replied. 'Hector loves his job; there is nobody on the payroll anywhere who's more dedicated than he is. Money isn't an issue either; he's on a director-level salary, a healthy six figures after tax, plus a performance bonus. For the last three years, he's been the highest earner in the entire InterMedia group . . . and that includes Joe and me. On top of that he owns a piece of the business. I said that the company is family owned, but over the years Pilar Roca has been rewarded with share options, to be exercised in the event of a sale, and since the digital revolution started, Hector's been on the same deal. Today, they own ten per cent of the business between them.'

'What's Hector's personal situation?'

'He's thirty-six, and he's single. He's had a few relationships, but he isn't in one at the moment; they've all broken up because he's so focused on his work. He has an apartment in Barcelona, but most of the time he lives in the family home. Pilar and Simon have a nice big house in Begur, and Hector has his own part of that, just as Joe has here.'

'Do you know for sure that he left home at eight?'

'One hundred per cent. His mother made him breakfast, then she heard his car leaving the garage. After that, as I said, he didn't arrive at the office and nobody has seen him or heard from him since then.'

'Are you sure he isn't in love, and just slipped off for a few days? Lust can do strange things to people, make them behave out of the ordinary. My boy Ignacio is living proof of that.'

'Pilar says no; she's sure she'd have known if there was anyone new around. She's going quietly mad over this, by the way. Besides, the one thing it would not have made him do is switch off his mobile phone. It never leaves him; it's an extension of his personality. He's one of those people who tweet everything, short of bowel movements, although I'm sure he's shared a few thoughts while sat on the throne. His Twitter account has been silent since last Thursday, and likewise Facebook.'

'Where's his office?'

'Hector's based in our group headquarters on the edge of Girona. So are Pilar and I, but we're not there every day, as he is.' The big guy smiled. 'I'm making up for the times when I was never away from the office.

'Everyone in the company reports to me ultimately but my hands-on involvement these days tends to be with our bankers and those people and organisations whose goodwill is important to us.'

'Politicians and civil servants?'

'Exactly.'

'Okay,' I said. 'If I understand you correctly, the group is run at top level by three people.'

'More or less. Pilar supervises all our newspapers and magazines, with each editor reporting to her. Hector's title is digital media director; he runs all the websites and has oversight of our radio and television stations, through assistants at sub-board level. We have a finance director, of course, Hilario Mendez. That gives us a six-person board, with Joe being the chairman, and Sheila as non-executive director.' He grinned again, and glanced at his wife. 'After we'd been here for a couple of years, I realised that I talked through every major business decision with her, and most of the smaller ones too, and that her input was pretty sharp, so we brought her into the circle.'

'I was the same with Sarah,' I confessed. 'Her being a forensic pathologist, we've had some very interesting conversations over the dinner table.' I looked at him. 'So that's your management structure?'

'Almost,' Sheila replied. 'Alongside the board we have an

internal audit department, run by Susannah Gardner, a Scots lady Xavi pinched from the *Saltire*'s accountants in Edinburgh. They scrutinise the finances of every component company within the group, right down to reporters' expense accounts . . .' she chuckled, 'and the managing director's when he's away on business.'

I looked at her husband. 'Since Hector disappeared, have you instructed a full audit of his department?'

He stared back at me. 'No, of course not. Why should I?'

'Probably because it's your duty as chief executive. You've just bounced this situation off me, as a cop. The man has gone, and there are no signs of violence or of any form of duress. I don't know him, so I am automatically objective, and I'm telling you, professionally, that in a case like this the first thing you do is look at the money.'

'Hector's not a thief!' Sheila protested.

'In which case there'll be no trouble demonstrating it. All I'm saying is that you have to check the company books. From what you're telling me the man spends his life online, doing stuff that's beyond your ken, and Xavi's. He lives in a different world from you. He could be the world's worst Internet poker player, and you would not have a clue about it.'

'Bob's right, love,' Xavi said, sadly. 'It has to be done.'

'What has to be done?'

The young voice that came from the far end of the room had a pronounced Catalan accent and yet still it took me back almost twenty years, to my Alex as an almost teenager. I caught the look in Xavi's eyes, and guessed it had been in mine too, around that time. Maybe it still is.

'Hello, Paloma,' he called out as the girl approached. 'Come and meet our guest. This is Mr Skinner, from Edinburgh.'

His daughter, as you'd expect, was tall for her age; her dark hair was long and tied in a ponytail. I glanced up at the central portrait of her namesake and saw a resemblance that should not have existed, since they were unrelated in blood.

'*Encantada, señor*,' she said. 'Pleased to meet you. I've been back to Edinburgh since we left, with Mama, but never with my dad. He says he doesn't like it any more. But he says', she added, 'that I can go to university there.'

'Let's get you through school first,' her father laughed.

A man had come into the room with Paloma. He was around the thirty mark, with a mop of dark hair and a black full beard; her stepbrother, I assumed, and this was confirmed when he spoke to Sheila.

'Mum, can I borrow the Toyota again?' he asked. 'There's a film being shown in English tonight in Girona and I fancy catching it.' He stopped then turned to me, hand outstretched. 'I'm sorry, no manners, I'm Ben McNeish.' He smiled, and I read a hint of shyness in him. 'You are the Mr Skinner, aren't you?' His tone underlined the definite article.

'I'm probably the one you're thinking about, yes,' I replied.

'It's an honour, sir.'

'My pleasure too, Ben. I hear you've had some bad luck on the job front . . . in which case, I know how you feel.'

'Mine was inevitable, the way things have gone in the book trade.'

'Mine too,' I countered, 'given the clowns that run our country just now.'

'The police could do it better, then, Bob?' Xavi challenged. 'Is that what you're saying?'

'We'd run it more efficiently, that's for sure. However, I'm for wider police accountability, not for none at all.'

'Dad, can I have some Playstation time?' Paloma asked, uninterested in Scottish politics. 'I've no homework.'

'In that case, my love, please do. We're in mid-discussion here. Ben,' he turned to his stepson, 'since you've got a woman to impress, why don't you take your mum's Range Rover . . . or mine, for that matter.'

'Thanks, Xavi,' he replied, 'but the Rav Four's fine. I'd be nervous in yours. How did you know I've—'

'Once a journo, always a journo; I have a nose for these things. Plus I noticed how long you spent on the fashion desk when I took you into the newspaper office yesterday.'

His stepson laughed softly. 'I'm that transparent, am I?'

The new arrivals went their separate ways and we returned to serious business.

'That's agreed,' Xavi said. 'I'll ask Susannah to take a close look at the digital department accounts first thing tomorrow. She'll find nothing, though.'

'I'm sure she won't, but it needs doing. You don't have to let his mother know.'

'Why not? It might do her good to see that something's being done.'

I raised my eyebrows. 'Do I need to spell that out too?'

Sheila had tuned in to the message. 'He means in case Hector has been at it and she's involved.'

'Jesus, Bob,' her husband gasped, 'do you suspect everyone?'

'The law says innocent until proven guilty. We cops don't go quite that far.'

'If that's so, you'd better investigate me too, in case I've done him in and buried him at the foot of the garden.'

'No, you're definitely innocent,' I said. 'If you'd done that, I'd be the last person you'd have called.'

'Thanks for that small vote of confidence,' he grunted. 'So, on the assumption that Susannah finds everything in order, what can we do to find Hector?'

'How about the blindingly obvious? You can call in the police.'

He shook his head. 'That I do not want to do, for now. As you've just pointed out, there's no evidence of violence, so they might laugh in my face if I ask them to investigate. But if they don't, if they take it on, then for sure it will leak. All our rivals . . . and that's the rest of the Spanish media . . . will run the story and they will use it to put the boot in.'

'And that's your fear, is it? That somehow, Hector's been taken by a business enemy to destabilise InterMedia?'

'Yes, it is; either that or for ransom. But if that was the case, surely we'd have been contacted by now?'

'Not necessarily,' I countered. 'A kidnapper might wait for a few days, to see how you react to Hector's disappearance. But in my experience . . . and it's limited, abduction not being a major industry in Scotland . . . you'd have heard something within forty-eight hours.'

I hesitated before I went on. 'When you suggest that a business rival might have taken him, do you have anyone in mind?'

Xavi considered his answer for even longer than I'd taken to put the question. Finally he responded.

'Over the last two years we have had three approaches from interested parties. The first was a German media group, who made contact through its lawyer. He asked if we'd be interested in selling, and I said there was no basis for negotiation. He accepted that and asked to be notified if the situation changed. I gave him that guarantee.

'The second was from an American investor, who said that he

wanted to establish a European media portfolio and thought that InterMedia would be a good place to start. I told him to start somewhere else. A few months later he bought an ailing newspaper chain in France.'

'And the third?' I asked.

'That was from an Italian conglomerate, an expanding business called BeBe, whose driving force is a youngish woman named Bernicia Battaglia. Have you heard of her?'

'Yes, don't they call her the "Warrior" because her surname means "battle"?'

'The one and only. She turned up unannounced in the office in Girona just over two months ago. I saw her alone, in my room. She told me that she was going to buy the InterMedia group for one hundred million euros in BeBe shares.

'I'm afraid I laughed in her face. I told her that I'm half Catalan, half Scots and because of that I only deal in stuff that I can take to the bank. She said, "Okay, sixty million cash."

'I said that if I was interested in a sale it would take a hell of a lot more than that, but that I wasn't going to play games with her, because the business was my life and I wasn't about to part with it.

'She looked back at me, across my desk, this tall jewel of a woman, dressed in her finest Versace, drop-dead gorgeous even though she wore hardly any make-up, and she told me, "In that case I will take your life, Señor Aislado." Then she got up and walked out.'

'Have you heard from her since then?'

'No, not a cheep. But if you're asking me who I've met in business that I reckon would be capable of attacking me in this way, it would be her. She's a very smart woman, and she will know that one person is crucial to the stability and success of InterMedia, and that it isn't me, it's Hector Sureda.'

'But she's only a businesswoman, not a warlord, for all her name.'

'Don't be so sure of that. Ten years ago, BeBe was the third-largest media company in Italy. The head of the second largest was an old bloke named Durante who was keeping it in shape for his son to run after he got over what Dad saw as a fleeting obsession with politics.

'One day Durante junior was walking home from the Chamber of Deputies when someone put a bullet through his head. The assassin was never traced and within three months, the Warrior had bought the old guy out.'

I confess that until that moment, all I had really been able to see was Hector as an unstable man, perhaps on the rebound from a broken romance, deciding on a total life change and buggering off to get on with it. The Durante story got my attention, not least because I remembered it.

By chance, I'd been in Rome, on holiday with Sarah, when it had happened. I'd understood none of the press coverage, but I'd mentioned it to the hotel barman, and he'd said the cops were denying that it was a Mafia job.

I didn't really want Sheila to hear what I had to say next, but I had no choice.

'If you're connecting that to Signora Battaglia,' I murmured, 'doesn't it follow also that you may be looking for a dead man?'

Xavi winced. 'The thought has occurred to me,' he admitted. 'But my hope is that she'll realise that Hector is so important to InterMedia that his death would diminish it to the point that it was no longer worth having. As I said, the man is a genius.'

'So your scenario is?'

'That he's been snatched and that he'll be held until I agree to sell our family shareholding in the group, with his contract in place.'

'But that would tie her to the abduction,' I pointed out.

'Not necessarily. She could wait me out. Hector's absence will be felt very quickly.'

'Okay,' I agreed, not entirely convinced that one man could be so important, 'but I still think it's a job for the police. If you suspect organised crime involvement it would be handled discreetly.'

'Nothing is leak-proof, Bob. My profession gets everywhere.'

'You could always sell out,' I suggested, bluntly.

'I could,' he agreed, 'but I'm not there yet. I want to try to recover Hector . . . assuming he's still recoverable. Resources aren't a problem. I'll hire my own people to find him and get him back safe. My hope is that you'll be able to tell me where to begin.'

'Mmm.' I scratched an itch on my right temple. 'A few months ago, I ran across a couple of guys who might have been useful to you on the recovery part. But they're no longer in the game.'

'Why not?'

'Let's just say that a colleague and I retired them; but let's not dwell on that. Before you get to that stage, you need to make sure of the situation. And for that you will need the best investigator in the business.'

'Where will I find him?'

'You're looking at him. Go and open another bottle of cava; my brain's a little rusty, and that's the best lubricant I know.'

Five

To this day I'm not sure why I said that, but in doing so I tossed the dice and crossed the river and did all the other symbolic stuff involved in stepping from one life into another.

It was the moment when I realised that in my heart I had always wanted to remain the hands-on cop I had been, rather than the civil servant . . . albeit a very senior one . . . that I'd become.

It was the moment when I realised that what I'd laughed off as the 'Sherlock Option' when considering my future was actually a possibility, and a very live one at that. I had skills and if someone wanted to hire them for a purpose within the law then why the hell should I not accommodate them?

After I'd made the offer, I felt as surprised as Xavi looked, but it was out there and I wasn't going to renege on it.

Once he'd popped the cork on another bottle of Freixenet and Sheila had left us while she looked after dinner (this is a fact; I know quite a few millionaires, and not one of them has a cook), he got down to business.

'What are your terms and conditions for this sort of assignment?' he asked.

I hadn't considered either, not at all, but my reply was

instantaneous. 'I have only one condition. Whatever I do I'll play by the rules; by that I mean I'll be bound by the same constraints that I was as a police officer. By that I mean I will not be hacking anyone's communications.'

'I wouldn't expect otherwise. And your terms? By that I mean financial.'

'In the future, I haven't a clue, but this is a favour for a friend.'

'You'll have expenses, surely?'

'Will I? I may make a couple of phone calls and it'll all be sorted.'

'Really?'

'No, probably not,' I admitted. 'We don't get that lucky very often. Xavi, I have no idea where this will go. If there are costs incurred, I'll let you know . . . but chances are you'll be involved in what I do. In fact the more people I have to speak to, the deeper in you'll be.'

'Fair enough,' he said, 'but why?'

'For one very good reason: I've had a place here for a long time but I only speak restaurant Spanish, at best, and a lot of that's got Catalan mixed in. I'll get by as best I can, but there will be times when I'll need a translator, and given the sensitivity of this business, that can only be you. Besides, you're a pretty damn good investigator yourself. You built a career on it, if you think about it.'

He frowned. 'I suppose I did,' he conceded. 'But journalists tend not to interpret, we simply establish facts and report them.'

'So do detectives; the remit's the same except we report to the fiscal, not the public. The only advantage we have is that when we want to interview people they can't slam the door in our faces. So, will you be my voice when I need it?'

'Of course. Where will you begin?'

'First off,' I responded, 'I'm going to look for Hector's car. He was last seen driving to work, you said. Generally you can make a person disappear more easily than a car. What did he drive?'

'A Porsche Boxster, a little yellow thing; looks like a fucking canary with wheels. It's not the most practical car for these parts, but it's what he wanted.'

'What he wanted?' I repeated. 'Does that mean it's company owned?'

'Leased,' he volunteered. 'All the directors' cars are, apart from Joe's Merc.'

'That could mean it's still in one piece; if it had been involved in an accident or dumped somewhere, the police would have contacted the leasing company, and they'd have been on to you. First thing tomorrow morning you should make a call.'

'To whom?'

I countered with a question. 'Who's your best contact in the Mossos d'Esquadra?'

'Comissari Canals in the Girona office . . . but Bob, you know how I feel about police involvement.'

'You can't avoid it,' I insisted. 'You only need to tell him that one of your cars is missing, and ask for his help in finding it. You don't need to say that the driver's missing as well.'

'Won't it be logged into their system as a theft?'

'Along with how many hundred others?' I pointed out. 'It's necessary, Xavi, or we'd have to find it ourselves. Once we have it, who knows what we'll find in it?'

'What's your guess about that?'

'I'll be hoping to see traces of anyone who was in that car, other than Hector.'

'Okay,' Xavi agreed, 'I'll call Canals. What else do you need?'

'I want to talk to Hector's parents.'

'Why, Bob? They can't tell you any more than I have.'

'Nonetheless, I want to hear it from them. They may recall something that's significant to us, something he said or did. But I really don't want to anticipate. You've told me what you believe, Xavi, and I can understand why you do, but I have to go into this with a completely open mind.'

'Then tomorrow I'll arrange a meeting with Pilar, in the office in Girona.'

I didn't fancy the idea. 'Why can't we go to Begur?' I asked. 'I'd much prefer that.'

He gave a huge sigh. 'There's a problem with Simon. He has a very bad heart condition; he needs a valve replacement, urgently. It's scheduled for next week; Pilar's been told that he must be kept calm and quiet until then. They have him on constant sedation, until they're ready to admit him to hospital in Barcelona. He can't know about this.'

'Then he won't,' I said. 'But I'd still like to go to Begur. You said that Hector has his own section of the house. Would it be possible for me to see it without Simon even knowing I'm there?'

He looked at me, a little sceptically. 'Do you really need to?'

'Open mind, Xavi,' I repeated. 'I have to start this from scratch, with Hector saying *adios* to his mum, and I'd like to see the rooms he left behind him. It may be that before this is done we'll need to go to his Barcelona pad too.'

'We won't find him there; I called his landline, no answer, and I even got someone from our office in the city to call round on some pretext or other.'

'But they didn't get in?'

'No,' he said. 'Nobody home.'

'Then we should go, unless we find him or he turns up in the next twenty-four hours.'

The big man nodded. 'If you say so.'

'I do; but first, the car. Can you make that call to your Mossos mate tonight?'

'I can try his office. He's a workaholic so he may still be there. Before I do, though, I'll need to check the Boxster's registration plate. I can access it through my computer, in my office upstairs.'

'Good. You do that. While you're at it, I promised Sarah that we'd speak tonight. If she's tried me on the L'Escala landline she'll be wondering where the hell I'm at.' I took my phone from my pocket, and switched it on. 'Do you have a decent signal here?' I asked Xavi as I waited for it to fire up.

He smiled. 'Of course. We have some influence with Movistar.'

Sure enough, my screen showed five bars. When I entered the pass code it also showed two missed calls, one from Sauce Haddock, and the other from someone I wasn't expecting to hear from; Mia, my secret son's mother.

I gave Sauce priority, and hit the return button. 'Chief,' he said as he came on line, but quietly. I guessed that he was not alone, and he confirmed it at once. 'I'm with Sammy.'

DI Sammy Pye is his boss; he's another of those I like to call 'my people'. The two of them work out of the Leith office and make a pretty formidable team. As their careers develop I expect Sauce to pass his gaffer by at some point, even though Sammy is famously ambitious. Young Haddock has that edge, a quiet determination that will not allow him to put the pieces of a puzzle back in their box until he's assembled the complete picture. Once he adds Pye's judgement to his arsenal, he'll be unstoppable.

'I had to let him in on it,' he continued. 'Your email used my force address, so he could have accessed it anyway.'

'I've got no problem with that,' I told him. 'I only called you because you owe me one after the help I gave you a couple of months back. Any progress?'

'Yes, some; Carrie McDaniels is her real name. She's twenty-eight years old and she's no more a journalist than I am. You were right, the story she spun you is pure fiction. The Belgian tour company does exist, but it never uses freelancers on its flight magazines. She probably used its name because it flew her to Barcelona, on a flight out of Brussels, last Saturday.'

'Do you know what she was doing there?'

'No more than connecting, as far as I can see. She caught an early-morning FlemAir flight to Belgium out of Prestwick.'

'Did she travel alone?'

'Yes, but she didn't pay for it; the booking was charged to the credit card of somebody called Linton Baillie, billing address in Edinburgh.'

'Do we know who he is?'

'The gaffer let me run a PNC check; it showed him as not known to the police, so I Googled him. Several hits came up, most of them on Amazon. He seems to be an author, specialising in what they call "true crime". There's no image of him anywhere that I can find, so we don't know if he's the guy in Carrie's photos. We could try the Passport Agency, but . . .'

'No,' I said, understanding his hesitancy. 'They'd want to know why, and if you told them the truth, that it's a private inquiry, then you'd be shafted by the Data Protection Act.'

'Exactly. But the DI says that if you want to make a formal complaint . . .'

I laughed. 'For what? The only thing we might have against him is indecent exposure on Gullane beach.'

'We could talk to his publisher,' Sammy Pye called out, close enough for me to hear him.

'Tell him no thanks, Sauce,' I said. 'If the guy's a serious nuisance I'll find him myself. Back to McDaniels: you've found out what she isn't. Got any clue to what she is?'

'Yes, believe it or not, she's a private investigator.'

'A what?' I exclaimed.

'No kidding, Chief. She's a licensed private detective. I found her CV online; it was pretty informative.

'It says that she started her career with an insurance company, straight from school, about ten years ago; as an assistant in its claims department. When she was twenty-one she joined the Territorial Army Military Police. She served mainly in Scotland but did a couple of short tours of duty in Germany and in Afghanistan.

'Two years ago, she left the TA, as a corporal, and got herself what they call a front-line licence from the Security Industry Authority. Armed with that she resigned from the insurance company and set up on her own as CMcD Investigations.'

'Working for whom?'

'According to the website, for her old employer, for a couple of retail chains, and for "a number of private clients". I'm quoting there, by the way.'

'One of those being Mr Linton Baillie,' I murmured. 'With tracking me as her brief, it seems. The bloody woman's had me under surveillance.'

'Looks like it, sir. Do you want us to look closer at this Baillie guy? Sammy's sitting here nodding, if you do.'

'No, I don't think so. For the moment, he thinks he's a secret. He can keep on believing that until I'm ready to deal with him. He's low priority at the moment; I've got something else to sort out here. Thanks for your help, both of you.'

Sauce's information would probably have driven Mia's missed call out of my head, had there not been a little red reminder on the screen of my phone. I thought about deleting it, for I wanted none of her in my life. But then I realised that she felt the same way about me, and that she wouldn't have phoned me just to pass the time. Shortly afterwards my scrambled brain recognised that we had exchanged mobile numbers for one reason alone: Ignacio, our son.

I made the call. When Mia answered she sounded more than a little agitated. 'Can't talk now,' she hissed. 'I'll call you back in five.'

'That's if you can get through,' I muttered, after she'd gone, then hit Sarah's number.

'Hello, my darling.' Her voice had an echo to it that told me she was driving. I checked my watch and saw that it was seven forty-two local time, an hour earlier in Scotland. I'd caught her on the way home from work, bound for Gullane. Our reconciliation is recent enough for us still to keep separate houses, although more and more she's been coming to mine, especially through the week when the kids are at school.

'Good flight? Settled in okay? Is L'Escala quiet?'

I smiled, as if we were speaking across the dinner table. 'Yes to the first; sort of, to the second; not as quiet as I'd like it to the third.'

'That last one sounds pretty mysterious,' she chuckled.

'It isn't really.' I decided to say nothing about Carrie McDaniels; not then at any rate. 'I was surprised by the number of ex-pats in winter, that's all. But I've been distracted.'

I told her about Xavi's call, and that I was phoning from his place. 'He's in a bit of a predicament and he wanted my advice.'

'What kind of advice?'

'Professional. He needs to trace a missing person, discreetly. I've said I'll help him.'

The chuckle became a full-throated laugh. 'Bob, since when did you do discreet?'

She had me there. For all my high police rank, I have a reputation for leaving carnage in my wake.

'This'll be fine. We'll trace the guy in a day or two, and I'll get back to what I came here to do.'

'Let's hope so. I want to see a man with a plan when you get back.'

'It's taking shape already,' I assured her. I wasn't kidding; I was amazed by the buzz that Xavi's situation was giving me. Furthermore, if somebody like Carrie McDaniels could set herself up as a licensed investigator, on the basis of a couple of years as a part-time Redcap, then what could I do?

'How's your day been?' I asked.

'Routine. This morning I did an autopsy on a fit and healthy twenty-six-year-old man who was found dead in his armchair. It was uncomplicated; the guy drank too much beer and ate too many pakoras, then fell asleep and inhaled enough of his own puke to see him over the line.

'This afternoon, I lectured to a couple of classes at the university, then wrote up my notes on the morning's subject for the insurance company that hired me to carve him up. He was insured for two hundred and fifty grand, double for accidental death. The argument will be whether it was accidental or self-inflicted.'

'Maybe the same insurance company should hire me,' I suggested, 'to find out who put heavy doses of Zolpidem and hydrogen peroxide in the pakoras, the first to knock him out, the second to make him vomit. I take it you're having the stomach contents and blood analysed.'

'The client isn't paying for that. See, I was right,' she said. 'You should write crime novels.' Then she paused. 'Do you really think I should?'

'I would,' I told her. 'In a thirty-year police career I've never heard of anyone dying like that, just from having a few beers and eating his dinner, least of all a young fit man.'

'Jimi Hendrix?' Sarah suggested.

'Go and read his PM report. He was drugged up to the eyeballs when he choked to death.'

'Hey, you've got me worried,' she murmured.

'No reason to be,' I said. 'Call the insurers; tell them you've consulted an independent source and been advised that tests are necessary.'

'Okay, I will; first thing in the morning. Got to go now; I'm almost home.'

'Give the kids a hug for me. Love you.' And I really do.

Mia had come back to me while I was speaking to Sarah. I was about to return both calls when she beat me to it.

'Sorry,' she began. 'When you called I was on air, just coming out of a commercial break.' She sounded nervous.

'Understood. How's the job going?'

'Very well, thanks. I'm building an audience already. Drive-time's a good slot to have, because a lot of people tune in for the local traffic info. The trick is to keep them listening once they're home, and I seem to be doing that. Healthy audience equals happy advertisers and sponsors . . . so happy that the boss has asked me if I'll do a Sunday morning show as well.'

'I'm very pleased for you,' I lied; I didn't begrudge her success, but I'd have preferred it to be happening in another country, 'but I doubt that you called me to give me a career update. What's up?'

'I had a creepy caller this afternoon,' she replied, 'around ten past four. I get all sorts of people phoning in, all ages, not just kids like I had on the Airburst station in Edinburgh, when you and I met. They're supposed to be vetted before they're put through, but this one got past.'

'How old was this caller? Was it a man or woman?'

'It was a man; I can only guess at his age, but the voice was mature, husky, like a smoker.'

'Did he give his name?'

'Of course. He wouldn't have got on air otherwise; he was called Linton, or so he said.'

I felt my eyes widen, but I did my best not to react in any way Mia could pick up on.

'First name or surname?'

She paused. 'I don't know; my producer didn't say before she put him through.'

'What did he say that spooked you?' I asked, trying to sound impatient.

'He said that he was calling on behalf of a female friend who was too nervous to phone in herself. He said that she had a son who's in prison, the product of a brief relationship back in the nineties. He said that the boy had been convicted of a serious crime, and that his father knew about it but was refusing to acknowledge him.'

'Fuck!' I whispered.

'I had trouble stopping myself from saying exactly the same on air,' Mia admitted. 'But I managed. Instead I asked him if he had a question. He said yes, how would I advise his friend.

Should she out the father, who's a prominent figure, even though he's threatened her, physically, if she ever does.'

'What did you say?'

'I told him that if his friend feared for her safety she should report the father to the police and ask for protection. He was going to come in with a follow-up, but I cut him off and cued up a song, three minutes ahead of schedule. As soon as it started I told my producer never to put the guy through to me again.'

Her voice rose as she spoke, and I could hear fear in it. 'Bob, what was that about?' she exclaimed.

'Maybe it was genuine,' I replied. I was trying to talk down her alarm.

'Are you kidding?' she snapped back at me. 'It was some sort of a weird message, to me, to you, I don't know, but he was telling me something, not asking. He knows whose son Ignacio is, Bob, and if he goes public with it, God knows what might happen to him in jail!'

'Calm down, Mia.' I wasn't feeling too calm myself; the mention of that name had wound me up tight. 'Did he try to get through again?'

'No.'

'Do you have a record of the call?'

'Of course; we have to record all our output.'

'Sure, but do you have the originating number?'

'Yes. I asked about it as soon as I came off air. It was an Edinburgh number. Do you want it?'

'Yes,' I said, 'text it to me as soon as we're done here. Mia, has there been any follow-up? Have you had any calls from the media? I know the press sometimes monitor live radio looking for controversy.'

'No, there's been nothing.'

'Then don't panic. Does your employer know about Ignacio?'

'The MD does; I told him my whole life story as soon as we began talking seriously about the job. But nobody else knows, and nobody here has ever linked me to the case or to my mother's death. I'm on the payroll here as Mia Spreckley; all the coverage referred to her as Bella Watson. Her maiden name was never used.'

She had a point: almost. When Ignacio Centelleos, a Spanish national according to his birth certificate and passport, appeared in court charged with the culpable homicide of Bella Watson and with disposing of her body, the trial judge, Lord Nelson, and the prosecutor, Moira Cleverley, knew the full story, but it was never told in open court.

It had been presented as a family dispute in which Bella had gone berserk with a cleaver and had been stabbed by the boy in his mother's defence. Mia's name had never been mentioned; neither had mine, but I had come clean to Archie Nelson and to the Lord Advocate, both of whom were due me a couple of favours. The affair had been kept as discreet as possible, for Ignacio's sake, not ours, but it wasn't watertight.

'But it was known,' I sighed. 'That's what her neighbours called her; all her household bills had that name too. If anyone wanted to find out who you were, it wouldn't take long. Even the world's slowest search engine would turn you up inside a minute.'

'Who would want to?' she wailed. 'This Linton character: does that name mean anything to you, Bob?'

'It does now,' I growled. 'If it's any consolation, I think that call was a message, but to me, not to you.'

'What sort of a message?'

I took a few seconds to think about that, and about the events of the afternoon, not least the timing of my encounter with Carrie McDaniels. That had happened a couple of hours before the call to Mia.

'A threat; the clear implication is that Linton – it's a forename, by the way; the other one's Baillie – thinks he knows who Ignacio's dad is, namely, yours truly. The guy's interested in me, for some reason; I believe that he got to know that I'd found out, and decided to send me a warning. It might even have been his way of introducing himself to me.'

'What are you going to do about it?' Mia asked. 'Find Mr Baillie and put the fear of God in him?'

'That would be difficult for me right now, since I'm in Spain. When I'm back, I'll deal with him, but as things stand, I don't believe it's in his interests to go public with the story that I'm Ignacio's dad. There wouldn't be enough money in it for him.'

'This is about money?' she gasped.

'Most things are,' I growled. 'Baillie will have to show his hand eventually. Until he does, he's not my biggest concern.'

'Then what is, for God's sake?'

'For one, a missing man here that I'm trying to find. For another, unless he's taken a wildly inspired guess and it's come off, I want to know how the hell he found out the truth about you, me and our boy.'

Six

Linton Baillie hadn't used his own phone to call Mia's programme. As soon as her text arrived with the number the station had logged, I couldn't resist dialling it, but something told me that if he was playing games, he wasn't going to deal me a good hand.

I let it ring for half a minute; just as I was about to give up it was answered. A male voice said, 'Hullo,' tentatively.

'Is Mr Baillie available?' I asked.

'How the fuck would Ah ken, mate?' the man replied, laughing. 'This is a phone box in John Lewis.' I killed the call, leaving him with a story to relate to his pals in the pub.

Did I consider withdrawing my offer to Xavi to help find Hector, and heading straight back to Scotland to pursue Mr Linton Baillie?

Well, yes I did, but only briefly. As I told Mia, I didn't believe there was an imminent threat to Ignacio's security in Jail. However, I'm far from omniscient; if all the mistakes I've made in my life could be turned into mileage, they'd circumscribe the planet.

As a failsafe, I phoned my daughter Alex, and asked her to call on the Governor of Polmont Young Offenders' Institution and let him in on the secret, so that the lad could be protected immediately, should the truth be leaked.

I tried to get away without telling her why I wanted it done, but she knows I'm not an impulse buyer, and that there's a specific reason for everything I do. When I told her about Baillie, and Carrie McDaniels, and the call to Mia's programme from a public phone, she went volcanic.

'Who is this man?' she shouted. 'I'll find him, I'll go to court and I'll tie him up in an interdict so tight his bloody eyes will pop out! He won't be able to come within a mile of you or any member of our family.'

'Thanks, love,' I said, 'but that won't help. The interdict itself wouldn't be secret; it would draw attention to the problem. When I'm ready, I'll make his eyes pop myself. But there's one thing you can do. D'you remember me telling you that I had a second DNA test done on Ignacio and me?'

'Of course I do. You used a lab in Glasgow, didn't you?'

'That's right. I went there in person, and dealt with the director of the clinic personally; I gave him the samples, but I didn't say whose they were. He assumed that it was police business, and I didn't correct him: but I did pay with my own debit card.

'I'd like you to have a chat with him; not a threatening chat, mind, just a conversation. Without saying why, ask him to check whether there's been any unauthorised access to the records of the tests.'

She was still fizzing with anger. 'Oh, I will, don't you worry,' she murmured. 'I won't threaten him with anything; I'll let him make another assumption, that's all.' She paused for a couple of seconds. 'Dad, can't I do anything about this man Baillie? Knowing he's out there, using Ignacio as a weapon against you . . .'

I understood her frustration. At that moment, I'd have liked to be standing on the guy's doorstep, with no witnesses.

'There is one thing,' I suggested. 'Sauce says that he writes true crime books. See if you can find any, and read them. They might give you some insight into the man.'

'I will do,' she promised. I heard her draw a breath. 'Pops,' she continued, although she sounded hesitant, 'is there any chance this could have leaked from within the police force?'

'That's a fair question, love,' I conceded, 'but I don't believe so. Yes, a DNA link between me and Ignacio was established during the investigation into Bella Watson's murder, when they ran his sample through the national database, but the only people who knew about it were Sammy Pye and Sauce Haddock, who investigated the murder, Arthur Dorward, the forensic team leader, and his technicians . . . and two others. When Arthur saw the findings he reported them directly to Maggie Steele and Mario McGuire, as chief constable and assistant chief. The knowledge went no further than that group and none of those would talk, none of them.'

'Not even the technicians?'

'No chance.'

Her silence told me that she wasn't one hundred per cent convinced.

'Trust me on that,' I insisted.

'You're sure?'

'Certain. Now go on, do as I asked.'

'Okay, I will, but you do one thing for me. Put this distraction right out of your head and focus on what you're in Spain to do; leave Baillie to me, and get on with considering your future. By the way,' she added, 'Andy said he wants to talk to you about that when you get back.'

I smiled as I pocketed my phone. Andy Martin, my daughter's partner, and first chief constable of the new unified Scottish police service, had talked to me about nothing else in the weeks since he'd taken up his post.

I hadn't ruled out all of the suggestions he'd made, but I was clear that whatever I did would be on my terms, and I wouldn't be calling anyone 'Sir' . . . the truth is, I was never very good at that . . . especially not him, the guy I'd given a leg up to as a raw young detective constable, twenty years before.

I had made my calls from Xavi's garden; there was a chill in the evening air, but nothing in comparison to December Scotland. I took a deep breath and then exhaled, gazing up at the stars. I've always liked dark skies; maybe, when finally I do retire, I'll take up astronomy . . . that's if I don't buy that boat I'm forever promising myself.

I heard the squeak of an unoiled hinge from behind me, and turned to see Xavi, standing in the open patio doors, his head touching the top of the frame. I strolled back towards him.

'All well at home?' he asked.

'Sure,' I replied, then moved on quickly. 'Did you call your Mossos friend?'

'Yes, and I caught him in his office, as I thought. I'm sorry it took so long, but here you don't simply ask for a favour. You make a bargain, and Comissari Canals is a bloody tough negotiator.'

'Even when you're reporting a potentially stolen car?'

'Particularly so, when it's me calling him: the managing director calling the police chief.'

'Did he ask the wrong questions?'

'No, he's a good guy; he's having a major raid on drug importers next week, and I've promised him a splash in all our outlets when he's ready to go public with the results.'

I smiled. 'I know how the game works,' I said. 'You and I played it ourselves a few times, in Edinburgh when you ran the *Saltire*.'

He nodded. 'I suppose we did,' he chuckled, 'but you always got a hell of a lot more out of it than I did. Come on, let's have dinner and talk over old times. I feel a lot better than I did before you got here, knowing that I'm actually doing something about Hector.'

He led the way indoors and through to a long dining room; there was a big pine table in the centre, and it was set for six, although it could have seated three times as many, easily. Sheila was waiting for us, and with her were Paloma, Joe and a woman I hadn't met.

'This is Carmen,' Xavi said, leading me towards her, 'Joe's partner.'

She smiled as she extended a hand; she was of medium height and slim, with dark hair and beautiful brown eyes. I knew that she had to be in her mid-fifties, but she'd have passed for ten years younger. In her presence Joe had a twinkle in his eye that hadn't been apparent earlier.

'The artist,' I murmured, as we shook hands.

She nodded. 'The policeman.'

'Señora,' I replied, 'your work is much more distinguished than mine.'

'Wow!' Xavi laughed. 'Dad, you'd better watch this guy.' He caught my surprise at the paternal reference. 'I thought he was my father until I was in my twenties,' he reminded me. 'I've never broken the habit completely.'

Dinner was a quiet family meal, a blend of local and British, with a salad of chorizo and other *embotits* (thinly sliced cold sausages; there are seventeen varieties in Catalunya) as the starter, followed by roast chicken and chips with fried onion rings on the side. Dessert was Crema Catalana, the local version of crème brûlée, but with more cinnamon; it was home-made, not shop bought . . . as most are, in most restaurants . . . and finished off by Sheila with a blowtorch, to melt and brown the sugar on top. I suspected that she had prepared it in my honour, for it's quite fiddly to make.

As we ate, I stuck to sparkling water; I don't like mixing cava with anything else, and besides, I keep an eye on my intake these days, particularly when I'm away from home.

As Xavi had promised, the dinner table chat was personal rather than business. Paloma was keen to hear about my family; I told her it was extended, and that my children with Sarah had a much older half-sister, just as she had Ben.

'Does she treat them like brothers and sisters?' she asked. The question surprised me and that must have registered on my face, for she added, 'Sometimes Ben treats me as if I was his niece, or even his daughter. Yes, he's eighteen years older than me, but still he shouldn't talk to me as if I was just a kid.'

'I suppose Alex does the same, sometimes,' I admitted. 'She doesn't have children of her own, not yet, so she does spoil them, especially Seonaid, the youngest; and she's very protective of them . . . all of them.' I had a flash recollection of her fury when I'd told her of the possible threat to Ignacio. 'It doesn't bother me; it's natural. The counter-question, Paloma, is how do they treat her? How do you think of Ben?' I asked her.

'Oh, he's my brother, that's all, and I remind him of that every time he gets stroppy with me.'

'When does he do that?' Sheila asked, with a trace of annoyance.

'Usually after I've beaten him on the Playstation. He's a bad loser.'

'Mmm,' she murmured. 'I must have a word with him about that; his father had the same unfortunate trait: I've never noticed it in Ben before . . .'

'Why should you have?' Xavi asked, with a grin. 'Dads and sons, it's different, but you don't have a pissing contest with your mum.'

'Good point,' she conceded. 'Nor should a grown man with his twelve-year-old sister.'

'You said "he had",' I observed. 'You spoke of your first husband in the past tense. Does that mean . . .'

She shook her head, firmly and quickly. 'No, it doesn't, not necessarily. I've thought of him in that way from the moment he walked out the door, seventeen years ago. He never left a forwarding address or got in touch. A year later, when I wanted to divorce him, I tried to find him through his employers, but they told me he'd changed jobs. I had to wait for another year before I could get rid of him legally. I have no idea where he is now, but I've never had any reason to think that he's dead.'

'Does Ben have any contact with him?'

'I'd be amazed if he has. Xavi, you talk about competition between fathers and sons, but Gavin McNeish was downright jealous of Ben right from the start, and it got worse the older he became. I don't know why I tolerated it for so long.'

Her frown deepened and then she added, 'No, I suppose I do. It was his job. He was a long-distance lorry driver, and he had routes that took him right across Europe. He could be away for as long as three weeks at a time, and when he came home he expected to be waited on hand and foot. "Me first", that was his philosophy. If anybody ever crossed him, or told him he was wrong about something, he'd go into a terrible huff.'

She sipped some wine. 'The bugger never spent a penny on Ben either, or on me for that matter. He paid the mortgage and that was it. When he was home, it was my salary that fed him and clothed our son. We never went on holiday as a family; I took Ben to Center Parcs once, when he was ten, but he wouldn't even go there.'

'You put up with it for too long, my dear,' old Joe said. 'I treated my wife with perfect respect, yet she walked out on me and on Xavi.'

'You treated her with total indifference,' Xavi countered, 'but I know you had your reasons; we won't go there.'

'I suppose I did, Joe,' Sheila agreed, 'but he was away far more often than he was at home, and when it was just the two of us, Ben and me, it was fine.'

'Why did he leave, in the end?' I asked.

She sighed. 'To this day,' she replied 'I don't know. Another woman? Possibly. The only thing he said was, "Look, Sheila, this isn't working for me any longer." Then he packed all his clothes in the cases I'd bought to take Ben on holiday, put all his other things in a box, and went off in the cab of his lorry.'

She smiled, suddenly. 'And did me a bigger favour than he could ever have imagined. Not that long afterwards, Xavi came into A&E having fallen off his bike, and we reconnected, twenty years or so after we'd met as teenagers.'

'Wherever the guy is now,' her husband said, 'I hope he knows how it worked out. I've often thought I'd like to meet him, just so I could shake his hand.'

'I could find him,' I murmured.

'I'll bet you could,' he said, 'but on balance I think it's best left as it is.'

'I'll still be having a word with my son, though,' Sheila

declared, 'as soon as he comes in. Getting stroppy with his little sister, indeed!'

Xavi winked; he was more relaxed than I'd ever seen him. 'If he comes in,' he murmured.

'Why shouldn't he?' she asked.

He beamed at her. 'You haven't met our fashion editor, have you?'

Seven

When I was very young, I regarded a direct instruction from my father as a basis for negotiation; since I've been an adult my attitude has hardened.

I'd heard what he said about not going after Mr Linton Baillie, but I knew full well what Pops would be doing if he was in the same country as the man.

At the very least, I was going to track him down. But first things first; he had asked me to do three specific things for him and they had priority.

I was at home alone when he called me; that was probably just as well, for Andy would have wanted to know what was up and either I'd have lied and said, 'Nothing,' or I'd have told him to mind his own business, or I'd have told him the truth.

None of these would have been good, but the last would have been the worst of all, because that would have made it official. He always did his best to draw a line between home and work, as did I, but if he knew the substance and implications of the call that I had received, the distinction might have been blurred, and he might have felt duty bound to do something about it.

Chief Constable Andrew Martin: the badges of his new

rank still sit uncomfortably on the shoulders of the black tunic uniform that he's taken to wearing.

To be frank, I haven't quite got my head round the truth that the guy I've known since I was a kid is the top cop in Scotland, that he's in the job that was sure to be my father's until he stunned the Scottish media, and a few other people too, by withdrawing his candidacy.

Publicly, Dad offered no reason for his decision. Privately, within the family, he said that when my half-brother Ignacio is revealed as his son, once he's done his time, the inevitable headlines would make his position untenable.

I've never believed a word of that excuse. My old man's come through bigger crises than that and swatted them aside. He'll never admit it, not even in the official memoirs that he's been offered a lot of money to write, but the day that he was persuaded to put on a chief constable's uniform, by people who didn't really know him at all, was the day he started to feel something that he'd never encountered before in his life . . . boredom.

When the Strathclyde force that he headed, however briefly, passed into history, and his job disappeared, friends and former colleagues felt sorry for him. I didn't, I felt relieved, because I knew that finally he could get back to being who he wanted to be . . . once he'd figured out who that is.

I knew that, because I find myself in the same situation.

My father's life and my own mirror each other. We were both young achievers, professionally. We were both emotional disaster areas. We both walked away from established relationships, me with Andy, Dad with my stepmother Sarah: in his case that was a major mistake.

Down the road, we both got back to where we had been,

albeit after causing pain to other people. Andy was a lousy husband to his wife, Karen, and I have to accept some blame for that, whatever they both say.

Dad was as bad with Aileen, in his brief third marriage, because he'd never left Sarah, in his heart. Okay, Aileen gave him grief too, but it doesn't absolve him.

Me? As good as I am as a lawyer, I was at least twice as bad at romance.

But it's in my professional life that once again I find myself as a reflection of my father.

As a law student, I had dreams of following him, not by joining the police force, but by becoming an advocate specialising in criminal work, just as he has done as a cop. However, after I graduated, I found myself, not manoeuvred . . . that would be too strong a word because it implies deviousness . . . but steered by him towards a trainee place with Curle Anthony and Jarvis, a big Edinburgh firm, and one which does purely civil work.

Before I knew it, I was fully qualified and on the ladder to promotion as a corporate solicitor. Before I knew it I'd been made a partner, one of CAJ's youngest ever, and was winning gongs. Before I knew it, I was 'Young Lawyer of the Year', followed by the ludicrously titled 'Dealmaker of the Year' . . . whatever the hell that means, for it's nothing to me.

All that success, and the big money I was earning, blinded me for a while to an uncomfortable truth: just like my dad, in his big remote offices, in Edinburgh and later in Glasgow, I was bored.

It dawned on me one night, after dinner with Andy at his place beside the Water of Leith. We were discussing our careers and our ambitions. His was quite clear: he wanted to succeed my father eventually as head of the Scottish police service.

'Okay, now you,' he said, after making his declaration.

I sat there nestling against him, listening to the little river ripple past beneath the balcony; I looked into the future, and I saw . . .

'Nothing,' I heard myself murmur. I was as if I'd been disembodied, for a moment, but I returned to myself pretty quick.

'I don't have one. I can't have one; all that's open to me is being head of the Corporate Department, which could well happen in five years. Beyond that, I suppose I'll be a candidate to chair the practice once Mitch Laidlaw retires, if he ever does.

'But Andy, I don't want either of those jobs,' I confessed. 'That means that all I can see in my future, as we sit here, is another thirty years of fucking deal-making, of helping people with lots of money make even more money!'

He eased himself away and stared at me, his green eyes wider than usual. 'I had no idea you felt that way,' he exclaimed.

'Neither had I,' I confessed, 'until this very moment.'

'What are you going to do about it?'

'What can I do about it? I have commitments.'

'You could have more; we could have kids.'

That is dangerous ground between the two of us, and I chose not to disturb it. 'That's a separate issue,' I replied. 'It wouldn't affect my career, not these days.'

'Then what do you want?'

'I don't know.'

And I didn't, not until my father did what he did, and

showed me the way forward. One week after he pulled his application papers from the Police Scotland job, I went into Mitchell Laidlaw's office and achieved what I'd thought was impossible. I took my urbane, unblinking, all-knowing boss completely by surprise.

'I'm leaving the practice,' I told him. 'I'm going to practise as a solicitor advocate. I want rights of audience in the Supreme Court.'

Mitch is the best lawyer I know, and one of the best thinkers; every word he utters has a point to it. It took him a full minute to frame a response.

'You can do that within this firm, Alex,' he said. 'I've been considering adding that string to CAJ's bow for some time now, having counsel in-house, and moving away from employing them as the need arises. Complete the training, and I'll transfer you to the Litigation Department. You can replace Jocky Scott as senior partner there when he retires.'

'I'm sorry, Mitch,' I replied, 'but I don't want to do civil law. I want to establish a criminal practice.'

That's when his mouth fell open and he stepped out of character. 'What?' he gasped. 'You're going to hawk yourself around the detention cells, like Frances Birtles and her crew?'

I smiled at his surprise. 'Think of it as me setting up in opposition to my father and my partner. They lock them up, I'll get them out.'

He fell silent for another minute, before saying, 'Then God help the Crown Office. The prosecution's in for a hard time.'

My partnership agreement specified six months' notice, but as I'd expected, Mitch put me on gardening leave as soon as I had handed over all my existing work; I don't have a garden, but that stuff is complex and confidential and couldn't be left with someone who was heading for the exit.

That evening, I told Andy what I'd done, and he was fine with it; after our head-to-head discussion, it didn't come as a surprise to him. As for my father, to avoid him trying to talk me out of it, as I knew he would, I explained my absence from CAJ by telling him that I was on a training course . . . as indeed I was, for the advocacy exams that were due in February.

He swallowed the cover story, and even gave me my first assignment without knowing it. When Ignacio was arrested in Spain and extradited to Scotland, accused of doing in his granny, Dad asked me to put together his defence team.

Although my first criminal client was my half-brother, I was able to keep our relationship secret, even from his counsel, the aforementioned Frances Birtles QC. She's the go-to solicitor advocate in Scotland, the woman I plan to become.

'Why you?' she asked, when I approached her. 'Since when did corporate whizz-kids get their hands dirty with criminal work?'

'I was born with that kind of grime under my fingernails,' I told her. 'No matter how hard I tried, I couldn't scrub it away.'

Frankie did a brilliant job of defending Ignacio, but even she was surprised when the Crown accepted a plea to culpable homicide, and again when the judge suspended half of his four-year sentence. If she suspected that another pleader had been at work, she was shrewd enough to keep that to herself and bask in the media glory of her latest triumph.

When Dad had finished briefing me on his latest problem, I went straight to my desk and switched on my computer.

Linton Baillie wasn't hard to find, as an author. A search showed work on Amazon, and on the websites of two other online retailers. I went to the first, because I have an account, and looked at his page.

There were three books listed, each with a garish title, and blood featuring heavily in its jacket design. Reader reviews gave three of them five stars, with the others scoring four and three and a half . . . a dodgy guideline, when you consider that Amazon readers also give four plus ratings to Hitler's *Mein Kampf* and even to *Struwwelpeter*, the only book I've ever read that I believe should be banned.

I skimmed through Baillie's synopses; one of them seemed to be set in gangland London, one was a biography of a Glasgow crime lord with a brutish nickname, and the third purported to 'unveil the deadly hand of the British security services in unsolved homicides'.

London didn't seem immediately relevant so I bought the last two . . . *Where the Bodies are Buried* and *The Public Executioner* . . . in eBook form.

While I waited for them to download on to my Kindle, I did a little more Googling. Dad had told me that Sauce Haddock hadn't come up with any images of the man, but I was looking for something else, for anything that might help me locate him.

Normally if you enter an individual's name into a search engine, you will come up with a website that gives you locations for everyone of that name in the UK, then offers to sell you the details.

'Linton Baillie' came up with nothing; while there were plenty of Linton references, and even more for Baillie, it seemed that if the person I was after lived in Britain, he wasn't on the electoral roll, and he wasn't a telephone subscriber.

The one thing that I did know about him was that he had a publisher. All his books had the same imprint, Donside. I searched for that and came up with a website. It was London-based, and seemed to specialise in non-fiction; it didn't offer an extensive catalogue but there was an address, in Titchfield Street, and a phone number that I would use when I was ready.

There was nothing else I could do there and then, and so I picked up my e-reader; it was a bit of a bugger, since I'd been approaching the conclusion of an enjoyable historical drama called *Mathew's Tale*, but I knew where my duty lay and so I settled down for an evening with *The Public Executioner*.

Eight

I woke at seven next morning, still in my armchair, in yesterday's clothes with my Kindle in my lap. My head felt like mush, and my right leg was tucked under me. I squeezed my eyes tight shut, then blinked, trying to clear the former, while freeing the latter and stretching it out, pulling my toes towards me in a vain attempt to fight off a pins and needles feeling so severe that I knew I wouldn't be able to stand for a while.

I was prepared to say one positive thing about Linton Baillie: he knew how to hold the reader's attention. Some of his allegations seemed far-fetched and poorly sourced, and his crime scene descriptions were graphic to say the least, but he had a decent prose style.

I'd finished the Secret Service exposé, which read like a series of *Spooks* episodes, and I'd been almost through the gangster yarn when I'd fallen asleep. That had been strewn with west of Scotland crime 'faces', as Baillie described them. None of them meant anything to me, not until a character from Edinburgh made his presence felt.

When I was a child, my dad never talked to me about his work, but when I reached my mid-teens he began to loosen up. A man called Tony Manson featured in a couple of his stories, and they didn't have a happy ending. While Mr Manson was one of Edinburgh's most notorious criminal figures, he must have been as good at his job as Bob Skinner was at his, if not better, for he was one of the very few that my father was never able to put away.

It took someone else to do that, a man who crossed him in business, then stabbed him to death in his mansion in the west of Edinburgh.

He'll deny it now, and always will, but Dad was affected by Manson's death. When I pressed him on the subject, all he would say was, 'Tony Manson had his own rules. There was a degree of perverse morality about them and he lived by them. I wanted to see him in prison, yes, but not dead.'

'You mean you liked him?' I persisted.

'No, I did not,' he insisted, vehemently. 'But criminality is a fact of life. When we put someone away, that's it; but when a guy is taken out, as Manson was, you don't celebrate too hard, because it creates a vacuum, and you know how nature feels about those.'

Manson was more than a peripheral figure in Baillie's story; if the author's assertion was correct, he was responsible for the murder of Gerry McGarrity, the oldest son of James McGarrity, the Godfather figure in the yarn. He seemed to disappear from the narrative after that intervention, but I still had a few chapters to go.

They could wait till later, I decided. I had things to do that day and I needed to look and feel presentable. To shake the stiffness out of my bones, and work off those pins and needles, I put on my thermals, my tracksuit and my trainers, and headed off for a run.

81

Leaving my apartment block, I jogged past the Scottish parliament building and into Holyrood Park. The morning was crisp and cold, and frost lay on the ground, but the pathway was lit well enough to be safe, and there was enough of a moon in the clear sky to let me see where I was going.

I wasn't alone; the Queen's Park is a popular location for runners and even at that hour the footprints of up to half a dozen people could be seen in the hoary white crystals.

I added mine to them, heading past Dynamic Earth, and *The Scotsman* office, then up the steep incline that leads towards the Dalkeith Road exit. On the way I passed three of the earlier runners on the way back. They seemed to be having problems with the frost on the way downhill, so I decided not to take that risk, leaving the park instead and choosing a longer way home.

As I ran, I contemplated several things.

I thought of my relationship with Andy, which had become just as comfortable as it was first time around.

Back then, he had visions of a perfect family unit with two kids, boy first, girl second; I had visions of an uninterrupted legal career until I turned thirty, after which I might get around to the children thing.

When I got careless and found myself pregnant at least eight years ahead of schedule, I had a termination. Andy was never meant to find out, but he did, and that was the end of us, for that time.

When we came together again, each of us had been wounded, and, far worse, had hurt others. We'd both learned from that, and second time around, we'd promised to be more considerate towards each other.

Andy's dynastic ambitions have been realised; he has two kids . . . girl first, boy second, but nobody's perfect. I've hit the thirty mark, but the only broodiness I feel is for the new career I'm planning.

We're both career-driven people, and our unspoken pact was that my job, whatever that might be, is as important as Andy's, however high and mighty he's become, no more, no less . . . or so I thought.

Running past St Leonard's Police Office, my mind turned inevitably to my father.

Poor Dad: a few weeks ago I was in the Cafe Royal's Circle Bar with Andy when we overheard . . . it was impossible not to . . . a loud-mouthed quantity surveyor in the midst of a crowd of his old school chums. (Why do people wear ties that advertise their education?)

'Hey,' he boomed, gleefully, to his conscripted audience, 'what do you think of the mighty Bob Skinner? It looks as if he's having a mid-life crisis, does it not?'

Andy went across to the group and had a quiet word in the clown's ear. They quietened down and left shortly afterwards. It was a pre-emptive strike by my partner; if he hadn't intervened I might have torn the guy a new one and he'd have been obliged to arrest me!

If the idiot had chosen to pursue his point, I'd have told him that my dad's been having mid-life crises since his mid-twenties. I know this because I've been witness to most of them, having been raised by him as a single parent since my mother's early death.

When I passed that police office on that cold morning I realised that I was happier for him than I have ever been. Okay, he was still confused about his future, hence the trip to

Spain, but for the first time in his adult life he had the chance to be truly his own master.

He's served the public for more than thirty years, often at great personal risk, and nearly always with emotional consequences.

He's always been there for me, and I'll always be there for him.

My eyes were misty with unexpected tears as I passed the Pleasance; I blinked them away as I took the turn that led me back home, and began to plan my day. It had the potential to be a long one, and it would involve travel.

As I stepped out of the lift and into my top-floor apartment, it was still a couple of minutes short of eight o'clock, and the day had yet to dawn, but I felt wide awake, for all my unconventional night's sleep.

The indicator light on my phone showed a voice message; I picked up the handset and took it with me into the bathroom. I reviewed it, as soon as I'd stripped off my running gear, and just before stepping into the shower compartment.

I'd expected it to be Andy, calling before he left for Glasgow to confirm our tentative arrangement that I'd cook dinner at his place that evening, or possibly my dad, who sometimes forgets time zone differences, ringing to tell me once again not to pursue Linton Baillie.

I had not expected it to be Mia Sparkles.

She and I had been in contact during Ignacio's trial and prosecution, but only out of necessity. The woman was in my life very briefly when I was a teenager, and I do not want her back any more than she has to be. By rights she should have gone to jail along with her son, but by some miracle there had been no evidence to corroborate her admission that she'd helped him dump her mother's body, and without that the Crown Office had been unable to charge her. As it played out, Cornton Vale Prison's loss was the Dundee listening public's gain.

Her voice gave the lie to her radio name; there was nothing twinkling or vivacious about it, instead she sounded tired and rattled.

'Alex,' the message began, 'I'm sorry to be calling so early, but I phoned your father and he said I should. He says he told you about the call I had on air yesterday, from this man Linton. I've had another, on my home phone this time. Please call me back.'

Standing naked in my en suite, with perspiration cooling on my body, I chose the recall option on the messenger menu and waited.

'This is Alex,' I said, probably a little testily, as soon as she answered.

'Thanks for calling back.' Mia sounded calmer than she had a few seconds before. 'I don't know what Bob thinks you can do about this, but anything you can will be welcome.'

'I'm going to be in touch with the institution later,' I told her. 'The more I can give them the better. Tell me about this call. When did you receive it?'

'At seven o'clock,' she replied. 'The bastard woke me. My home number's ex-directory, Alex. How the hell did he get it?'

'Bribery sounds like a reasonable guess to me. A guy like this has contacts.'

'A guy like what? Do you know something about him?'

'Yes, but tell me what he said.'

'Very little,' she replied. 'He didn't have to tell me who was calling, not after his first few words; I recognised his voice straight off. "You got the message, I take it." That was how he began. I asked him what exactly that message was, and he said, "I know your whole story: you and Skinner, and your boy. I want to talk to you."

'I said, "And I want you to fuck off and leave me alone, or I'll have you done for harassing me." He laughed. He laughed at me, Alex! "Do you think Skinner will let you do that?" he asked me. "Does he want it all to come out, and does he want his son identified to every hard kid in Polmont Young Offenders? If he is, he'll have an arsehole like the Clyde Tunnel by the time he comes out, that's if he makes it out alive."

'Come on, Alex, tell me. Who is this man? He doesn't know who he's messing with. He doesn't realise I'm descended from a line of psychos on my mother's side.'

This was not Mia Sparkles as her fans know her.

'Will you calm down,' I snapped, 'and cease the hysterical threats. I know who and what he is, but that's all at the moment; "where" has still to be determined. Obviously he has an agenda, but we have no idea what that is, not yet. I'm dealing with this for Dad, Mia, and keeping Ignacio safe is my first priority. After I've done that, I'll try to answer all the other questions. All I ask of you is that you let me get on with it; I definitely do not want you getting involved.'

I paused to give that time to sink in.

'Okay,' she murmured. 'I'll trust you, for now. How can I help?'

'You can begin by telling me how your call ended. Did you agree to meet him?'

'Hell no. It ended with me slamming the phone down, after I'd promised to rip his scrotum off.'

'Did you check last caller number on your phone?'

'No, sorry, I wasn't thinking that straight. I didn't and when you called me back, it'll have wiped it out.'

'Pity . . . although the chances are he used a public phone, as he did yesterday. If he contacts you again . . .'

'Do you think he will?'

'If he really does want to talk to you, there's every chance. If he does, I want you to agree to it . . . but,' I added, heavily, 'only in person, not over the phone. Make an arrangement, let me know straightaway and I'll be there too. What you said earlier was true; he doesn't know who he's dealing with.'

'What can you do to him?' she asked, with a trace of scorn.

'I'm a lawyer, Mia. I can rip his balls off too, but I can do it through the court, and through his wallet.'

She laughed at that notion, and our discussion ended more calmly than it had begun.

An hour later I was showered, breakfasted and in my car, heading for Polmont Young Offenders' Institution, where the Scottish government locks up seriously bad boys under the age of twenty-one. They don't call it a prison, but it is; I'd been there on a few occasions as Ignacio's lawyer while he was on remand, and once after he'd been sentenced. I'd never been to a prison before; I know already that it's the one part of my new career that I am not going to like.

I was expected; I'd prepared the way by phoning the Governor (yes, they still use that archaic title) and asking for an urgent meeting on behalf of my client, Ignacio Centelleos.

His secretary had begun by offering me ten minutes at ten o'clock next morning.

'Bring that forward by twenty-four hours, and you'll meet

my concept of urgency,' I told her. 'It's a matter of personal security.'

People in my former professional world did not sigh and say, 'Hmph!' but she did, followed by a very grudging, 'Hold on.'

I did, until she came back on line, with another sigh, and said, 'Very well, Mr Kemp will see you, but for five minutes, maximum, that's all, Miss . . . er?'

'Skinner; Alexis Skinner. Ms.'

I took the West Approach Road out of Edinburgh rather than risk being caught in traffic on its tedious bypass, and reached Newbridge and the motorway with time in hand to make my appointment without putting my foot down too hard. Before police unification, speed enforcement used to vary from force to force, but since my dear Andy has been in charge of the whole bloody country, it's uniformly rigorous. Given our history, any speeding tickets I get would be irrevocable for me and potentially embarrassing for him.

Polmont Young Offenders' Institution has been part of the Scottish prison system for over a hundred years, and some of it was in use before that as a private school; nevertheless it presents a modern face to visitors.

I left my eco-friendly hybrid sports car in the visitors' car park, and went through security, where a couple of the female staff recognised me from previous visits. They'd been told to expect me, and to escort me straight to the Governor's office.

I'd never met Christopher Kemp before, but my father had mentioned him on a few occasions, their paths having crossed when he was Governor of Saughton Prison in Edinburgh.

He didn't stand up when his po-faced secretary showed me into his room. His considerable bulk stayed firmly lodged in his big executive swivel rocker, behind his big desk, as he pointed at a straight-backed chair on the other side.

'Have a seat,' he began, raising a heavy eyebrow, 'and tell me what's so bloody urgent.' Then he leaned back, giving me an appraising look as I set myself down.

'No,' he exclaimed, 'before you do that, answer me one question. Alexis Skinner: any relation to Bob Skinner?'

I gazed back at him, without blinking, and I'm sure without the hint of a smile, for by that time I was feeling bloody angry.

'I'm his daughter,' I replied, just as he broke eye contact.

'I thought so,' he grunted. 'You've got his bearing about you. You're better-looking though, if I may say so.'

'I'm not sure that you may,' I replied, icily. 'Why do you ask about him?'

'I like to know who I'm dealing with, that's all. I may as well tell you, Ms Skinner, your father and I don't get on. He may have told you that.'

'No, he hasn't; he's never said anything about you, one way or the other. What's your problem with him?'

'He was bloody rude to me once, back when he was deputy chief in Edinburgh. A high-security remand prisoner killed himself in his cell at Saughton when I was Governor there, and your father bloody well blamed me for it. He told me to my face that it was my fault.'

The incident came back to me; the man had been a rapist, one whose guilt was so easy to prove beyond any reasonable doubt that he intended to admit it, in the hope that the judge would go easier on him for sparing his victim the ordeal of the courtroom. Dad had been pleased about that, but furious when he learned that the brute been able to spare himself too.

'As you say, Mr Kemp,' I murmured, 'you were the Governor; who else would he blame?'

'I can't watch every bloody prisoner all the bloody time,' he protested, 'not personally. Someone slipped up on the remand wing; he was disciplined for it.'

'How?'

'A formal reprimand.'

'Wow.'

Kemp bristled, and glanced at his watch. 'You're using up your five minutes, Ms Skinner, so get on with it. Let me warn you though: if you're here to ask me for some sort of favour for your client, you'll be out of luck. Your old man is history now; he's on his way out of the force, yesterday's man. He cuts no ice with me, not any more.'

I smiled; if that was how he saw it . . . 'How about Chief Constable Andrew Martin?' I asked. 'He's very much today's man. How does he rate in the ice-cutting department?'

The Governor frowned, less sure of himself. 'Obviously . . .' he began.

'Obviously he's someone you don't want to fall out with. Then take note: I'll be cooking his dinner this evening, and he'll probably make my breakfast tomorrow.'

Kemp frowned, shifting in his chair.

'If you really want to make this personal,' I told him, 'so be it. I can still play that game, but I don't want to. I expect no favours from you. I expect you to do your job, that's all. If what happens to that man in Saughton should happen to my client, after the information I'm about to give you, there will be no shuffling off blame, and there will be no token reprimand.'

The man ran his thick fingers though his straggly grey hair. 'Okay,' he sighed. 'We've got off on the wrong foot, Ms Skinner. What is it you have to tell me about your client and why do you believe he's in jeopardy in my institution?'

'He's not only my client,' I said, abruptly. 'He's my half-brother.'

Kemp's mouth hung open for several seconds, before he snapped it shut. 'He's what? I've got Bob Skinner's boy in here? Is that what you're telling me?'

'Exactly that. Ignacio Centelleos is my father's son, from a brief relationship almost twenty years ago. He knew nothing of him until a few months ago; his existence was only revealed by the investigation of the crime that put him in here.'

'Now it's my turn to say, "Wow"!' Kemp conceded. 'Who else knows about this?'

'No more than a dozen people; outside the family, only a handful of police officers, and three scientific officers. Not even Frances Birtles, his counsel, knew who she was representing.'

The Lord Advocate and the trial judge knew also, but I felt no need to share that with Kemp.

Kemp nodded. 'I can see the risk to the boy if it becomes known in here that he's Skinner's son, but if the loop's so small why should that happen?'

'There's a chance that we've had a leak, that's all I can tell you.'

'What do you want me to do?' Kemp asked.

'I want you to keep him safe,' I answered. 'How you do it, that's your business, but if there's as much as a scratch on him, there will be consequences, and not only for the scratcher.'

'I could put him in isolation this morning,' he suggested, then paused. 'The problem with that is, he's got another nine months to do. Whenever we take an inmate out of the general population, the rumour mill starts, so if you're happy with it, my inclination is to do nothing until I have to.'

'I'll accede to your judgement on that, Governor. Hopefully you'll never need to take action.' I frowned. 'Can I take it that you're not recording this conversation?' I asked.

He recoiled at my question. 'Ms Skinner . . .' he protested.

'Fine, just thought I'd ask. I haven't known my brother for very long, but I want the chance to get to know him better.'

'You will, don't worry. I'm pleased you've chosen to confide in me. Is there anything else I can do for you?'

I nodded as I rose from my uncomfortable chair. 'Yes, two things, if you would. I'd like to see Ignacio now, and also, if anyone asks for a visiting note other than his mother or me, or asks for any information about him, I want to know, soonest.'

'Are you saying I should refuse all visits other than the two of you?'

'Not necessarily. I want to know about them, that's all.'

'How about his father? Will he be visiting?'

'No, because that would raise eyebrows in security, and people would talk.'

I didn't need to go any further.

'Understood, understood. Let me set up your visit, Ms Skinner. We'll call it a legal consultation, shall we?'

In his new spirit of cooperation, Mr Kemp arranged for me to see Ignacio in a small room in the office area of the institution, rather than in the hall where visits normally take place.

As he stepped through the door, my half-brother wore an expression of puzzlement, which changed to surprise when he saw me. 'Alex,' he exclaimed, as his escort closed the door behind him, waiting in the corridor outside. We were really favoured; privacy is a rare privilege for people visiting prisons.

The Governor had even arranged for coffee; two mugs and a plate of biscuits had been delivered on a tray a few minutes earlier. 'This was not expected,' Ignacio said, as he took a mug in one hand and a Jaffa cake in the other. He frowned, as he added, 'There is no bad news, is there?'

'No,' I replied. 'Something's come up, that's all.'

'The screw said that it was legal business.'

I laughed. 'The screw, indeed; you're picking up the slang quickly enough. They prefer to be called prison officers.'

'Not by us. Prisoners call them Sir or Miss . . . apart from me; to me they are Señor or Señora.'

Ignacio was born in Spain and raised there, but his mother made sure that he grew up bilingual. His English is excellent, but a little over-formal, and his strong accent gives away his roots.

The meeting room had a window with a view of the area beyond the prison; he stood by it, mug in hand, looking at a world he was not due to see again for months. His profile still gives me goosebumps; I could be looking at a younger version of my dad, as I remember him from my childhood. He's the same height, a couple of inches over six feet, slimmer, although it struck me that his frame seemed to have thickened a little since the first time I'd met him three months before in the Polmont remand wing following his extradition.

'How is *mi madre*?' he asked me, quietly, still gazing through the window.

'Your mother's fine,' I assured him. 'Her new radio show is very popular.'

'That is what she said when she was here at the weekend; we can't get her station here. I have heard her on radio in Spain; she is like another person. On air she is very . . .' he looked for a word, 'confident, but not so much at home. There she is much more anxious.'

That struck a chord with me; on the few occasions in my teens that I'd seen my father in a professional situation, it struck me that he wasn't the man that I knew at home, but another, more confident, assertive, at ease with himself.

Christ, Pops, I thought, was I that much of a burden?

'Is everything okay in here?' I asked.

He turned and looked at me, eyebrows raised, with a light, quizzical smile.

'They lock me up every night, and four times during the day too; that is not okay. But the food is better than I expected, the uniform,' he glanced down at his blue shirt and brown trousers, 'is clean and it fits, and they change the sheet on the bed once a week. I am in Dunedin Hall so I am allowed outside for an hour every day, and I exercise in the gymnasium too. There is education, so I am studying chemistry, physics, English and maths, to sit the Scottish examinations next year. Our father said I should, even though I did my baccalaureate in Spain last summer. I have a television in my room, and I watch the news to learn about Scotland. I even watch *River City* to learn about Glasgow.'

'That's more than I do,' I laughed. I have never quite taken to the BBC Scotland soap, or any other for that matter.

'Alex,' he said, 'I am here; I have no choice but to be okay, as you say. If it wasn't for you and Señora Birtles, I might have been here for many years, not just one.'

'That's good,' I told him, 'and I'm glad to hear it, but do you feel physically safe? You're a stranger here, in a way; an outsider in the midst of some bad young people.'

'Hey, *hermana*, I know where I am. Yes, when I came here I was worried. I've heard stories of prisons in Spain. They say that in some, half the people have AIDS and the rest will have soon. It's not like that here. Yes, there are a few guys here who are not nice, but most of them are like me, just trying to get through with no trouble.'

He smiled. 'I am not a pussycat, Alex,' he said. 'I am not yet nineteen but I can bench press one hundred and fifteen kilos, that's about one and a half times my body weight. That means something in here. And besides,' he frowned for a second or two, then grinned, 'I am just a little bit of a legend among the inmates, even though it's for a terrible reason. I'm the kid who killed his own granny.'

As quickly as his smile had come, it disappeared. 'Not that I ever talk about it. People have asked me; I tell them all politely to fuck off. I don't tell them that it was her or my mother, and maybe me too. I don't tell them that she was a crazy woman or that *mi madre* had nightmares all the time I was growing up, about her and the life she had left in Scotland.'

'You understand why Dad can't come to visit you?' I asked.

'Of course. Alex, I would understand if he didn't want to know me, ever. Jesus, he hardly knew my mother, yet here I am.'

As I looked at my brother, I felt a great sadness for him. He was a nice lad made older than his years by his casual parentage and by an upbringing over which he had no control, and which had led him to a terrible place. I felt the guilt that I know is within my father.

Ignacio moved away from the window, drained his tea and put the empty mug back on the table. 'Now,' he continued, 'what is the legal matter the screw . . . sorry, the officer, told me about?'

I decided not to tell him the whole story; if Linton Baillie or anyone else leaked the truth about him he would know soon enough, but by that time Kemp would have taken action.

'Nothing,' I said. 'I said that so that it won't count against your monthly visit ration; I was passing on my way to a meeting and I blagged my way. Otherwise I wouldn't have got to see you before Christmas.'

I gave him a sisterly hug, and opened the door to call his escort. Less than five minutes later I was pulling out of the car park, knowing that I'd put Ignacio's security in Kemp's hands, and trusting that the Governor's ego wasn't so big or his enmity towards my father so great that he would be unable to resist the temptation to talk about it.

Nine

Stop one hundred people and give them one hundred seconds to tell you what deoxyribonucleic acid is, and you will receive at least ninety-five blank stares.

Ask the same hundred what DNA is, and most of them will tell you in a variety of ways that it's a long molecule from which every individual's genes are made, the architectural drawing that determines what we are. It contains the hereditary information that's handed down from one generation to another.

That's the signature that we leave behind us everywhere we go, every time we lay down a fingerprint, or leave a follicle behind on a hairbrush.

It's the means by which Ignacio Centelleos was determined, not once but twice, to be the son of Robert Morgan Skinner. The first test was done in Spain, when Mia managed to get hold of samples of Dad's DNA . . . she's a cunning and devious woman.

The second he commissioned himself, although he was in no real doubt given the likeness between Ignacio and him. There is no such thing as certainty in a positive DNA test, only in a negative, but he chose a lab that offered the smallest possibility of error.

Forest Gate Laboratory Services is in the centre of Glasgow, close to the university of which I am a graduate. It's existed for decades and in its earlier days was the go-to place for people accused of driving under the influence, to have their half of the blood or urine sample independently tested.

Those customers declined in number with the introduction of breath testing, but the drop-off was more than replaced by the DNA business.

I found the office without difficulty. It's just another name on a brass plate in a long Victorian terrace where residential use has given way almost exclusively to commercial.

The lady receptionist gave me a sweet, comforting smile as I approached her desk. Her hair was just too jet-black to be natural and she wore spectacles with an ornate winged frame. Her face seemed familiar, until it struck me that she had a strong resemblance to an auctioneer I've seen on daytime telly since leaving CAJ.

'Good morning, madam,' she greeted me, in what I recognised from my Glasgow student days as the twisted twang of a Kelvinside accent. 'How can we help you today?'

She glanced at my capacious shoulder bag. 'I hope you haven't brought samples for testing . . . because if you have, you might have had a wasted journey. Many people do, but for security, our technicians have to take them personally from the people involved, or they have to be certified by a lawyer.'

'I am a lawyer,' I told her. 'Does that mean I can certify my own sample?'

'Well, eh, no, eh,' she drawled, the smile still in place.

'Maybe that'll be useful knowledge at some point in the

future,' I said. 'But it's not an issue right now. My father commissioned a test here, three months ago. He arranged it through your director, personally, and delivered two DNA samples . . . which were not taken by your techies, incidentally, because the identity of the donors was confidential. You were asked to confirm the relationship between them.'

'Did that happen?' she asked.

'Yes, it did; you certified that the two were father and son, with a margin of error of no more than one in one hundred thousand.'

'Very good.' She nodded, pleased with herself. 'How can we help you today? Do you want to commission another test?'

'No, but I do need to speak with your director. I'm sorry to turn up on the doorstep like this, but it is urgent.'

Kelvinside Woman smiled again; I sensed that it wasn't just painted on, that there was genuine kindness behind it. 'Then let me see, dear, what I can do. Dr McGrane is very busy, but I can usually twist his arm if I have to. You haven't given me your name yet.'

'It's Skinner, Alexis Skinner.' I took a business card from my bag and handed it to her. I had them printed the day after I left the firm, my first gesture of independence.

'Take a wee seat then, dear, I won't be long.'

I settled into a leather bucket chair in the small waiting area; there was a table littered with past copies of *OK*, *What Car*, and some golf magazines, the kind I've seen in every doctor's or dentist's surgery I've ever been in. I settled on a year-old copy of *Golf Monthly*, because Rory McIlroy was on the cover and he has a nice smile.

I hadn't made it past the first few pages of ads for

equipment that was already outdated, before the lady returned, with a cup of coffee . . . a cup, note, not a mug . . . and the good news that Dr McGrane would see me as soon as his meeting was over. 'About ten minutes, he thinks,' she added.

I thanked her and tried the coffee. It was pretty damn good; my guess was Nespresso, the brand George Clooney advertises.

I looked out of the window as I waited. The city skyline has changed considerably in the ten years since I lived there, and for the better. Some of the new buildings I could see were offices; another was an arena, the massive new Hydro, but most were blocks of flats, much like mine in Edinburgh.

My eye settled on one of them, one that I knew. Aileen de Marco, the more recent of my two official stepmothers (there were a couple of unofficials during my childhood and adolescence) has an apartment there. She kept it even when she was married to Dad, and even though she's gone from Scottish politics now, to a safe Westminster seat in the north-east, I've no doubt that she'll have kept her foothold in the city where her personal power base still lies.

'I wonder who's kissing her now,' I hummed, quietly, then realised that I was scowling and drove further thoughts of the Witch from my mind, concentrating on Sarah, the one stable presence in my father's life since Mum died . . . although even she's had some pretty flaky moments. I forgave her those a long time ago, though, as she's the mother of my younger brother and sister, who may be the reasons I have never felt the need, as yet, to raise kids of my own.

'Ms Skinner?'

A voice broke into my contemplation. I turned to see a tall

man, in a perfectly tailored charcoal-grey suit that any football pundit would have been proud to wear, standing beside the reception desk.

'Roger McGrane,' he announced. 'I run this place. Please, come through to my office.' There was no Kelvinside about his accent; it was pure Oxbridge.

Aesthetically speaking, Dr McGrane was a bit of all right. His hair was dark, but with the kind of natural highlights that I pay my stylist hundreds to fake, he was clean-shaven and so clean-cut that he could have advertised a coffee brand on television any day of the week.

His features were fine, but the hand that shook mine was broad and strong, and used for something more energetic than placing slides under a microscope. As for his age, there's ten years between Andy and me, and I guessed that he slotted in somewhere around the mid-point.

'What's your doctorate?' I asked as he ushered me through the door behind reception. 'Medical?'

'No, it's a PhD: genetics. I did it at Massachusetts Institute of Technology, after I graduated from Cambridge.'

'Cambridge England to Cambridge Mass,' I said, 'That was a nice move. What lured you to Glasgow?'

'The climate.' He smiled as I stared at him. 'Not! I was going to add.

'This place is American-owned,' he explained. 'I worked for the parent company in Atlanta, and was more or less inserted here when the vacancy arose.'

'You were drafted?'

He grinned, flashing a couple of gold fillings, 'You could say that. The Forest Gate group talent-spots in several universities. It contributes research funding and gets the

101

inside track on recruitment. They chose me from MIT, and got me a Green Card straight away. Other foreigners can wait years.'

'Can you go back?'

'Oh yes, and I will, in a couple of years probably, once I've got our new premises up and running. We're expanding, moving across the river to a purpose-built centre on Pacific Quay.'

We'd reached his office; he opened the door and showed me into a small room with a window that looked out across a back yard and beyond to the spiky Gothic building that is Glasgow University.

I pointed to it. 'That's my alma mater,' I said. 'I lived not far from here for four years; hall of residence for a while, then Dad bought me a flat.'

I took a seat, facing across the desk, but he joined me on the same side. He picked up my business card and peered at it.

'Not very informative,' he ventured. 'Just "Alexis Skinner, LlB, Solicitor", and a mobile number.'

I explained my career move, and told him what I'd been doing before.

'I know,' he murmured. 'I read the business press, Alexis . . . may I call you that?'

'That's my Sunday name, Roger. It's Alex on the other six days. I only use the full version on my card to avoid the assumption that I'm a bloke.'

'I imagine that could be a disadvantage in law these days. Aren't most new graduates female?'

'So I believe.'

'And you've been a trailblazer. Why should the "Dealmaker

of the Year" decide to change tack? You're not following in your father's footsteps, are you, joining the police force?'

'They call it "Police Service" now,' I tutted. 'They're very precious about that.'

'Is that why your father did what he did? Was the new set-up too touchy feely for him?'

'The opposite, funnily enough; he thinks it's divorced from the people.'

'I can understand that view.' He smiled again. 'Your father is a very impressive man, Alex. He seemed to fill this room when he was here. I was taken completely by surprise when he turned up and asked to see me. Strathclyde Police has always been, or rather was when it existed, our biggest client, but in the five years I've been here I had never met the chief constable, not until then.'

'Another reason why he's opted out,' I told him. 'He's a hands-on guy.'

'Even so, I was surprised, when he explained the commission, that he should be bringing it to me personally. I still don't know why he did; my assumption has always been that state security was involved, hush-hush stuff, because he did impress on me the need for confidentiality. Even the invoice had to go directly to his office, so marked.'

I shook my head. 'No, Roger, it wasn't security, nor was it counter-terrorism, nor any police matter: it was personal.'

For the first time, Dr McGrane looked unsure of himself. 'I don't understand,' he said.

'It was a family matter; that's all I need to tell you. However, the need for secrecy, yes, that was about security: the personal security of an individual. And now that may have been compromised. That's why I'm here.'

'Do you think we've breached it?' he exclaimed. 'Is that what you're saying?'

'No, I'm saying no such thing. I'm here on my father's behalf to eliminate that possibility, that is all.'

'Fair enough,' he said. 'I'll help you do that if I can. But Alex, I have to point out that it would be difficult for us to leak a secret when we don't know what it is. The samples that we analysed were anonymous.'

'You can remember the detail of every single test?'

'I remember that one because of the man who commissioned it; plus, I looked up the details while you were waiting in reception. That's what the ten minutes were about.'

'That being so, what can you tell me about it?'

'Your father visited me twice: the first time was to give me the commission, and the second was to deliver the samples. When he did, he told me that they had been taken by a medical professional.'

That made me smile. I enlightened him.

'My stepmother: she's a forensic pathologist.'

'Then she's very good; they were presented and labelled perfectly. Chief Constable Skinner asked for a minimum fifteen loci analysis. You probably know that we can test to various levels and various degrees of certainty; the more loci, the greater. I did the comparison myself, and I have no doubt that I was looking at father and son. There's always a statistical possibility of error, but at that level, it's utterly remote.'

'Especially if the two individuals have a close resemblance?'

'That underlines it.'

'How were your findings delivered to my father?' I asked.

'Mrs Harris, the lady you met in reception, delivered them to his office in Pitt Street, by hand. His personal assistant came down and took possession.'

'No other links in the chain?'

'None at all; and let me head off your next question by telling you that Yvonne Harris is absolutely trustworthy; she's been here for fifteen years, and worked for three directors, me included. The invoice for our services was included with our report. I see from the record that your father called our account department that same afternoon, and made payment. I didn't know until today that he used a personal debit card.'

'How are your records kept?' I asked.

'For DNA testing, the reports are filed electronically. The samples are destroyed unless there's a specific request that they're retained; there was none in this case and so all the slides were incinerated.

'For added security, reports are always filed under the client's number rather than his name, or its, if it's a corporate entity. Without that key, suppose some genius was able to hack into our system looking for a specific file, he wouldn't know where to begin.'

'You must keep a record of client names surely, otherwise you won't know which is which yourselves.'

Dr McGrane grinned. 'Very true. It would be a shambles otherwise. Our numbered client list is kept the old-fashioned way, on paper, in a safe in this building: in this room, as a matter of fact,' he pointed to the wall behind me, 'behind that large photograph of President Obama, which my bosses in Atlanta display in all our offices to make our parentage clear. We've had no break-ins here, ever.'

'Suppose someone did hack into your server, what would happen?'

'It would set off a huge alarm. Alex, we are paranoid about security; given the nature of much of our work, we have to be. I have an IT security consultant; she earns nearly as much as I do . . . and I don't come cheap.'

'Thank you, Roger,' I said. 'I have no questions left.'

'I have one,' he replied. 'Would you consider having lunch with me?'

The loss of my mother in my infancy and my single-parent upbringing combined to make me precociously cynical. I am notoriously difficult to surprise. It happens maybe once in every year, and that may have helped to make me a good lawyer. Three months earlier I'd learned that I had a teenage half-brother. That came out of the blue, and I'd reckoned that was my annual quota, but Roger McGrane's question set me back in my seat.

I stared at him, for longer than I should have, and he read it wrongly. 'I'm sorry,' he said, 'I've embarrassed you, forgive me.'

'No,' I replied slowly, as I recovered my composure, 'you haven't embarrassed me at all. You asked me a straight question, would I consider it, and I'm doing just that. The answer is, yes, I would consider it. Having done that, I have no urgent appointments this afternoon, it's that time of day and the alternative would probably be a sandwich at Harthill service area on the motorway. So, did you have anywhere in mind?'

He smiled, in a different way than before, giving me an opportunity to admire the most perfectly aligned set of teeth I've ever seen on a man of his age.

'There's a place I go nearly every day. I have a lunch table permanently reserved there. It's not gourmet dining, but I like it. Normally I walk, but today we might drive.'

'A mystery restaurant,' I said. 'I'm up for that. We'll take mine; it's parked outside.' That was not a suggestion, and Dr McGrane realised that. Accepting an impulse lunch invitation from a strange man is one thing, but to get into his car as well is a step too far for any cautious woman.

He led the way through reception, passing Mrs Harris at her desk. 'Usual place, Yvonne,' he told her, 'and my mobile will be on if you need me.'

I thanked her for her help; as we left, I had the impression that her smile was just a little less warm than before. I was about five years younger than her boss and she was maybe five years older. Did she have a crush? Might there even have been history? If so, sorry but tough luck; I was going to lunch and she wasn't.

'Nice car,' Roger murmured as he eased his tall frame into the passenger seat of my Honda. He glanced in the rear-view; from his angle he could see the child seat in the back.

I read his thoughts. 'I have a half-sister,' I told him. 'She's approximately twenty-five years younger than I am. I took her to see Santa Claus last weekend. My young brothers are no longer believers, so I left them behind. Seonaid and I are bonding, now that she's starting to turn into a human being.'

'You're not married?' He glanced at the plain gold ring on the second finger of my left hand.

'No. I'm a career woman, in a comfortable long-term relationship with a career man. You?' I asked quickly to deflect supplementary questions.

'Was. Kendra-Jane couldn't hack Glasgow. She's a Californian; anything below twenty Celsius and she gets hypothermic. She left after a year, and divorced me in Reno a year later.'

'How did you feel about that?' I asked as I started the car.

He shrugged. 'I signed the papers and sent them back express delivery.'

His directions took me out on to Sauchiehall Street, where it becomes two-way, turning right, away from the city centre. We hadn't gone half a mile before he told me to turn right, and directed me into the car park of Kelvingrove Art Gallery and Museum.

'I love this place,' I exclaimed as I got out. 'I used to come down here to study, believe it or not. I'd sit in the central hall; it was quiet and nobody would ever bother me.' I looked up at the great red-stone building. 'I haven't been here in years.'

'It was refurbished a few years ago,' he said.

'I know; I gave them a donation.'

'I don't know if they put the restaurant in then, but it's nice, particularly when the day is sunny, like today.'

He led the way inside through the Grand Entrance. There is a Glasgow urban legend that the thing was built back to front and that the architect jumped off one of the baroque towers when he saw what had been done, but it's not true. The building was designed to look across Kelvingrove Park, as it does, and up towards the university spire beyond.

The restaurant is in the lower ground level, and Roger's reserved table was beside a floor-to-ceiling window, taking full advantage of the view. He barely glanced at the menu, then smiled across the table.

108

'I have haggis once a week, and today's the day.'

'Suits me too. I take it Kendra-Jane didn't like haggis either,' I ventured.

'She genuinely believed that the haggis is a creature.'

We ordered our lunch, and sparkling water. 'How much time do you have?' I asked.

He gazed into my eyes. 'As much as you like, Alex.'

I gazed into his. 'Are you trying to pull me, Roger?'

'Are you pullable?'

'Do you mean am I the sort of woman who meets a single guy, fancies him, and isn't averse to a quick, no consequences, afternoon shag at his place, which I'm guessing isn't too far from here?'

He grinned. 'I suppose I do. You're wonderfully direct.'

'I was brought up by my dad, on his own,' I said. 'He doesn't do subtle, and that's rubbed off on me. As for your question, a few years ago I might have been, but now I'm not. However much such a prospect might interest me . . . not that I'm saying it does . . . I'd have to tell Andy afterwards. It would hurt him very much, and I wouldn't do that for the world, because I care for him.'

Neither of us had broken eye contact. 'Why do I not feel embarrassed or ashamed of myself?' he murmured.

'Why should you? You're being honest. So am I; I wouldn't be sitting here right now if I didn't feel some . . . let's call it personal curiosity.'

'Can I see you again?'

Of all the questions he could have asked, it was the one I feared. My relationship with Andy was long-term, and as I'd told Roger, I saw it as comfortable and loving, even if it had become predictable. He made me feel safe, most of all because he never crowded me, even if we did little together but eat, talk and have sex.

And yet . . . people say I'm my father's daughter, but none of them ever met my mother.

I frowned as I turned my head to look up at the university building that dominates the west of Glasgow.

'I don't know,' I murmured. 'My number's on my card; call me in a week and ask me then.' Then I smiled. 'But you'll probably have pulled some other lady visitor by that time.'

He smiled, a little gauchely. 'That's very unlikely. I'll be in touch.'

Lunch arrived then, perfectly timed and very well cooked. Roger did most of the talking, about Forest Gate and how it operated internationally, about the new centre he was building, and about himself. I'd pegged him mentally as a public school boy, and he was, but through a scholarship. His father was a motor mechanic, he said, and his mother a nurse. Dad had died of cancer when he was fourteen, and his mother had raised him alone from then on.

'My story's the same,' I told him, 'although I was much younger than you when I lost my mum. With her it was a car crash. My father didn't remarry until I was through university. He's a great cop, but a lousy husband; his first divorce and his third marriage were both mistakes, but he's corrected them both.'

Right on cue my mobile sounded in my pocket, as if he'd known I was talking about him.

'Hi,' he said. 'Can you talk?'

'Yes, up to a point.'

'Not alone?'

'No.'

'Okay. How are you getting on with those things I asked you to do?'

'The reading part, I'm progressing. The security situation is taken care of. The man Kemp is no fan of yours, but he's sorted. As for the third task, I'm with Dr McGrane now, and I'm happy that Forest Gate is watertight.'

'Water will get through anything if you let it drip long enough. I can hear crowd noise. Where are you?'

'Glasgow. We're having lunch.'

'You sound as if you're enjoying it. You watch yourself, girl.'

'Pot. Kettle. Black.'

'Stop winding me up. That's all good news, though. It could be that Mr Baillie is on some kind of fishing trip. Maybe he's put some random numbers together and come up with the right total, only he isn't sure, so he's dropping hints to see how we react. Even so, I don't like him phoning Mia, and on an ex-directory number at that.'

'Yes,' I agreed, 'she was pretty angry about it when we spoke.'

'She's not the only one. But don't worry. Once I've sorted out some other business here in Spain, I'll take care of the fucker myself.'

'That's what worries me more than anything else. What other business, by the way?'

'Nothing you need bother about. A favour for a friend, that's all. Thanks, love. Keep Mia calm, if you can.'

'Your father?' Roger asked, as I pocketed the mobile.

'Yes. He's supposed to be on a mind-sorting mission in Spain, but he's a magnet for crisis, wherever he goes.'

'While you were speaking,' he said, 'I remembered

something, about the second time he visited me. When we'd done our business I showed him out. I expected to see a police car at the door, but there wasn't, he'd come on foot. That's understandable if he wanted the exercise. The headquarters building in Pitt Street isn't very far from here.

'I watched him from the window as he walked down the steps, and then I saw the strangest thing. A little way along the road there were two people in a car, a man and a woman. I took them for police, for she had a camera and I'll swear she was photographing your father.

'I couldn't work it out and I still can't. If I was right in my assumption about them, why would two cops be photographing their own chief constable?'

Ten

Xavi's place isn't very far inland from L'Escala, or more than a few hundred feet above sea level, but when I opened the window to clear the stuffiness in the well-heated bedroom they'd given me, I felt a crispness in the air that was instantly refreshing.

It was welcome, for I was a shade beyond grumpy at the time. I'd been woken from the best sleep I'd had in a week by Mia, on my mobile, which I'd left charging by my bedside. She was raging because she'd had a call from the man Linton Baillie, on her ex-directory landline.

I was pretty angry myself after Mia had given me a word-for-word account of the guy's message, and frustrated because there was nothing I could do myself, other than tell her to call Alex and let her know.

I put the annoyance out of my mind, as best I could, and got ready to face a day that I had not expected at all less than twenty-four hours before. The weather helped improve my mood. The sun was only just over the horizon, but the sky was a clear blue and the few clouds were wispy. My room was at the back of the house, giving me my first daytime view of the bulk of the Aislado estate. I could see the place properly for the first time, and was impressed.

It was set on what might have been a volcanic plain, below a huge, layered escarpment that made me think of the Grand Canyon. Xavi had told me that it covered just over eighty hectares; that's big enough for a golf course. More than half of it was woodland, not a wild forest but tall trees that had been planted in straight lines by the previous owner, half a century before, as an investment.

Closer to the big house I saw an olive grove, and to its right a citrus orchard. Even from that distance I could tell that it was heavy with oranges, reminding me of a February break that Sarah and I had enjoyed in Seville, with our then infant son. James Andrew was unimpressed, but we loved the place.

The rest of it was devoted to vegetables: potatoes, carrots and calçots, a type of winter onion that's a Catalan delicacy, and, by the way, one of the messiest dishes I have ever encountered.

Three buildings stood beyond by the stone wall that enclosed the *masia* gardens; one was either a barn, or it was a garage for the vehicles needed to manage and cultivate the place. The second was a white-painted cottage, where Carmen lived, I'd been told, and just beyond, there stood an older building that I guessed was the studio she had mentioned when we'd spoken at the dinner table.

She and Xavi were the only people in the kitchen when I got there. I'd found them by following their voices. 'Ben's in deep shit,' the big man said, as I joined them. 'Sheila was expecting him to do the school run with Paloma this morning, but he didn't come home. She's taken her instead. Normally I'd do it, but with our business . . .'

'What would you like for breakfast?' Carmen asked, in Spanish. She started to repeat in English, but I headed her off by replying, 'Scrambled eggs and orange juice would do it for me;

but let me make them, please, for all of us. More often than not I fix my own in Scotland.'

She protested, but I insisted. The eggs were fresh from the chicken run behind the studio. Way back, even before Joe's time, Carmen's parents had been the *masia*'s caretaker and gardener. The old studio had been their home until Joe had built the cottage, and she had looked after the hens even then.

I scrambled nine of them, and fried a few mushrooms, with some sliced potatoes left over from the night before. I'd assumed that Joe would be joining us, but Carmen explained that these days he goes to bed late and rises late, and that his daily breakfast is bread, olive oil, and coffee.

'The same as Grandma Paloma,' Xavi said. 'She baked the bread herself even when we lived in Scotland, as I do here. She taught me.'

She taught him bloody well, because the bread was excellent.

Our breakfast conversation was mostly about Joe, and the influence he'd exercised over everyone's life, Xavi included. 'He made me a businessman,' he said. 'Without him, the *Saltire* would have gone down the pan years ago, and I'd still be a journalist in Edinburgh, squeezing out a living in a declining market.'

He was being hard on himself. If Joe hadn't been around to save his paper, Xavi would have taken one of the many offers that came his way from rival titles, and would have been a major player wherever he'd gone.

'He made my career too,' Carmen added. 'There are many, many very good artists in Catalunya. It is very difficult to be successful nationally. Joe helped me to break through by paying for exhibition space, first in Barcelona, then in major cities around Spain . . . Valencia, Bilbao, Cordoba . . . and finally in Madrid. Everything was planned by him, I had a new collection everywhere I showed and of course his newspapers and radio stations gave me lots of publicity.'

She smiled. 'At every exhibition, Joe ensured that the local mayor did the opening ceremony; and of course, having done that, they all had to be seen to buy a picture, and after them, all their friends and hangers-on.

'I did mostly still life in those days, but with one or two portraits included. These *alcaldes* and businessmen, they are vain people; several of them commissioned portraits.

'When the president of the government, what you would call the prime minister, Bob, commissioned one of his wife, that was it: everyone had to have a Carmen Mali portrait over their fireplace.'

She rose from the table. 'And now I must take breakfast to the man who made it all happen.'

She looked down at me. 'He told me to go away, you know. Fifteen years ago he said to me, "Carmen, it's time for you to leave me. Find a young guy, make yourself happy, get a life." I told him, "Joe, I have the life I want." And I have.'

As she left the kitchen carrying a tray laden with a cut loaf, a bowl of olive oil and a cafetière, Xavi gazed at her back. 'That's him,' he murmured. 'And to think, Bob, for the first twenty years of my life I thought he was an arsehole.'

How many people in the world feel about me the way Carmen does about Joe? I wondered. Their numbers must be in single figures, and for sure, far more think that I'm an arsehole . . . the good news being that many of those are in jail or even lower down the scale of social acceptability, in politics.

'So,' the big fellow continued, 'what's the plan for today?'

'Pilar Roca,' I replied, 'Hector's mother. I want to go to Begur, see her and see where he lived.'

'What about Battaglia?' he asked.

'What about her?' I replied. 'I know what you think, that she's behind Hector's disappearance, but we can only do one thing at a time. Let's find the man himself first, alive or dead; after that, if we have to, we'll look at her.

'Go on, phone Pilar, tell her we're on our way. Christ, man, you never know, Hector may have phoned her by now to tell her he's holed up with a chick in the Caribbean.'

Xavi laughed softly. 'You don't know Hector. His relationships all collapse because he won't take his chicks any further than the Palau de Musica.'

'Where's that?'

'Two streets away from his apartment in Barcelona.'

Eleven

While I cleared away the breakfast dishes, Xavi made the call to Señora Roca.

'We're on,' he announced as he came back into the kitchen.

He said that he would drive to Begur. That was sensible on two grounds: he knew where we were going and he's so damn tall he wouldn't have been comfortable in my car.

I insisted on packing my overnight bag before we left, as I had to go home that evening, whatever happened during the day, but I had another reason for wanting a little privacy.

Back in my room, I took out my phone and called a number that was listed simply as 'Amanda'. Mrs Dennis is an old friend of mine; she's a middle-aged divorcee who is listed in public files as a Grade Two civil servant. In fact, she's the head of the security service, and I'm one of the very few people outside her circle in Whitehall to have her mobile number.

It was ten minutes to nine in London when I called her, but I knew she'd be at work.

'Bob,' she greeted me brightly. 'This is a surprise; I didn't expect you to call me back so soon. You said you wanted some time to think about my offer . . . or have you decided to say "no" already?'

As I've said, I had a few career options to consider, and one of them was a role that she had offered me, with her beloved service. 'Think about the principle,' Amanda had said when we had lunch during what was ostensibly a routine visit to the Glasgow out-station. 'If the idea of working in Five is attractive to you, we can work out a precise role later . . . or possibly an imprecise role.'

'I haven't decided anything yet, Amanda,' I told her. 'I'm calling because I'm helping a pal in Spain with a situation that he has in his business, and a name's come up.'

'British?'

'No, but I know that you talk to your counterparts in other countries so I thought I'd try it on you. Ever heard of Bernicia Battaglia?'

'The Italian media person, the one they call the "Warrior"? Not quite in the Berlusconi class yet, but with ambitions of getting there?'

'That's the lady. She has her sights on my friend's business; he doesn't want to sell, but "No, thank you" isn't a phrase she's used to hearing, or understands when she does. There have been rumours about her ruthless way of dealing with people who oppose her. I'd like to test the strength of them, if possible.'

'I'll see what I can discover. Mind, if I do come up with something useful, I'll be looking for something in return.'

I laughed. 'I thought I had a credit balance in favours between the two of us.'

'This one might wipe it out; my opposite number in Rome doesn't give things away either. Somewhere along the line there's always a trade involved. We'll speak again, when I have something for you . . . or when you have some good news for me.'

I went downstairs and slung my bag into the boot of the Suzuki, just as Sheila arrived back from her school run. Xavi was waiting as she parked beside his car. She looked around as she stepped out of her Evoque.

'Is that son of mine not home yet?' I heard her say as she reached up to kiss him. 'Dirty little stop-out; wait till I see him.'

'Come on,' her husband laughed. 'He's a grown man.'

'So what? Wait till your daughter's grown up, and see how you feel about her.'

'D'you hear that, Bob?' he called to me. 'You've got a daughter Ben's age. How am I gonna feel?'

'Do you want the flip answer or the honest answer?' I asked.

'Let's try honest.'

'You're going to feel the same way you feel now, but you'll realise she's what you made her, so you'll stand back and let her get on with her life, however she wants to live it . . . up to a point, that point being, if you know that she's making a huge mistake or worse, being abused or exploited, you will do something about it.'

'And that something being?'

I thought back to a very dangerous time in Alex's young life and how I'd handled that. 'Whatever's necessary.'

'Hey,' Sheila exclaimed, gazing at me, 'you look as though someone's walked over your grave.'

Actually it was the other way around, but I didn't tell her that. Instead I told her, 'Nobody's exploiting or abusing your Ben, and he's not doing anything unseemly under your roof. In fact, he sounds a lot like me when I was his age.

'The best thing you can do for him is dig out a couple of cans of Red Bull. He'll probably need them when he gets home.'

I climbed into Xavi's Range Rover and we set off for Begur.

His chosen route wasn't the one I'd have taken, south towards the port of Palamos, then veering north past Palafrugell, but the highway was good and it was quick.

Like many old Catalan towns, Begur is built on a hill. Normally the church will be the highest point, but Begur is dominated by the ruins of a castle. I'd been there before with Alex, in her childhood, and been impressed by the views from the old battlements. No enemy was ever going to take its occupants by surprise, unless they were brave enough to climb steep and stony slopes on a very dark night.

'We'll leave the car here,' Xavi announced, pulling into a parking area beside a road junction. 'The village roads are too narrow for this thing.'

He wasn't kidding, I realised, as we left the main drag and turned into a street called Carrer de Santa Reparada. (I've researched the saint's story since then: I don't believe a word of it.) Not very far up, Xavi stopped at what looked at first like no more than a big yellow stone wall with a few slit windows and a double garage entrance, until I saw, slightly inset, a polished oak door, with a buzzer beside it and a name tag, 'Sureda/Roca'.

We had to wait for a full minute before the call was answered. No one asked who we were but that's what video cameras are for. 'Xavi, *cariño*,' a woman said, as the door swung open, squeaking slightly as it caught on a raised tile beneath.

I knew that Pilar Roca was pushing seventy, but no way did she look it. She's a tall, grand lady who managed that morning to maintain her elegance in a housecoat that might have been bought in the Palafrugfell market . . . and probably was, given the famous thriftiness of the Catalan people.

She greeted me with a polite smile and an appraising look. If

I'd been sold as the man who'd find her son, as I was sure I had been, that was something she wanted to decide for herself.

'*Bienvenido, señor*,' she said, and I thought, *Oh shit, a translation job*, but mercifully she switched to English. 'Welcome. It's fitting that the two words mean exactly the same in each language, Castellano and English. You will be even more welcome if you can help find our son.'

Her anxiety was written all over her face, in lines and in the dark bags under her eyes.

'If I can, I will,' I replied. 'That's all I can offer, or say.'

'How is Simon?' Xavi asked.

'He's asleep. He's turning night into day; even with his sedatives, he is always awake in the *madrugada* hours, even though he hates the darkness. It has got to the stage when he does not try to go back to sleep any more. Instead he gets up and he watches television; anything, movies or yesterday's sport on Canal Plus, even the rolling bulletins on the twenty-four-hour news channel, the same stories over and over again. As soon as the sun rises he goes back to bed and sleeps until midday at least. I tell you, his operation cannot be soon enough, for either of us.'

'Is it possible, señora,' I asked, 'that Hector's having difficulty dealing with his father's condition?'

I knew that I was taking a chance with the question, so I wasn't surprised when she flared up.

'Are you suggesting that my son is a *pollo*?' she snapped. 'That's he's too chicken to support his father. It's the opposite that is the truth. When Simon began to be ill we were both ignoring it, he and I. It was Hector who said, "Papa, something is wrong here and you must deal with it." He made all the appointments with the doctors and he went with Simon to every one. I didn't have the cojones to do that; he did.'

I smiled. 'I'll take that as a "no", then,' I said. 'I apologise for upsetting you. I wasn't implying anything, only asking what any investigator would.'

She softened immediately. 'No, I say sorry to you. A good journalist would ask the same question also.'

'Xavi says that Hector has his own rooms in this house. Can I see them?'

'Of course.'

She led the way up a flight of stairs that opened into a hallway, on what seemed to be the ground floor of the house, and then another. On that level, there was a door with a barrel lock which she opened.

'More steps,' she said. 'They are bad for Simon; he can't take them any more. He sleeps on the garden level, the first one that we came to. Hector's place is in the *atico*.'

When finally we reached it, Hector's place was pretty damn impressive. It had only one bedroom, with an en suite bathroom, but the rest of the living area covered the whole width of the house below. It was open-plan, with a terrace that had a view across the neighbouring beachfront town of Sa Riera, and all the way up to the Islas Medas.

It was a young man's apartment, no mistake. The furniture was modern and expensive. The kitchen area was state of the art, with an induction hob and twin fan ovens, an American-style fridge freezer, and Miele white goods. In the rest of the living space there were the inevitable toys, a wall-mounted fifty-inch flat screen TV, an X-Box One, and some hi-fi equipment that I recognised as Cyrus, because I have some myself, although not nearly as new as Hector's.

There were only two photographs on show. One showed Pilar flanked by two men, one young, the other older, their likeness marking them out as father and son, as clearly as Ignacio and I are, once you've seen the right shot of me at his age.

The other showed the man I took to be Hector, with a woman. She was in the same age group as him, and she was beautiful, a real traffic hazard on any pavement, in any city; she had an oval face, dark hair and brown eyes that seemed to reach out and grab me. The pair were both clad for the ski slopes, and they were standing against a background of deep snow.

'That was taken in Andorra, in January of last year,' Pilar volunteered.

'Who's the girl?'

'Her name is Valentina; she's a Russian girl. She was his big romance at the time, but he broke it off.'

He did? I thought. *What a mug.*

'Would you mind if I looked around, señora?' I asked, when I had finished being impressed.

'Of course not; that's what you're here for.'

I thanked her and headed straight for the bedroom. The only furniture was a bed and two side tables. All the wardrobes and storage had been built in when the attic apartment was created, and was hidden behind three large mirrored doors. I slid them along to reveal as much as I could.

His shirts were folded and stacked on a shelved area. They were quality, real designer labels, not market copies. His socks and underpants were stored in drawers, all laid flat, not scrunched into balls as all of mine are. 'Very neat, Hector,' I murmured.

Jackets, trousers and suits, including the ski costume I'd seen in the photograph, and one other, same brand different colour, all hung on a rail. There were three spare coat hangers, and two of the trouser clips that I always ask the Marks and Spencer assistants to put into the bag. Hector bought his own, it seemed;

they were metal, with padded grips to make them easy on the garments.

'For sure,' I murmured, 'this is a very well-organised guy; a place for everything and everything in its place. The clothes he wore to work, fair enough. That accounts for a couple of empty hangers, but the others?'

I looked at the shirts once more. A dozen were short-sleeved, summer wear, four were heavier, long-sleeved, and ten were formal business shirts. 'Should there be twelve of those?' I wondered.

I slid the doors along to reveal the rest of the long wardrobe. It was split between shoes and storage. Again the footwear had been placed carefully in a fold-down rack, left foot, right foot, side by side, each in its proper place, even the ski boots. Two slots were empty.

Alongside there was a rack holding five ties, all silk, all plain colour, no stripes or patterns; three shades of red, pale green and yellow.

In the storage area two pairs of skis stood on end, beside two matching four-wheeled cases. One was the size of a cabin bag, the other much larger, the size that few people use these days because of weight restrictions. Had there been a third in the set?

I was in Hector's bathroom when Xavi's voice came from the doorway.

'How are you doing? Pilar's gone downstairs to check on Simon,' he said, then added, 'I'm worried about her, Bob. The very fact that she's dressed like a bag lady tells you how strung out she is.'

I made the appropriate reassuring noises. 'She'll be fine. We'll find her boy, her husband will have his dodgy heart valve replaced, and she'll be back to normal.'

'Simon's operation is high risk,' he countered. 'And as for Hector, we'll find him, but in what condition?'

'Hey!' I said, sharply. 'Don't go all fatalistic on me. You're assuming the worst, that the guy's been taken, or simply taken out. It's not as easy as that. He left here in his high-performance sports car as if he was going to your office in Girona.

'We've just covered the same road that he would have taken; it's wide open and there appears to be constant traffic. Suppose someone was targeting him, how would they get him to stop?

'I say they, because the scenario needs at least three people: one to keep him subdued and under control in a getaway vehicle, one to drive it and one to get Hector's car off the road. Even then, how exactly do you hide a canary-yellow Porsche?'

'What do you think happened?'

'I don't know for sure, but I do know that your abduction theory is wild, fanciful and plain fucking wrong. Mostly, my friend, I deal in evidence, as you do as a journalist. Instinct can come into my work, but I've never been able to arrest and charge someone on that basis alone. I've always had to prove it. I've found no evidence here, so far, that we're looking for a victim.'

I smiled at his grim concern. 'In fact, it's the opposite. He hasn't been taken; he's fucking gone.'

I closed the door of his bathroom cupboard and went back to the living area, just as Pilar returned.

'Señora, can you tell me,' I began, 'when you last saw your son; literally, the very last time.'

'Friday morning,' she replied, looking at me as if I was daft. 'Xavi told you that.'

'No, I mean where, on that morning, in this house.'

She frowned. 'It was in the kitchen, downstairs. Simon was awake at that time and the three of us took breakfast together.'

'How did he seem? What was his mood?'

'What do you mean? I don't understand.'

'Was he happy? Was he preoccupied? Did he seem different in any way from his usual self?'

'I would say,' she ventured, after a few moment's thought, 'that he was positive; you say in English, in a good place. He talked to his father of his operation. He said that he had researched the surgeon on the Internet, and had found that his success rate for this type of surgery is much better than others. He told him the names of famous people who have had heart surgery and recovered from it. President Clinton was one of them, Burt Reynolds, the actor, was another. Yes, he was happy. Then he left to go upstairs and be ready for the day.'

'Was he dressed as he usually did for work?'

'No, he was wearing a casual shirt and jeans. But as I say, he went upstairs to change.'

'What does he wear in the office?'

'He dresses properly, as a senior executive should. A suit, and in the winter he will wear a necktie with his shirt . . . always the same one, his favourite colour, *azul*.' I formed a mental picture of the rack in the wardrobe: no blue tie there.

'How did you know that he was leaving?'

'He called from the hall. "*Adeu, Mama y Papa*." Then I heard the garage door open and his car start. You cannot mistake its noise for another.'

'Between him going back to his apartment and him leaving, how long was it?'

'Not long,' she replied, at once. 'Four minutes. Because you ask I remember it. The kitchen clock was showing exactly half past when he go upstairs, and a little before *ocho y triente cinco*.'

'Okay,' I murmured.

'What are you thinking?' Xavi asked.

'I'm thinking that was a hell of a quick change. Señora, Pilar, there are two matching *maletas* in his wardrobe. Do you know how many there should be?'

'*Tres*.' Her eyes widened. 'Do you say . . .'

'I'm saying nothing yet. Come and look at this, please.'

I led her back into the bedroom and slid the mirrored doors open.

'Can you tell me what should be there that isn't?'

She peered at the hanging garments, then at the shirts on their shelves.

'A suit,' she declared, 'three shirts, maybe four, I am not sure, and his black leather jacket, the one I bought for him in a shop in Torroella de Montgri.'

'He packed a case,' I said. 'When the three of you had breakfast, those were travel clothes he was wearing.'

I looked at my friend. 'As I said, Hector wasn't taken anywhere, mate, he went. There's no shaving gear, wet or electric, in his bathroom, and no deodorant either.'

'But why would he do that?'

'Jesus, Xavi, this is a wealthy young man with a sports car and an apartment in Barcelona. It was a Friday. Does the phrase "Dirty weekend" translate into Catalan or Spanish?'

'That's what you think? He's gone off with a woman?'

'It's the most logical conclusion I can draw from the evidence.'

'No!' his mother insisted. 'My Hector, he would not . . .'

'Come on, señora. Are you telling me that your son has never done anything unconventional, or that he's open about every aspect of his sex life? He was upbeat over breakfast, he was positive about his father's prognosis. He was happy with life, and I believe with something that was about to happen in it.'

'I talk to him a lot, Bob,' Xavi said. 'He's dropped no hint of a new woman.'

'Why should he? We all like a bit of privacy.' I turned back to Pilar. 'Does your son keep a paper diary, a list of engagements?'

She shook her head. 'No. Hector's office is in his laptop, in his phone, and in his iPad. I can see by looking around that they are all gone, as I would have expected.'

'I don't see a landline phone anywhere,' I pointed out.

'He does not have one, not in the apartment. He only has his hand phone, as many people do today.'

'Okay. Señora,' I said, 'here's what I recommend: that you stop worrying about your son and devote all your attention to your husband.' As I spoke, Xavi's mobile sounded, and he stepped out on to the terrace to take the call. 'Let him have his break,' I continued, 'and the chances are he'll come back even happier.'

She smiled. 'I will, although when he comes back there will be hell for him. I go downstairs now to make coffee; you and Xavi please join me when you wish.'

I thanked her, then turned to look at my friend. He seemed to be in a conversation that was unusually animated, by his standards. As I watched he nodded, vigorously, said something that I lip-read as '*Gracias*', or the Catalan equivalent, then ended the call and came inside, closing the door behind him.

'That was Canals,' he said. 'He's found Hector's car. A Mossos patrol spotted it in a public car park in the centre of Girona.'

'Do they know how long it's been there?'

'Since Friday morning; the entry system photographs the number plate as each car checks in, and gives it a unique ticket. It's part of the security; stops the wide boys from pulling a ticket from the entry barrier then stealing any car they can get into.'

'We should look at it,' I told him.

'What's the point, if you're right and he has buggered off for a few randy days in Barcelona with his mobile switched off?'

'I only said that for his mother's sake, Xavi. The girlfriend notion may still be right, but I'm having trouble seeing the man you've told me about being that irresponsible. A long weekend is one thing, but it's fucking Wednesday now: five full days and no contact?'

'Mmm.' His earlier elation vanished. 'That's true. Okay, there's a spare key for the Porsche in the office. We'll pick it up and take a look at it.'

'Yes, but before then there's something else we should do. Does he have a computer in your office?'

'Yes, of course. It's an iMac; the entire business runs Apple.'

'Then let's get into it. Maybe he's left a hint there of what he's up to.'

'That might not be so easy. Each of the directors sets his own password.'

'Sure and yours is probably your wife's name and birthday.'

He smiled, and nodded. 'Pretty damn close,' he admitted.

'Who manages your IT?'

'Julia Gutierrez. She controls the systems right across the group.'

'Out of your head office?'

'Yes. Her department is on the floor below mine.'

'Then we'll find out how clever he is, and how quickly she can get us into Hector's desktop.'

Twelve

I had expected the headquarters of InterMedia to be in the centre of Girona. Instead I discovered as we arrived there that it was located on an industrial estate on the western outskirts of the city, beside a massive printing hall that produces half of the group's daily newspapers in Catalunya and all of its weekly magazines and supplements. The factory was a grey, rectangular building, with an adjoining circular office pod that seemed to be built of dark, smoked glass, and reflected distorted images of everything around it.

'We moved here ten years ago,' Xavi told me as he pulled up in a space in the car park, with his Sunday name, 'Sr Xavier Aislado', on a sign. Joe's classic Merc was parked in the next bay.

'This is our biggest production centre,' he said, 'but we've got others spread across the country. I'd give you the grand tour but we don't have time; maybe later, when everything's sorted.'

I opened the passenger door as he spoke; as it swung, the wing mirror caught a glimpse of a sleek, silver, medium-sized car, pulling into a bay in the general park, fifty or sixty yards away. It was a Skoda Spaceback, and it was the second time I'd seen one of those that morning. There aren't too many of them around in Spain and I am not a man who believes in coincidence . . . not when they happen to me, at any rate.

The big man led the way inside, then, with a nod and a '*Bon dia*' to a blonde woman heading in the other direction and to the uniformed guy on security, across the big hallway, past the stairs, towards the lifts. 'That's the girl Ben was chatting up yesterday,' he murmured. 'She looks tired.'

He pressed a call button and the elevator on the right opened at once. 'The first floor's for the print hall managers,' he said as we rode upwards, 'second floor's accounts and specialist departments, and the third floor is us. There is a fourth level, but we only use it for board meetings, hospitality and such.'

We stepped out into a central area that should have been dark but wasn't, because light funnelled down from a cupola, through a glass ceiling. Xavi saw my upward glance. 'Cost a fucking fortune, that thing,' he growled. 'The bloody roof's a smoked-glass dome, with a watering system that keeps it clean on the outside and cool inside.

'That's what happens when you give a Catalan architect carte blanche, but this one's father's a big wheel in the Generalitat, the regional government, and he's done Joe a few favours over the years.' He grinned. 'Is that corrupt, Bob?'

'Possibly,' I replied, 'but who's looking?'

He laughed. 'That's exactly what Joe said when I asked him the same question.'

The old man's office door faced the lift entrance, and it was open. I could see him seated at his desk, with a newspaper in his hand. Xavi stuck his head inside. 'What brings you in today?' he asked.

Joe pointed upwards. 'Lunch: with the president, captain, senior players and coach of FC Barcelona, and our sports editors and football columnists. Two o'clock. Remember?'

My large friend slapped his forehead; the blow would have stunned a normal man. 'Shit, I thought it was tomorrow.'

'Fuck me,' his half-brother sighed, theatrically. 'And to think I'm the one who is supposed to be the geriatric.'

'Can you handle it without me?'

'Don't be daft. I know bugger all about football, whereas you used to be a pro. You can talk to them as an equal . . . more or less. You must be there.'

Xavi turned to me. 'Bob, this might change things. I'd invite you to join us, but these guys might not open up with a stranger there.'

'It doesn't worry me,' I assured him, although the football fan inside me was lying in his teeth. 'I wouldn't understand three-quarters of it anyway. Let's get on with what we came here to do, and see what time we have afterwards.'

We stepped into the office next door, which was Xavi's own. I hadn't seen properly inside Joe's, and so I was taken by surprise. The internal walls were solid rather than glazed, panelled in dark rosewood that blended traditional and modern. The furniture matched the walls, apart from the leather swivel behind the desk and two guest chairs, and the floor was carpeted in a smooth British Wilton. There was one painting on display; it was of Paloma, aged around ten, a Carmen Mali original.

To everyone who meets them the Aislados are ordinary guys; every reminder of their wealth comes as a shock.

Xavi dropped into his chair, picked up his phone and gave a series of instructions in Catalan to whoever was on the other end of the line, a secretary, I guessed. Then he rose to his feet once more and motioned me to follow.

Hector Sureda's room was on the other side of the pod,

behind the lifts. It faced north, and was less brightly lit, but fitted and furnished in the same style, although the rosewood desk was much smaller; big enough, though, to take an Apple iMac with a twenty-seven-inch screen, and still allow space to work in comfort. Xavi pushed a button in the rear, to switch it on, then swung it round so that we could see it from where we stood.

'The IT manager's on the way up,' he said. 'And my assistant's getting hold of the spare key to Hector's Porsche.'

The machine booted up, quickly, then stopped in its tracks as a window asked us for a password. Just then, when we needed her most, Julia Gutierrez, the technical wizard, arrived, five feet tall with frizzy dark hair and energy that seemed to radiate from her. She smiled at her boss, looked at the screen, reached for the wireless keyboard and tapped in a few letters.

The window vanished, and the desktop appeared.

Xavi looked at her in blatant astonishment, and muttered something to her that I couldn't hear, in Castellano. Her reply was spoken faster than I could hope to understand.

As she left, I asked him what they had said.

'I asked her how she did it so fast,' he replied. 'She told me it was no magic; that she made Hector give her his password, just in case he was involved in an accident and she needed access to his files. She added that I shouldn't worry, that she only has his. Getting into my computer or the finance director's would take her much longer. She could do it, though,' he added.

I looked at the screen, and at the desktop wallpaper. 'Does that remind you of anything?' I murmured.

'Should it?' he replied.

'It's a snow scene; the same as in the photo of his Russian girlfriend in his apartment. The same place, I'd say.'

'Is that significant?'

'Only in that it must represent a happy memory for him.'

'You still think he's gone off with a woman?'

'As I said, it's the most obvious answer. But I'm still wondering why he hasn't come back, and why he hasn't switched on his phone at the very least. There could be one good reason for that. You can pinpoint someone through a mobile, but only when it's active. Come on,' I said, 'let's see what the iMac tells us.'

Xavi pulled up a chair, reached for the mouse on the keyboard and clicked on a compass icon at the foot of the screen. Instantly a window opened, showing what I realised almost at once was the homepage on the InterMedia website. 'We use Safari as the search engine because it's built into the system. Julia won't let us download any other in case it causes conflicts. She's a bit of a control freak.'

He clicked on another icon and the screen changed to show a selection of windows. 'These are his top sites,' he said. 'They're very straightforward, only the web pages of our own electronic newspapers. This feature monitors your usage and tells you where you go most often.' He moved the mouse again and the windows became smaller, showing more, with five blanks at the foot of the screen.

'This should open his diary,' he murmured as he clicked another icon. It did; the whole of December was set out.

'Look at that!' Xavi exclaimed, instantly animated as he pointed at the screen. 'Last Thursday.'

I followed his pointing finger and saw an entry, an evening engagement timed at eight. '*Sopar: B.*' Supper; no venue, no companion named, only that initial.

'Now look at today,' I said. There was one entry; the same lunch with FC Barcelona that Joe had mentioned. 'That means he was expecting to be back. Who's B?' I asked.

'I haven't a fucking clue,' my friend admitted. 'Let me look at his history, see what he's been looking at, see if there's a clue in that.' He moved to the top of the main window and clicked again. All the icons disappeared.

'Eh? He's cleared his bloody history. Now why would he do that?'

'Because he's a good housekeeper?' I suggested.

'Or because he doesn't want Julia, or anyone else, to see where he's been looking. She can override this system if she's asked, and get into his programme. Wait a minute, let's look at his email.'

He moved to the menu bar and hit 'Yahoo'. A new page opened: top right, he selected '*Correu*', and a mail folder opened. He leaned forward and worked though a series of sub-folders, one by one. 'It's all business. There's nothing personal on here, nothing at all.'

'Should there be?'

'For staff, no, it's forbidden, but the directors exchange personal emails.'

'But don't necessarily store them.'

'No, I suppose not. But hold on.'

He picked up the phone on the desk and hit a single button. 'Xavi,' he said as his call was answered, then spoke in Catalan.

'That was his assistant,' he told me as he hung up. 'I asked him whether he makes Hector's travel arrangements. He told me no, he does it himself, and that his trips should be kept somewhere on his computer, so that Susannah, the auditor, can compare them with his expense claims if she wants to make a snap inspection. Mmm, let me check something.'

He went back into the list of folders, muttered, 'Ah!' then clicked on an icon.

'There was something I'd overlooked,' he said. 'A sub-folder in a file called "Regional offices"; it's called *"Viajes"*, that's journeys in English. I'm looking at it now, and it's odd. It shows his travel and hotel booking on business trips, but there's nothing there that's less than three months old. Hector goes away quite often, at least once a month.'

He opened one more folder, then whistled. 'Look at this.' I did. The folder had no heading, only a familiar 'Trash' icon, and it was empty.

'He cleared the history,' Xavi murmured, 'and here he's emptied his trash bin too.' He turned and looked at me. 'Bob, this isn't normal behaviour for Hector. I'm beginning to wonder . . . is he coming back at all?'

Thirteen

For all the anomalies in Hector's computer, I remained unconvinced that there was anything sinister in his disappearance. He hadn't been kidnapped and buried in a shallow grave, as Xavi had imagined in his worst nightmare; I couldn't imagine that, not at all.

Wherever he had gone, it was of his own free will. Why he had gone there, that was the mystery, but I didn't really see it as one that concerned me. His motive was either personal, in which case it was none of my concern, or it was business . . . in which case I wasn't too bothered either.

But, bugger it, I'd volunteered my help in a fit of enthusiasm and although I was beginning to regret it, I felt honour bound to see it through, or to carry on until my friend told me not to bother any longer.

I gave Hector's desk and filing cabinets a full professional search but found nothing that took us any further forward. While I did that Xavi went to see Susannah Gardner, to be told that she had done a check for financial discrepancies in the digital media department, and found everything as it should be, no cash shortfalls.

He was pretty deflated when I met him back in his office.

'Have I misjudged this man completely, Bob?' he asked. 'I can't believe that I would. I've known him for most of his life.'

'I don't know, chum,' I replied, 'but look at it this way. We're a long way from the black scenario that you painted for me last night. We know that he didn't disappear between his home and the office, but drove into Girona, with a suitcase in his Porsche.'

I asked him a straight question.

'Do you want to look any further, or will you wait for him to resurface, and in the meantime take what precautions you can against the chance that Hector might have sold you down the river?'

'Sold us to whom?'

'You're fixated by the Italian woman, but if not her, then to the highest bidder.'

My large friend's face darkened. 'If that's happened, I want to know,' he said in a voice like distant thunder. 'I've been betrayed once in my life, Bob. If it's happened again, I think I might do something drastic about it.'

'That's not something you should be saying to me, buddy. If he's done something criminal, I'll help you hand him to the police, but nothing else.'

'Understood,' he said, softening. 'Don't mind me. I haven't lost faith in Hector; I respect his parents too much and as I said, I've known him since he was a kid. Carry on with this for a little longer, Bob, please. I must find out what he's up to, for Pilar's sake, and Simon's.'

'Okay, I'll stay with it. First up, we should take a look at his car, and see if that tells us anything.'

'Could you do that alone?' Xavi asked. 'Joe's right; I can't miss this football lunch, so I can't chance being held up in Girona.'

'Sure, but how am I going to get there?'

'Take my car.' He tossed me the keys. 'You won't find it complicated.'

'Here, mate,' I retorted, 'I passed the police advanced driving course in a Range Rover.'

'That does not fill me with confidence,' he chuckled. 'I've seen you guys on the skid pan.'

'Me neither; it was about a hundred years ago. By the way,' I added, 'I'd like a photo of Hector as well. I might do some nosing around while I'm there.'

He nodded. 'I'll have one printed out for you.'

As soon as he left to make that happen, I took my mobile from my pocket. I'd set it to silent earlier and it had vibrated while we were searching Hector's computer. It showed one missed call, and I chose the ring-back option.

'Bob,' Amanda Dennis said, briskly, 'this will have to be quick. I'm alone at the moment but I have a section heads meeting in two minutes. I spoke to my equivalent in Italian domestic security, the AISI. As I'd suspected he takes a healthy interest in Bernicia Battaglia, and her doings. She's attracted a lot of attention in recent years, and a macabre mythology has grown around her.'

She paused. 'Do you remember the Durante assassination? An Italian MP, the son of one of her business targets?'

'Yes.' I did, only too well after hearing Xavi on the subject the night before.

'She didn't do it,' Amanda said abruptly. 'The son was a member of a parliamentary security committee investigating the influence of organised crime in the industrial cities of the north. In fact, he was its driving force; he made a real nuisance of himself, and for that reason he was removed.

'Battaglia was seen as a useful means of distracting attention from the people who ordered his death, and the rumour of her involvement was spread . . . to her great delight. She used her own newspapers and TV outlets to publicise the stories, obliquely, and she even issued an oddly worded denial that did nothing to deflect them. But the fact is she was never suspected of having Durante killed, and she was never investigated over it or in connection with anything else. She's mostly a myth of her own creation.'

'So why's your Italian spook friend so interested in her?'

'Because he's concerned that the myth may have just a little substance to it. Her editorial line against the Sicilian Mafia and the Neapolitan Camorra has been less than robust at times. It's very cynical about the state's efforts to curtail them, and on occasion her editors have been allowed to ask whether they might actually be economically useful to the Italian state.

'Successive Italian governments have thought she might be a mouthpiece of the Dons. However their biggest fear is that she might go into politics, and if she did, that Italy's big but slumbering fascist vote might unite behind her. Ideally, they'd like her out of the way, but they certainly don't want her getting any bigger.'

'Can't they stop that?'

'At home, yes. Italian and European competition law won't let her expand further in her own country. However, she's looking abroad. She's stake-building in medium-sized media companies in France and Germany, getting ready, it's said, to launch takeover bids. She has a target in Spain too, but that's not so easy, because it's family-owned. I think you know the company I'm talking about, Bob. That's right, is it not?'

'Yes, it is,' I murmured.

'And that your interest might be sharpened by the fact that your mobile phone shows up on our tracing as being in Girona?'

'That's not impossible either.'

I heard her chuckle. 'I might have known you wouldn't sit on your hands for long. I have to go now,' she said, 'but I'll tell you this. If you do happen to come up against this woman, you'll have friends in Italy if you need them.'

'In that case,' I replied, 'you might ask them a question from me. Do they know where she is now?'

'I'll run it by them. You really should join us, Bob,' she added. 'It would be such fun.'

And what would Sarah say to that? I asked myself as I ended the call, and as Xavi returned, photograph in hand.

'That's the most recent we have,' he said. 'What are you going to do with it?'

'I'm going to show it to some people,' I replied, as I took it from him. 'Enjoy your lunch. If you can get the players' autographs for me, my son James Andrew will be forever in your debt. I'll bring your car back in one piece, I promise.'

I headed for the door, then stopped. 'Is there a back way out of this place?' I asked.

He frowned, puzzled. 'Yes. Just along from the lift, there's a doorway with a red "Emergency Exit" sign above it. It's a fire escape. But why?'

'Call it a fire drill,' I replied.

I followed his directions; the exit door opened on to a spiral staircase alongside the lift shaft. I jogged down, feeling bulky and aware of the weight I'd gained since I didn't have an office to go to every day. The door at the foot opened with a crash bar; there was no handle on the outside, but it closed itself automatically.

The estate was laid out like a small town, with proper roads and pavements. I took a look around, working out the geography of the site, and planning my moves. When I'd decided, I headed to my left, still jogging. I crossed the road at the first junction then turned left at the second. Two hundred yards later I found myself, as I'd calculated, at the edge of the general car park.

I looked back towards the InterMedia building. That silver Skoda Rapid was still there, pointing at a slight angle away from me. You couldn't miss its distinctive panoramic sunroof. I approached it indirectly, two or three car widths away so that I couldn't be spotted in any of its mirrors. The rear windows were dark glass, so I couldn't get a clear view inside until I was almost level with the front doors. When I could, I saw, as I'd expected, the back of a blond head. I closed on the car quickly, opened the passenger door and slid inside.

Carrie McDaniels jumped in the driver's seat, spinning round to face me. 'Hello again,' I said, laughing at the shocked look on her face. It gave way to anger almost at once.

'What do you think—' she began, but I cut her off.

'I don't think, lassie, I know; I know who you are, what you are. Did you think I wouldn't be curious after I'd had a look at that photo album of yours? I might not be attached to the force any more, but I'll always have clout there. It took me one phone call to find out about you and about Mr Linton fucking Baillie. What's his game, Carrie?'

'I can't tell you that,' she snapped. 'He's my client and it's confidential.'

'You don't have that sort of privilege,' I told her. 'You're a licensed investigator, that's all. I could make one more phone call and have that licence suspended, so don't push your luck.

'As of now, you're only a nuisance to me, but your client, he's something else. He's been making oblique threats to someone I know, and I won't let that go unanswered. Next time you report to him you tell him that. We may be sitting here having a nice wee chat, but that doesn't mean to say I'm helpless in Scotland. I've got someone on Baillie's tail, and if he doesn't stop what he's doing, she will.'

'You're pretty good at threats yourself, Mr Skinner,' she hissed.

'No, I'm not,' I retorted. 'In fact, I never make a threat; all I do is tell the future, and spell out consequences. You think on that when you're sitting here, after I've gone. Before I do go, I really have to tell you that you're not very good at your job, whatever your experience was in the part-time Military Police.

'If you're going to tail somebody in Spain, the car of choice is an old white Seat Ibiza, not something as bloody obvious as this. You should keep a change of clothes handy, too, and some deodorant. This is a pretty stuffy car, which tells me that you slept in it last night, somewhere near the Aislado estate, I'd guess.'

I said that only to wind her up: it wasn't really true. She looked a little crumpled, but she smelled okay, and my crack about her sleeping in the car had been no more than an educated guess. She'd followed me all the way to Xavi's, and she must have stayed close to see us leave in the morning.

'Thanks for the advice,' she said, grimly. 'I'll take it on board. But what makes you think I'll be sitting here after you've gone?'

'This does,' I replied, as I opened the door and stepped out. In the pocket of my jacket, I still had the knife that I'd taken from Carrie's Moroccan minder the day before. I opened it and stuck the blade into the right-hand front tyre.

'Hey!' she screamed, as it deflated. 'You can't do that.'

'That's obviously wrong,' I remarked, affably, leaning back into the car. 'I just did.'

'I'll call the police!'

'That would be a mistake, Carrie, even if you could get over the language difficulty. Your front-line investigator's licence is worth sod all in Spain. What you're doing constitutes stalking and it's illegal. I'm saving you all sorts of bother, really.'

I smiled. 'I don't know if this thing has a spare wheel or not. If it does, I'm sure it won't be too hard to change. Alternatively you could flutter your eyelashes at the security guy in the InterMedia building and he might help you. Failing all that, you can put the rescue call-out charge on Linton Baillie's bill, with my compliments. Either way, don't let me see you again, lass.'

I left her to contemplate the unfairness of the world, and the inadequacy of her surveillance techniques, and walked across to the waiting Range Rover, giving her a farewell wave as I climbed in and drove away.

Along with the photograph, Xavi had given me a note of the address of the car park in Girona. I stopped at the exit from the estate, programmed his satnav system, without too much difficulty, and set off.

The route I was given took me into the city by a road I'd never used before, close by the thousand-year-old Romanesque cathedral and then across the river to my destination. The car park was on a big broad avenue, and unlike most in Girona it was above ground, with six levels.

I took a ticket and eased the wide four-by-four through the entrance barrier, then began to cruise slowly through the first aisles, looking out for anything yellow.

Hector's Porsche was on the third level. I looked around for an empty space where I could park, but there were none; in fact

I had to go up two more floors before I found a slot that was big enough to take Xavi's precious motor. I eased it in there, then took the stairs back down.

In my teens and early twenties I was keen on sports cars, and so was Myra. In fact, before Alex was born she talked me into buying one, an MGB Roadster in British Racing Green, with a soft top. That was enough to put me off the damn things for life. My dear first wife, whose need for speed proved to be the end of her, loved it but I couldn't stand the little monster. The driving position was cramped, it was cold in the winter, and damp in the rain, and worst of all I had the devil's own job getting in and out of the thing with the rag-top in place, which it had to be for all but a few weeks of the year.

I remembered that car as I looked down at the daffodil-coloured Boxster, and the relief I felt when I handed over its keys in part-exchange for an Austin Princess, once a pregnant Myra had finally accepted that two-seater cars are for childless couples only.

There was a button on the Porsche's entry key with an icon that looked like a roof, I pressed it and sure enough the fabric top disengaged and stowed itself away, meaning that I could inspect the inside of the car without having to squeeze myself in there.

Hector kept it immaculate, no question about that; there was hardly a speck of dust on the dashboard, and no grit in the floor well, only a small heel print beneath the pedals to indicate that it had ever been driven. The passenger seat was pristine. There was a water bottle, half-empty, in a socket in the central console, and a small tray close to it that was filled with coins, ready no doubt for parking machines or motorway tolls.

I played with the remote until I found the button that lit up the dashboard, and the satellite system. It was broadly similar to the one in the Range Rover, so I was able to search its memory for previous journeys. It was empty; young Señor Sureda was a man who knew where he was going and didn't need help to get there.

I flipped open the central console cover and leaned over to peer inside; driving gloves, small box of peppermints, a Spanish brand I didn't recognise, and some scraps of paper that turned out to be credit card slips when I took them out. There were four; three were for petrol and the other was from a very famous restaurant in Girona.

There was no bill with it, only the card slip. I know that place is expensive, but if Hector had been dining on his own, he must have had a hell of a lot to drink, or made a very top-end choice from the wine list. I checked the date, and raised an eyebrow. It was timed at half an hour before midnight on the previous Thursday, the day before his disappearance, the day before the Porsche had been left in the car park.

I called Xavi. He took the call, but I could hear a buzz of noise in the background. 'Bob, what's up?' he asked.

I told him what I'd found. 'I'd like you to call the restaurant,' I said, 'and ask them if they recall who he was with. The bill's over four hundred euro; it could be that there was more than one person at the table, or that he was out to impress someone in particular. I could make the call myself, but I doubt if they'd talk to me, even if they understood me. You, on the other hand, have got some clout around here.'

'I will do, as soon as I get a chance. We're still at the warm-up stage here. The club president's a very cautious man, until he settles into his surroundings.'

'Going by the stories I've heard about that restaurant,' I

continued, 'it couldn't have been a spur-of-the-moment dinner date. Don't you have to book months in advance?'

'Normal mortals do,' he agreed, 'but InterMedia has an option on a table there; we have a business relationship with them. Why?'

'I dunno, really. I'm just trying to establish a picture, to assess possibilities.' As I spoke, my eye hit on something I'd overlooked; more paper, crumpled on the floor of the car almost out of sight beneath the driving seat. I reached down, picked it up and smoothed it out between my fingers; not a card slip this time, but a bill.

'Hey,' I exclaimed, feeling a sudden smile cross my face, 'the woman theory has definitely moved up a gear. Just before he parked on Friday morning, Hector stopped off at a place called Flores Elena, and spent sixty euro on roses.'

'Eh? Hector? Flowers? This is not the man I know. Bob, you're right and I was very wrong. This has nothing to do with business sabotage, it's a guy following his dick, as simple as that.'

'It looks that way, but I'm even more curious now; I'd like to know where it's taking him. While you're tucking into the Serrano ham and the beef filet, I'm going to see if I can find out. Give me a call when you can, if you get anything from the restaurant that helps us.'

I left him to his football schmoozing and secured the Boxster, then went back up to the Range Rover. I was focused on my next task and about to pull out of my parking slot when my other situation forced its way into my consciousness. I smiled grimly at a vision of Carrie McDaniels trying to find the jack on her hired Skoda. Then I thought of Alex and the things I'd asked her to do.

I'd been worrying about my daughter, in the midst of my own

self-absorption. She'd seemed unsettled ever since I'd given her the task of putting together a criminal defence, in which she had no experience, for a half-brother she'd never met before or even imagined his existence. That had been a lot to ask of her, but she'd handled it as professionally as I'd known she would.

Yet there had been no triumph about it, and that had surprised me. When Alex gets a result, usually the world knows about it and she celebrates, but not that time; maybe the new sibling thing had gone badly with her after all, or maybe it was that mysterious training course she was on. Or could it have been something else, something away from work and family, something personal?

In the midst of my own relationship upheaval, it had become clear to me that while she and Andy Martin were very comfortable together and, on the face of it, happy, they weren't actually going anywhere. What they had was how it would be, for neither of them had time for one hundred per cent of the other.

I dug out my phone again and called her. There was background noise when she answered, but it would be lunchtime with her so I wasn't surprised. I asked her how she was getting along with the things I'd asked her to do.

I'd forgotten that an old adversary of mine, Christopher Kemp, was Governor of the Polmont YOI. From what Alex said he still carried a grudge, but she said that she'd sorted him out, and that Ignacio wasn't at risk.

With no one knowing of our connection, I hadn't been worried about him being picked on in there. He's a big lad, and charming with it, the sort who doesn't invite aggression but looks as though he could deal with it should the need arise. But after what the creepy caller had said to Mia, I had been just a little concerned that he might have contacts in there, the sneaky kind who don't believe in what we from the west of Scotland like to call 'a square go'.

I was pleased that she'd visited the Glasgow lab too. Again, I hadn't expected any leak to have originated there, but that had to be confirmed.

Something else I hadn't expected was her having lunch with Roger McGrane. I was his age once. Back then, I was a ladies' man too, and so I can spot one a mile off . . . or even a thousand miles off, as I was then . . . especially when he's focusing on my daughter.

She was being quietly impressed; it wasn't anything she said that made me certain, it was the change in her voice when she told me she was with him, and her subtly defensive tone when she told me they were having lunch.

I told her, casually, to take care, and she put me in my place. I accused her of winding me up, but Alex doesn't defend on the back foot, so I didn't win there either.

I changed the subject, and floated the notion that perhaps there had been no leak. Was it possible that Baillie had done some thorough background research and had put two and two together, coming up with a remarkably lucky total of four, which he was tossing at Mia like a baited hook, to see if she would bite?

If I'd been in Scotland at that point, I'd have found Baillie within a few hours, but I wasn't, so I let it lie until I did have time to attend to him. Instead I thanked Alex and asked her to keep Mia calm, then got on with my own day, and with my business in hand.

The Porsche had been in the car park for five days, during which time there had been no sign of Hector. That meant that he was either holed up with a chica somewhere in Girona, in a hotel or possibly an apartment, or that he and she had left town.

Of those choices the hotel option seemed least likely; they all have private car parks, so why would he have dumped his very expensive motor in a public multi-storey if he was staying in one of them?

On the basis of the information I had, which was none, checking the apartment option wasn't possible, and so I did the only thing left open to me. I fired up the Range Rover and headed for the railway station. I knew that it was a long shot, but if they didn't come up from time to time, nobody would bother gambling and bookies would be poor.

I found a vacant meter bay a few hundred yards from the station, in a wide avenue. It was lined with trees that would offer shade in the hottest months, but they had been cropped right back for the winter, and so the low sun shone brightly and unimpeded.

As soon as I stepped into the booking hall, I sensed that I really was wasting my time. There were a dozen people there and all but a couple were queuing at a bay of ticket machines.

Fuck, I thought. *If only I had a warrant card here; I could check this guy's credit card transactions and waste no more bloody time.*

But I didn't, so I went up to the only booking window that was attended, by a dour, bespectacled man with a black moustache that seemed to emphasise the sourness of his expression. The first two fingers of his left hand were stained a rich nicotine brown.

'*Hablar Ingles?*' I asked.

'A leetle.'

That was a start.

I showed him Hector's photograph. 'This man,' I said. 'I need to find him. Have you seen him here? Probably last Friday,'

He looked at me as if I'd caused him physical pain. 'Señor,' he sighed, 'so many people's *aqui*.'

I nodded. '*Si, intiendo*. But please, look.'

I pressed the image hard against the glass that separated us. His shoulders sagged in a half-shrug, but he did as I asked, frowning wearily.

He gazed for at least ten seconds before his expression began to change, and for as long again before the light went on finally in his eyes.

'*Si!*' he exclaimed, underlining the affirmative with a nod. '*Este hombre*, *si*. I remember, señor. He is the crazy man who ask if there is Club Class on the AVE to Barcelona. I tell him no, the train takes only *quarante minutos*. So he buy tickets *Preferente*.'

'Was he travelling alone?'

'No, no.' My new friend was in full flow, pleased to be of service to someone, to anyone. 'He had a lady. I remember her, she had flowers, *rosas*. And she was *guapa*, *muy guapa*.'

'Did he buy return tickets?'

'*Ida y vuelta?* No, only the one way.'

I pocketed the picture and dropped a ten euro note on to the tray in the service opening.

'Where you want to go, señor?' he asked. 'Barcelona be more than that.'

'I don't want to go anywhere, not yet. Have a drink and a cigar on me.'

Finally, he showed me that he could smile.

Fourteen

When a Catalan invites you to lunch, it is not advisable to have any other appointments for that afternoon. The midibus that had brought the FC Barcelona contingent was still outside as I eased the Range Rover, still pristine, into its parking place.

Reception had been briefed to send me straight to the third floor, but I had to wait in Xavi's office for another half-hour before he reappeared, with a smile that seemed to belong in another place.

'Good lunch?' I asked.

He nodded. 'Interesting. When I think of my own football career, such as it was, and the world those guys live in . . .'

'In that world, you could have been the Barça goalie.'

'Not a prayer,' he chuckled. 'I'd have been okay with the catching and the punching stuff, but I'd never have been quick enough on my feet, or skilful enough with the ball. The modern keeper has to play sweeper as well. I did think about going back to rugby, before I turned fifty . . . there are a few clubs around here, and I'd have got a game, no worries . . . but Sheila put the kybosh on that.'

As he lowered himself into his chair, I caught his eye.

'Speaking of Barcelona,' I said, 'that's where Hector's gone.' I told him of my lucky strike with the ticket seller at the station.

'The woman he was with was very beautiful, he said. He remembered the flowers as well. You told me you called his apartment, but it may be that he had the phone off the hook.'

'I'd understand that for a couple of days, Bob, but . . .'

I was on the point of asking him if he'd forgotten what it was like to be young but I stopped myself. In truth, Xavi never really knew. He was with Grace from his earliest adult days, until it all went horribly, horribly wrong, and she died: youth passed the poor bloke by.

'Did you have a chance to call that restaurant?' I asked.

'Yes, he dined there all right, and with a woman. They didn't arrive together, though; she arrived after Hector, by taxi. The owner said he'd never seen her before. He's sure she wasn't Spanish, but that's what she spoke.'

'Who made the booking?'

'Oh, Hector did. As we know, he paid, and then they left together, in his car.'

'And he dropped her somewhere,' I said, 'with an arrangement to meet next day, and go to Barcelona. He goes home to pick up some stuff, leaves on Friday morning, and the rest we know.'

'It sounds like a blind date,' Xavi observed, 'like two people who met online or through a dating agency. They had dinner, fancied each other . . .'

I picked up the thread. '. . . and Hector says, "Fancy getting to know each other better in my place in Barcelona?" Yes, I can see that. Maybe they only went down for the weekend but they've been eating each other ever since.' I looked at my friend. 'So what do you want to do?'

'Let's go down there and pound his fucking door down if we have to. Are you up for that?'

'Sure. Now?'

'Now. We can be there in an hour and a half.'

That suited me; as soon as we'd solved the Hector mystery, I could concentrate on my other problem.

We had just joined the autopista when my phone sounded. I checked the caller and saw that it was Amanda. 'Your question,' she began. 'As to Battaglia's current whereabouts, she seems to have dropped off the radar. She hasn't been seen in her office for a week, and she doesn't appear to be at home. Her PA is fielding all her calls. Whenever she leaves Italy, she uses her private jet, but it's parked at Leonardo da Vinci Airport, and no future flight plan has been filed.

'Let me know if you find her,' she concluded, with a laugh in her voice. 'I'd have fun telling the Italians.'

'Who was that?' Xavi asked, as I thanked her and disconnected.

'A friend,' I replied. 'I've been doing some checking up on the Warrior.'

I gave him a quick précis of Amanda's information, without naming the source.

'And this is reliable?' he asked, knowing better than to pry.

'Rock solid. Although she had nothing to do with the Durante assassination, Battaglia's been living off the rumour ever since, and using her dark reputation to intimidate guys like you.'

'I wasn't fucking intimidated!' he protested.

'You were impressed, though; she left her mark on you.'

'Maybe, but she didn't scare me,' he said quietly. 'I'm an Aislado, the son of a man who had to leave Spain in the thirties because he killed one of Franco's men who threatened him and his family. Anyway, fuck her; she's an irrelevance. She may have enough stock market leverage to let her take over her French and German targets but she can't lay a finger on me because my family owns ninety per cent of InterMedia.'

'All of that's true,' I conceded, 'but twenty-four hours ago you were suggesting to me that she might be behind Hector's disappearance.'

'And now you've persuaded me otherwise,' he countered. 'Thanks to what you've discovered, the likelihood is that Hector is entrapped by the power of the furry purse, to borrow one of Joe's more colourful phrases.'

'In which case, what are we going to do when we find him?'

'I told you. We're going to knock until he lets us in.'

'And after that?'

'That will depend on how contrite he is.'

'Suppose he isn't; what then, will you sack him?'

'Hell no, he's too valuable to the company . . . and besides, he's like family. Och,' he exclaimed in a burst of Scottishness, 'I suppose I'll just give him a bollocking for worrying all of us, then tell him to take as long as he needs.' He glanced at me. 'I suppose also that there's no need for you to be here for that. I'm really imposing on you, pal.'

'No, you're not. I offered you my help, remember; you didn't ask me. Once we get to Barcelona we'll see whether I'm needed or not. We might have to kick the door in, and that used to be one of my specialities as a young cop.'

'There'll be no need. Pilar has a key to the apartment; she gave it to me.'

For the rest of the journey we talked mostly football. Xavi's a big Barça fan, and although he'd never admit it, he'd been star-struck by his lunchtime guests. I am a big Motherwell fan. Since we won the Scottish Cup for the second time, I've ceded bragging rights to nobody . . . nobody from Dundee, that is.

Although I've been a regular visitor to Spain for almost thirty years, I'm not very familiar with the layout of Barcelona. However, I do know that it's bisected by two great avenues, the Meridiana and the Diagonal. We entered the city by the former then joined the latter, but not for long, before we turned left. After two more turns Xavi announced, 'This is it,' as he pulled up and parked in a bay that was miraculously empty, in the busy Wednesday evening traffic.

I glanced up at a street sign that was only just visible in the deepening darkness and was mildly amused to see that we were in Carrer de Trafalgar. I suspect that a Catalan mayor of another era had enjoyed naming a street after a Spanish naval defeat.

Hector's apartment was on the top floor, the fifth of a classic city block; not a Gaudi building, but one of a similar vintage, which meant, no lift. By the time we reached the top we were going slowly, as Xavi's old football injury took its toll.

'One day,' he said, as we reached the top landing, 'I will need a knee replacement. When my consultant told me that, I didn't believe him, but now I do.'

He pointed to a door that opened almost directly on to the stairs, then stepped forward and pushed the bell button. We heard it ring inside and listened for the sound of feet approaching; there was only silence. Xavi rang again then thumped the door with the side of his huge fist.

'Hector,' he boomed, 'don't piss me about, let me in.'

He waited for another half-minute, before muttering, 'Fuck it,' then reaching into his pocket.

He found the brass key that Pilar had given him, slipped it

into the lock and twisted it; nothing happened. He frowned. 'Bloody thing's . . .' he muttered as he turned the handle and opened the door.

I can no longer remember the number of times in my police career that I've opened a door without knowing what was behind it, only for my copper's instinct to kick in.

Xavi was about to step inside when I put a hand on his sleeve. 'No,' I said. 'Wait. This is for me; it's why I'm here.'

The hallway was dark, but I didn't feel for a light switch; I knew where I was going. Another door faced me and it was ajar, letting in enough light from the street outside and beyond to guide my way, as I followed my nose.

It doesn't take long for the smell of death to gather, but after a couple of days in a centrally heated apartment it's unmistakeable.

The light in the big reception room had an orange tinge, from the street lamp that was fixed to the wall not too far from the window and the balcony outside. There was enough of it to let me see that the figure lying face down in the centre of the room was not Hector Sureda.

No, it was a woman, elegantly dressed, dark-haired, face down in a pool of dried blood that was big enough for me to know I didn't want to see the exit wound left by the bullet that had killed her. Splatters of red, streaked with brain matter, spread outwards and across the room, in a pattern that almost matched the roses that were scattered on the floor.

It took me back six months, to another place, another time, and another dead female.

The central chandelier exploded into light; Xavi, behind me, had hit the switch.

'Who the hell . . .' I murmured.

'I can tell you,' he said, softly. 'You don't even have to turn her over. That's Bernicia Battaglia.'

I don't know why but I remembered a promise made. I took out my phone and made a call.

'Amanda,' I murmured as it was answered, 'you are going to have such news to pass on to your Italian.'

Fifteen

As I drove back to Edinburgh, my head was full of Roger McGrane. I hadn't been chatted up (girlie term) like that in longer than I could remember. In the aftermath I was surprised that I felt not a trace of annoyance at what I might have seen as presumptuous behaviour, only pleasure at what I decided was flattery. He'd made me feel desirable, and nobody, male or female, is ever going to object to that.

I'd asserted my independence by insisting on paying for lunch; he'd understood that and hadn't argued about it. As we left Kelvingrove, I'd offered to drop him at his office, but he said that he'd rather walk and get some fresh air into his lungs.

We parted with a handshake. 'I will call you,' he promised, his eyes holding mine.

'You do that,' I told him. 'But give me that week.'

The guilt began to kick in as I left Glasgow. My dad can read me like a book; when he told me to watch myself, I knew he hadn't been kidding. He likes me to be safe; that's why he's always been cool about my relationship with Andy, apart from when it all started, when I was, as he saw me, barely out of school uniform. No, he was not cool then.

Dad's seen too many women preyed upon in his life, and like most alpha males he's never been able to consider the possibility that some of us might be predators ourselves. He still can't, not even after his experience with the recently departed Aileen.

If I did see Roger again, he wasn't going to be very pleased.

However, I wasn't thinking only about how he'd look in the shower first thing in the morning. I found myself dwelling on what he'd said about the two people in the car, who seemed to be photographing Dad.

A man and a woman; two people he'd taken for plain-clothes police. I'd asked him if he could describe them, but all he could recall was that she was blonde and he was dark, and as for age, 'youngish'.

My immediate assumption was that they had been the McDaniels woman and Baillie, working in tandem. I thought about calling my father, but decided that his blood pressure was probably high enough, without me adding to it by telling him about stuff he was unable to deal with.

Instead, I decided that as soon as I was home, I'd make tracing Linton Baillie my number-one task.

As I drove I remembered something Dad had mentioned: Baillie's name came into the frame when Detective Sergeant Sauce Haddock discovered in his unofficial inquiry that he had paid for McDaniels' flight to Barcelona.

As soon as I hit the outskirts of Edinburgh, I pulled into a lay-by and called Leith CID where Sauce is based. I don't know him all that well, but I guessed he'd talk to me.

'Alex,' he said as he came on line. 'Two calls from two different Skinners in two days: can I take it they're connected?'

'Yes, you can. I'm looking into the problem my father has.'

'With the McDaniels woman?'

'Yes, but I'm more interested in the man Baillie. Do you have anything more on him?'

'Nothing,' he replied, 'but we haven't been looking. There's no grounds for an official inquiry. We did try to put a name to a face in a photo your father sent us, but no joy. No match on our database.'

'You told my father he paid for the flight by credit card,' I ventured.

'He did; the airline gave me a billing address. Since I last spoke to the chief, I've followed that up. It's in Edinburgh like I told him, but it's a PO Box number. They said also that the card itself is a Visa, issued by something called First National Mutual. That's an offshoot of a Chinese bank and it does all its business online. That's as far as I can go, until the guy does something illegal. He hasn't, has he?'

'No. I wish to hell he would.'

I heard a deep breath being drawn. 'Alex,' Sauce murmured. 'What's this about? The gaffer said he thought he was being stalked, but he didn't say why.'

I frowned, thinking about a very small loop. 'There's something you know,' I replied, 'something very personal and pretty secret that came out of the Bella Watson investigation. I don't want to spell it out over the phone, but are you with me?'

'Yes, I am.'

'Right. There have been a couple of phone calls that suggest it may be known to Baillie as well. So far it's a family affair, but the guy's going to find out that he's up against the wrong bloody family.'

'Jesus, Alex. Listen,' he sounded agitated, 'if that's been leaked, it isn't through me or DI Pye. I haven't mentioned it to a living soul, not even my girlfriend, and I'm certain it's the same with Sammy.'

'Nobody's even thinking that, I promise you. If you've got any ideas, I'd like to hear them, but for now, all I'm really interested in is finding Baillie.'

'Thanks for that, Alex. Do you want me to have a word with George Regan, in Special Branch?'

'Christ, no,' I exclaimed. 'If it gets that serious I'll leave that to Dad. If there's anything else I need checked, discreetly, I'll come back to you. Meantime, thanks for your help.'

I switched off and re-joined the traffic; it was beginning to build up as evening approached, and it took me as long to cross the city as it had to cross the country, but eventually I pulled into our underground garage, parked and took the lift up to my apartment.

As I closed the door behind me, the 'Incoming message' tone sounded on my phone. I took it out; a text from Andy. 'Stuck in Glasgow tonight, sorry. We need to talk; maybe tomorrow.'

'Yes,' I whispered, 'maybe we do.'

I needed a reviver after the drive, and so I went through to the kitchen and poured myself a glass of an energy-packed smoothie that's like Red Bull without the caffeine. I took it with me into my office and booted up my computer.

I'd read as much of Baillie's work as I wanted to but I went back into the downloaded books, looking for the standard author bio that you find in most. Not in those, though; there was no personal information at all.

I logged on to the Internet and looked up Amazon. That

was slightly more helpful, but not much; the blurb for each of his titles volunteered only that he was an allegedly best-selling author, and that he was Scottish, nothing more.

However, I did have one place to go: I searched through the notes on my desk until I found the number that I'd noted for Baillie's publisher. It was closer to six o'clock than five, so I had no great hope of an answer as I dialled, but I came up lucky.

'Donside,' a female voice drawled in my ear, managing to fit an extra syllable into the name. 'Denise speaking. How can we help? Unsolicited manuscripts will be destroyed.'

'I'll bear that in mind when I finish mine,' I said. 'I'm trying to contact one of your authors, a Mr Linton Baillie.'

'One of ours, is 'e? Do you know who his editor is?'

'No, Denise, but I'm hoping you can tell me.'

'Hold on a minute then, madam; I'll look though our list but whoever it is, she'll pro'lly have gone by now.'

I held on, for longer than a minute. I was beginning to suspect that she'd hung up on me and pissed off herself when she restored my battered faith in human nature by coming back on the line.

'You're in luck, madam. Mr Baillie's edited by Clarissa Orpin, and she's still 'ere. One moment and I'll put you through.'

'This is Clarissa.' The new voice on the line was as clipped as Denise's had been languid. 'To whom am I speaking?'

'My name is Alexis.'

'You're interested in one of my authors, I'm told: Linton Baillie?'

'That's right.'

'You're not a reviewer by any chance?'

'Sorry, no.'

'Pity, he could always use a few more. A journalist, then?'

'Not that either, I'm afraid; I'm a lawyer.'

'Oh my God,' she sighed, wearily, 'not another one. Listen, let me spell something out for you. Donside is a small publisher; no way can we afford to be on the wrong side of a libel action or even to be caught up in one. We insist on all our non-fiction authors giving us specific indemnities, on the basis of legal opinion, against that possibility. What that means is talk to Mr Baillie, not me.'

'No, Ms Orpin, it means you're jumping to conclusions, although it does suggest this has happened before with this particular author. I do want to talk to him, but not about defamation.'

'Then what is your purpose?'

'I can't say, I'm afraid. Client confidentiality, you understand. My hope is that you can give me an address, or a contact number for him.'

'I would if I could, Alexis,' she said, 'if only to get you off the line, and me on the tube, but I don't have either. Truth be told I have never met the man.'

'But you're his editor,' I observed.

'No matter. I don't need to see him to do my job; sometimes it's better not to. One might form an opinion of a person, good or bad, that might colour one's attitude to his work. Baillie's manuscripts arrive in my in-box, I edit them and send back my observations and the final text is agreed. That's how it works.'

'That may be so, but you must have contracts, yes?'

'Yes we do, but it's always the agent's address on those. In Baillie's case it's the agent who forwards the manuscript, and responds to my queries.'

I frowned. 'What you're saying to me in effect is that for all you know, Linton Baillie might be a pseudonym. There might be no such person of that name.'

'That hadn't occurred to me,' she admitted, 'but it is the case. An author can call himself what he likes. Indeed, given some of the areas that Mr Baillie discusses in his work, that might a sensible precaution.'

'He has a credit card,' I told her.

'So what? As long as he services the debt the issuer won't give a damn if his real name is Joe Bloggs.'

'Point taken,' I conceded. 'Tell me, Clarissa, am I the first person to come looking for Baillie?'

She sniffed. 'No, you're not. I had a very nasty phone call last year from a chap with a Scottish accent. I reported it to the police; they investigated and told me that the man's objection was to his name being used in Linton's first book. They pointed out to him that he didn't hold the copyright on it and that if his namesake happened to be a dead East End gangster, that was his unfortunately tough luck.'

She paused. 'There was also a call after the publication of *The Public Executioner*, from a chap in the Home Office. They weren't too pleased by the content, but as the book didn't make the *Sunday Times* top ten, they didn't make a public fuss.'

'Lucky old Linton.'

'He'd agree with you. I never expected that book to ever earn out its substantial advance, but it has done, and then some.'

'Does he have anything else in the pipeline?' I asked.

'We have an option on his next work, through a clause in his previous contract. His agent promises me that it will be special, but after the success of *Executioner*, he isn't going to commit to a contract until he's finished the manuscript.'

'When is it due?'

'He didn't give me a specific date, but I've been told to expect it by the end of April, next year. I have to tell you, my dear, I am holding my breath; Baillie has kept our head above water for the last couple of years.

'This business is very risky. True crime sells, no question, but there's more and more of it around, and readers tend to be going crazy for anything Scandinavian. My best advice to an aspiring author these days is to write in a Nordic language and then have it translated into English.'

She chuckled at her own joke. I didn't because I didn't get it.

'And now,' she said, 'I really must go. The only help I can offer is the name of Baillie's agent. It is Thomas Coyle, of the eponymous literary agency, and this is his number.'

She dictated eleven digits. The first four were familiar. 'He's based in Edinburgh,' she added, but I'd worked that out. 'I can't recall the address, I'm afraid, and I don't have time to look it up.'

'That's all right,' I said. 'I do. Thanks.'

'Will I be hearing from you again?' Clarissa Orpin asked. Her tone was cautious rather than curious.

'That may depend,' I replied, 'on what Mr Baillie is up to.'

I left her wondering and reached for the Edinburgh Yellow Pages. I found four literary agencies listed, alphabetically: Thomas Coyle was the second, and his address was shown as Bengal Place. I had never heard of it, but Google maps soon showed me that it was a very small street between Canonmills and Stockbridge, where I used to live.

I called the number Clarissa had given me. It rang out five times then voicemail picked up.

'Congratulations,' an over-enthusiastic man exclaimed, in a husky voice. 'You have reached the Coyle Literary Agency. The slightly bad news is that I can't take your call at this moment. However, if you leave a message, and a contact number, I will get back to you soonest. That's a promise. While you're waiting, you might like to check out my website, www.coylelitagency.com.'

All that phoney sincerity must have infected me, for I put on my best girlie simper and ad-libbed, 'Hello, Mr Coyle. My name's Lexie Martin and I'm an author. I write these really terrific detective novels. I'm trying to get them published and a friend said I should call you. I've got some free time tomorrow morning, and I'd really, really appreciate it if you could see me then.'

I left my mobile number, then hung up. A few keystrokes and couple of clicks later and I was in his site.

I plan to set one up myself as soon as I've passed the Bar exams, but I haven't got around to choosing a web designer. When I do, it won't be the one who set up Coyle's. The wallpaper was a miscellany of bad taste, a mix of images that I guessed were meant to demonstrate the categories of work he represented; gambolling bunny rabbits and bloodstained corpses are all very fine, but not side by side.

There was a photograph of the man himself; he looked as unctuous as he sounded, a chubby-cheeked middle-aged man with what looked like a toupee in a garish blue jacket with big lapels. Add in some sparkles and I could have been looking at a reincarnation of Liberace.

I looked along the menu bar and selected 'Bio'. It told me

that Coyle was thirty-seven . . . I didn't believe that for a moment; even in a studio photo, he looked forty-five, minimum . . . and that after a 'stellar' career in entertainment management he had set up an agency dedicated to 'the best of Scottish literary talent'.

His client list was also available. I opened it and looked for recognisable names among the two dozen or so listed; Linton Baillie was there, and a couple of people I knew as newspaper columnists, but the rest were unknown to me.

I searched on the Internet for half a dozen of them; two names cropped up on Amazon, but of the other four, one was a proctologist in Dallas, Texas, another was a lifeguard on the Australian Gold Coast, a third ran a very dodgy 'get rich quick' business in Wales, and the fourth was a foreign exchange dealer. Maybe everyone who called Coyle wound up being listed as a client, or, just as likely, he had made up half of the names. If that was so, Lexie Martin would fit in very nicely, for there wasn't a single 'M', an oddity for a Scottish agency, where 'Mac' should abound.

I clicked on a name on the site, one of those I'd recognised, Jean Shields: 'Freelance journalist and now the celebrated creator of Jimmy the Sheepdog, beloved by children around the world.' The accompanying image showed a woman with a shy smile; it was off-centre, probably an iPhone selfie.

Finally, I moved on to Baillie, hoping to put a face to him, but no such luck; there was no mugshot on display, and very little text, only, 'The man who took the lid off MI5 with his best-selling *The Public Executioner*.'

'Time for me to put the lid on him,' I murmured to the empty room, as I closed my computer.

I was in the kitchen, wondering what to do about dinner,

given that all I had in the fridge was the MacSween's haggis I'd forgotten that I was taking to Andy's when I chose my lunch with Roger, when I had an incoming text.

'Delighted to see U 2moro. 10 am, 10 Bengal Place. OK? Tommy Coyle.'

I flashed him a response. 'Super. Thanks a million. C U then. Lexie.' I grinned at my phone, and blew it a kiss.

Sixteen

I had a plan for my meeting with Mr Coyle, but there was a flaw in it. Even though the man was, on the face of it, something of a bullshitter, I wasn't going to last long with him if I walked through his door empty-handed.

I'd told him I wrote 'really terrific' detective novels. I needed something to back that up.

The solution came to me after half an hour's fretting over a home-delivery pizza and half a bottle of white wine. I went back into the Amazon website, and copied the headline information on half a dozen bestsellers in the crime fiction list, pasting it into a Word document, piece by piece.

When I was satisfied that I had enough, I edited it down, taking a little bit from here, a little bit from there, blending it all together until I had what I reckoned was an acceptable synopsis for a debut mystery novel.

I was printing it out next morning when the phone rang. I picked it up and went out of the office, away from my noisy printer, saying, 'Hi, this is Alex,' as I walked.

'Hi, love,' Andy said. He sounded weary. 'I'm sorry about last night. There was a hijacking threat on a Russian aircraft over the Atlantic; Ukrainians. The pilot told the hijackers they could shoot him if they liked but he was landing at Prestwick, not on top of the fucking Kremlin, as they demanded. He did too, and we had armed police and negotiators on the ground waiting for him.'

Instantly, I felt ashamed of my annoyance the night before. 'What's the situation now?' I asked.

'Sorted. The negotiating team talked them out without bloodshed. I've only just lifted the news blackout, so you can expect the telly to go crazy shortly.'

'Well done the good guys,' I said. 'You sound whacked.'

'I am.'

'Too whacked to talk? Your text said we need to.'

'Later, maybe tonight.'

'Give me a clue, at least,' I insisted. 'I may have plans for tonight for all you know.'

'Exactly. That's part of it. I can't do this any more, Alex, this commute between Edinburgh and the west of Scotland. Bob might have managed when he was in Strathclyde, but even he would have had to give in eventually.'

'What are you saying to me?' I asked him.

'That I'm moving to Glasgow.' He let the words hang in the air for a few seconds. 'That's where my new headquarters will almost certainly be when I move out of Tulliallan, but even if it's not, that's where the bulk of the job is. I need a place there, and it doesn't make economic sense to keep on the Edinburgh house too. I've made an offer for a place in Clarkston, so Dean Village goes on the market next week.'

I felt myself go cold inside; something else was coming, and I knew what it would be. 'I like that house,' I said, quietly.

'I know, and so do I, but it can't be.'

'Maybe I'll buy it.' The coldness crept into my voice.

'Come on, you like your place too.'

'That kind of defines our relationship, Andy, doesn't it? What are we? Lovers or best pals?'

'We're both, aren't we?'

I let my silence speak for me.

He broke it. 'Come with me?' he ventured. That's what I'd anticipated.

'Stay with me,' I countered.

'I can't,' he protested. 'Edinburgh doesn't work for me any longer. I need to do this. Alex, you can practise criminal law in Glasgow as easily as you can in Edinburgh. Most of your work will be in the High Court and that goes on circuit.'

'The Appeal Court is in Edinburgh,' I countered. 'Anyway, that's not the bloody point. Couples discuss major issues, and they agree what's best; that's how it's meant to work. One party doesn't bugger off and take a decision on his own. You just did that, Andy, which means only one thing to me . . . we aren't a couple.'

I heard something on the line that sounded very much like a growl.

'I seem to remember you taking a decision a few years ago,' he said, 'a very big decision, without discussing it with me.'

'You got me pregnant, Andy,' I snapped at him. 'It wasn't meant to happen but it did. If I'd discussed it with you, and said I wanted a termination, you'd have screamed the place down. You'd have rediscovered the Catholic principles that you use when it suits you, and demanded that I sacrifice my career. You'd have done that, and I'd have listened to you, then I'd have had the abortion anyway. So all I did was avoid the confrontation.'

173

'Thanks.' That one word was dripping with irony.

'Don't mention it. You're getting your own back now.'

'Come with me,' he repeated.

'On what basis?'

'Come and be Lady Martin. I had the letter from the palace this morning; the knighthood's been offered and I've accepted.'

I astonished myself by exploding with laughter.

'Fucking hell, you've done it again. Leaving aside the fact that you've just made the clumsiest marriage proposal in history, you didn't stop for one second before accepting to consider whether I might prefer to be Mrs Martin.'

'Can I take that as a "No"?' He sounded as cold as I'd felt earlier, before he'd fired up my anger.

'Andy, you can take it as a "Fuck off"!' I yelled.

I pushed the red button on the handset and threw it across the room, so hard that it shattered against the wall.

Alexis Skinner doesn't do tears very often but I did then. I dropped into my red armchair and buried my face in my hands. I didn't know whether I was crying out of anger, out of frustration, out of loss. All I knew for sure was that inside I felt as I had when I walked out of hospital after having the abortion; something was gone and it could never be replaced.

I got it all out of my system in the shower, then with an effort of will turned my thoughts back to the business of the morning.

My first consideration was how to dress. I had presented myself in my voicemail message as an ingénue would-be novelist. The power suit that I had worn the day before would hardly fit that image.

After a brief rummage in my casual wardrobe, I came up

with a pair of hipster cords that I'd last worn when I was in my mid-twenties but had never got around to sending to the charity shop. I settled on them and was pleased to discover that they still fitted; indeed they hung a little loose, but not perilously so.

I topped them off with a 'Yes for Scotland' sweatshirt, worn bra-less, ruffled my hair a little, and appraised myself in the mirror.

'Well, get you, Lady Martin,' I murmured, with a small chuckle and a raised eyebrow.

I retrieved my fake synopsis from the printer, and read through it again. It would do, I decided; it didn't need to be a work of art, for all it was doing was getting me through the door.

Street parking is never fun in Edinburgh, so I decided to take the bus to Bengal Place. I'd been doing that a lot more frequently since leaving CAJ. I've become an expert; I buy M-tickets online and store them on my phone.

The route took me to the foot of Dundas Street, where I got off and turned into Henderson Row. My bust-up with Andy was still on my mind; being Lexie seemed to help keep it at bay, although I was kicking myself for giving him Martin as a surname.

He called me again, just as I reached Bengal Place, but I didn't take it. I guessed that he'd be looking to calm me down, but I knew for sure that he wouldn't have changed his mind, or even come up with a compromise. He doesn't do that.

It isn't one of my strong suits either, probably the main reason why I was dealmaker of the year. I don't blink first.

Earlier, I'd thought of phoning Dad, the master of the icy

stare, to cry on his shoulder, but he didn't need it at that moment in his life, and besides, he seemed to be busy with something in Spain, hence my involvement in the Baillie affair. There was also the complication that if he'd asked me what I was doing, I'd have had to confess that I was exceeding my brief by searching for the man.

The office of the Coyle Literary Agency wasn't hard to find. Bengal Place is no more than thirty yards long and is made up of tenement buildings on either side, all the doors being controlled by entryphones.

There was no brass plate, or anything grand, simply a card trimmed and fitted into a slot, beside a button. I pressed it and waited for a few seconds until a male voice, one I recognised, intoned, 'Yessss?'

No receptionist, I guessed.

'It's Lexie Martin, for Mr Coyle.'

'Of course, my dear, first floor.' There was a buzz and I pushed the door.

The stairwell was presentable, by which I mean it had been painted fairly recently and it didn't smell of piss . . . the main benefit of remote entry systems in central Edinburgh . . . but food odours made it clear that I was in a residential rather than commercial building.

Thomas Coyle was waiting for me at the door. He was an inch or so shorter than I am, and looked older in the chubby flesh than in his photograph. The odd toupee was in situ but the garish jacket had been replaced by a sweater; maybe cashmere, but probably not.

He smiled, giving me a quick glance up and down, his eyes widening not quite imperceptibly at one point. It had been cold in the shaded street, my Hippie Hanna Afghan coat was hanging open and I could feel my hardened nipples pressing against the sweatshirt. I squared my shoulders to make them stick out a little more and grinned back at him.

'Come in,' he said, ushering me quickly through a shabby hall and into a room that looked down into Bengal Place. It was set out like an office, with a desk by the window, but there was a television in the corner, and two old leather armchairs on either side of the fireplace, in which a coal-effect gas fire flickered.

'Let me take your coat.' He reached out as if to help me out of it, but I beat him to it, slipping it off my shoulders, and handing it to him. He copped another quick glance at my temperature gauges, before hanging my coat on a hook behind the door.

'It's very good of you to see me at such short notice,' I gushed. 'You must be terribly busy with all your other clients. I looked at your website this morning; it's very impressive.'

'Thank you, Miss Martin.'

'Lexie, please.'

'Thank you, Lexie, but think nothing of it. 'Helping aspiring writers is my *raison d'être*. It's what I'm here for. But first,' he exclaimed, 'it's my coffee time. Will you join me?'

'I'd love one,' I lied. 'Do you have Nespresso?'

He may have thought that I thought that he looked like George Clooney, for he beamed. 'Normally yes, my dear, but I'm out. It's only inst, I'm afraid.'

'That will be lovely.'

He went back into the hall, heading for the kitchen, I assumed, leaving me free to look around. There was very little business furniture, only a three-drawer filing cabinet, on top of which sat a printer, connected by cable to a computer on the desk. Wireless technology hadn't reached the Coyle Literary Agency.

I'd have loved to sneak a look into the cabinet for Baillie's file, but I couldn't take the risk, in case Coyle had a quick-boil kettle. Instead I retrieved my 'synopsis' from my coat and smoothed it out.

I had just finished when he returned with two mugs of coffee. Each one featured a book on the outside, promotional material, I surmised, handed out by publishers to plug an author or a new title.

The image on the one he'd given me was the jacket of *The Public Executioner* by Linton Baillie.

He saw me inspect it. 'Impressive, aren't they. Who knows?' he added. 'One day your work might be on one of those.'

'Mmm,' I murmured. 'If only . . .'

' "If only" is why you're here, my dear,' he gushed. 'My job is to turn "if only" into reality. Tell me something about yourself, Lexie.' He tried to look at me in an avuncular way, but still his eyes missed mine, settling lower down.

I sipped my coffee, hoping that it might warm me up and soften Cheech and Chong . . . we all have pet names, don't we? It was as dodgy as I'd expected from the cheesy little bugger, supermarket value brand, most likely.

'I'm thirty,' I began, 'and I'm single. I've worked in a big office for ten years, but now I've chucked it to do what I really want, and that is, become a best-selling novelist.'

'Have you any writing experience?'

'I've been doing it for years,' I bullshat. 'I tried poetry, then I tried children's books, then I tried fantasy romance . . . I'm a huge Twilight fan . . . but now I've switched to crime fiction, and I know that's the way to go.'

'Do you have a manuscript?' he asked. 'Most writers who come here have a book to show me.'

'No, I don't, not yet, but I have an outline of what I'm working on.' I handed him my printout, with the most nervous smile that I could muster.

'Then let me look at it.' He took it from me and studied it, reading it through once, then a second time, with a gravitas that reminded me of my old university tutor studying a paper on civil law that I had handed in.

The similarity ended when he smiled.

'This is marvellous, Lexie,' he announced. 'You have a wonderful, unique imagination; if you can match it with your writing as you turn this into a complete manuscript, you have a big future in front of you. And even if you can't, the agency can help you with its editorial services.'

I frowned. 'I don't know if I can afford that.'

Coyle laughed at my apparent naivety. 'There's no cost, my dear lady. It's included in our twenty per cent commission.'

If I'd been for real I'd have squared him up there and then. I don't know a hell of a lot about the publishing business, but I do know that twenty per cent is at the top end of the range. But I wasn't, so I looked relieved and said, 'That's very reasonable.'

He nodded, as if that was true. 'How soon do you think you can complete the book?'

I frowned. 'Three months?' I ventured.

'That would be admirable. I believe I can help you, Lexie. My terms are set out in a standard letter. We both sign it and it serves as an agreement between us. You can terminate it by giving three months' notice at any time, but my rights in any agreement I negotiate on your behalf will continue in perpetuity. Is that acceptable?'

'Is it ever!' I gushed.

'Give me your address and I'll print it out now.'

We were several steps beyond anything I'd anticipated. No way was I giving him my actual address, so I gave him Andy's instead.

He went to his computer and played with the keyboard for a while, then moved his mouse and clicked. The printer hummed into life, and a few minutes later, Lexie Martin had an agent, even if he was the most gullible guy in the book trade.

'Now that I'm part of the team,' I said, as I handed him the signed letter of agreement, which was serviceable legally but didn't bind me actually to produce anything, 'would it be possible to meet one of your writers? I'm a huge fan of his work. Being new to this I'd love to pick his brains, and get any tips he might give me.'

'I'm sure that's doable,' he replied. 'Who would this author be?'

'Linton Baillie. I think *The Public Executioner* is just sensational.'

Coyle sucked in a quick breath. 'Oh, Lexie, I'm not sure about that. Linton's a very private person. As a fan you'll know that his work deals with some very sensitive areas, so he has to be careful. On top of that he's naturally shy.'

I gave him a quick eyelash flutter, and a smile. 'I'll be gentle with him, I promise. Honestly, I am his number one fan. It would be a privilege to meet him.' I leaned towards him, so that C and C, who were still showing the effects of my being underdressed in Coyle's under-heated office, stood out boldly against their covering. 'I'd be very grateful,' I purred, 'to you both.'

His eyes widened, emphasising the bags beneath them. For a moment I was afraid he was going to ask for a quick flash. I'm not sure how I would have dealt with that, but I wasn't put to the test, for he nodded, and said, 'I'll consult with Linton and see what he says. I'm sure I can persuade him to meet you, especially when I tell him how, er, enthusiastic, you are. I'd do it now, Lexie, but,' he sighed, as if he'd been anticipating a little gratitude in advance, 'unfortunately I'm meeting another client, Jean Shields, in the Sheraton Hotel at eleven, and I must be going there now. But I do promise I will speak to him as soon as Jean and I have finished our business. I'll call you later on today, I promise.'

Two minutes later I was back in Henderson Row, heading for the bus stop. My Hippie Hannah Afghan was pulled around me very tight indeed.

Seventeen

When I stepped back into my apartment, just after eleven fifteen, my voicemail indicator showed that I had three messages. Unfortunately I couldn't access them without the handset, and I'd broken that beyond repair.

There were missed calls and voice messages on my mobile also, two of each. I resisted them for as long as I could, but finally I gave in.

The first caller wasn't as expected. No, it was my old boss, Mitch Laidlaw, asking me if I'd call him on his mobile, urgently. He'd been in touch a couple of times since I'd gone, to see if I was wavering, but on each occasion it had been through his PA, not on his private phone.

I rang him back straight away. 'Thanks for calling, Alex. I have a job for you, if you'd be prepared to take it on.'

I sighed. 'Mitch, I appreciate that you're trying to help, and that I owe you a lot. Call me an ungrateful cow if you like, but I am determined about this.'

'I know you are,' he said, 'but it isn't our kind of job. It's one that might kick-start your new career.'

That was intriguing. 'Then tell me about it, please.'

'The son of a friend has landed in a spot of bother,' Mitch

began. 'He was picked up in a nightclub last night for possession of cocaine. The story I've been given is that he was in the gents and someone he knew offered him a line. The lad swears he's not a habitual user, but he'd had a couple of drinks and thought he'd try it, to see what all the fuss was about, as he put it. He was bent over it, snorting, when a man stepped out of one of the toilet cubicles . . . a police officer.'

'A cop on his own?' I asked.

'Yes. I think he was genuinely off duty, but chose not to turn a blind eye. When he challenged the two of them, Jamie's so-called friend denied all knowledge of the drugs, and now the sod's given a statement corroborating the officer's story.'

'That's tough luck on the kid, Mitch, but where do I come in?'

'Jamie's surname is Middleton. He's eighteen years old. His father's Easson Middleton.'

'As in Easson Middleton QC.'

'Exactly. The top man in the criminal Bar, and Vice-Dean of the Faculty of Advocates. He can't act for the boy himself, and he doesn't want to go to an established firm of solicitors, because he's instructed by most of them and doesn't want to be seen to be playing favourites. I've told him about you and he's asked if you'd be prepared to take him on, in the early stages at least.'

'Mitch,' I said, 'I don't know if I can.'

'There's no reason why not. This is a relatively minor offence and it'll never get past the Sheriff Court. Ideally it won't go to court at all, if the fiscal can be convinced that one of his witnesses is lying.'

'Where's Jamie now? In custody?'

'No, he was charged this morning then bailed on his own recognisance, to appear in court on a future date.'

I was tempted, but uncertain. 'Are you sure I'm up to this?'

'If I wasn't we wouldn't be speaking. Alex, if it goes to court, so be it; you won't have made things any worse. If you can cast doubt on the corroborating witness, and the charge is dropped, great. If not, and you can persuade the Crown Office to ask the sheriff for an absolute discharge in return for a guilty plea, that would be second best.'

'What's behind this?' I asked. 'The kid snorted the coke, that doesn't seem to be in dispute, but a minor drugs conviction is hardly career-wrecking these days.'

'It might be in this case. Jamie's a golfer, a very good one. He has a sports scholarship lined up with a university in Florida, beginning next year. I don't have to tell you that the US authorities take a very hard line on admitting people with any sort of conviction.'

'Okay,' I said. 'I'll do what I can. Where can I see him?'

'You can use this office . . . you're still a partner of record here.'

'No thanks, I don't want people getting confused.'

'Mmm, maybe not. Tell you what, I'll have Easson book one of the faculty's rooms, in the consultation centre. How soon can you see him?'

'This afternoon if his dad can fix it.'

'I'll get on it and let you know. It should be okay.'

'Fine. I have just one question. Who's the arresting officer?'

'I'm told his name's Montell, Detective Sergeant Griffin Montell. Can't say I know him.'

I grinned from ear to ear; my day had just taken a turn for

the better. 'I do,' I chuckled, 'and something tells me that our boy is going to be all right.'

I was still smiling well after Mitch had gone. From out of nowhere I had two jobs, putative novelist and criminal defence solicitor, one fantasy, the other very real. I was so pumped up that I forgot about my other voicemail message until I'd finished dressing in my business clothes.

I picked up my phone to access it, but before I could do so, an incoming call interrupted me. It was Mitch again; Easson Middleton had moved fast. I had an appointment to meet him and his son in the Advocates' Consultation Centre at two o'clock that afternoon, in less than two hours.

Finally I got back into my mailbox; the second message was from Andy, as I'd expected.

I'd been hoping for a little contrition, but I didn't hear any.

'Alex, I hope you've had time to calm down,' he began. 'I'm sorry that I told you what I've decided on the phone and not face to face, but I don't think it would have made any difference. I'm doing one of the most important jobs in Scotland, possibly the most. I have to be properly located for it. I'd hoped you'd accept that, and accommodate me, but it seems that your selfish streak will never go away.'

'You bastard!' I hissed.

'To be frank, I've been concerned ever since you embarked on this career change. With all your connections, I've got no doubt that you'll be successful and that before long you'll be a top defence lawyer. If you can't see the conflict between that job and mine, then you're walking around with your eyes closed.

'I've loved you from the moment we got together, but I don't believe we've ever been compatible. If you think about it you might come to agree with me. It's best that we agree to be friends from now on, and back off from everything else.

'You don't need to return this call, unless you want to scream at me some more. When you're ready, perhaps we can meet over dinner. I assume you weren't serious about buying the house, but if I'm wrong, call my solicitor before next week, and he'll sort out terms.'

I stared at the phone. For the first time since I was sixteen years old, I'd been chucked.

'I'll never be ready, Andy,' I whispered. 'I don't care how important your job is, or how menial. It's more important than me, and that's all that matters.'

I was still gazing at it when the ring tone sounded again, and Coyle's number showed on screen. I accepted the call, switching into Lexie mode.

'Tommy,' I chirped. 'I wasn't expecting to hear from you so soon. Have you found me a publisher already?'

'I'm still working on that, dear. I'm calling to say that Linton's agreed to meet you. He isn't normally interested in helping other writers, but when I told him what a sweet girl you are, and how grateful you'd be, that did the trick. He says he'll be at home this evening if you'd care to call on him, any time after eight. His address is twenty-seven slash two slash c Portland Street, in Slateford.'

'Really?' I gushed. 'Really' seemed to be Lexie's favourite word. 'That's wonderful of you, Tommy. He's going to teach me lots of stuff I didn't know, I'm sure. Thank you so much.'

And I'm going to give him a couple of lessons in life, I thought as I closed the mobile.

I checked my watch. I'd time for a quick salad lunch before

my meeting with the Middletons; time for that, and one more phone call. I threw some Chinese leaves, peppers, corn and a couple of quail's eggs into a bowl, dressed them with a mix of extra virgin, balsamic vinegar and a little mustard, then put it on a tray with a bottle of water and took it into the living room.

When I was finished, I made that call.

'Alex,' Griff Montell exclaimed, 'this is a surprise. Should I be talking to you or will it come back to bite me if the big boss man hears about it? It took me long enough to get my promotion; I wouldn't want to blow it.'

'You're in no danger of that,' I promised him.

Griff and I have history, of a friendly kind. When I was in Stockbridge, he and his twin sister lived next door, having come to Scotland from South Africa, for personal reasons. He needed to make enough money to support his kids from a failed marriage, and she left because she'd been unhappy there as a gay woman.

Griff got me out of a difficult situation once, and I was duly grateful. As I said, we were friends, but sometimes the journey from my place to his was just too long for him to contemplate, so he stayed over.

Those days are well behind us. He's never been in my new apartment.

'How are you and Alice?' I asked. I'd heard on the grapevine that he's involved seriously now with a former colleague, a woman called Alice Cowan.

'We're good, thanks, better since she left the force. So,' he said, briskly, 'what's this about? Need a shoulder to cry on?'

'Hell, no! What was that Amy Winehouse song?'

'"Love is a Losing Game"?'

'Close but I was thinking about "Tears Dry on their Own". No, chum, this is business. It has to do with a client of mine, Jamie Middleton.'

'Him? How? Why? You're corporate.'

'Not any more. I've just been retained by his father.'

'Then listen carefully, Alex; the boy's done. I caught him with a tube full of blow up his nose. Wrong toilet, wrong time and tough on him but I couldn't walk away.'

'Your witness did, though.'

'No. He swore he was clean. The first thing I did was pat him down, and he was.'

'What did Jamie say?'

'That the boy had provided it.'

'Why didn't you believe him?'

He laughed. 'Because it didn't matter. Your client still had the tube in his fucking nose while he was telling me!'

'Did you have the tube tested?'

'No, but there was no need.'

'I'm going to want that done; when I do, your witness's prints and DNA will be all over it. I'm going to kill your corroboration, Griff. This case is going to trial.'

'You're pulling my chain!' he gasped.

'I'm pulling nothing. I'm going to plead him "Not guilty"; the fiscal's going to need you as a witness. That's going to be awkward, is it not?'

He knew what I meant, only too well. He's Special Branch, and the force doesn't like them to be identified. 'Only if you choose to make it that way,' he countered.

'That's true, but I won't have a choice. The fiscal has, though.'

'What do you want?'

'A slap on the wrist, no more; an informal police caution, but nothing that goes on his record or can ever be used against him.'

'I can't do that deal, Alex, you know that.'

'I know but the fiscal can. I'd like you to speak to whoever's handling the case and explain the facts of life. I'm seeing Jamie at two; a call shortly after that would be appreciated.'

'I'll see what I can do. Lizzie Baines is the depute involved.'

'I know her,' I told him. 'We were in the same year at university. We got on all right.'

'Then let's hope that helps your boy. Like I said, flower, I've got nothing against him. I saw what I saw, that's all there was to it.'

'Understood. Thanks, Griff.'

''S okay. It's great to hear from you again. You sound different, somehow.'

'You mean older?'

'No, I mean the opposite. You come across as happy, in a good place; I like that.'

'So do you,' I replied. He might have been flattering me, but I meant it.

'I hope so,' he said. 'I've moved in with Alice.'

'That's nice. Take care of her.'

While he made his call to the fiscal, or so I hoped, I left for my meeting. I walked there, three-quarters of the way up the Royal Mile, and arrived with five minutes to spare.

Easson Middleton QC was waiting for me; a tall, stick-thin, austere man, dressed in senior counsel clothes: dark jacket, pinstripe trousers and a blue and white striped shirt.

'Ms Skinner,' he greeted me, 'this is an unexpected turn of

events. In other circumstances it would be a pleasure. Is there any part of Mitch's brief that you don't understand?'

I shook my head. 'I have a grasp of it, I believe. This is about damage limitation.'

He sighed. 'In a bloody nutshell; silly young bugger.'

'How far do you want me to take this?' I asked. 'If I can't keep it out of court, do you want me to plead the case, or will you appear for Jamie?'

'I can't do that. I have too many enemies on the Bench, even at Sheriff Court level. It's your brief, and you take it all the way . . . as I fear you'll have to. The lad was caught bang to rights; because I am who I am, I can't see the fiscal being lenient.'

My first criminal client, a stocky kid, was waiting for us in a small consulting room. He was wearing a school blazer with a familiar crest, and a worried expression. His father asked me, properly, if I wanted to see him on my own, but I told him I was quite happy for him to sit in.

'Do you know what's at stake here?' I asked the boy as soon as we'd been introduced. 'Uncle Sam's a real arse-hole when it comes to letting convicted felons into the country.'

He nodded. 'College is really important to me, Ms Skinner. Would they really cancel my scholarship?'

'In favour of a clean-cut all-American boy, with an unblemished record?' I said. 'What do you think?' I didn't let him dwell on it. 'You told the police that you'd never done drugs before. Was that true?'

He reddened. 'Well . . . I've smoked a wee bit of puff,' he admitted. 'Hasn't everybody?'

'I haven't, Jamie. But when I was a kid my dad was head

of the drugs squad, so I had a powerful disincentive. Your story is that the boy you were with supplied the cocaine. Is that true?'

He frowned and shook his head. 'No, we bought it between us from a dealer in the club. Donnie made the buy though,' he added.

'But you paid for your share?'

'Yes.' Middleton senior buried his face in his hands.

That's really going to impress the sheriff, I thought.

'Am I in serious trouble?' he asked. 'Could I go to jail?'

I looked at his father. 'Given the amount involved, no,' he said. 'But the fact that you went there with the intention of buying will not help.'

'How will anybody find out?'

'They'll find out if I put your friend Donnie in the witness box and he tells the whole story. So I can't risk that.' I turned to Easson again. 'We've got one chance here.' I checked my watch, twelve minutes past two.

'Failing that, though,' I continued, 'I'd say our best chance is to plead guilty and for me to get down on my knees before the sheriff and beg for an absolute discharge, which means no conviction is recorded. But that will bring your relationship with the Bench into play, Mr Middleton.'

'It looks as if I'll have to risk that, Alex. You're right beyond a doubt. If you put Donnie in the box, then it's a car crash waiting to happen and, worse, Jamie's seen to have made a false statement to the police.'

He was glaring at his son when my mobile sounded. I checked the screen. 'Excuse me, I have to take this.'

'Is that really Alex?' Lizzie Baines exclaimed in my ear.

'It sure is.'

'The same Alex whose boyfriend I pinched in the second year?'

'In your dreams, woman; I'd binned him before you came along.'

'Did you bin the dishy DS Montell too?'

'No, that just came to a natural end. We're still pals but it won't stop me putting him in the box and asking him what his police duties involve, and why he happened to be where he was when he was.'

'So he says. I've just had a call from his boss, a man called McGuire, telling me he wouldn't like that. He said that if necessary the next call that he'd make would be to my boss. Cut to the chase time, Alex?'

'Yes, what's your proposal?'

'Official police caution?' she suggested.

I'd thought that one through since mentioning it to Griff. 'Nah, Lizzie. What would be the point? He's sitting here crapping himself, plus he has a sore nose from snorting the stuff. You drop the case, but retain the file. That way, if he ever does it again . . . which he won't . . . you can refer to it in any subsequent court proceedings.'

'Okay,' she conceded, 'you've got it . . . but make sure Easson kicks his arse good and hard.'

'I think that's happened already. Thanks, cheers.'

'No worries. See you around.' She paused. 'You never binned him, did you? He said you were broken-hearted.'

I laughed. 'He lied, Lizzie. They all do.'

I pocketed my phone and looked at the younger Middleton. 'Go in peace, young man, but think yourself very lucky that it wasn't another cop . . . any other cop . . . in that toilet.'

And that's how I got a result in my first criminal case, and made a lifelong friend of Easson Middleton QC, a man who's sure to be a judge within the next two years.

He told me to send my fee note to his home address; I told him to consider it a favour to Mitch Laidlaw. In fact there hadn't been any real legal work involved.

I was passing John Knox's House on my way home when Griff called me.

'All sorted?' he asked.

'Yes, it is, case closed. Thanks, mate, I owe you one. If you ever need any help involving my new best friend Easson Middleton, let me know.'

'I'll pass that on to George Regan. When I told him what had happened he went straight up to see Mario McGuire. I'd have been in big trouble if Lizzie Baines had dug her heels in.'

In fact, he wouldn't. After my candid conversation with young Jamie, there's no way I'd ever have entered a not guilty plea, so Griff wouldn't have been required as a witness. But that wasn't something he needed to know, so I didn't tell him.

However, I did feel like sharing with someone: my dad. My day had been freakish, with two positives that only just balanced a very large negative, and I felt an urgent need to talk about it. There was also the small matter of my new career; now that it had been launched in a way I hadn't imagined, I knew I had to tell him before the Edinburgh legal grapevine got to work and word got to him.

After I'd plugged in the new phone I'd bought on my way home, I called the L'Escala number. There was no reply; I left a short message, 'Pops, if I don't get you on the mobile, call me.'

As it happened, I did reach him on the mobile. There was background noise, but he came through loud and clear.

'I know what you're going to tell me,' he said, before I had a chance to utter a word.

Bloody hell! I thought. *Has Middleton spread the word that fast? Or has Mario McGuire spoken to him?*

Neither, it transpired.

'Andy called me this morning,' he continued. 'So you two have come to the parting of the ways again.'

'So it seems. What did he tell you?'

'That he's leaving Edinburgh and you're not, and that it got pretty heated.'

'That's a fair summary. Did he ask you to talk sense into me?'

'Not in so many words.'

'Are you going to try?'

He took an extra second to respond. 'Do you want me to?'

'No. You'd be wasting your time and mine. I didn't realise it until very recently, but he's boring. Since I've turned thirty and he's turned forty we've become different people. I've outgrown Andy, and what with his job . . . his very important job, he was at pains to tell me . . . and his kids, he doesn't really have time for our kind of relationship. So he can bugger off to Glasgow with my blessing.' I paused. 'Does that upset you, Pops?'

'Me? No, kid, why should it? You sound cheerful enough. I may be the wrong guy to be saying this, given that Sarah and I are second time around, but I never thought you should have got back together.'

'Why not?'

'Because Andy's a throwback; he believes in a stable family unit, but one in which the man is the head of the household. He's had one go at it and that didn't work, but it hasn't changed him. If anything it's made him harden his attitude. He can't help it, but you'll never be the dutiful little wife who knows her place. I'm glad you worked that out for yourself, without me having to tell you.'

'It's as well you didn't try,' I retorted.

'I was sure I'd never have to. I wasn't surprised when he called me, you know. I've been aware that things weren't right. I could sense it.'

'Could you indeed?' I said. 'I told Roger McGrane yesterday that I was in a comfortable long-term relationship, and I meant it.'

'Sure, and which of those words doesn't work for you? "Comfortable", Alex. You're higher maintenance than that. Move on, enjoy your life . . . and your new career.'

I felt myself redden. 'How did you . . .' I began, and then I realised. 'Andy. He let it slip.'

'He did.'

'I'm sorry, Pops, I was going to tell you, honest, once you'd sorted your own life out.'

'I appreciate that. Again, I'm not going to give you grief about it. I understand exactly why you're doing it, and I'll do everything I can to help you.'

'I don't know if I want that,' I told him. 'I want to make my own name, not be dragged on your coat-tails.'

I heard him sigh. 'Look,' he said, 'I am who I am. I can't change that and neither can you, so if my reputation and contacts can do you some good, accept it and benefit from it. Things are changing now, but the Edinburgh legal establishment was built on nepotism for a couple of hundred years.'

'There's a new establishment,' I said. 'I've just met one of its pillars.'

I told him about Mitch Laidlaw's surprise call, and how things had played out.

He was laughing before I finished. 'Priceless. "Of all the gin joints" and all that, it had to be Montell in that crapper.'

'I know. My client was as guilty as sin, too. "First time buyer"? His dad might have accepted that, but I didn't.'

'You did your job, though, and you saved the daft laddie's skin.'

'It was pure luck.'

'No, you had the nous to know that Montell would be at worst a reluctant witness and that at best Mario or someone like him would veto him ever being called.'

'What if it had been someone I didn't know?'

'Hell, you'd probably have asked me,' he chuckled, 'and I'd have looked for a weakness in him. I can do that, now I'm a free agent.' Before I had a chance to react to that remark, Dad ploughed on. 'How are you getting on with the other thing, the man Baillie?'

'You told me not to do any more than advise Polmont and check out the lab in Glasgow.'

'I'm well aware of that, but you haven't done exactly as you were told since you were twelve years old. That being the case, what have you found out about him?'

'Nothing yet,' I replied. 'But I am seeing him tonight.'

I explained how I'd gone about tracking down the mysterious Linton, although he seemed less than keen to be found.

'You're seeing him at his place?' he exclaimed. 'Alone?'

'Pops,' I said, 'I'm a big girl and I can look after myself.'

'I know you can, but you will have blagged your way into the man's home, a stranger's home. When he finds out who you are . . .'

'He may not. I may stay as Lexie Martin all through the meeting. It depends what he volunteers when I get round to asking him about what he's doing currently.'

'Alex, he may recognise you as soon as you walk through his door. Take someone with you, for Christ's sake.' He was as close to pleading as I'd ever heard him.

'Do you have anyone in mind?' I retorted. 'Andy's out of the picture . . . not that I'd ever have asked him . . . Ignacio's in the nick, and James Andrew, although he's a bruiser, is just a wee bit too young.'

'Then have somebody drive you, even if they wait outside. I'll call Sarah and ask her.'

'Pops, I will have my pepper spray in my pocket and my black belt handy to strangle the man if need be. I will be fine.'

'Bloody hell, Alex,' he sighed. 'You have to do this while I'm away.'

'Pops, if you were here, you'd be water-boarding the fucker to find out why he's been having you followed, even though in Glasgow.'

'In Glasgow?'

Oh shit! He hadn't known about the two in the car outside Forest Gate. When I told him, that did not improve his mood.

'Sauce Haddock has a couple of images,' he said. 'I'm going to have him forward them to you. When you get them send them to McGrane and ask him if they look anything like the people he saw.'

'Who are they?'

'One's the woman McDaniels, that I told you about. The other might be Baillie.'

'Okay, but you'd better do it quickly if you want me to catch Roger today.'

'I'll do it right now,' he said.

All the time we'd been talking he'd sounded tense, and throughout, that strange rhythmic background noise had continued.

'Are you all right, Pops?' I asked.

'I'm fine. In fact, I think I've got my mojo back . . . whatever the fuck that means,' he chuckled.

'Where are you?'

'At the moment? I'm on a train, heading for Madrid.'

'Madrid? Why?'

'That's a long story, which I'm not going to go into right now. Let me get on with phoning Sauce.'

He left me holding a dead phone, with nothing to do but wait for an email. It arrived within ten minutes, and this was fortunate, because when I rang Roger McGrane, his guardian, Mrs Harris, told me that he was on the point of leaving. It might have been my imagination, but when she came back on line to say he'd take my call, I thought she sounded a little disappointed.

'Alex,' he said, 'I thought we left it that I'd call you.' His voice sounded more honeyed on the phone than across the lunch table.

'We did, and that still stands, but this is more business than personal.'

When I explained what I wanted him to do, he was intrigued. 'Are you telling me those people weren't police?' he exclaimed.

'That'll depend on whether you recognise either of them from the images I'm going to send you.' I had taken his email address from his business card, and was ready to go.

'Let me see them,' he said. 'I'll keep the line open.'

I clicked to send my message and attachments on its way.

'There's a show in the Festival Theatre in Edinburgh just now,' he murmured, as we both waited for their arrival. 'It's a musical, and I can get tickets for tomorrow. If that's too soon, how about next week?'

'Call me next week,' I replied, firmly.

'The tickets might be gone by then.'

'Something tells me they won't.'

'I . . . Hold on, your email's here. Let me have a look.'

I waited while he downloaded the pics, and studied them.

'It's been a while since I saw them,' he said, when he was ready, 'but she's a yes. Him, I'm not so sure about. He was on the far side of the car. There's a vague similarity, but I didn't get a good enough look at his face to be able to say one way or another.'

'Thanks anyway. She's a bonus.'

'Not cops, then.'

'No, private sector.'

'And following your father? They must have been out of their minds.'

'She still is,' I told him. 'She hasn't gone away.'

'What are they after?'

'I hope to find out later on this evening.'

'Can I help in any way?'

If he'd been handy, I might have asked him to drive me to my meeting with Baillie, but he was fifty miles away, so all I said was, 'You just did.'

199

'Anything to oblige. I will call you next week, possibly Sunday.'

I smiled at his persistence, and decided to reward it. 'Oh, all right,' I laughed. 'If you're keen enough to come to Edinburgh, tomorrow's a date. But I tell you now, don't pack an overnight bag, because you will be going home.'

I called my father back, to tell him what Roger had said about the photos, but the train must have been in a tunnel, for his phone was unavailable. I left a message instead, then turned my attention to the remainder of the day.

'Any time after eight,' Coyle had said. That gave me a couple of hours to hit the books. I'd been a little nervous that full-time study would come hard to me after such a long break, but I'd surprised myself by the ease with which I'd taken to it.

In a big law firm, you have to account for almost every minute of your working day; you're judged more than anything else by the fees you bring in, and as much of your time as possible has to be chargeable.

Freed from that pressure, I've rediscovered my interest in the law for its own sake, and I enjoy the cramming to which I've committed myself.

I do most of my work in the Signet Library, of which I'm a full member, but that closes at four thirty, so I dug out my own textbooks and immersed myself.

By seven o'clock I was a little wiser, and also hungry; time was a consideration, so I stuck a two-minute rice dish in the microwave and sufficed with that, washed down by an energy drink.

That done, I turned myself into Lexie Martin. I was amused to discover that I enjoyed being her. She may have been a part of me that I'd suppressed for years, or she may have been a projection of my image of my mother, to whom I'm closer than anyone could imagine, for all that she's more than a quarter century dead. Whatever, Lexie's gaucherie was fun, and a contrast to the serious worldly-wise woman that I've become.

Since my meeting with Coyle, I'd begun to fantasise that I might actually try to turn the shamefully pirated ideas that had formed my synopsis into a full-length manuscript, and see how it read. I know enough about the law of copyright and plagiarism to know if I stepped over the line.

I took a quick shower and dressed in Lexie-style clothes . . . with the addition of a bra . . . smothered myself in scent that my lovely brother Mark bought me for my last birthday, and set off to meet Linton Baillie.

My bag matched the Afghan coat, more or less; it was soft and floppy, not huge but big enough to hold my purse, keys, another printout of my outline, a digital recorder with a microphone sensitive enough for covert use, and of course my pepper spray.

I knew roughly where Portland Street was, but before leaving I checked it out on street view, to get a feel for the place. It looked as if it had been built this century, and was made up of three-storey blocks of flats on either side.

Parking is less of a problem in the evening in Edinburgh, and so I took the car. When I reached my destination I found a space on Slateford Road, and walked the final few hundred yards. I reasoned that Baillie was expecting a naive, starfucking, would-be writer; if he happened to be looking out of a window and saw her climb out of a swish sporty model, he might begin to wonder.

Number twenty-seven slash two slash c was on the first floor. There was no secure entry at street level, and so I walked straight in and up one flight of carpeted stairs.

There was no name tag, only the flat number, by Baillie's door. It was half-glazed and I saw light inside, not in the entrance hall itself but spilling in there from another room. I reached into my bag and switched on my voice recorder, then pushed the bell button. I heard the first few bars of the *Star Trek* theme ringing out inside the flat.

I waited for a minute but there was no sign of Mr Spock. On the basis that even a Vulcan might be in the toilet, and might not have heard the first time, I tried again, but again, no response.

I was on the point of calling Coyle and asking him in my best Lexie voice whether he'd been pulling her chain, when I noticed that the door was very slightly ajar. Less than half an inch, but it was unlocked, no question.

'Leave it alone, Alex!' Three voices spoke in harmony in my head: Dad's, Andy's and my own sensible self. I ignored them all, and pushed one of the glass panels. The door swung open, very gently.

'Mr Baillie,' I ventured, Lexie-like. There was no reply, but I could hear a sound, a man's voice, then a woman. As I listened more closely, I heard him counter, 'Many a good hanging prevents a bad marriage.'

Not casual conversation in Slateford; no, a line from *Twelfth Night*. Linton Baillie liked Shakespeare; I wouldn't have guessed that from his bland prose style.

I stepped inside the flat, closing the door behind me, and headed for the source of the light, as the play unfolded. The first thing I saw in the living room was a Bose radio, on a sideboard. The sound was as good as the maker claims.

'Mr Baillie,' I called out again, a little more firmly than before. *He must be lost in it*, I thought, for again I went unanswered.

Tentatively, I stepped through the door.

The room was capacious, big enough for a dining table to the left and for a two-seater couch and a swivel chair in the centre of the room, facing a wall-mounted flat screen TV between two windows.

The chair was occupied. A man was sitting in it. He had a leaf-shaped birthmark on top of his bald head, which lolled sideways on to his right shoulder. His arm hung over the side, the hand touching the carpet. His neck was exposed, showing a raw red circle, the skin broken in places.

'Mr Baillie,' I said yet again, but by then I had no hope of an answer.

I stepped close behind him, standing on something dark and rodent-like as I put my hand on the black leather, and swung it round.

Glazed dead eyes stared up at me. The eyes of Thomas Coyle.

Eighteen

'What's happened here?' Xavi asked, of nobody in particular, as I finished my call to Amanda Dennis. I doubt that he'd even noticed me making it.

'Seems rather obvious to me, mate,' I grunted. 'Wait here.'

I left him and did a quick check of the place, to make sure that Bernicia Battaglia was the only dead person there; she was. The apartment had two bedrooms; one was untouched, but the other was a mess, with drawers left open as if someone had grabbed clothes in a hurry. It was in stark contrast to the neatness of Hector Sureda's *atico* in Begur.

When I re-joined my friend the situation had caught up with him; he was starting to hyperventilate.

The big man had seen violent death before, up close and very personal, but he wasn't nearly as inured to it as I was. He was shocked and trembling as he stared at the figure on the floor. I took hold of him by the arms and made him look at me instead, waiting for his heart rate to get back to normal.

'What do we do?' he asked, when he was steady and in control of himself.

'One of two things: either we fuck off out of here and get back up to Girona, or we call the Mossos d'Esquadra. The first of those options is tempting, but you in particular are not a guy that even the most casual observer is likely to forget, and the car we've got parked outside, that'll draw attention too, even in a city this size. Besides, it would run against all my instincts. So we make that call.'

I looked up at him. 'Do you have your friend the comissari's number stored in your phone?'

He blinked. 'Yes, but it's not his territory.'

'All the better. Look, Xavi, we should assume that we've been seen coming in here. If we call one one two, we could have first responders on scene in a couple of minutes. Report it through Canals and it'll take longer. That way we'll have kept ourselves on the angels' side, and I'll still have time for a quick look round.'

Xavi nodded. 'I'll make the call.'

'Tell him who I am, and lay it on thick. It'll save time having to explain it to the people who turn up.'

'I will . . .' He paused. 'But Bob, like I said, what's happened? Who killed her?'

'I'm a detective, Xavi, not a bloody psychic, but we have to start by looking at your man Hector.'

'Surely you can't think . . .'

'Jesus, Xavi, it's the only thing I can think at this moment. We're standing in his flat having followed him down here. We know that he came with a woman, having bought her a dozen red roses in Girona. Look on the floor and join the fucking dots.'

He stared at the body, his mouth hanging open 'Not Hector, surely. I can't believe it.'

Even in those grim surroundings I was able to laugh at the shocked incredulity of a man who had once opened a parcel in his office in Edinburgh to find a pair of severed human hands.

'I have a teenage son I didn't know about six months ago,' I reminded him, 'who's currently in jail for killing his granny. I'll never be surprised in my life again. You're a journalist: neither should you be.'

'Why would he?' Xavi protested.

'We'll ask him when we find him. Make that call.'

I left him to it, while I got on with what I do best.

I began by taking a more detached look at the crime scene, as if I'd walked in cold, as the local investigators would do, sooner rather than later. Battaglia was on the floor; the angle at which she lay told me that she'd been killed with her back to the door, and that if she'd ever known what hit her, it was only as her brains were exiting through her forehead. Beyond any doubt she'd been holding the flowers at the time, so she couldn't have been long in the flat before she was shot.

'After you, dear,' I murmured. 'Bang!'

I crouched beside the body and looked for the entry wound in the back of her head. Her hair was so dark, thick and glossy that it was hard to spot, but the blood that had matted around it acted as a marker, around a small hole at the base of the skull. It was close to the hairline, but the skin was unblemished, with no sign of scorch marks.

I forced myself to turn the dead woman's head slightly to see the exit wound; it was where I'd anticipated, smack in the middle of her forehead.

I glanced up at Xavi. He had just finished his call to Comissari Canals. 'You met the woman,' I said. 'How tall was she? I can't assess her height properly like this.'

'Even with those heels, no more than five eight.'

'And Hector. How tall is he?'

'He's six feet, give or take an inch. Why?' he asked.

'Because the bullet seems to have taken a slightly upward

trajectory through her skull, and it isn't a contact wound. Do you know if Hector has ever done any shooting? Did he do army service?'

'No, he missed out by a couple of years. It wasn't a hobby of his either. The only guns he ever fired were on Playstation, of that I'm sure. Does that help?'

'It might,' I said. 'This was either a very good shot or a very lucky one.'

I left him to chew on that and went through to the bathroom. The first thing I saw was a hand towel on the floor, in a corner by the shower, lying there as if it had been used and then discarded, the way you might in a hotel room. I picked it up and saw telltale blood-red smears.

'Think, Skinner, think,' I murmured. 'How was this done? Battaglia had taken about three steps into that room, carrying her rose bouquet, when she was shot in the back of the head, almost certainly by someone standing in the doorway. If it was Hector, how the hell did he get blood on him? He wouldn't have been that close.' I frowned. 'But suppose he went into the room first . . . what did he do?'

I put myself in there, in Hector's place, assuming his innocence for the purpose of the exercise. What did he do? What did he say?

'We need something for those flowers,' I said, aloud, on the move already.

The kitchen was off the dining room, separated by double doors; one was closed, the other lay half open. It had been refurbished fairly recently, possibly by Hector when he'd bought the place. The sink was against the far wall, and beside it, on a work surface, stood a heavy crystal vase; it was half full of water.

'He didn't do it,' I called out to Xavi. 'The way I see it,

someone was waiting for them in the flat, or much more likely followed them in, very quietly, via the newly unlocked front door. Hector went to fill that vase and the gunman stepped into the doorway and shot Battaglia.'

'But what the fuck was he doing with the bloody woman in the first place?' Xavi yelled, in an unusual show of temper and frustration.

'I fear, my friend,' I replied, 'that he might have been selling you out.'

'Where is he now?' he demanded, as if I would know.

'He's not here, that's for sure. Either the intruder took him with him . . . At gunpoint, into a busy city centre? Unlikely . . . or job done he ran for it, leaving Hector here with the body, and a choice to make.'

'Okay,' Xavi said, interrupting me. 'Hector didn't shoot her, but could he have set it up? What if he knew the gunman was here? What if they left together?'

I shook my head. 'I might buy that but for a couple of things. He got blood on himself, for he washed it off in the bathroom, and left some on a towel. How did he do that? By kneeling beside Battaglia, I'd say, to check that she was dead, to see if he could revive her. Also, his bedroom is a mess, as if he's packed a case in a great hurry.

'Apart from that.' I added, 'there's motive. Why in God's name would he want to kill the woman? No, Xavi,' I continued, 'this was an ambush and she was the target, not him. That raises a question. How did the shooter know she was here?'

'How could he have known?' he asked. 'Whether Hector planned to bring her here or not, how could he have known?'

'I have no idea. My best guess is that they were followed all the way from Girona.'

'Why bother? Why didn't he kill her there?'

'He may not have had an opportunity. She stayed in Girona on Thursday night, having arrived from Italy. How did she get here? She didn't use her aircraft, and she didn't have a car here, so she must have taken the train, a very public form of transport.

'Where did she sleep last Thursday? It must have been a hotel, five star for sure. The best hotels have CCTV coverage all over. So he followed her, next morning, to the station. He saw her meet Hector, again . . . you can bet he trailed her to the restaurant . . . and he saw them buy tickets to Barcelona. He did the same, then he followed their taxi from Sants to here. The rest . . . is lying on the floor.'

'But why not kill Hector too?'

I shrugged. 'We have to assume that he wasn't paid to kill Hector. If he'd had to, to get to Battaglia, he probably would have, but if I've read it right, he had a clear shot, and with Hector in the kitchen he was able to get away without being seen.'

Xavi frowned. 'I suppose that works,' he conceded. 'But it still doesn't explain why Hector's missing now, and why he didn't call the police himself.'

I nodded. 'Agreed. That's what any half-rational, innocent man would do, once he'd got over the shock. But he didn't. Instead he got out of here, as fast as he could, without even bothering to lock the door. Look,' I pointed to the table, 'his keys are still there.'

As he glanced across at them, a large metaphorical kite offered itself to me, but before I had a chance to fly it, we heard the door swing open. A few seconds later the room was full of cops, pistols drawn and our hands were in the air.

Nineteen

The man in charge was an intendant; a slightly built guy, around the forty mark, with a look of Rhett Butler, right down to the pencil moustache. He came in after the footsoldiers had secured the scene, and calmed things down.

'Who is Señor Aislado?' he asked, in Catalan, as we lowered our hands. The big fellow nodded.

'My name is Reyes, señor,' the officer said, in a respectful tone, then added something in which I caught the name Canals, and my own.

'Yes, that's him,' Xavi said in English, for my benefit, then switched languages again and said something about me being police chief in Scotland. In the circumstances I didn't object to that, even though it was somewhat out of date.

With my friend's help I explained to Reyes that we'd done as little as possible to fuck up his crime scene. That wasn't quite true. We should really have backed out of there as soon as we found Battaglia's body. He accepted our good faith, though, and then asked us to minimise further damage by accompanying him to somewhere we could talk while his CSIs got to work. That turned out to be a bar across the street; it was fairly busy but his uniform ensured that we had plenty of space around us.

Xavi's call to Canals had been brief; he had given him no more than the address and the fact that we'd found a woman's body there, so we had to start from scratch. We gave him the basic facts that we had come to Barcelona on the trail of a missing colleague, and that we were still looking for him.

We talked him through the timeline, and were doing fine until he asked if we knew who the dead woman was. When Xavi told him, and explained where Bernicia Battaglia stood in the Italian hierarchy, his eyes narrowed and his moustache dropped a little as he spoke.

'Intendant Reyes says this has suddenly gone way above his pay grade,' the big man explained. 'He thinks we should all go to the director general's office.'

'That would seem eminently sensible,' I remarked.

It was going on for midnight before we were clear of Barcelona.

I hadn't wanted to pull rank on Reyes, so I hadn't mentioned the fact, but I know the head of the Mossos d'Esquadra, Julien Valencia, having met him at a policing conference two years ago. We'd hit it off then because of my special interest in Catalunya, and had kept in touch afterwards.

Julien greeted me like an old pal, in English, then had his most senior available officer take formal statements from the two of us. I avoided speculation, but offered my theory that Hector Sureda had been in the kitchen when the woman had been shot.

I volunteered nothing else, though. Instead I suggested that it would be unhelpful to name Hector at that stage of the investigation, or to put out any public appeal for sightings. The murder of one of the highest-profile media figures in Europe would give the press plenty of meat to chew, while his forensic investigators looked for traces of the unknown little man who'd stood in the doorway of Hector's living room, sighting his pistol on the back of Battaglia's head.

Valencia went with that. Indeed he ordered that no formal statement was to be made until the following morning, when he would hold a press conference himself.

'Something funny happened, Bob,' he said, as his deputy left us. 'I just called Italy, to tell them what we got here, an' they knew already. How could that be?'

'Maybe they had her killed,' I suggested, with a smile. I didn't believe that, but it did no harm to throw that pebble into the pond.

He didn't react at all; Julien's a good cop, open to all possibilities until they're proved to be impossible. So am I, but my thinking was that if the Italian security apparatus wanted her dead, they'd have done it on their own ground, in a much more subtle way, rather than make a big mess in another country.

He gave us dinner in his office, then took us back to Xavi's Range Rover in his own car, complete with driver. Just before I stepped out, I had a quiet word with him.

'We're not going to give up looking for Hector,' I told him. 'We won't get in the way of your investigation, that's a promise, but I'd appreciate being kept informed of your progress. Young Sureda is very important to Xavi's business, and more, he's almost family.'

'I'll arrange that,' Valencia said, 'on the understanding that if you find him, I want him.'

'You'll have him,' I promised, 'if only to prove his innocence.'

The director general smiled. 'Or his guilt, my friend. None of us are infallible; you could be wrong about him. Is there anything I can do to help you look for him, since it is in both our interests?'

'There have been places I haven't been able to go,' I replied, 'while we've been looking for him, information that hasn't been open to me. For example, it would be useful to know if his personal credit cards and bank debit cards have been used. So far the only things I've had to go on are a couple of card slips that I found. You can access that stuff; I'd appreciate it if you could share it.'

'I have no problem with that,' Valencia said. 'I'll keep you informed.'

Neither Xavi nor I had anything to say on the way out of the city. In fact it wasn't until we passed the prison, on our right as we headed for the Granollers autopista station, that either of us spoke.

'Where has he gone, Bob?' my friend asked. 'And who's he running from?'

'He could be almost anywhere in Europe,' I replied. 'We know that his passport is still in Begur, for I saw it in one of his underwear drawers, but he wouldn't need it to go to any of the Schengen countries. When Valencia accesses his card activity that might tell us.'

I paused, as that metaphorical kite came back into my mind, the one I'd been about to fly when the police burst into the apartment.

'As for the who, Xavi . . . the gunman ran away from him, so I can't imagine that the threat of immediate physical danger made him go. But consider where he was; in Barcelona, having a fling with Bernicia Battaglia.' I studied his profile in the dark. 'When she approached you and offered to buy you out, did you share that with the rest of the board?'

'I told Sheila, Pilar and Hector. We laughed about it, about the sheer cheek of the bloody woman, and her colourful threat.'

'Are you sure that all four of you laughed?'

'Mmm. Now that you ask,' he murmured, thoughtfully, 'maybe not. Where are you going with this?'

I didn't answer directly. 'You told them, and they knew how you felt, yet a few months later we find Hector having dinner with Battaglia and then taking her to his fuck-pad in Barcelona. As I said earlier, that suggests that he was considering selling you out.'

'How could he? He doesn't have a controlling interest.'

'Come on, sunshine. You told me yourself that he runs the growth areas of the company and that he's invaluable to you. If Battaglia bought Hector Sureda, with his skills and his unique knowledge, and had him set up a rival Spanish digital network, what would happen?'

'We'd probably be fucked if he got it right,' Xavi admitted.

'It's not going to happen now, but if it had, would that have made you angry?'

'Oh yes,' he murmured, his face a blue shadow in the light from the instrument panel, 'it would have made me very angry indeed.'

'And maybe you don't know how formidable you can appear,' I said.

'Now consider this,' I continued. 'There he is, in his apartment, potentially about to fuck both Battaglia and you, simultaneously, when there's a shot, he goes back into his living room and she's dead. A few scenarios must have run though his mind, Xavi, but which one scared him the most? I believe that I know. I suspect, my scary big pal, that Hector's running from you.'

Twenty

I stayed at Xavi's place for a second night. Sheila was still up and wide awake when we got there, well after one o'clock. She hadn't been told what had happened in Barcelona, only that we had been delayed, but when she saw how tired we looked she wouldn't be fobbed off any longer.

As a result, my head didn't hit the pillow until two thirty; it proved to be a waste of time, for I doubt if I managed more than two hours' sleep. It doesn't matter how many dead people you find in a career, they always hang around for a while.

We were all up and about by eight. I was uncomfortable, as I hate wearing the same clothes two days running, but I hung around, for there was a lot to discuss.

As soon as Ben had left for the school run with Paloma, we got down to it over breakfast, with Sheila sitting in.

'You have to see Pilar,' she said, 'and straight away too, before Señor Valencia has his press conference. It's bound to be live on the news channel.'

'He promised to keep Hector's name out of it for now,' Xavi countered. 'She won't be too bothered that Battaglia's dead, but there's nothing to link him to her.'

She raised an eyebrow. 'Oh no, Mr Journalist? Every crime

215

reporter in Barcelona will be covering this story, including ours. They will know already that there's a crime scene at an address in Carrer de Trafalgar, and as soon as the city offices open for business, they'll know who owns the place. Our staffer will know for sure who Hector Sureda is, and it won't take the rest long to make the connection.'

'True,' he sighed. He reached across the table and squeezed her hand. 'I've been management too long, honey. When this is sorted, I think I'm going to put myself back on the news desk.'

'I will go and see Pilar,' I volunteered, 'as soon as we're done here. I have to get back to L'Escala, and it's more or less on my way. It'll give me a chance to pick her brains. If anyone's likely to know where Hector's potential boltholes might be, it's his mother.'

'I'm not so sure about that,' Sheila laughed. 'Ask me the same thing about my son and I wouldn't have a bloody clue. Nonetheless, Bob, it's very good of you. We all appreciate the help you've given. I am so glad that Xavi wasn't on his own when he walked into that apartment.'

'Hey, I've not done yet,' I promised. 'I'm out of clothes, that's all. Wherever we go next, I'll be there.'

'But where will that be?' Xavi grumbled. 'I'm tired, and I'm stumped.'

I punched him, gently, on the shoulder. 'Like you said, you're out of practice, investigator, that's all. Me? I'm getting my second wind.'

'Why?' he asked. 'Two days ago you'd never heard of Hector Sureda.'

'But I have now,' I retorted. 'And there's more. I have this compulsion, you see. Every time I see a dead body, and I don't know who made it dead, or why, I have an irresistible urge to find out.'

'To give them justice?'

I looked at Sheila as she spoke. 'Not any more,' I told her. 'These days I'm just plain curious.'

I was on my way fifteen minutes later. We'd debated whether Xavi should tell Pilar that I was coming, but in the end we decided that I should go in there unannounced.

As I drove out of the estate, I paused, looking left and right for any glimpse of any part of a Skoda. When I was satisfied that my follower had given up, I re-joined the highway and set off for Begur.

The morning had turned dull and damp by the time I reached Carrer de Santa Reparada, and cold too, for I felt distinctly chilly as I stood waiting at the Sureda/Roca door. I had to stand there for a full two minutes; *maybe I should have let Xavi make that call*, I thought, *to give the lady a chance to make herself presentable*.

She certainly was when she opened the door, dressed in slacks and a heavy shirt. 'You've only just caught me, Señor Skinner,' she said as she let me in. 'I've decided to go to the office today, if only to clear my in-tray.' She must have read something in my expression for suddenly hers changed.

'Is there news?' she asked, urgently. 'Have you traced Hector?'

I was about to answer, 'Yes and no,' when my phone sounded. I checked the screen and recognised a Barcelona number from the code. 'I'm sorry,' I said, 'I need to take this.'

It was Julien Valencia, the Mossos DG himself. 'I have a little news,' he said. 'First, our crime scene people have done a good job. They have found a left handprint on the front door that doesn't match anything we have on record, or the victim. Also they have found a couple of hairs in the doorway, and a DNA profile is being prepared. When it is ready the technicos will do a check against the database.'

'Very good.'

'There is more. They found an ejected cartridge casing, and they have identified it as coming from a Russian automatic pistol called a Makarov or possibly from a newer weapon called a Pernach. So maybe the killer is Russian.'

'Not necessarily,' I countered. 'There are Russian guns all over Europe now. You should know that.'

'I suppose. That's the crime scene, Bob, but I have news on Sureda. We know now that he withdrew six hundred euro, the daily limit, in cash from his bank account from a machine at Barcelona Sants station on Friday afternoon, six hundred more in Lleida the following morning, and six hundred more on Sunday, in Zaragoza. Since then there has been nothing, and his credit cards have not been used at all.'

'Thanks, Julien,' I said.

'*De nada.* I must go now to prepare for my press briefing. The news will be released simultaneously here and in Italy. It's going to get crazy.

'You must realise the press will identify the owner of the flat very soon, so I don't think I can hold off identifying him any longer. Already I have passed his name and the image you left with me to the Policia Nacional, since my authority does not go beyond Catalunya.

'Publicly, I will try to treat him as a witness, rather than a suspect, but my colleagues may not be so subtle . . . also I may not be my own master at the briefing,' he added, as if in warning. 'Does any of that help, Bob?' he asked.

'It does. When I make progress, I'll let you know.'

'Good. I am relying on you to an extent; I have a feeling you may have a better chance of finding Señor Sureda than the police have. That's why I am letting you run with it.'

'You understand that finding him may not clear up your crime?'

'Yes, but to be brutal, if it comes to it, I will have someone to pacify the media, and our bosses.'

And do huge damage to Xavi Aislado's business in the process. That's what I thought, but I needed Valencia onside, so I kept it to myself.

I'd been aware as I spoke that Pilar's eyes were fixed on me. 'Was that about Hector?' she asked.

I nodded. 'Let's sit down somewhere, I have a lot to tell you and it's not pleasant.' Her hands flew to her mouth; I continued, quickly, 'Hector's still missing, but he's safe. I believe he's hiding somewhere.'

She took me into her kitchen, and offered me coffee. I needed a caffeine boost, so I accepted. As soon as she'd made it, I went through every detail of what had happened since I saw her last.

When I reached the part of the drama that was set in her son's apartment she began to tremble. When I told her who we'd found dead on the floor, the news that was soon to be announced on national television, she stared at me, and gasped, her mouth forming a perfect O shape.

'It was her? What was my Hector doing with her?'

'I can hazard a guess, señora, but only he can tell us.'

'This will kill his father,' she wailed. 'Simon must not know.'

'Must not know what, my dear?'

The hoarse question came from behind me. I turned to see a man in a dressing gown framed in the doorway. He walked with help from a carved stick, and carried in his free hand an oxygen bottle, from which a fine tube led behind his back and into twin feeds inserted in his nostrils.

'Simon,' Pilar exclaimed. 'What are you doing?'

'Looking for food; I'm hungry. Why are we speaking English? If it's for the benefit of our visitor, you might introduce him.'

'Let me introduce myself,' I said, standing. 'My name's Bob Skinner; I'm a friend of Xavi Aislado.'

'Ahh,' Sureda grated, 'he has spoken of you for many years: the fearsome policeman.' He smiled. 'You don't look so fierce to me, but the deceptive appearance can be the most dangerous.'

'Simon!' his wife snapped. 'You must go back to bed.'

'No, my dear. I see the way you're dressed. You are going to Girona. As soon as you were gone I would have got up anyway and made myself a *bocadillo*. You want to save me some energy, you can do it for me.'

She frowned at him but moved towards the fridge.

'And while you do that,' he added, easing himself into a carver chair, and laying the oxygen bottle by his side, 'Señor Skinner can tell me what it is that has you so anxious, this thing you say will kill me to know.' He smiled, and I could see the charm of the man. 'Pilar, my curiosity is aroused, and if it is not satisfied that will be more dangerous for me than knowing what has happened with my son.'

Simon Sureda looked me in the eye, and I understood at once why Xavi revered him: there was an intangible quality about him, a calm wisdom. 'I know something is wrong,' he said, 'because I have not seen him since Friday morning, when he left here with an excitement in his eyes that has not been there for a while. I know he is not dead, because his mother is not prostrate with grief, only anxious. So what is it, señor? What is this mystery?'

I glanced at Pilar. She sighed, then nodded, giving up the fight.

'Let's begin on Friday, then,' I said, 'with what we know so far. But first, do you know the name Battaglia?'

'The Warrior? Of course I do.' He grinned. 'She wants to buy us all out, the stupid woman. As if there was a chance of that happening. Never, while Xavi Aislado breathes.'

'That's more true than you realise,' I told him.

As I had done with his wife, I led him step by step through the story, ending with the discovery that Xavi and I made in Hector's apartment, and our subsequent meeting with Julien Valencia.

'I know Valencia,' Simon murmured, interrupting me. He was calm, a man in control of his emotions. 'He's an ambitious man, as much of a politician as a policeman, but overall, I believe you can trust him.' He paused for a second, before adding, 'And that is everything, señor, *si?*'

I nodded. 'Almost, but I'll get to the rest in a minute. First, I want to ask you . . . did you have any idea that your son had been in contact with Bernicia Battaglia?'

He moved in the chair, and his oxygen bottle started to roll away from him. I reached down to stop it, and stood it on end.

'No,' he replied, 'none at all.'

'I understand that he knew about her offer to buy InterMedia?'

'Of course he did. Xavi reported her approach to the directors, quite properly, even though he had already taken the decision that it was unacceptable.'

'I understand that you're not a director, señor,' I ventured.

'That is correct.' He smiled. 'You wonder why, since my wife is and my son is, and I have been there from the beginning of the Aislado ownership?' I nodded.

'The answer is simple: I chose not to be. I am a journalist, señor, not a manager. Pilar is comfortable with being on the company board, of course she is. When Josep-Maria Aislado bought his first newspaper in Girona, he brought her in as its editor because he saw her as an ally as much as an employee.

'We were together even then, she and I, but I preferred to be a simple reporter, for that was my strength. I was happy to mentor others, but I believed then and I believe now that as a senior manager there would be a danger of my integrity being compromised.

'Xavi, he was the same. When he worked for the *Saltire*, in Edinburgh, before InterMedia bought it, he discovered that its owner was a crook. He ran the story; he exposed the guy in his own newspaper, and then he saved it, by having Joe take it over.'

'Xavi's a manager now,' I pointed out.

'That's true,' Simon conceded, 'but only because it was forced on him by circumstances. He hasn't written a news story in years, yet I'll bet if he found a scandal and chose to shine light on it, he would do so fearlessly, even if it struck at his own heart.'

His wife interrupted him, by placing before him a sandwich on a plate; it was half a baguette, filled with lettuce, tomato and tortilla.

He smiled. 'Thank you, my dear. Now you should go.'

She said something to him in Catalan, that I took to mean, 'Are you sure you'll be all right?' He nodded. 'Three hours,' she added, 'then I'll be back.'

'I will try not to die while you're away,' he chuckled, in Castellano, which I understood completely.

'It's better she's gone,' he said, as soon as he heard the door close behind her. 'I can guess what you are going to ask me, and Pilar might not like to hear it.'

'Indeed? What would that be?'

'Whether my son was as resolutely opposed to the idea of a sale to BeBe as Xavi was . . . am I correct?'

'Spot on,' I murmured. 'Was he?'

'The fact is, no, he wasn't. Hector is a child of the Internet. He believes in growth and global markets. His preference would be for InterMedia to absorb BeBe, but he knows that Xavi has no ambition to do that, so he would accept the alternative. He has gone as far as he can in the company as it stands; it cannot contain him any longer.'

'Xavi has never mentioned any of this to me,' I told him.

'Xavi does not know how Hector feels; nor does his mother. He has only spoken of this to me.'

'How did you react when he did?'

The frail man shrugged his shoulders, weakly. 'I didn't react. I cannot take sides between my son and his mother, or for that matter between him and his patron, the man who has made him what he is today.'

'Between us, how do you feel?' I asked.

'I understand him. If you stand still in a world that is moving constantly, everyone will pass you by.'

'Have you said that to Pilar?'

He flashed me a crooked smile. 'In my condition I don't need the grief it would bring me. Once the surgeon gives me my new heart valve, I will write an editorial on the subject and I will insist that it is published in *GironaDia*. Hector asked me to do it. I didn't commit myself, but I said I would consider it, when I am well.'

He frowned. 'Maybe I will talk to Joe Aislado as well. With

Battaglia dead, BeBe will be ripe for the plucking, and he is not so old that he has lost his eye for a business opportunity.'

I dragged him back to the moment. 'Let's just focus on the fact that she is dead, and on Hector's predicament. He had given you no clue that he was meeting her?'

'No. I think back over the last few weeks but I can recall nothing. However, as I told you before, he was excited the last time I saw him, on the day when you say they met. Which of them do you think made the contact?' he asked.

'My assumption is that she did. They met on his territory; that's as good an indicator as we have.'

'From what they say, she's a very attractive woman,' he mused. 'And my son has always been fond of the ladies. Nature must have taken its course, for him to take her to Barcelona. He's only ever brought one woman here, and that was the Russian girl. Yes, they must have been getting along.'

'Or he simply took her there to discuss business,' I suggested . . . and then I thought of the roses. 'But we don't know, for it's all a mystery from then on.'

'What did you hope that Pilar could tell you?' Simon asked. 'And why, señor, if you will forgive me, are you even interested in my son?'

'I promised Xavi I'd help find him,' I replied, instantly, 'and I haven't done that yet. Yes, I know I could leave it to the police from now on, but a promise is a promise. As for your wife, I was going to ask her if she knew where he might have gone.'

'You would have been asking the wrong parent.' His laugh was weak, but his smile was wide.

'To his mother,' he continued when his voice returned to normal, 'Hector is a model of virtue. But no man can be that good, and stay normal. His successes have always been reported to Pilar, but his failures and his faults have been confessed to me.

'The truth is that my boy was a little wild in his college days. He drank more than he should have, he smoked marijuana in industrial quantities, and as for the women in his life . . . I met a couple of them when I visited him in Oxford.'

'Oxford?' I repeated.

'Yes, he studied there. Its computer science course is rated the third best in the world, after two universities in the US. It is very expensive, but his godfather paid his tuition fees. Joe,' he added. 'Joe Aislado is his godfather.'

He paused. 'Anyway, those women, they were pretty loose. They were not students, more . . . camp followers, I think is the English phrase.'

'But he graduated in spite of it all?'

'Oh yes, with first class honours. He really is a genius, Señor Skinner.' He looked at me. 'Do you have sons?'

I gazed at him. I nodded. 'I have three. My youngest . . . he's a bit young to be showing special skills, other than on the golf course. His older brother we adopted after he was orphaned; he looks like following in your Hector's footsteps.'

I hesitated, then decided to be frank; after all, the guy was no better than even money to see Christmas. 'There's a third one, from an old relationship; he's something of a genius too, in chemistry, but he used his talents unwisely, and it caught up with him.'

'He is a burden to you?' Simon asked, gently.

'I hardly know him, señor . . . but that is something I will rectify. Is Hector your only child?' I asked, moving on discreetly.

'Yes, he is. We'd have liked a daughter too, but it never happened.'

It was my turn to laugh. 'I have two of those; they're challenging . . . regardless of their age.'

'And so is my Hector, it seems,' he sighed. 'As I said, he had a few troubles as a student, and also as a younger man in Barcelona. There were a couple of occasions when I had to use my influence with the police there to keep him out of court, but those were minor adventures, scuffles in nightclubs and such. In recent years, however, as he has become more and more important to the InterMedia group, he has become a responsible citizen. I think his girlfriend Valentina helped too; I wish she was still around.'

'Your wife told Xavi and me that he ended the relationship,' I said.

'Because that is what Hector told her. I do not know what happened, but he was upset by it. He brought her here to meet us; there was talk of a future together and then . . . she was gone. He told me very little, but as I understood it she left him, not the other way around. What he told Pilar, it was only to stop her thinking badly of Valentina.'

He sighed, as deeply as he could. 'If only . . . if they were still together he would not be in this trouble.' He frowned then looked me straight in the eye. 'You are telling me the truth, Señor Skinner, yes? You do think he is innocent?'

'I do,' I assured him. 'I'm not being partisan either. I don't know Hector, so I have no inbuilt bias in his favour. My opinion is based on what I saw at the crime scene.'

'And Valencia? And the Mossos investigators? What do they think?'

That was a good question. 'Valencia is looking for Hector as a witness, not a suspect; that's what he told me yesterday. Whether he still feels that way today . . .' I glanced at my watch, 'we should know very shortly, when he has his press conference. He'll face some tough questioning, especially when the journalists there realise who Hector Sureda is, and what he is to InterMedia.'

'He will face some tough questioning from the examining judge too,' Simon pointed out. 'In Spanish law he is the head of the investigation; he will want to complete it as quickly as he can.'

He didn't have to explain in any more detail. Structurally the system is like our own in Scotland, where the police investigate as agents of the Crown Office, but in practice the Spanish system is more hands-on. Whoever the *juez* was, he was faced with an internationally famous victim from another country, found dead in the apartment of a man who had been at the scene and whose reaction had been to go into hiding.

As Simon had been on his way to suggesting, whatever the crime scene had said to me, it would tell the judge that he had an acceptable prime suspect. And would the judge be at the press conference? For sure he would. That was what Valencia had meant when he talked of not being his own master there.

I'd been kidding myself. Valencia's open-minded attitude was irrelevant, because he wasn't in charge. The judge would lead with what he had, and Hector would be a fugitive, his face plastered across every newspaper and TV bulletin in Spain. Once he was caught, he would disappear into a judicial system that can take a year to bring a man to trial, with the presumption of guilt firmly planted in the public consciousness.

'I expect,' his father continued, 'that the police will be here soon, wanting to know the same thing you do. With Pilar absent, I can deflect them by the simple means of going to sleep, as my doctors say I should whenever possible . . . even though each time I do I wonder whether I will wake up again. So let me see how much of a head start I can give you. Has there been any trace of my son since last Friday?'

'Three bank withdrawals,' I told him. 'In Barcelona, then Lleida, then Zaragoza, on successive days. I guess he drew the maximum each time.'

'In that case, I suspect . . . no, I am certain . . . that he was heading for Madrid.'

'Over two days or more?'

'Yes, if he went by slow train or even by bus; high-speed train journeys can be traced. He's a resourceful man; that's the sort of thing he would do if he didn't want to be detected.'

'So why do you think he's gone to Madrid?'

'Because that is where Jacob Ireland lives, his closest friend . . . in fact his only close friend outside of the business. They met at Oxford, where Jacob was studying Spanish. They were . . . how you say . . . kindred spirits, each as unruly as the other, each as clever.'

He smiled, remembering. 'When they were in trouble it was always together; in England and in Spain, when Jacob moved here. One time in Barcelona when I had to get them both out of jail!' He nodded. 'That's where he's gone. Madrid.'

'Do you have an address for Ireland?'

'Calle de la Cruz, *numero doscientos quarante dos*: sorry, two hundred forty-two. It is an apartment in a street between Puerta de la Sol and Plaza Mayor . . . in the heart of the city, like Hector's is in Barcelona.'

'Does this Jacob live alone? Is he single?'

'Sometimes,' Simon chuckled. 'He has changed less than Hector from his younger days. I can give you his mobile number.'

'Do that, but if we go there I doubt if we'll give him advance warning. What does Jacob do? What's his job?'

'He is a translator. When legal and other documents have to be converted into Spanish from English, they will be accepted by the authorities only if they have an official stamp. Jacob has one of these. He is also a tour guide, for the British and Americans. He gets a lot of work, because he knows all the places that are not in the tourist guidebooks.'

He looked at me. I sensed that his limited energy was all but exhausted and that he was more affected by his son's predicament than he had cared to show me.

'Find him for us,' he whispered, 'if you would be so kind. When you do, tell him that his mother will kick his ass big time when he gets home.'

Twenty-One

I called Xavi as soon as I got back to my car. He was surprised to hear that I'd been talking to Simon. 'For the last few weeks Pilar hasn't let anyone see him,' he said, 'not even me.'

'She didn't have a choice this morning,' I explained. 'He walked in on us. Don't get me wrong,' I added, 'he's a sick man, but he's a long way from comatose. She's more scared of his condition than he is. Simon sees the light at the end of the tunnel; she sees the proverbial train coming.'

'I hope he's right, not her.'

'They also see their son in different ways.' I gave him a precis of Simon's account of Hector's youth. 'You never told me that Joe paid his way through Oxford,' I added.

'It wasn't relevant.'

'Are they close, the two of them?' I asked.

'Close enough for Hector to have told Joe that he was meeting Battaglia?'

'That's what I'm wondering,' I admitted. 'Simon reckons there are a couple of barks in the old dog yet. He reckons he might be talked into having a go at acquiring BeBe, now that she's out of the way.'

'I'll ask him,' Xavi growled, 'as soon as we're done. What else did Simon tell you? I don't suppose he knows where Hector is.'

'He reckons that he does.' I told him about Jacob Ireland.

'That's his name, is it?' he murmured. 'Pilar's mentioned an old university pal of his from time to time, usually with a frown on her face.'

'Maybe, but Simon's dead sure that's where he'll have headed: to friend Jacob, in Madrid. Valencia called me earlier. He said that Hector's pulled three slabs of cash out of ATMs; the locations point in that direction.'

'Then we should go there,' he declared. Then he paused. 'I say "we" but . . .'

'Fuck's sake, man,' I exclaimed. 'Of course I'm coming. I'm hooked now; you couldn't keep me away. There's only one thing you should know. If I'm completely wrong, and I find that Hector Sureda did shoot Battaglia, then I'll give him to Valencia, gift-wrapped.'

'I'll buy the wrapping paper,' Xavi said. 'I'll take what we saw yesterday to my grave. Nobody deserves to die like that, not even the Warrior. Suppose you're completely right, Bob, I'm going to find it hard to forgive him for running out and leaving her lying there, undiscovered, for the best part of a week. I don't care how good he is at his job; I'll find him for his parents' sake if I can, but he's finished with InterMedia.'

'Let's see what we find,' I told him, 'before making any judgements. How do we get to Madrid?'

'We take the AVE from Girona, like he did. Can you be ready to leave this afternoon? There's a train round about four o'clock. We should get there not much after seven.'

'Go for it. Let me know the exact time and I'll meet you at the station.'

I left him to get on with it and headed for home. I hadn't got very far before my phone rang again. I'd have ignored it, had there not been a parking bay just ahead; I pulled in and took the call.

It was Andy Martin. 'Gimme a break, pal,' I moaned. 'I'm out here to do some thinking about the future, please give me time to do it.'

'Sure, Bob,' he replied, a little tetchily. 'That's not why I'm calling.'

It disappoints me to have to say this, but since he's become chief constable of the whole fucking Scottish world there's been a change in my long-time friend. He has a stiffness about him that's never been evident before; it's as if he's distanced himself very slightly from everyone, even from me.

It's a significant factor in my hesitancy over accepting a role within his force. I backed his candidacy, and lobbied for him with all the decision-makers that I know, but now that he's there I'm far from certain that I could work under his leadership.

'What is it, then?' I asked, suddenly irritable myself. 'Have the traffic lights packed in at the foot of Lothian Road in the middle of the rush hour?'

'No, nothing as dramatic as that; it's tedious, in fact, and entirely domestic. It's Alex and me; we've had a row.'

I said nothing; I let a void of silence develop between us until he had no choice but to fill it.

'I'm selling the house in Edinburgh, Bob, and moving to Glasgow. As I told her, I need to live closer to the heart of the action.'

'No, you fucking don't,' I said, abruptly. 'You are the heart of the action. You're the policing equivalent of the queen bee. You can be anywhere in the hive you like. Your office base is in

Clackmannanshire at the moment, and you're under no real pressure to move. That's easily accessible from Edinburgh.'

'In that case you've taught me too well. You know as well as I do, better, that most of the action is in greater Glasgow. I have to be hands on there when necessary.'

'Which will be very rarely,' I countered. 'Listen, if I had gone for your job and got it, I might have set up my HQ in the old Fire Training School in Gullane, now that Fire and Rescue Scotland has decided in its dubious wisdom to shut it down. I could have walked to work and been just as efficient. You could do much the same thing. Edinburgh's the capital; you could argue that the chief's office should be there.'

'I could, but I choose not to,' he said, coldly.

'Sure. And having made that choice, you assume that Alex will just say, "That's nice, dear," and follow you. When she doesn't you have a hissy fit. I'm assuming that's what's happened.'

'She's the one who was doing all the hissing,' he retorted.

'I'll bet. So what do you want me to do about it?'

'Nothing,' he replied. 'I'm simply calling to tell you what's happened, and to say I'm sorry it hasn't worked out between us.'

'Again.'

'You sound as if you expected it.'

'I've had bigger surprises in my life,' I admitted. 'Sarah and me, for a start.'

'I hope that works out for you two this time around. At least your careers won't be in competition, unlike Alex's and mine.'

'What do you mean?' I asked, puzzled. 'What's the clash between a senior police officer and a corporate lawyer?'

'But—' He stopped abruptly, then murmured, 'Oh shit, Bob. Don't tell me she hasn't told you.'

'Told me what, mate?'

'That she's leaving CAJ to become a solicitor advocate, specialising in criminal work.'

If we'd been on a Skype video call he'd have seen my jaw drop. As it was he heard me burst into laughter a few seconds later.

'So it never went away,' I chuckled. 'When she was in her last year at school, getting ready for uni, it was all about being the first woman Lord President of the Court of Session, but somewhere along the line she got sidetracked.

'Maybe that was my fault, for I had a vision of her in court ten years later, cross-examining people she'd known for much of her life: you, Mario, Neil, maybe even me . . . although a judge would have had something to say about that.'

'Aren't you still worried by that now?'

'No. Why the hell should I be? I want what she wants, if it's going to make her happy. And that, my friend, is where we differ, and why it will never work between the two of you.'

I had nothing more to say to him, other than, 'So long,' so I did, and ended the conversation. I almost called her, there and then, but decided against it. There was no telling how long we'd have been on the line, and I had a deadline. Instead, I put the Suzuki back into gear and headed for L'Escala.

A north wind had arisen out of nowhere, the fearsome tramontana; it was strong enough to rock my unladen car on open stretches of road, so I drove more slowly than usual, making a brief stop at a supermarket to buy some food. As I drove into the old town I heard the church bell strike noon . . . or two minutes past, given the peculiar local habit of ringing the hour twice, in case anyone lost count the first time.

I slipped off the main drag and took the sloping road that leads to Puig Pedro. When I turned into my street, I drove right past a grubby white Seat Ibiza that was parked a few yards along, It was only as I stepped out of my car and locked it that I noticed it, and saw that it was occupied.

I shook my head, despairing rather than angry, and walked towards it.

'You might as well come in,' I said to Carrie McDaniels.

'Will I ever come out again if I do?' she asked, fiercely.

'There's a fair chance of that,' I promised. 'When you do you'll have had lunch.'

She glared at me for a few seconds, then sighed and climbed out of her car. 'I lost my deposit on the Skoda,' she grumbled, then adding, as if she'd done me a favour, 'but I didn't drop you in it. I told the company I'd been at a meeting and come out to find that my tyre had been done. They still slapped an insurance excess charge on me.'

'Which you will pass on to your client,' I said, as I unlocked the front door and let her in.

'Too right,' she agreed.

'What's he after?' I asked her.

'I can't tell you that.'

I laughed. 'Come on, Carrie, don't give me that client confidentiality crap. You're not a doctor, you're not a lawyer; you've got no legal privilege.'

'Maybe not, but I have ethics.'

'What? Ethics? To the likes of you that's an English county with a fucking lisp.'

'The likes of me, indeed,' she shot back. 'You cops think you're special, but you're not. We do the same job . . . but my hourly rate is better.'

'No you don't,' I said as I led the way into the kitchen. 'You follow people around, you take sneaky photographs, you intrude into their lives, and your only motivation is money. Police officers keep people safe in their homes. What do you do? You took telephoto images of mine.' I glared at her. 'My children live there; imagine how I feel about them being spied on.'

She flinched a little, started to speak, but thought better of it.

'No, don't deny it,' I snapped at her. 'I have the evidence, and maybe grounds for a civil action against you. I'll need to consult my daughter about that.'

'Look . . .' Carrie protested. I ignored her and started cracking eggs into a bowl.

'Look . . .' she tried again.

'Who was the guy on the beach?' I asked, abruptly, cutting across her. 'Was that Linton Baillie?'

She frowned. 'Him? No, that was just a guy I know, a boy-friend. He had no idea what I was doing . . . well, not specifically.'

'How long have you been doing this job on me?'

'Seven months . . . no, make that eight. Baillie emailed me, out of the blue, and asked me if I wanted an unusual job. I was a bit doubtful when he said I'd be running surveillance on the chief constable, but money speaks my language, and business hadn't been great for a while.

'It hasn't been twenty-four seven, though. Baillie hires me by the day; he calls it Skinner-time. He's been watching you himself, and hires me to cover for him when he has other things to do. I'll get a phone call, with instructions to follow you, sometimes to specific places, others, just in general. When I'm done I forward reports, and the best shots I've taken, to a Gmail address.'

'How do you get paid?'

She watched me as I beat the eggs, with a little milk, and put a pan on the hob. 'I invoice him, monthly, to the same email address. He pays me by credit card.' She smiled, briefly. 'I add on five per cent to my rate to cover the Visa commission.'

'So what's he up to?'

'Honestly, Mr Skinner, he's never told me.'

I transferred the eggs to the pan and began to stir them slowly, with a wooden spoon, making sure they didn't stick. 'Describe him,' I said.

'I can't. I've never met him.'

'Are you serious?' I asked, looking her in the eye. She nodded; thirty years' experience made me believe her.

'What did he tell you about himself?'

'Only that he was a writer. He gave me the name of a couple of books he'd published so I could check him out. I didn't ask him directly why he wanted you followed. I just assumed . . .'

'That it was for another book, one about me?'

'Exactly. An unauthorised biography, I reckoned.'

That was a reasonable assumption, but those calls to Mia had raised an alternative possibility.

As I thought that through, I asked Carrie to cut a couple of slices from a round loaf that I'd bought and spread them with Flora. When they were done, I put them on plates and piled scrambled eggs on top.

We sat on stools and ate at the breakfast bar. I let her finish before I resumed my gentle quizzing.

'Has the surveillance pattern been the same all along?' I asked when I was ready.

'Mr Skinner,' she said, 'I still feel awkward about this. Mr Baillie's my client; strictly speaking, I need his permission to talk to you.'

'You need to understand something,' I countered. 'Your

front-line investigator's licence doesn't give you any sort of immunity if your client has asked you to do something that might prove to be illegal.'

'There's nothing illegal about taking photographs.'

'That could depend on the use to which those photographs are put.'

Her eyes narrowed. 'Such as?'

'Extortion is one possibility.'

'What are you talking about?' she exclaimed, just a little rattled for the first time.

'I may get to that later. For now, tell me, over the last six months has the surveillance pattern always been the same?'

'No, it changed a few months ago. I was following you one day, when out of the blue, you took me by surprise and went to Edinburgh Airport. I thought no more of it, until a couple of days later Baillie called and said he wanted me on you full time till further notice. I told him that would be expensive, but he told me it was okay.

'You were in Glasgow by that time, Chief Constable of Strathclyde; I thought we were pushing it a bit, but I carried on. Nothing unusual happened for a while, until one day you left your office on foot. I was parked up in a car, but I was able to follow you, to an address next to Sauchiehall Street. I checked the plate on the door; it was a laboratory called Forest Gate. I photographed it and sent it to Mr Baillie with the rest.'

'Shit,' I whispered. I thought through some possibilities, then asked, 'Did you ever follow me to the High Court in Edinburgh?'

She stared at me, then blinked, taken aback by my question. 'No,' she began, hesitantly, 'not directly, but there was one day Mr Baillie asked me to go there and photograph everybody going in and out of the public entrance. And you showed up. You were in civvies, very casually dressed; I hardly recognised you. You went in on your own but when you came out you were with a woman, very attractive, forty-something. The pair of you went for a coffee and I followed you.'

She paused. 'Is that why you're talking about extortion? Are you shagging her and is Baillie blackmailing you? Is that it?'

'No to both of those,' I retorted. She'd put her questions in the present tense, so I didn't have to lie. 'Did you photograph us? I didn't see anything like that on your memory card.'

'I used another camera. Come on,' she said, suddenly urgent, 'I'm trying to be upfront with you. Give me something back. Just between the two of us,' she added, hopefully.

'I've got nothing to give.'

'Who was the woman?'

'She's an old acquaintance, and that's all I'm telling you.'

Carrie shot me a quick smile. 'I could find out. I know where she lives.'

'And how would you know that?' I murmured, letting my eyes burn into her.

'While you were in the coffee shop, I called Baillie. He told me to follow the woman if the two of you split up. I did. After you left, she caught a taxi in Bank Street, and I got into the one behind and followed it, all the way to a big house at the foot of Blackford Hill. I photographed it and sent it off to Mr Baillie with the other stuff.'

If Baillie was any sort of an investigator it wouldn't have taken him long to find out who owns that house: Alafair Drysalter, daughter of the late and very unlamented gangster Perry Holmes. She's Mia's foster-sister; yes, I reckon that's the best way to describe her. If Baillie was any sort of an investigator he'd have made the jump to . . .

'A few weeks before that,' I said, 'I went to Spain, at short notice. Did Baillie know about that?'

'Yes. I was supposed to follow you one day, but he called me the night before and said not to bother because he'd seen you board a flight for Barcelona that afternoon. He told me that you had a house here.'

And two days later, a young man named Ignacio Centelleos had been extradited from Spain to Scotland to be charged with the murder of Bella Watson, his grandmother, labelled 'Cramond Island Woman' in an investigation that had made headlines way beyond Edinburgh. The press had reported that he had been arrested in L'Escala.

Baillie might not have been able to prove conclusively that I'm Ignacio's dad, but he'd observed a set of circumstances leading up to my incognito appearance at the High Court and my meeting with Mia that had made him confident enough to speculate, accurately.

As I saw it, only one question remained. How much did he want?

'Why did he send you out here?' I asked. 'He couldn't have known I was coming.'

'He wanted me to photograph your house, places around the town, and a restaurant in the Marina called La Clota. I tried,' she volunteered, 'but it's closed for the winter. When you turned up here yourself two days ago, I couldn't believe it.'

'Why did you tip your hand to me?' That puzzled me.

'I didn't think I had a choice. Like I said, I was taken by surprise. I was less careful than I usually am, and I was sure you'd seen me photographing you while you were eating. I realised, when I took those pics as you were passing by, that you hadn't, but it was too late by then. As for those idiots that I'd hired . . . I'm sorry about that.'

I shrugged my shoulders, and cleared away our empty plates. 'Not as sorry as them.' My face twisted as I recalled the man with the knife. 'A few years ago, I was stabbed, and nearly died. When that geezer pulled his blade on me . . . he's lucky I didn't dislocate his fucking neck.'

'I know about that,' she said. 'Mr Baillie mentioned it once in an email. He told me lots of stuff about you, going way back. He said that he's the world expert on the career of Bob Skinner.'

'I doubt it. The world expert would be me.' I frowned. 'I thought you said you've never met him.'

'I haven't, but we had long talks on the phone. He has a nickname for you: he calls you "The Secret Policeman". That would be a good book title, wouldn't it?'

'It would, if it was ever published.'

'Do you think you can stop him? I read his last book, about MI5. I don't imagine they're too pleased about it, but it's still out there.'

'Probably because it's bullshit; if he was spilling any classified information it would never have seen the light of day.'

I went into the fridge, produced two cans of Coke Zero and handed one to her. 'You've had your fun, Carrie,' I told her, 'and you've made some money. If I give you some advice, will you listen to it?'

'If it's good advice, yes.'

'It is, and it's this. You've had as much out of this place as you're going to get, so you should go home. Go back to Edinburgh, send your client an invoice, as quickly as you can, and ask for immediate payment. I have private business here that'll keep me occupied for the next few days, but when I'm done, I'm going to turn my full attention to your Mr Baillie, and I'm going to put him out the game.'

'Will I tell him that?'

'You can if you like, but if he hasn't worked it out for himself he's not nearly as smart as you think he is.'

Twenty-Two

As I headed for Girona, with enough clothes for three days packed in a cabin bag, I didn't bother to check whether Carrie had taken my advice, or whether she was still there in my rearview, following me.

Truthfully, I didn't care about her any more. She'd told me enough to confirm my suspicions about Linton Baillie, and about the motivation for those calls to Mia. I was confident that I'd find out in due course how much money he hoped to extort from us as his price for keeping the secret that he'd stumbled across.

Shortly after that I'd nail his hide to the nearest available wall.

Xavi was waiting for me in the concourse of Girona railway station, with two AVE tickets clutched in his hand, and a case of similar size to mine by his side. He didn't look too happy.

'Have you seen Valencia's press conference on telly?' he asked, as I approached.

I shook my head. 'No, I didn't have time. Another part of my life intervened.'

Instantly he was contrite. 'I'm sorry, Bob. I keep forgetting that you've put a lot of stuff aside to help me in this.'

'I'm happy to do it, so don't be bloody sorry. What did he have to say?'

'Not as much as the fucking judge,' the big guy growled. 'Valencia was fairly circumspect, but Gonzalez, the *juez*, made it clear that he was at the head of the investigation and that he was happy to charge Hector with murder as soon as he's caught. The deputy interior minister was there too, promising the Italians that Battaglia's killer will be in jail before the week's out.'

'That's brave of him, given that he doesn't have a clue who or where he is. What did they say about Hector, and about InterMedia?'

'Oh, we were named right up front. There was even an implication by the judge, in answer to a question by a reporter who used to work for us until Pilar fired him a couple of years ago, that the murder might be a falling out between business rivals.'

'Ouch!'

'Indeed,' Xavi muttered. 'I'm not having that, Bob.'

'What can you do about it?'

'Joe's issued a public statement, as group chairman. It points out that there's no physical evidence that Hector shot Battaglia, but there are indications that a third person was in the apartment. He's also said that there's no business rivalry between InterMedia and the BeBe group, and demanded that the interior minister remove Miguel-Angel Gonzalez as presiding judge, on the grounds that he's demonstrated bias against Hector Sureda.'

'Will the minister do that?' I asked.

'Probably not,' he admitted, 'but I'll be surprised if Gonzalez isn't reprimanded.'

'How's Pilar taking it?'

'She's in shock. When you told her what had happened she

didn't really take it in, but the press conference absolutely floored her. She's locked in her office, and her secretary's guarding her, savaging any poor bastard from another newspaper that tries to get through to her on the phone.'

'And Simon?'

'He's okay. He's going into hospital in Barcelona this afternoon to prepare for his op. I managed to persuade his surgeon that with everything that's going on, and the possibility of an unfriendly media besieging the house in Begur, that was the best place for him. They're bringing his operation forward to tomorrow.'

'Was there any hint given at the press briefing,' I asked, 'of Hector heading for Madrid?'

'No, thank Christ. Valencia was able to keep that under wraps. I have to assume he didn't tell Gonzalez about it, or it would be public knowledge.'

He was still grumbling as the train came into the station, fifteen minutes behind schedule. 'Spanish trains are never late,' he moaned. 'This one started in fucking France and look at the difference.'

I smiled as we boarded. Clearly he hadn't been on a British train in a while.

Our *preferente* coach was furnished as well as first class on any airline, although the seats didn't convert into beds as far as I could see. We had barely left Girona when we were offered a drink. With a three-hour journey ahead of us, I couldn't think of a single reason to refuse, so I chose a Mahou from the beers on offer.

There was a movie showing on the carriage screen and Xavi seemed focused on it, so I rang Sarah. It seemed like an age since I'd spoken to her.

'Hi, lover,' she said cheerily, as she answered, 'have you called to gloat?'

'Me? No, why should I?'

'Remember the autopsy I told you about last time we spoke?'

I hadn't, until she mentioned it. 'Go on,' I said, interested.

'I ran the tests you suggested, on the stomach contents and blood. It was Zopiclone, not Zolpidem, but otherwise you were right. The victim's food was drugged then he was given an emetic as he slept. Ingenious. His partner's a nurse; she's under arrest for his murder.'

'And the insurance company's delighted, I'll bet.'

'So delighted that I've got you a consultancy fee. One per cent of the policy's payout for accidental death: five grand. Is that okay?'

'Okay?' I laughed. 'It's bloody magic.'

'Where are you?' she asked. 'That's an odd background noise.'

'Odd but pretty quiet, considering we're travelling on rails at damn near three hundred kph. I'm still with Xavi.'

'So his problem hasn't gone away?'

'Hell, no, it's grown teeth.'

'In that case, don't let it bite you.'

'I won't, I promise. The chances are it'll be out of our hands soon.'

'Will you find his missing person?'

'If we don't, someone else will. Then I'll come home; the future's a lot clearer now.'

'Good. Your younger daughter's missing you.'

I smiled at the thought of my wee Seonaid. 'That is mutual. I think my older daughter is as well.' I told her about Andy's call.

'Oh dear,' she said. 'It sounds like curtains this time. What are you going to do?'

'About Andy and Alex? Nothing. About me? When I get back, I'm going to issue a press release, and then we're going to have a party.'

I was mentally drafting that press release an hour and a half later, with the remains of a meal on a tray before me, when Alex called me. If I'd expected her to be despondent, I'd have been disappointed. She was indignant when she found out I knew about her break-up, but there wasn't a single note of regret in her voice.

Still, I told her that she'd done the right thing, thinking that if I felt that way, maybe I should have said something before. Then I dug her up slightly about the career change that she'd kept secret from me. I was slightly concerned by the gamble she was taking, but she put my mind at rest with a crazy story about her first criminal case, involving an advocate's son, a line of cocaine in a nightclub toilet, and Detective Sergeant Griff Montell.

That put a smile on my face, one she wiped off straight away by telling me she had traced Linton Baillie, and had arranged to see him that evening. I was worried about that, but I couldn't talk her out of it.

She'd done good work on Baillie, even discovering that he'd had me watched in Glasgow. I was surprised when she said that McGrane had seen two people in the car that had been observing me. I told her I'd arrange for Sauce Haddock to send her the images from the beach, for her to run past him. I did so, without hoping for much, but if McGrane could identify the guy as having been in the car as well, that might have interested me.

I'd expected a call back fairly soon but it wasn't until we were approaching Madrid that my phone told me I had a voicemail message. I checked it, to hear Alex telling me that while

McGrane had identified Carrie, he hadn't seen enough of her companion to make any judgement.

On Xavi's advice, I'd worn my heaviest jacket for the trip; I was glad of it when I stepped off the train. The Spanish capital is more than two thousand feet above sea level, and is significantly colder there in winter than on the Costas.

He had booked us into a hotel on Calle Atocha, which he said would leave us only a short walk to Jacob Ireland's place. We checked in, dropped our bags and then set off to find him.

I'd been in Madrid once before in my life, and my memory of the place was vague. I recognised Plaza Mayor when we came to it, though, a huge open rectangle surrounded by restaurants. Most of them had tables outside, with a forest of gas-fuelled space heaters among them. Very few were occupied, but Xavi assured me that it would be much busier later.

He had a hand-held navigation app on his phone, but didn't switch it on until we reached the plaza. That proved to have been an oversight, for it took us back in the direction from which we had come, then across a much smaller square, called Jacinto Benavente. Calle de la Cruz opened off that, sloping down towards what my friend told me was the true heart of Madrid, Puerto de la Sol.

We headed in that direction, counting off the numbers until we reached two hundred and forty-two. It was about half-way down, an entrance door alongside a restaurant that was distinguished by an absence of open-air tables.

The stairwell was lit by a series of wall lights on timer switches. They seemed to be on minimum setting, for we were plunged into virtual darkness twice before we reached a door on the third floor with the name 'Jacob Ireland' on a card in a brass holder.

Alongside it was a scribbled note. Xavi peered at it.

'According to this, he's out,' he announced. 'It says, "Sorry, Thais, I'm on a night tour. Won't be back till midnight."'

I rang the bell anyway, in case he'd posted his notice the day before and forgotten to take it down, but it seemed he wasn't kidding. Xavi even called out, 'Hector, it's me. Open up if you're in there,' but he was wasting his breath.

We went back downstairs more quickly than we had come up. Outside, in the street, Xavi cast an eye over the restaurant. 'I fancy this place,' he announced. 'No outside tables means they don't hawk for tourists; that's usually a good sign.'

It was called Fatigas del Querer. I asked him what that meant in English.

'It's hard to translate,' he replied. 'The closest I can get is "The tiredness of desire" . . . or something along those lines.'

'Sounds familiar,' I murmured. 'Let's give it a go.'

Anybody who is two metres tall always attracts instant attention, and so it was when we stepped inside. Not for the first time on our travels together, I felt invisible beside Xavi as the guy I took to be the head waiter, by the sash around his waist, headed towards us.

'Bienvenido, señores,' he greeted us. 'Una mesa para dos?'

We were spoiled for choice, because the restaurant was very quiet. Looking around the empty tables I began to doubt the place, and whispered as much to Xavi.

'Trust me, mate,' he said. 'It's early yet, by Madrid standards. In an hour you won't be able to move in here, you wait and see.'

An hour later he looked around, then grinned at me, across the table. 'Well?'

By that time there wasn't a single unoccupied table, and people were sitting up at the bar, waiting in hope. That was no wonder, for the food . . . mine was a Caesar salad starter followed by pig's cheek . . . was excellent, the portions were vast, the wine list was extensive and everything was reasonably priced. I remarked on all of it to my friend.

'I was thinking exactly the same thing,' he conceded. 'If we were sitting under one of those space heaters up in Plaza Mayor, we'd be eating mediocre pizza, drinking wine that tasted like vinegar, freezing our nuts off and paying through the nose for the privilege. Hector's friend Ireland is a lucky lad to be living above a place like this.'

Nobody pushed us for our table, and so we had a second coffee (don't tell Sarah) and a half-bottle of a very decent red called Alion, from Ribera del Duero. We were still there when the place began to thin out.

Eventually, I made the 'Bill, please' sign to the head waiter. He nodded and brought it across, on a tray with a bottle of Torres Gran Reserva brandy, and two shot glasses. I grabbed the slip while he poured, waving off my friend's protests. He'd paid for everything else, so no way was he buying me dinner as well.

'Was good?' the waiter asked me in English, as I punched my PIN into the card terminal.

'Was excellent,' I replied.

'How you hear of us?'

'We didn't,' I confessed. 'It was pure luck. We came here looking for a man who lives above.' I pointed to the ceiling. 'He wasn't at home. I'm glad about that. If he'd been in we might not have eaten here.'

'Ah,' he exclaimed. 'You mean Jacob, the English guy? He eats here, mos' days.' He smiled. 'He's crazy, Jacob.'

On impulse I reached into my pocket and took out the photo of Hector that I'd been carrying for two days. 'Do you ever see this guy with him?'

He seized it from me and peered at it. 'Sure, is his amigo. He come here sometimes with Jacob. He as crazy as Jacob.' He returned the image. 'He very well dressed in that,' he observed. 'Here he dress like, like . . .' He grinned. 'Like Che Guevara. Usually he wear this shirt with Che's face on it.'

'When was the last time you saw him? Can you remember?'

'Sure I can remember, señor. It was two days ago; it was . . .' he searched his English vocabulary, but gave up. 'It was *Martes*, in the afternoon. Jacob, him and a *mujer*; I'd never seen her before. Don' know who she was. *Guapa*, she was. Blond hair, short, pointy, and she wore big *gafas de sol*, even in here.'

'Did she seem to be with either of them?'

He frowned at me. 'Sorry, señor, I don' understand.'

Xavi repeated my question, in Spanish.

The waiter shrugged. 'I dunno. I couldn' tell. She didn' kiss either of them if tha's what you mean.'

I thanked him and downed the brandy shot . . . out of politeness, and doing my best to miss my taste buds, for I've never cared for the stuff.

My throat was still burning as Xavi and I stood outside. 'That was a bonus,' he said. 'I really am slipping. I've always believed that a good reporter and a good cop should be asking the same questions, but it never occurred to me to ask what you did, or to show him that picture. I've gone soft, Bob. All these years in the fucking boardroom . . .'

He crossed the narrow street and looked up, at the third floor. 'There's a light up there,' I heard him murmur, to himself rather than me. 'It could be Jacob's place, but I'm not sure. Should we go back up?'

I looked at him. He'd probably had more of the wine than I had, and the waiter had poured him a second brandy shot.

'Better not,' I told him. 'As you say, the light might be in another flat; his note said he wouldn't be back till midnight, remember, and it's only just gone ten. But even if he is in . . .' I paused. 'From what our pal said, Hector could be with him. Given that he might have been in the act of selling you out to Battaglia before she got killed, things could get confrontational between the two of you. It's better that we come back first thing tomorrow, when our heads are clearer.'

'My head's fine,' Xavi growled, but it wasn't and he knew it.

'Come on,' I said, and we headed up the slope, back towards our hotel.

'Who do you think the woman was?' Xavi asked, out of the blue, as we crossed the Plaza Mayor.

'How the hell should I know?' I replied. 'Jacob's note was for someone called Thais. I suppose it could have been her.'

'I suppose,' he conceded, then stopped, almost in mid-stride. 'You know,' he continued, 'that second coffee's given me a hell of a thirst. Do you fancy a beer?'

'Do I what?' I laughed. 'Look at the two of us. Gentlemen rankers out on a spree. Why the hell not.'

'I thought it was gentlemen songsters,' he retorted.

'You don't know your Kipling,' I countered.

'Then come and tell me about him in that bar over there.'

I couldn't top that, so I followed him, like a large lost lamb.

As we sat at the table, my phone buzzed in my pocket. I checked it and saw two missed calls from Alex, but when I tried to return them my battery indicator went red and the thing died on me.

'Fuck it,' I whispered. 'It's been a long day for my mobile too.'

One beer led to a second, but that was it. Even so, Xavi was well the worse for wear by the time we got back to the hotel. 'I never could handle too much,' he confessed, just before almost falling into his room. 'Those fucking brandies were a very bad idea.'

There was a gym in the basement. Every time I go on a trip I pack trainers and shorts just in case, but they've never come in more handy than they did next morning. We had agreed to meet at eight next morning, but I knew there wasn't any chance of him making it, so I headed down there at seven and put in a good hour on the treadmill and the weights, before going back upstairs for a shower.

I was in the breakfast room for eight thirty, but had to wait for another ten minutes before Xavi joined me. His eyes were a shade slitty, but otherwise he looked human.

'Don't tell Sheila,' he muttered as he came over from the service counter with his third glass of orange juice in his hand, the first two having disappeared in an instant.

Even with that delayed start we didn't imagine that we would miss Jacob Ireland. Other than banks, public offices or cafes, Spain doesn't switch on much before ten. We lingered a little over breakfast, but even so, when we set out for Calle de la Cruz it was twenty past nine, still relatively early in the daily cycle of Europe's third largest city.

Before we left, Xavi just had to buy a paper. 'I'm sorry,' he said. 'It's my profession, and I can't go a day without getting ink on my fingers.'

'Fine,' I replied, 'but you can get it on your pocket for now, and read it later.'

He nodded, bought a copy of *El Pais* from the stall in the foyer, and rolled it up without so much as a glance.

'We should have checked the television last night,' he grumbled, 'for coverage of Valencia's press conference.'

'We should,' I agreed, 'but we didn't. We know the story anyway.'

In the grey morning light, Calle Atocha had shed the glamour of the night before; it was just another city street, heavy with traffic as what passes for a morning rush hour in Madrid approached its peak. It was cold, but not desperately so; the clouds overhead were threatening rain rather than snow, and made good on their promise just as we reached our destination.

Fatigas del Querer, or 'Shagged out', as I had decided to call it, was locked up; clearly it was not a breakfast destination. It seemed diminished also, in the daylight, and we barely gave it a glance as we stepped into number two hundred and forty-two.

There was a little natural light in the stairway, coming from a skylight that we hadn't seen the night before. 'Thank Christ for that,' Xavi muttered as he glanced up at it. 'Running upstairs between these bloody miser switches is not good for my knee.'

The note was still pinned to Ireland's door. 'Looks like Thais stood him up,' I observed as I pressed the buzzer.

I pressed hard, but not enough to break the lock, so I was surprised when the bell didn't ring, and instead the door swung open. It had a ball socket rather than a latch, a mortise lock and two bolts, top and bottom, on the inside. All of them were unfastened and a security chain hung from its keeper, twin screws still in their holes in the fastening that had been ripped from the wood.

'Not good,' I whispered, as I felt an old familiar tingle running down my spine.

'What?' Xavi exclaimed behind me, not having seen the damage.

I held up a hand. 'Hold on,' I ordered, as quietly as I could. 'Stay here and stand to the side, so that you can't be seen from inside. If anyone gets past me, let him go if you aren't spotted. Otherwise grab the fucker and throw him down the stairs.'

He stared at me, as if he was struggling to understand, but finally he nodded.

I left him there and moved inside. I didn't have to do a full search; I only needed to follow my nose, as I had in Barcelona.

In Madrid, it led me to a sitting room off the hall. I stood outside, very still, for almost a minute, listening for the faintest sound from inside, a rustle of movement, a tense breath.

If I wasn't the only intruder in that flat, I didn't want to be making myself an easy target. Instead I steeled myself and stepped across the doorway, hoping to make it to the other side. I did, without incident, and from that position I could see a wide wall mirror: it told me that there was no threat. I stepped inside.

The man that I assumed had been Jacob Ireland was tied to a dining chair, by the wrists, with plastic restraints. His head was lolling on his left shoulder; he seemed to be staring at something on the floor beside the door, but that was an illusion because the third eye, the bullet hole in the centre of his forehead, made it very clear that he was staring at nothing.

The poor bastard hadn't died well, though. He was sitting in his own mess, with a small pool of blood on either side of the chair and a third by his right foot. He was wearing a white, long-sleeved shirt and tan trousers, clothing that let me see, very clearly, what had been done to him.

He had been shot through each elbow, and through the right knee. They must have been contact wounds, for each joint was shattered. The man had been systematically tortured, his screams . . . and there would have been many . . . silenced by a blue hand towel that had been jammed into his mouth. It lay in his lap, but I could see fibres caught between his teeth.

'What the hell is this about?' I whispered.

If I'd been at home, and I'd been carrying a warrant card, I would have been in a position to find out. But I wasn't: I was a civilian in a foreign land, staring at my second cadaver inside forty-eight hours. That was at least one too many, by any objective standard.

I could have taken a minute or two to search, but someone had done that before me. There was a six-drawer unit in a corner of the room; its contents lay all over the floor. A laptop sat on a table by the window; it was powered up and the screen showed an open file; it seemed to be a list of names, addresses and contact details. I reached for my phone to take a photo of it, then remembered that the damn thing was dead, and I'd forgotten to pack my charger.

I checked the rest of the place; two bedrooms, bathroom and kitchen. There was no one else, dead or alive, nor any sign of another person's presence, other than the lethal visitor, for he had tossed each room, quickly and thoroughly.

That was the point at which I went off the straight and narrow. All my training, all my experience, all my sense of what was right and what was wrong told me that I should pick up the landline phone that sat on top of the chest of drawers and call the European emergency number, one one two.

But it told me also that if I did phone the police we were there for as long as they wanted to keep us, and, putting myself in their shoes, I suspected that would have been quite some time.

We weren't there for Ireland; we had come in search of Hector. He was the link between the two crime scenes. It was also possible, I reminded myself, that he was their perpetrator, but if he wasn't, as I still believed, he could be in greater danger than we had ever supposed.

He had been left alive in Barcelona, but had he been the target in Madrid? He had been there, we knew. Then Ireland had been tortured. Why?

To me the answer was obvious, but it was convoluted. To the Policia Nacional, who would be likely to look at circumstances first, motive second, if at all, the simple solution would be that Hector Sureda was their man, a killer on the rampage, covering his tracks.

Best that we had a head start, I decided; I left the phone untouched.

Meanwhile, Xavi was obeying orders, keeping out of sight from the hallway.

'I'm coming out,' I said, not wanting to be thrown down that flight of stairs.

'What's up?' he asked, tense as he stepped into view.

'Go,' I retorted, pausing only to wipe the surface of the door buzzer with the sleeve of my jacket. 'Out of here, now.' I pushed him ahead of me.

'Where are we going?' he asked, bewildered, as we hit the street outside.

'Anywhere,' I replied, turning right and heading down towards Puerta de la Sol.

As we emerged from Calle de la Cruz, I saw a taxi approaching, its green light showing, and flagged it down. It was only when we were inside and heading for the Prado Museum, a flash of inspiration by my friend when the driver asked 'Where to?', that my heart rate began to slow to somewhere near normal.

We sat in silence all the way there. I could tell that Xavi was bursting to ask me what had happened, but he had the sense to stay nothing that the driver could overhear.

He dropped us at the main entrance to the gallery, not far from a bronze statue on a high plinth; it immortalised a guy in a long coat with a top hat tucked under his left arm; Goya, I saw from the lettering beneath its feet.

'Let's go in,' Xavi said.

I had no objection to that, for a steady drizzle was falling and it was growing no warmer, but as I pointed out to him, there was a long queue of determined tourists huddled under umbrellas, stretching from the ticket office to the corner of the building and beyond.

'That's okay,' he replied. 'We don't need to do that.'

He led the way, past a great stone staircase, towards a second entrance where there was no queue at all. 'InterMedia is a supporter of the Prado,' he explained. 'I have privileges here.'

These turned out to be strong enough for us to be waved straight through the revolving door, into a foyer that was dominated not by works of art but by a souvenir shop, and a cafeteria. We headed for the latter, past a great marble sculpture of what appeared to be a son protecting his father from an unseen assailant. The younger man had suffered some damage in his time: a significant part of him had fallen victim to a hammer, and was no longer to be seen.

Xavi went to the counter, leaving me to choose a table as far away from other visitors as I could find. When he returned he was carrying a tray with two cafes con leche, and four large bottles of water. He drank two of them by the neck, one after the other, straight away.

'Dehydrated,' he explained. 'I can't remember the last time I got tanked up like we did last night. You Scots guys, you're fucking lethal company. Now tell me,' he continued with barely a pause, 'what was in there?'

'Jacob Ireland,' I told him. Then I described the condition in which I'd found him, in detail.

His eyes widened. 'But only him? Not Hector?'

'Hector had gone. He's like fucking Macavity, the mystery cat; when a crime's discovered, he's never there.'

'How do you know that it was Ireland you found?' he asked, not unreasonably. 'Neither of us have ever seen him.'

'There was a framed diploma on the wall,' I explained. 'I think it certified him as an official translator. There was a photo in it.'

'I don't understand, Bob.'

'Neither do I. The what, I reckon I know, but how and why are missing. Someone came looking for Hector, in Madrid, of that I'm sure. He wasn't there, so Ireland was tortured, to make him tell where he could be found. But how did whoever it was make the link between them? And if Battaglia was the target in Barcelona, why are they coming after Hector now?'

'Who can tell?' Xavi exclaimed. 'Surely, though, he's still safe?'

'I'd like to think so,' I said 'but one thing has me worried. Ireland was shot three times; each elbow and one knee. When he was killed, he wasn't gagged.'

'So?'

'Why wasn't he shot in both knees? The way I read that, the poor bastard finally had enough. He talked, hence the gag being in his lap, not in his mouth. And when he had told his interrogator what he wanted to hear, he was finished off. We've still got to find Hector, Xavi, but I'm worried that we haven't got much time . . . indeed we might not have any. For all we know he could still be in the city . . . and if he is, he could be dead by now.'

My friend's eyes seemed to sink back into his head, as he contemplated that prospect.

'What's this about, Bob?' he murmured. 'Battaglia, Ireland, both killed: what's all this about?'

He picked up a third bottle of water and leaned back in his chair; as he did so, the newspaper he'd bought in the hotel fell from his pocket on to the floor. He retrieved it and laid it, still rolled up, on the table.

'What are we going to do about Ireland?' he asked. 'We can't just leave the poor guy sitting dead in his own shit. What if the Thais woman he mentioned in his note walks in and finds him?'

He had a point. 'Do you have your phone?' I asked. 'Mine's as dead as Kelsey's nuts, and I've left my charger in L'Escala.'

'Sure,' he nodded and handed it over, then picked up his long-forgotten copy of *El Pais*, and unrolled it.

I went into his browser and looked up the number of the Mossos d' Esquadra headquarters, then keyed it in. It took me a minute or so to convince the communications room that I really did want to speak to the director general himself, and two more for his secretary, who did know who I was, to pull him out of a meeting.

'You have news for me, Bob?' he asked. 'Have you found Sureda?'

'No,' I replied, dousing his enthusiasm, 'but we have found his best friend. Sadly he was no help to us.'

I explained why, imagining his expression as he heard the news. I thought he might go off the deep end about our delay in calling in the murder, but he had something else on his mind.

'The presiding judge will go to town on that,' he sighed. 'He went too far at the press conference yesterday, and he has been rebuked by the Interior Ministry, but he is still in charge of the case. To have Hector Sureda implicated in a second murder, that will make his day.'

'He's an idiot, Julien; you can tell him that from me if you like. Sureda's now the target, or so it seems. There's an easy way to prove it; you and the CNP should compare ballistics on the bullet and cartridge case from the Barcelona crime scene to those you'll find at Calle de la Cruz.'

'You think they'll be the same?'

'I'd bet your life on it, Director General.'

'In that case,' Valencia said, 'if Sureda is as smart as your friend Señor Aislado thinks he is, he should walk into a police station and give himself up. A police cell might be the safest place for him right now.'

'Could be,' I agreed.

'I'll suggest that in my next public statement,' he continued, 'but now I must call my opposite number in the Policia Nacional and pass on your message. I'll keep your name out of it.'

'No, don't do that,' I said. 'You should be upfront with him. If you're not, then very early in the investigation his officers will waste time trying to find two mystery men – one of them very large – who were asking questions last night in the restaurant below Ireland's apartment.'

'Were you given any answers?'

'Yes. The two guys, Hector and Jacob, and a woman, ate there together, a couple of nights ago.'

'I'll pass that on. For sure, he'll want formal statements from you both. Where are you staying in Madrid?'

I told him. 'We're booked in for tonight also, but . . . if we get a lead to Hector, we're liable to take off after him.'

'No, Bob, we are at the stage where, if you have such information, you must pass it on to us.'

'Okay,' I conceded, grudgingly, 'we'll share what firm information we have, but we may also act upon it ourselves.'

I heard a soft laugh in my ear. 'In Scotland were you also as unruly?'

'In Scotland, Julien, I made the rules, more often than not. You and your colleagues can contact us on this phone if we're needed.'

I ended the call and handed the mobile back to Xavi. He laid down the paper and took it from me.

'I heard some of that,' he said. 'We don't have anywhere else to go, do we? When we came here we were hoping that we'd find Hector with his pal, or at least get a steer to where he was. No chance of either of those now.'

I couldn't deny that. The man we were trying to find was out in the jungle with a hunter on his trail, someone who probably had a better idea of where to find him than we had, after his interrogation of Jacob Ireland.

'We might as well talk to the police here,' my friend sighed, 'and then go home. Unless you'd like to spend a couple of hours here, like bloody tourists, then maybe visit the Real Madrid stadium.'

'Only if there's a game on,' I retorted.

I picked up my coffee; it was cold but I drank it regardless. I frowned. Xavi was right. We were stalled, helpless. There had to be a reason for Battaglia's killer to leave Hector unscathed on the previous Friday, but I couldn't see it. We knew all there was to know about the circumstances: the killing, Hector's slow journey to Madrid, his sighting with the ill-fated Ireland, everything, except one thing.

'Who was the woman?' I whispered.

I was still wondering when my eye fell on Xavi's discarded *El*

Pais. All I could see was a headline, '*Barcelona Asesinato: Magnate de la Prensa Italiana*', but I didn't need a translation to know that it was the Battaglia murder, writ large.

I reached for it and unfolded it, so I could see the report. It covered half the front page. I scanned through it as best I could, focusing on the words whose translation was obvious, and on the quotes in the story. Some were attributed to Valencia, but most of the limelight seemed to have been grabbed by Miguel-Angel Gonzalez. There was a very small contribution at the end, by Intendant Reyes, in which he said that the forensic team had made important discoveries, but no detail was offered.

There was nothing remarkable that I could see, until my attention shifted to the photo that accompanied the piece, fighting with it for domination of the page. It was a full-face portrait of a woman; she was more than attractive, she was beautiful, in her mid-thirties, with compelling brown eyes, full lips beneath a strong but not over-large nose, and dark hair shaped around an oval face.

I stared at her as if I was hypnotised, my head spinning as I tried to grasp a significance that I knew was there, but couldn't quite see . . . until it hit me, like a sledgehammer, and everything made sense.

Xavi was staring too, at me and at my reaction. I turned the page towards him, showing him the image. 'This is Battaglia?' I murmured.

'Of course,' he replied. 'Why the surprise? I told you she was a looker.'

He'd met her before; clearly she'd made something of the same impression on him that she seemed to have on Hector. No wonder he'd bought her roses.

'You're right, beyond a doubt,' I said. 'There aren't too many like her to the pound. And yet why am I thinking I've seen the woman before, when I know that I haven't? Come on, Xavi, tell me.'

He shook his great big head, looking like a bloodhound with a blocked-up nose. 'Sorry. I don't know what you're talking about.' Then he paused, to peer more closely at the page. 'But then again . . .' He kept looking at it, frowning, until his eyes switched back to me. 'No,' he sighed. 'Tell me.'

'Think back to Hector's attic,' I challenged, 'in Begur. The photograph. His girlfriend, Valentina, the one he chucked. Maybe I'm kidding myself but I don't think so. I'm not saying they're twins, but is there not a significant resemblance between Battaglia and her?'

He frowned as he considered my question. 'I suppose . . . yes, now that you mention it and now that I consider it, I suppose there is. But so what, Bob, so what?'

'So what?' I laughed. 'So what? You are definitely going back to being a journalist after this. Your brain's fried if you can't see it. Look at the sequence. Battaglia was shot, in Barcelona, last Friday; and she lay there for five days, and nothing else happened. Then she was found, and yesterday, her death was reported, in all the news media in Spain and, you can bet, all across Europe. That's the sequence, agreed?'

'Yes. So?'

'So, following that, before yesterday was out, her killer shows up at Hector's hidey-hole in Madrid, and shoots holes in his mate. It's fucking obvious, man! Battaglia was never the target. It was her resemblance to Valentina that got her killed. Hector's girlfriend, the one he's supposed to have chucked, was the target all along . . . and she still is.'

'Are you certain about this?' he asked

'As sure as I can be.'

'Then you should tell Valencia.'

'Maybe, but not yet. There's something I want to do first. I'm sorry about the walk around this place, and the Real stadium tour, but we need to be somewhere else. Come on.'

'Okay,' he agreed, 'after we've done one thing. Come with me.'

He led the way out of the cafeteria, heading for a doorway. The Prado is quite a complex building with many galleries, but Xavi seemed to know exactly where he was headed. He made three or four turns, through a couple of galleries then into one that was busier than all the others. The reason was a large exhibit on an end wall; it was a triptych, a painting in three parts. A couple of dozen people stood staring at it; many of them had audio guides pressed to an ear, and a glance told me that they were listening to the commentary in Japanese.

I was taller than any of them and Xavi towers over me, so we were able to stand behind them and have a clear view.

'I never visit the Prado without coming here,' my guide told me. 'Every time I look at this thing, I see something new.'

'What is it?' I asked, although I felt that I should know.

'*The Garden of Earthly Delights*, by Hieronymus Bosch; here they call him El Bosco, mainly because it's a bloody sight easier to say.'

It was a big piece, seven feet high, and around twelve feet wide in total. 'The panel on the left is Eden,' Xavi continued, 'and it shows God introducing Eve to her date, Adam, who's short of one rib by that time. The centre painting shows the same place, well after nature had taken its course.'

Further explanation was unnecessary. Adam and Eve had gone forth and multiplied, and the nature of the delights in the garden was pretty clear. There was a whole lot of cavorting going on, and mankind seemed to have been too busy up to then to have got round to inventing clothes.

The third panel, the one on the right, told a different story; it was El Bosco's grim vision of Hell, presumably the final destination of all those revellers in God's garden. He had spared his public some of the detail, but the message was clear enough.

'What do you like about this?' I asked my friend.

'Like is the wrong word,' he replied. 'I'm fascinated by the power of its imagery, maybe most of all by its age. It's over five hundred years old, in one of the greatest galleries in the world, and yet it's still the most visited piece here. What do you see when you look at it?' he threw back at me, abruptly.

By that time, I had been seized by that dark panel on the right; I shuddered, involuntarily. 'I see my fucking life, mate,' I muttered. 'Let's go.'

Outside, the rain had eased, the crowds had diminished and there were taxis waiting at the rank. We took the first; I told the driver Puerta de la Sol. I should have added 'pronto', because he took us for something of a scenic tour by comparison with our earlier trip.

He dropped us in the middle of the semi-circular plaza, around a hundred metres from Calle de la Cruz. When we got there, and looked up the street, we saw two police cars parked at the top, and a third vehicle, a van, also with a blue light on top. The inevitable crime scene tape had been placed over the entrance to two hundred and forty-two, where a uniformed officer stood guard.

'Valencia's made his call,' I said, 'and the cavalry's arrived.'

'Shouldn't we find the officer in charge,' Xavi suggested 'and volunteer our statements?'

'Yes we should,' I agreed, 'but we're not going to. I need to talk to our waiter pal before we decide our next move. I'd like to do that discreetly, which means, on my own. No offence, pal, but I've seen totem poles that are smaller than you.'

'What do I do in the meantime? Just stand around like a spare?'

'No, find another road that takes you up to Plaza Mayor, and I'll meet you there.'

Grudgingly, he agreed. As he walked back the way we had come, I headed uphill, towards the blue lights, and the knot of curious pedestrians who had stopped to watch the action.

I hadn't been certain that Fatigas del Querer was open, but I was in luck. I stepped inside, nodding, as I did, to the guardian cop in the adjacent doorway. He ignored me.

My second stroke of luck was that the head waiter was on duty, morning and evening. He spotted me at once and came across. 'Hola, señor. You see what happen above us?' he asked, breathlessly. 'The cops. You know what happen? The guy at the door, he no say.'

'I think you'll find you've lost a customer,' I said. 'Listen to me, I need to show you something, and ask you something.'

He shrugged. '*Si.*'

I showed him Battaglia on the front page of *El Pais*. 'Think of the woman you spoke of last night, the woman who was here with Jacob and his friend. Forget her hair, and think of her only when she took off her *gafas*. Could that have been her?'

He took it from me, and studied it, for a little while . . . then for a longer while. Finally he handed it back.

'No,' he declared, firmly.

Bugger, I thought.

'It could not have been her,' he continued, 'because here it

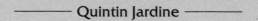

says this woman was killed on *Miercoles, la semana pasada.*'
Then he looked at me, with a teasing grin. 'But if there are such
things as *espectros*, señor, this was definitely her.'

Twenty-Three

'It was Valentina. What Paco said makes me sure of it.'

'Who the fuck's Paco?'

'The waiter from last night; that's his name. When he looked at the paper he said that the woman he saw with Hector and Jacob could have been the ghost of Bernicia Battaglia.'

I'd had no trouble catching up with Xavi. I'd spotted him, sitting at a table on a covered pavement, in a corner of Plaza Mayor, nursing a tall glass of orange juice and a half-litre bottle of carbonated water.

'What's her story, do you think?'

'Dunno,' I replied, 'but she's upset somebody, that's for sure. Is your phone still charged?' He nodded. 'Then call Pilar for me, please. I'd like to speak to her.'

He did as I asked. They spoke briefly, in Spanish, before he handed me the phone. 'She's at the hospital,' he whispered. 'Simon went into the operating theatre two hours ago. Be careful with her; she's fragile.'

I nodded. 'Good morning, señora,' I said, as I took it from him. 'This is a nervous time for you, I know, but I'm sure that Simon will come through this strong and fit. In the talk I had with him I realised that he's a very determined man, with a lot more to do in life.'

'What he wants most of all is to see his son.' She sounded very different from the woman I'd met in Begur. 'Will he? That judge yesterday, he frightened me.'

'From what Xavi tells me,' I said, 'that judge is an idiot. Don't worry about anything he says. There have been developments in Madrid. We believe that Hector may be with his old girlfriend, Valentina, so we need to trace her. For that we have to know her family name; it's essential. Can you recall it?'

'No, I cannot, I am sorry. I only ever called her by her first name; I was never told the other. That may sound funny to you, being British, but it's the way we are.'

'How did you correspond, the two of you?'

'We didn't much. When we did it was by email.'

'Do you have that address on your phone?'

'Yes!' She brightened up, instantly. 'I can text it to you. I will do that as soon as we finish.'

'In that case, do it now. Thank you, señora, we'll be thinking of you and Simon, all day. Please call Xavi when he comes out of the operating theatre.'

'I will, thank you.'

The call ended; I held on to the phone and I waited, for less than a minute. Then it buzzed and a text appeared in the window: 'Valbar913@ Hotmail.com'.

I handed it to Xavi. 'There. Send her a message; say that you're Hector's boss and you need to contact him urgently.'

'In what language? She's Russian, remember.'

'Does Hector speak Russian?'

'No.'

'So, unless their relationship was conducted by sign language . . .'

'My brain's still mush from last night,' he muttered, and began to key in a message.

The reply came instantly. Xavi held the mobile up so I could see the screen. 'Delivery failure.'

'Doesn't surprise me. Somebody wants to kill the woman; she's a fugitive. She'll have changed more than her hairstyle. Everything will have gone, name, home, phone, email; we're not looking for Valentina, but for somebody else.'

'In that case, why is it so important to know her surname?'

I frowned at him. 'Keep up, Xavi. Her danger doesn't come from who she is now. We need to know who she was.'

'Could her given name be Thais?' he asked.

'It's possible,' I conceded. 'But if she's still around, and Jacob left that note for her on his door last night, then where the hell is Hector? She did know both men, though, and Hector was always in contact with her. He headed here after Battaglia was killed, and they met up.'

'Did Hector know why she was shot?'

'He must have. If I worked it out, so did he.' I tried to form pictures in my mind, to make a pattern of the things I knew. 'He came to Jacob, his best friend,' I said aloud, voicing my thoughts. 'Did he have a relationship with the woman also?'

'Or was he just a conduit, a go-between?' Xavi suggested.

'Hopefully time will tell. What we know for sure is that someone is after Valentina; there's a kill contract out on her, and the person who placed it is patient.'

I had a clear picture.

'They'd lost her, so they watched Hector. And she must have been friendly with both of them, for they watched Jacob too. One killer . . . if ballistics confirm it . . . but more than one watcher, in Girona and in Madrid.'

'How do you know that?'

'It's simple, Xavi. Until yesterday they thought she was killed last Friday. When they realised they'd shot the wrong woman, the killer came straight here, straight to Jacob's place, and went to work on him. They must have been watching both men. You with me?'

'Up to a point,' Xavi replied. 'They couldn't have followed Hector round the clock.'

'They wouldn't have to,' I retorted. 'You know, as soon as I get home from here, I'm going to dig out my old Filofax and put it back into service. From what I've been told, Hector's whole life is in his laptop and his iPad. My bet is they've hacked into his diary, probably into his voicemail and his email too; he's been under electronic surveillance. Ring Pilar again,' I instructed. 'Ask her when Hector and Valentina broke up, as exactly as she can recall.'

I finished off his fizzy water, straight from the bottle, as he made the call. I was feeling hungry again . . . the buzz of a hunt always does that to me . . . but there was no time to do anything about it.

'February the twelfth,' Xavi announced, once he was done. 'Hector told his parents two days before Valentine's Day that he had finished with her. He said that he'd be obliged if they never mentioned her name again. Pilar was struck by the timing . . . Valentine, Valentina, get it? . . . so the date stuck in her head. By the way,' he added, 'she's just had word from the theatre that the surgery's going fine.'

'That's good,' I said, distracted momentarily from the main business at hand. 'Fingers crossed for him. I liked Simon a lot, when I finally got to meet him.'

Then I got back to business. 'So we have a period of less than a year,' I said. 'In February, he said he never wanted to hear Valentina's name again; now, less than ten months later, a lookalike woman is killed, and he goes running off to find her. Who is she, Xavi, and why does someone want her dead? Let's say you really are a reporter again. Who are you going to ask?'

'I'm going to start with the police,' he replied at once.

'Then let's do that.'

I called a waiter across and paid for Xavi's refreshments, then led the way out of the Plaza Mayor, back to Calle de la Cruz. The lone guard was still at the door, but the atmosphere around the crime scene had changed. The street had been blocked off to vehicle traffic and other uniformed officers were stationed at the junctions, interviewing passers-by.

'You do the talking here,' I murmured as we approached number two hundred and forty-two. 'Tell the guy at the door we're witnesses and we want to see the man in charge.'

The cop had ignored me earlier, but he looked up second time around. My large friend has that effect on people. He spoke rapidly as we reached the man, in Spanish. Even I could tell that it was heavily accented; the door warden looked puzzled, and had to hear his request for a second time before he understood. He nodded towards the restaurant as he replied.

'He says that the guy in charge is in there,' Xavi said. 'His name is Inspector Jefe Sala.'

We followed his direction, into Fatigas del Querer. The place was a customer-free zone and the chief inspector was in plain clothes and had his back to us, but I'd have known what he was even if it had been jam-packed. He was standing with Paco, listening to him. I've interviewed thousands of people over the years, and in most of them there was a kind of eagerness to please that is visible; the eyes a little wider, the smile that says, 'Please believe me, I'm speaking the truth.' The waiter was sending those messages, silent and clear.

He looked at us in the doorway, and his eyebrows almost pushed his forehead out of the way, so high did they rise as he shopped us to the detective.

The man turned slowly; he was around forty, a couple of inches shorter than me, with the shoulders of a weightlifter, and the attitude of one who's used to being obeyed. He looked us up and down, slowly and deliberately, as if to demonstrate that he was unimpressed. He glared at me, then barked out a question. Its speed, its aggression and its accent were too much for my Spanish.

Whatever he was saying, I didn't react well to the way he said it; it's not in my nature, I'm afraid. I returned his glare with one of my own, raising the animosity stakes. 'Repeat that in English,' I retorted, 'and a lot more politely, or we're off to a bad start.'

Xavi stepped forward, as if to keep the peace, and spoke to Sala. The chief inspector's expression, and his attitude, seemed to soften, but only a little. The big man produced a Spanish national identity card and offered it for study. The cop looked at it, shrugged, and handed it back.

Xavi carried on; I heard my name mentioned, and the phrase, '*Jefe de policia en Escocia*'. That was a mistake. The chief inspector might have been able to relate to me on the basis of one tough guy to another, but he'd never have yielded to the slightest suggestion of a foreign policeman pulling rank on him on his own patch . . . any more than I would.

It didn't go downhill after that, not exactly, but the Book was produced and adhered to, line by line. That was how I played it too, when Sala decided that he and his deputy, Inspector Raimat, would interview me formally. The other guy spoke decent English, but I decided to forget any Spanish I ever knew and insisted on Xavi translating for me.

It was clear from the start that the inspector jefe knew, courtesy of Julien Valencia, the answer to his first question, why we'd come to Madrid, but I replied anyway. I told him that a colleague of my friend, the media proprietor Señor Aislado, was missing and that he and I were trying to find him.

He asked why we had gone to Jacob Ireland's apartment. I said that we'd been told he and Hector were at university together, no more than that.

He asked why we'd left the scene after finding the body. I told him that I'd known as a detective not to risk any further contamination.

He asked why we'd reported the murder through the Mossos d'Esquadra, and not directly to the Policia Nacional. I replied that I knew its director general, and reckoned that he could get word to the right people in Madrid faster than I could.

He asked and I answered, but I volunteered nothing. I didn't share my belief that the killings in Madrid and Barcelona might be linked by the firearm involved. I said not a word about Valentina, because neither he nor Raimat asked me. Their omission led me to assume that Paco hadn't told them about my visit earlier that morning, or about the photograph I'd shown him.

If he hadn't he wasn't about to, because as soon as the interview was over, the detective told him that he could open for business once more.

He ordered us, again through Xavi, to leave him contact numbers and then to get the fuck out of Madrid and back to where we had come from. That suited me fine, for it was what I'd intended to do.

Why hadn't I been more forthcoming with the Madrid detectives? Professionally, I had no reason to doubt them; they held senior ranks in a major force and, as such, I accepted their competence. Personally, it wasn't that I didn't trust them, rather that I couldn't afford to.

It may be denied by both parties, it may be deplored by governments and courts, but it is a fact that in most countries there is a relationship of mutual back-scratching between the police and the media. Cash or gifts should never change hands but information does, in both directions, on a barter basis. It had been an issue in Barcelona, and so it was in Madrid.

If I had mentioned the name of the mystery woman Valentina, there was an excellent chance, life being what it is, that it would find its way into the public domain within twenty-four hours, either officially, though a press statement, or through the back door, whispered into the ear of a media contact of Inspector Jefe Sala or Inspector Raimat.

I was certain that she and Hector were in hiding . . . unless they were dead already . . . with a killer on their trail. It would not help for the whole of Spain to be on the lookout for both of them.

'What do we do now?' Xavi asked, as the detectives left, leaving us alone at a table.

I shrugged. 'I don't know about you, chum, but the menu del dia chalked on that board over there is calling out to me, loud and clear. I'm going to have some of that, and then we're going to grab the first AVE back to Girona.'

And that's what we did. (For the record, I had paella starter, followed by hake in the Basque style.) Once we'd eaten, we went back to the hotel and checked out.

We validated our return tickets at Estacion Atocha, but we had a couple of hours to kill, and so at Xavi's suggestion we spent them in the Reina Sofia art gallery, where the national collection of modern art is displayed. That includes Picasso's huge mono-chrome masterpiece, *Guernica*, his condemnation of the Spanish Civil War. It was on my bucket list, and I'd missed it on my previous visit to Madrid.

It did for me what El Bosco's work in the Prado had done for my chum; it grabbed me and held me to it. I stared at it for twenty minutes, until it was time to head for the station. If ever I visit the Spanish capital again, and I plan to do so, I'll be back to do it homage.

I waited until we were on the train before calling Julien Valencia, to keep my promise to get back to him with any new information I had. Xavi's phone had been on its last legs too, but there were power terminals by our seats and he was able to plug in his charger.

When I got through to the head of the Mossos, he was not a happy man. The presiding judge's wings might have been clipped, but the Italians were giving him grief, demanding progress on the murder investigation. Piled on top of that, he had a new gripe. He had asked Madrid to liaise with Intendant Reyes and the team investigating the Battaglia shooting, but no contact had been made. As a result, when I said that I'd been less forthcoming with Sala than I might have been, that cheered him up a little.

'It's the woman,' I told him, 'the one who was seen with Hector and Jacob on Monday night. She's at the heart of it.'

'How?'

I explained my thinking, that Battaglia had been killed by mistake, and that it was the discovery of the error that had triggered the torture murder in Madrid. Valencia's an administrator, not an investigator, so it took me a little while to convince him, but eventually I did.

'Who is she, this lady?' he asked.

'That's what you need to find out,' I replied. 'She's Russian and her given name is Valentina, but that's all I know for sure. Her old email address suggests that her family name begins with the letters B, A, R. That's all I have to go on.'

'I'll pass it on to Reyes.'

That didn't fill me with confidence; a middle-ranking officer might not command sufficient top-level attention.

'You might want to make that search yourself, Julien,' I suggested, 'you or your deputy; someone with command authority.'

'I do not like to undermine my subordinates.'

'I appreciate that, and your own database might give you the answer, but you may well need a wider search than that. This woman is not a Spanish national.'

'Where do you suggest?'

'If it was me, I'd be talking to Europol and possibly Interpol too, although I know they pool their intelligence.'

'Okay,' he agreed. 'I will try them. I will keep you informed, out of courtesy. Thank you for all your help, Bob, and for what you discovered in Madrid. We will handle it from here.'

Will you indeed? I thought as I put the phone down on the tray table. *And what exactly will you do with it?*

Twenty-Four

We hadn't even reached Barcelona when Valencia called me back, on Xavi's recharged phone. Within a couple of seconds I realised that he was rattled.

'I have a message for you,' he said. 'It comes from my boss, the Justice Minister in the government of Catalunya; it came to her from the Interior Minister in Madrid. The woman you told me of . . . I'm not going to mention her name over the phone . . . you are to forget you ever heard of her.'

I couldn't help it; for all his intensity, all I could do was smile. 'As messages go,' I chuckled, 'that's right up there with the stupidest I've ever had. But since it comes from two politicians,' I added, 'that's not as surprising as it might be. How can I forget that which I know already?'

'You know what they mean,' he retorted sharply.

'Did your boss say why her *bragas* are in a twist?'

'She didn't want to be questioned about it, but you are right about the underwear. From the way she acted it must have been damp to say the least,' he chuckled.

'As soon as you and I had finished speaking,' he continued, 'I called my opposite number, the Director General of Europol, in Brussels. I told him what you have told me and asked if he could identify the woman from the information you had given me. He said he would call me back, but he didn't. Instead, only fifteen minutes ago, I had this tirade from Marte Negredo. She didn't call me, she actually came to my office from the Justice Ministry.'

'What did she say, exactly?' I asked.

'I told you; she said that we should forget the woman Valentina, we should stop looking for her and we should not mention her name again.'

'Wow,' I exclaimed, 'now there's a coincidence. Hector Sureda said exactly the same thing to his parents last February.'

'Coincidence or not,' he sighed, 'we have to obey. I have been told directly that this woman is not part of this investigation. I have to concentrate on finding the person who killed our very important Italian visitor, and nothing else. In that respect, the minister has come down on the side of the judge; she has declared that Hector Sureda is the only suspect in the murder.'

'You may have to obey, Julien,' I countered, 'but I don't. I'm a private citizen trying to find a man who's gone missing, as a favour to a friend. I was ready to leave that search to your people, but not any longer. I'm not going to let Hector be arrested for something he didn't do, or shot while resisting.'

'That's not going to happen!'

'Too fucking right it's not, because I'm going to find him before your people do.'

'The Mossos is not a death squad, Bob,' he protested.

'I know that, but Madrid's involved, and all national governments have previous in that respect. I hear your minister's message, and I choose to ignore it. I won't compromise you, though. I won't call you again until I have something positive to tell you.'

'I'm sorry, Bob,' he said, sincerely, 'but as one cop to another, you know how it is.'

'That's where we part company, Julien,' I replied, as gently as I could. 'I'm a cop; you're a civil servant.'

'What?' Xavi asked as I gave him his phone back.

I gave him a rundown of the conversation and of Valencia's orders.

'What's the fucking mystery?' he exclaimed. 'Why's she off limits?'

'If I knew that it wouldn't be a fucking mystery, now, would it?'

He sighed. 'Bob, I know I started this thing off with my daft theory about Hector being kidnapped, but I had no idea it would turn out like this. You've done more than enough for me as it is. Just walk away now and let everything run its course.'

'That course, if it's left unaltered, is going to leave your friend with a bullet in his head. I can't let that happen. I've met his parents; I like and respect them. I'm not doing this for you any longer, big man. I'm in it for them.'

'We have nowhere else to go,' he pointed out. 'We're at a dead end.'

'Bad choice of words, but no, we're not. They're in hiding, we have to find them.'

'And how do we do that?'

I smiled. 'I'll tell you a story. When I was a kid, till I was about nine or ten years old, I had a cat. His name was Figaro, and he was my only friend. He was a right wee rascal, always getting into bother; whenever he did, he always went to the same place, under the sideboard. That was where he felt safe and secure. Then one day, he started making funny noises. He headed for the sideboard but he didn't make it. He died, half in, half out of his place of safety.'

I gazed at him but I wasn't really seeing him, no, I was looking back in time.

'People are the same. Your place of safety, after Grace died, used to be the *Saltire*; now it's here, in Spain. Mine was my job, and I can see now that's why I'm having such trouble walking away from it. But I will, though; I'll make Sarah and my kids my refuge, as they should have been all along.'

Xavi nodded. 'Good idea,' he said quietly.

'What we have to do now,' I continued, 'is to find Hector's citadel, the place where he feels safe from all the bad stuff.'

'A week ago,' he remarked, 'I'd have said that was inside his computer. But now I'm not so sure.'

'I have an inkling,' I told him. 'To find out whether I'm right or not, we have to get off this train, not in Girona, but in Barcelona. That's where Pilar is right now, at the hospital. We need to talk to his mother, because if there's one person in the world right now who can tell us where he is, it's her . . . even if she doesn't realise it.'

'I could phone,' he suggested.

'You could,' I agreed, 'but you should go there anyway, to support her.'

He frowned. 'You're right, of course. If all this shit hadn't happened I'd have been there with her during the operation.'

We surprised the conductor by leaving the AVE at Estacio Sants. The taxi rank was busy when we got there, but there are a hell of a lot of cabs in Barcelona, so we didn't have to wait for long.

Simon's life-or-death operation was being performed in a university hospital in Vall D'Hebron on the outskirts of the city. It's very large, and we'd have been struggling to find the surgical section, but our driver had been there often and knew exactly where to drop us.

Xavi led the way inside, and straight to reception; the woman in charge was cautious at first, to the point of frostiness, but he dipped into the well of charm that he keeps for special occasions, until she thawed and directed us to level two. 'Your friend will be there, somewhere,' she promised.

- She was, in a quiet place reserved for patients' families. It was a large room, with a large window looking down on the city; it was comfortably furnished and there was a coffee machine and snacks in the far corner, not unlike an airport VIP lounge, minus alcohol.

She didn't notice us at first, for she was talking to the only other person there, a woman . . . another anxious wife, I guessed from the tension that lined her face. Her own relaxed smile was in stark contrast, and it told us all we needed to know.

'Pilar.'

She turned towards us at the sound of Xavi's voice, excused herself to the other lady, and came across to join us. '*Hey, sorpresa,*' she exclaimed: in Catalan, but I had no trouble with that translation.

She switched to English. 'Thank you both for coming; everything is okay. They have replaced the aortic valve, and carried out a quadruple artery bypass. The chief surgeon came to see me half an hour ago. He says he expects Simon to make a very good recovery, considering the condition that his heart was in. We will not dance the tango for a while, but a gentle *sardana* should be possible before too long.'

'That's great,' I said. 'When will you see him?'

'Tomorrow morning. They will keep him sedated overnight then let him waken gradually. Tonight I stay in a hotel; I would go home, but I am exhausted.'

She paused, her eyes on us, going from one to the other, studying our faces. 'Is that all the good news I will have today?' she asked, quietly.

'You'll have no bad news,' I replied. 'Hector is still missing, but we still have reason to suppose he's with his girlfriend, with Valentina. What we don't know is where they might be.'

'Maybe at her place,' she suggested. 'It was near Sitges, as I remember.'

'No, they won't be there, that's for sure. They'll have gone somewhere else, a place where they would feel secure, that nobody else would know about.'

She sucked in a deep breath. 'In that case. "nobody else" would include me. Apart from Begur, there were only two places Hector went: his apartment in Barcelona and Jacob's, in Madrid.' She frowned a little. 'He's not with them? Jacob?'

'No,' Xavi said, a little too sharply, then added to still any curiosity, 'He's still in Madrid.'

'Can I make a guess?' I murmured.

She looked up at me. 'Of course.'

'The photograph we saw in Begur, in Hector's attic, of him and Valentina in winter, in the snow. I noticed that he uses the same scenery as the screen wallpaper on his computer in the Girona office. Do you know where they were, where those were taken?'

Pilar's eyes widened a little. 'Yes!' she exclaimed. 'It was a ski lodge in Andorra. They went there last winter for *Cap d' Any* . . . New Year. When they came back, they both said that it was beautiful. Valentina even said that if they ever married she would like it to be there, in that hotel. I have never thought of Andorra as an attractive place, but they did.'

'Can you remember the name?'

'It was called the Hotel Roc Blau. It is not large. Hector said that it has ten rooms and also some chalets; they had one of those. They told me the chalets are built right into the side of the mountain, and that the place is as high as the road goes.'

'Did they go back there afterwards?'

'They broke up six weeks after it.' She paused before adding, 'But for that, they would have gone. They called it their special place. They made me promise never to tell anyone what it was called . . . not even Jacob.'

'Is Jacob a skier?'

Pilar laughed. 'In no way, any more than Hector is. Those two, they are not sportsmen, either of them.'

'Do you know how they discovered the hotel?' I asked.

'Valentina knew of it. Now her, she does ski. She is very good, Hector said, champion class. He told me that the Hotel Roc Blau does not advertise, and it has no website, because it has no need. All the top skiers know of it, and only they go there. Most of them don't even tell their families about it, according to Valentina. That's why I had to keep it secret.'

'Let's hope it still is,' Xavi murmured.

'Will you go there to look for him?'

The big guy glanced at me, repeating Pilar's question with a raised eyebrow.

'Yes,' I replied. 'It sounds like the best bet.'

'Will you find them both there, do you think? I hope you do, for I would like them to be together. She has a lot of mystery about her, that woman, but she made my son happy. He hasn't been the same since he stopped seeing her.'

'A lot of mystery,' I repeated. 'In what way?'

'She never talked about herself, or about her family. I asked her about them, but she always managed to reply without ever telling me anything. My business is getting information from people, but I never managed to do it with her. I have never known a woman who will not mention her mother, at some time or other . . . or rather, I hadn't known one until I met Valentina. I began to think that she was raised in an orphanage.'

'Maybe she was.'

'Who knows?' She smiled. 'I have one guilty secret; I did try to find out her family name. She was in Begur one time and she left her bag lying about. I looked inside: her passport was there and I took a look. Yes, there was a second name, but it was no use to me. It was in Cyrillic script, and I can't read that.'

'Did she have a profession?' I asked.

'She told me that she was an accountant. When I asked her for whom she did her accounting, it got mysterious again. "For an entrepreneur," she said, "who likes to keep his affairs very close to his chest." It was her very polite way of telling me to mind my own business.'

Xavi looked at me, over Pilar's head.

'Damn nuisance,' he said, 'our cars being in Girona.' He thought for a few moments. 'We could hire one,' he suggested.

I checked my watch; it was ten minutes before seven. 'By the time we get that sorted, we could be back up there. Besides, if we really are going as high as the road goes up in the mountains, I'd rather do it in your Range Rover than anything else. How long's the drive?'

'Two and a half hours minimum,' Xavi replied, 'probably more. This is Friday, remember, and there's plenty of snow up there. The road will be busy with skiers.'

'Okay,' I declared. 'We go back to Girona, pick up the cars, grab a few hours' sleep at your place, then leave at sparrow-fart, about six o'clock, looking to get there for nine.'

We settled on that as a plan.

'When you find Hector,' Pilar asked, 'what will you do? The police will want to talk to him about Battaglia.'

'So will I,' Xavi said, ominously. He hadn't forgotten that his younger colleague had been consorting with the enemy. 'But that can wait. We will keep him right with the Mossos. Bob doesn't believe they'll have enough evidence to hold him, but if he needs a good lawyer I'll find him one. You trust me to look after him, my dear; you look after Simon.'

We left her there in the family room. Outside, taxis were coming and going all the time; we hailed the first one that was free. I'd have settled for the train, but Xavi asked the driver if he'd take us to Girona. With the promise of a decent tip, he agreed.

'The killer will have a twenty-four-hour head start on us, Bob,' my friend pointed out, as soon as we were on the Ronda de Dalt, and heading north. 'He could have found them already.'

'You're assuming that he's heading in the same direction as us,' I pointed out. 'Jacob, poor bastard, took at least three hits before he talked . . . that's assuming he did, and that the gunman didn't simply get fed up and shoot him. He could have sent him south, east or west. But suppose it is the worst case, and he did give up Andorra, he doesn't know about Roc Blau.'

'We don't know a hell of a lot about it either,' Xavi pointed out. 'All we have is the name, no address, no postcode. Tomorrow's Saturday, so all the public offices will be closed in Andorra la Vella, like everywhere else.'

'We'll ask when we get there. Or maybe . . .' I paused for thought, and the obvious reared up and bit me. 'You own a couple of dozen newspapers,' I exclaimed, 'including several in Catalunya. Skiing's a sport, so you must cover it.'

'Of course we do. We have specialist writers.'

'In that case, call one of your people, a sports editor or

whatever. Tell him we want a location for Hotel Roc Blau, where the top sliders hang out.'

'Good idea,' he conceded. 'I'll call Andrea Graciana, on *GironaDia*. She's my best. But she's a reporter, mind, she'll want to know why I'm asking.'

'And you're the boss, mind,' I retorted. 'Just fucking tell her to do it.'

He laughed, a great rumbling sound in the darkened cab. 'That would really get her going. I'll tell her I want to take Sheila and Paloma up to Andorra for a break, and that someone mentioned the name to me.'

The day staff in Girona had gone home, but he managed to track the woman down on the contact number held by the sport desk. I listened as they spoke, and heard him chuckle a couple of times.

'What's the joke?' I asked when they were finished.

'A Real Madrid footballer's been caught shagging a teammate's wife. They can't decide which one to sell in the next transfer window. That would never have happened in my playing days; most of our guys were paid so little they couldn't afford wives.'

The taxi trip took a couple of minutes under an hour. We retrieved both cars and I followed Xavi back to his place. As I parked the Suzuki I did a quick, unsuccessful search for my phone charger, in the vain hope that I'd left it there. I was beginning to feel completely isolated, something I'd never known for as long as I could remember, and I didn't like it.

I was going to ask Xavi if I could call Sarah and Alex from his landline, but he had called Sheila from the road and she had dinner ready for us . . . just the three of us; Paloma had eaten earlier, and Ben was off with his woman . . . and by the time that was over, I judged that it was too late.

Next morning we set off as planned, a few minutes after six. The *masia* was in darkness when we left, and we had to take it easy on the country roads, but once we hit La Carretera, heading for Vic, and then Manresa, we were able to make decent time.

We'd started off with no firm destination, but that changed just after eight, as the sun started to rise on what promised to be a clear morning, when a phone call interrupted the radio programme that Xavi had selected . . . one of his own stations, naturally.

I could hear Andrea through the car speakers; she had a nice voice, even though nearly all of her message was lost on me. It made sense to Xavi, though, for he kept nodding, and repeating 'Vale, vale' . . . that's 'Okay, okay' . . . as she spoke.

He thanked her when they were done, then lowered the volume of the radio as it kicked back in. 'We head for a place called El Serrat,' he announced, 'then go north from there. She says we'll find a *camino* that leads up to the hotel. We've to look for a sign that says "HRB" at the turn-off.'

'Sounds like the end of the universe.'

'There's no way out, that's for sure.'

'Does it have twenty-first-century facilities? For example, a phone?'

'Not that Andrea could find, I asked her. It may be too high for a landline.'

The closer we got to Andorra, the more dense the traffic became; there were lots of off-roaders and lots of roof racks, some holding coffin-shaped boxes and others with skis clipped into special holders. The higher we climbed, the lower the outside temperature dipped, until it was down to zero and snow flanked the highway.

We were ten kilometres short of the border with the micro-state when the radio died once more and the phone rang again.

'*Hola*,' Xavi exclaimed as he accepted the call.

'Who's that?' Julien Valencia asked. He spoke Castellano, but even in that language I could tell that he was confused.

'Julien,' I said quickly, 'Bob Skinner here. I'm on the road.'

'You're not alone?'

'No, I'm with Xavi Aislado.'

'I can't speak on hands-free, Bob.'

'No problem,' Xavi said. He dug his phone from a breast pocket in his jacket, handed it to me, then killed the Bluetooth.

I nodded my thanks to him. 'Okay now,' I told Valencia. 'What's the panic?'

'There is no panic, but I have some important news for you. What you said to me last night, Bob, that got to me. I am not a civil servant, but I understand why you felt that way, because I have been behaving like one of those. You made me feel ashamed of myself for letting the Justice Minister push me around. Also I am angry that the guy in Holland, in Europol, my equal, went over my head to the fucking politicos.'

'Good,' I agreed. 'I'm glad to hear it. So what are you going to do about it?'

'I have done it already. I have friends too, as I am sure you do, in the criminal intelligence community, people I can talk to who know I can be trusted with what they tell me. I called one, a former colleague of mine when I was in the Guardia Civil. She's in Madrid, and she hates the Interior Ministry, so she was very willing to talk to me. I asked her the same thing that I asked the guy in The Hague, about a missing Russian woman, Valentina, then something beginning with B, A, R.'

'And?'

'And she didn't even pause to think about it. The lady's *apellido* is Barsukova. She is the daughter of a Russian oligarch, Veniamin Barsukov. This man was super-rich in minerals, but he got that way by criminal means, by persuading people to sign over assets to him at gunpoint, for nominal amounts. Naturally these crimes took place in private and could never be proved.' He paused. 'Are you with me?'

'I'm so with you that I think I can guess what's coming next. He upset the people in power at home?'

'Exactly, so he left the country and moved to Spain, where it is a lot warmer, and a lot safer for him all year round. When he did so, he took a lot of secrets with him, business dealings like his own that would embarrass those powerful people in Russia. Barsukov is no fool, he did not walk around unprotected, but a year ago, his brother was assassinated, and that scared him. So he did a deal.'

'With whom?'

'With the Americans, of course; he told them what he knew and they gave him a new identity and laundered his assets, so that he cannot be found, ever.'

'Hold on,' I said. 'What was the value of this information to the Yanks?'

'In the short-term, none, while the regime is strong, but in time it can be used against it, to destabilise it.'

'Valentina,' I asked, 'where does she fit in?'

'She was a problem, it seems. She is Barsukov's only child; she could have vanished with him under the deal but she refused. She was in love, she said, and she would not leave Spain. With our help, she also was given a new identity, and stayed here. However, she was told that she had to lie low, and that she and her lover had to be very careful. She knows none of her father's secrets, but his enemies will kill her anyway, simply to punish him.'

'As we've seen,' I murmured. 'Was there a leak? Did they know she was still in Spain?'

'Not necessarily. It is clear that they have been watching Hector Sureda, but that may only have been a precaution, against an outside possibility . . .'

'. . . which was real all along, that they were still in touch. And when they hacked into his diary and saw that he'd arranged a dinner meeting, with someone referred to only as B, they thought they might be on to a winner.'

'It's even better than that,' Valencia exclaimed. 'My friend is a Russian speaker; she told me that in the Cyrillic alphabet, our letters V and B share the same character. A Russian might read B as V and think Valentina.'

I whistled. 'So goodbye Bernicia, by mistake.'

'Exactly. The rest of the story we can work out. They must have been watching Jacob Ireland also.'

'That's what I've been thinking, but it's not necessarily the case, Julien. Any decent profile on Hector would show Ireland as his best friend, and that would mark him as the first port of call for anyone trying to find him. Poor bastard.'

'And poor Valentina and Hector if the assassin got what he needed from Señor Ireland.'

For a moment I thought our conversation was over, until he asked, 'Bob, where are you and Señor Aislado going now? Do you know where they are?'

'We might. We're heading for Andorra.'

'That is out of my territory: it's another country.'

I laughed. 'I did know that, chum. What can you tell me about its police force?'

'It's very small, as you'd expect. I know their director; we have an informal understanding that if he has a major situation, he can call on me for extra manpower.'

'And if one of your investigations crosses into his territory?'

'We work together. When you get to your destination, Bob, should you need police help, call me. If you find Señor Sureda and Señora Barsukova . . .' He hesitated.

'We'll bring them straight to Barcelona, whether they like it or not. Until this hit man is caught, they'll be safest in your custody.'

Unless he's ahead of us.

That scary thought was preying on my mind as the Andorran border came into sight, until it was replaced by another worry.

'Hey,' I called out to Xavi over the sound of some early Christmas music on the radio, 'we don't have our passports.'

'We won't need them,' he assured me.

The ski-slope traffic was thick by then; it slowed to a crawl as it approached the crossing, then speeded up. There were two Spanish booths on either side of the single carriageway, and two Andorran, twenty-five metres beyond, but none of them was manned. There were few cops to be seen and all of them were on the other side of the road.

'They might stop us on the way out,' Xavi said, 'but only to check that we're not smuggling. They don't give a shit about what goes in.'

He had programmed El Serrat into the satnav; he let it guide us and I looked at the scenery. I don't get claustrophobic but I pity anyone who does and who finds himself in Andorra. Mountains towered above us, on either side; I had a mental image of the Almighty pausing in his work of creation to take an axe and whack it into the Pyrenees, leaving a great gouge that would become an anomalous state.

We followed the traffic up to Andorra La Vella, the main town, then gave our digital navigator free rein. The roads had been slush-covered until then but as we drove higher, that gave way to hard-packed snow. Xavi stopped to fit chains to the tyres, and the Range Rover began to do the job that it had been built for.

There were poles on either side of the road and as we climbed they showed a depth of snow that became steadily greater. We passed through El Serrat almost without realising it, carrying on, still climbing until we reached a hairpin junction, with a sign.

'We turn here,' Xavi announced. 'Andrea said we should head for the national park.'

For the next ten minutes I wished she hadn't; I'm a lousy passenger, even at the best of times. The road was narrow, and on my side of the car the mountainside seemed precipitous. Yes, it was forest, but that was no consolation. If we'd gone off, there would have been nothing but catastrophe. At one point we had to overtake a very slow-moving bus; I listened for the sound of its passengers screaming, but they must have been struck dumb by terror.

At last, at very long last, Xavi called out, 'That's it. See?' He pointed. 'The HRB sign. The *camino*.'

Sure enough, it was there, a few metres ahead, so small and insignificant that we'd never have spotted it without Andrea's guidance.

The word *camino* means 'road' in English but these days there's less to it than that. Most that carry that name are simply dirt trails, with no blacktop. The one that led to Hotel Roca Blau was narrow, and very steep. I have no idea what lay under the snow, but at least that had been ploughed since the last fall, and the surface was firm and passable.

After a hundred metres or so the trees began to thin out, and we had an idea of where we were going. A significant climb still lay ahead, but we could see all the way to a bend around the mountainside.

When we reached it we found that it took us out on to a plateau of sorts, a level stretch of ground on which there stood a three-storey building, with a roof that sloped sharply on either side of a central ridge. In front of it were four smaller, similarly shaped buildings, two on either side.

Two off-roaders, a Skoda Yeti and a Grand Cherokee, were parked in a small compound with a high wooden fence on three sides, strongly built to shield against avalanches from the mountain behind. Xavi pulled into an empty space, beside a small tracked Bobcat vehicle, with a snowplough blade attached and raised off the ground.

I jumped out of the Range Rover and stretched my back, breathing so deeply of the cold air that I felt my head spin for a second. My winter weight jacket had never been put to such a temperature test, but it was up to it, for that moment. Xavi joined me, finishing yet another bottle of mineral water; his fourth on the journey.

'Impressive,' he murmured. 'What a view.' He was right; it couldn't be overstated. We were facing due south, and with no pollution we could see right over the top of Andorra la Vella and its protecting hills, far into Catalunya. 'I can almost see my house from up here.'

That reminded me of an old, bad taste joke, but I decided not to sully the moment by sharing it.

'I can see why the skiers like this place,' he added. 'Look.' I followed his pointing finger and saw, stretching upwards from a point behind the main building, a cable, with a couple of small pods suspended. 'I'd guess that goes straight to a slope; this hotel's practically on piste.'

Roc Blau appeared to have a small garden laid out. Like everything else, it was buried under at least a foot of snow, but there were shapes that hinted of hardy bushes, set in orderly lines. A pathway had been cleared from the parking area to the main building. We followed it all the way to a flight of five steps that stretched across the hotel's full width, accessing a terrace that was protected by the overhanging roof. Heavy wooden tables and chairs were set out, each grouping below an electric heater fixed on the wall.

As we entered a small reception hall, through a revolving door, a bell tinkled; a few seconds later a tall, middle-aged woman appeared; she had a broad open face, blue eyes and her hair was bleached, but not chemically. 'Good morning,' she said, in English. 'Welcome to Hotel Roc Blau.' I tried to place the accent: not Spanish, not French; German, Austrian or possibly Swiss. 'I am Magda.'

'Nice to meet you,' I responded. 'How did you know we're Brits?'

She smiled. 'I can tell at a glance. Your friend, I am not so sure, but you, certainly.'

Her grin demanded to be returned. 'You'd have been half right with him,' I said.

'How can I help you?' she asked. 'I was not expecting any British guests to arrive today. If you made a booking, then I apologise, for it has not been registered, and we are full for the weekend.' I must have looked puzzled, for she added. 'I know, you only saw two cars there, but most of our guests choose the easier drive to the ski slope reception, around the mountainside. They park there and come down here in our own cable cars.'

'I wish we'd known that,' I told her, sincerely. 'No, we don't have a booking. My name is Bob Skinner, and my large friend is Xavi Aislado. We've come here looking for a friend of his, a friend and a colleague, Hector Sureda. He may be travelling with a woman, Valentina Barsukova.'

'What made you imagine they would be here, Mr Skinner?' Her smile didn't waver.

Neither did mine. 'I'm good at imagining. Maybe you don't get Spanish TV up here, but if you do and you watch the news, you'll be aware that the Mossos d'Esquadra in Barcelona are very keen to talk to Hector, and have been since a body was found in his apartment a few days ago. What isn't public knowledge are the facts that he may be travelling with Señora Barsukova, and that someone's trying to kill them.'

'Really? This is Andorra, such things don't happen here.' Still the smile held steady . . . but her eyes didn't.

'Let's skip what I suspect or imagine,' I said, 'and concentrate on what I know. Hector and Valentina saw in the last New Year here. It was his first visit but she'd been here before; he came to love it as much as she did. They were happy then, but they're in hellish trouble now. Magda, three people are looking for them; the two of us and somebody with a gun. If we don't find them first, and he does, they're dead. Look at me and tell me you don't believe me.'

She did, her expression serious at last. 'Am I the first person you ask about Valentina?' Her question was murmured. 'My husband, Horst, he runs the ski lift. He called me half an hour ago to say that someone had come there asking about her. Was it you?'

I felt my spine stiffen. 'No way,' I replied. 'If you don't believe us, ask him to come down here. Magda, that makes it all the more important that you trust us. If they're here, or if you know where they are, please tell us.'

She looked at me, weighing up a decision; finally she made it.

'We are managers here,' she began, 'Horst and I. We are employed by the company that owns Roc Blau. Until the beginning of this year, that company belonged to Valentina's father, Mr Barsukov. Then without any warning, we were told by the lawyers that it had been transferred to a new owner. We were told not to worry, that our jobs were safe, but we would not be seeing Mr Barsukov, or Valentina, again. And we didn't, until she and Hector arrived here three days ago, on Wednesday.'

'They're still here?'

She nodded. 'There is a fifth chalet,' she said. 'You can hardly see it from here, but if you stand on the terrace outside and look to your left, you will just have a glimpse of the top of the roof. It was kept for use by the Barsukov family alone, and because we have received no orders otherwise, it is still never rented. That is where they are. I will take you to them.'

Beside me, Xavi let out a great sigh. 'Thank you, señora,' he said.

She led us outside, along a path that led to a small building we hadn't noticed before. 'The supplies hut for the maids,' she explained, casually, as we reached it. There, a small flight of steps led to a lower level, where the fifth chalet was situated. One set of footprints, and twin wheel tracks, led to the door.

Magda saw me looking at them. 'Only the chalet maid has been here since they arrived. They have not been outside. When the snow is on the ground you cannot come and go from here without being noticed.'

The door was in the centre of the building and there were windows on either side. There was a floodlight set in the wall with a photo-sensor, and close to that a video camera.

'There is a monitor inside, and another camera hidden in the door. We had better stand here for a moment, so we can be seen clearly. I don't want to panic them.'

We did as she suggested, until she decided that it was okay to approach. 'I'll leave you now,' she said.

The door opened before we reached it. A man stood there, a man I'd never met but knew from the photograph that I'd been showing people for most of the week gone by.

'Xavi,' Hector Sureda exclaimed, as the short distance between us closed. 'Am I glad to see you.'

'Maybe you shouldn't be,' the giant beside me growled. 'I might have come to kick your arse off this fucking mountain, you treacherous little shit.'

Then he seemed to soften, and enveloped his young friend in a great bear hug.

It might have been a relief to them, but it made me feel exposed and uncomfortable. 'Hey, you two,' I called out, 'can we go inside?'

They got the message; Hector stood to one side and ushered us into a big living area, flooded with sunshine, where Valentina Barsukova waited. She was staring at us fearfully, as if we were invaders rather than saviours, and her short spiky dyed blond hair stuck out as if she had been shocked. '*Amor, quién estes hombres?*' she asked.

'They're friends,' he replied, in English. 'This huge fellow is my boss, Xavi . . . I've told you about him often enough . . . and this is . . .'

I took over. 'My name is Bob Skinner, señora. I'm a friend of

Xavi, and I've been helping him find you. I used to be a cop,' I added, in validation of sorts.

'Did Jacob send you?' she asked, then frowned. 'But how could he? He doesn't know where Roca Blau is, or even its name.'

'But he did know about Andorra, yes? And the fact that you two were together here?'

'Yes, we mentioned it to him.'

'In that case,' I said, 'he may have sent someone after you. Thank Christ we got here first.'

Hector frowned, bewildered. 'Why would he do that?'

'To stop the pain.' It couldn't be sugar-coated. 'Jacob's dead. He was murdered in Madrid on Thursday night, but not before he was tortured. No question that the person who did it was looking for the two of you, and we believe for Valentina most of all.'

'Then I was right,' he whispered. 'Bernicia was shot because she looked like Val.'

I nodded. 'Now let's all sit down, and calm down.'

I took a moment to look around the chalet. It was much bigger than had seemed possible from the outside. There were two doors off the living room, and each lay open, one showing a kitchen, the other a bedroom. Between them a spiral staircase led to a lower level. The far wall was glass, with double sliding doors leading to a terrace, enclosed by a timber surround; they lay open and yet it wasn't cold inside, for in a hearth, in the centre of the space, a great log fire was blazing.

Valentina, Hector and Xavi all sat on a long sofa of soft brown leather; I bagged a chair on the other side of the fireplace and turned it round to face them.

I looked at the digital genius. 'Did Battaglia contact you, or was it the other way round?'

'She got in touch with me,' he replied. 'Not directly at first, but through a guy who was one of her aides, a lawyer, I think.'

'What was the pitch?' Xavi asked, grimly.

'They pushed the benefits of a link-up between BeBe and InterMedia.'

'And you listened?'

'Yes,' Hector replied, animated. 'They had a point, Xavi. We can't stand still in our industry, not any more. We can't dig in our heels and say, "This is how it's going to be in five, ten, fifteen years," because we just don't know. The truth is, we don't know how it will be in one year. This is not a period of change, this is a time of revolution, and anyone who doesn't keep pace with it will be crushed.'

'You might have told me, chum,' Xavi sighed. 'It is my company, after all, mine and Joe's.'

The younger man shook his head, in denial. 'No, you're wrong,' he retorted. 'You may be the majority shareholders, yes, you may own the physical business, but it has stakeholders too . . . all the people you employ, who have put their careers in your hands. You have a duty to them to do what's best for them, and that definitely does not include laughing in the face of Bernicia Battaglia. I would have told you, really, but in my own time, after I'd heard Bernicia's proposal.'

'Did you have time to hear it?' I asked.

He glanced at me, across the fireplace. 'As it turned out, no, I didn't, not properly. I met her for dinner in Girona, but that was no more than an ice-breaker. I couldn't concentrate on business, not at all, because my mind was blown by how much she looked like Valentina.

'Instead of getting down to detail that night, we agreed that we'd go to my place in Barcelona next day for further talks, in private. And yet I was still thinking of Val next morning. I bought roses; in my mind I was giving them to her, not Bernicia.'

He paused, shuddering. 'Then we got to Barcelona, and . . . I can't describe it.'

'You don't have to,' Xavi told him. 'We've been there. It was us that found her. We've spent the last few days clearing up after you.'

'I'm sorry,' Hector moaned, 'but when it happened . . . I was putting water in a vase for the roses,' he began to explain, 'when I heard a noise.'

'We'd worked that out, son,' I said. 'And worked out why you bolted too.' I looked at Valentina. 'Were you two always in touch, even after you and your father went off the radar?'

She stared at me, astonished by what I knew.

'I wasn't just any old cop,' I murmured.

'Yes,' she whispered. 'They told me I shouldn't because I would be in danger if I was discovered, but I had to. I couldn't risk email, so I wrote to Hector instead. I used Jacob's box number in Madrid, and he forwarded my letters to the office in Girona. He did the same thing in the other direction. I have a box too, where I've been living, in my new name.

'On Saturday, Hector wrote to me directly, and asked me to meet him at Jacob's, as soon as I could. I received the letter on Monday, and went there next day.'

I frowned at him. 'Why did you do that? You'd just seen Battaglia's brains on your carpet. Why reach out to Valentina after that?'

He took a deep breath, puffing out his cheeks. 'Until then,' he began, 'neither of us had been completely convinced that there really was a threat. Our plan was to give it a year, then if everything was okay, we'd meet up again casually, Val with her new name and her new hair, as if it was a completely new relationship.

'When Bernicia was killed, I panicked. I decided that we had to run for it, before the Russian people got lucky. I thought this was safe, so we came here as a first step.' He frowned. 'How did you know about it?'

'You left a couple of leads behind. Your mother gave us the rest.'

'My mother,' Hector exclaimed. 'How is my father? Do you know?'

'He's going to be fine,' Xavi said. 'Now we have to make sure that you are.'

'How the hell can you do that? Battaglia is dead, Jacob is dead. How can we be safe from this person?'

'You're going to jail,' I chuckled, 'both of you. But it'll be short term, until this hit man is caught. They'll move you on from there. Right now, we're going to get into Xavi's car and get the hell out of here. There's a police officer in Barcelona who's very keen to meet you. Pack, as fast as you can.'

The big man stood. 'Yes,' he declared. 'But first I have to take a leak. Where is it?'

Valentina pointed to the bedroom door. 'Use the en suite.'

He left us, closing the door behind him.

'I'll tidy up in the kitchen,' Valentina said, and went off to do just that, leaving Hector and me alone for the first time. I looked around the place, taking the chance to appraise it properly. It had a homely feel to it; the furniture was polished in places from regular use, and there were pictures, ornaments and sculptures all around. I spotted some nice paperweights on a sideboard; one was a snow scene, solid glass, not the kind you shake up. I picked it up to admire it, feeling its smooth solidity in my hand.

'Why are you doing this?' Hector asked, out of the blue. 'You don't live in Spain. Xavi's mentioned you, sure, but I know he hadn't seen you in years.'

I shrugged. 'Simple, I'm here and he asked for my help. I had nothing else to do, and I love a challenge, so . . .'

'I'm glad you did. I doubt if he'd have found us by himself, without you. These Russian people are very scary, señor. They seem to be capable of anything.'

'You'd better believe . . .'

I was interrupted in mid-sentence by a chime from the front door. I followed Hector's eyes as he gazed at a screen on the wall, and saw a woman in the frame, in uniform and carrying a mop and pail. There was a trolley behind her with an array of cleaning products.

'Chalet maid,' Hector said. 'I'll tell her to go away.'

I didn't bother to watch him as he went to the door and opened it. I was looking through the open doors at the spectacular view beyond, and so I didn't even notice him backing into the room, not until a woman's voice called out, '*Donde es la mujer?*' Her accent was rough and definitely not Spanish.

I spun round, and as I did, I shouted, 'Stay where you are, Valentina. Block the door if you can.'

The woman was small and dark-haired, with a broad forehead, above a sharp nose and a narrow, mean mouth. She shoved Hector backwards, with greater force than her slight frame suggested she possessed, sending him sprawling as she turned her silenced pistol on me. I know a bit about guns, having fired a few in my time, and I can spot a Russian weapon, as opposed to, say, a Glock, or a Smith and Wesson.

'You should tell her to come out, mister,' she hissed. 'She will anyway, when she hears your scream after I've shot off your prick.'

As I've said, I don't react well to threats, not even from a little woman with a gun. She was two or three yards away from me, but I was armed too. I was still holding the paperweight.

At that range I didn't need to wind up to throw it; a strong flick of the wrist was all it took to send it flying towards her. It would have caught her in the right eye, but her reflexes were good. She jerked her head to her left, just in time, and so it only skidded off the side of her head.

By then I was halfway towards her, but only halfway, and I knew that wasn't going to be enough. The seconds were flowing like treacle, and she had ample time to refocus her aim and to put a nice neat hole in any part of my body she chose. She would have too, if the bedroom door hadn't opened at exactly that moment, distracting her yet again, as Xavi appeared. It was only by a fraction of a slow-moving second, but it was enough.

I grabbed her arm with my left hand, seized the pistol with my right, ripped it from her grasp and hurled it behind me into a corner of the room.

Never in my life would I have let a bloke do what she did next. She kicked me with the toe of her small, black-shod left foot. She missed what she was aiming for, but she did catch me on the inside of my thigh, sending a spear of pain shooting through it, followed by numbness.

My grip on her loosened; she wrenched herself free and started past me, after the gun. Xavi was useless; speed was never his strong point. Hector wasn't, though. He was still on the floor, but he grabbed her ankle, delaying her long enough for me to do my best to ignore my dead leg and get some movement going.

She kicked Hector too, on the jaw, then stamped on his wrist to free herself. By that time the only way to the pistol was through me. She tried it too; her right hand went to the pocket of her chalet maid's tunic, and came out with a flick knife, the sort of weapon that was banned in Britain fifty years ago, the sort of weapon that Carrie McDaniels' Moroccan had pulled on me a few days before.

'You shouldn't have done that,' I warned her as she feinted a thrust with the blade. 'You've picked the wrong man to pull a knife on. Drop it now, and you can walk away from this. Come at me with it, and you won't like what happens.'

Her eyes blazed at me. A movement behind my back told me that Xavi had recovered the pistol.

'Come on,' I murmured. 'You're a pro. You're beat and you know it, so don't be silly.'

'I'm never beaten,' she whispered, then lunged at me, lightning fast.

She expected me to step outside the line of the thrust as most people would, so when I stepped inside, and twisted my body round, it threw her off guard, and off balance. I seized her by the elbows, immobilising her arms, and then lifted her clean off her feet, as I turned and stepped through the open doorway, on to the terrace.

'Don't say you weren't warned,' I whispered, as I looked her in the eye. Then I threw her, up and outwards.

Maybe I'm stronger than I realise, or maybe the distance was less than I thought; or maybe I knew exactly what I was doing.

She flew backwards until her calves caught the timber guard rail, then she tumbled backwards out of sight, soundlessly, without a whimper, far less a scream.

I stepped up to the edge of the terrace and looked over. Hector and Valentina hadn't been kidding when they told Pilar that the chalet was built into the side of the mountain. In fact it stood on the edge of a precipice, a sheer drop of at least three hundred feet, probably more.

The killer woman was still falling. As I watched she smashed into an outcrop of rock, bouncing off it and on to another, head first, then finally through a tall snow-laden tree at the foot of the cliff, before disappearing from sight into the Andorran forest.

When I turned, the two guys were staring at me. I shrugged as I stepped back into the chalet, leaving the doors open behind me.

'What would you have done?' I asked. 'She wouldn't have stopped until she killed me, and then you two and Valentina.' I looked at Xavi, the gentle giant. 'Could you have shot her, my friend?'

He lowered his eyes, then shook his head.

'What do we do now?' Hector asked, his voice tremulous.

'You leave everything to me.'

Twenty-Five

I called Julien Valencia, on Xavi's phone. He was at home, anticipating an afternoon at the football with his son . . . the poor sod turned out to be an Espanyol supporter . . . but when I told him my story, he arranged for the kid's granddad to take him instead.

'We found them in a chalet in the mountains,' I said. 'We hadn't been there long when we were interrupted by the killer. It was a woman; not what we were expecting, but her height matched the forensic clues from the Battaglia murder.

'She was dressed as a chalet maid, so Hector let her in. She held us at gunpoint, and she would have shot Valentina, but the poor lass panicked and jumped off the balcony.'

'What happened to the killer?' he asked.

'She ran for it. She stole a car, as far as we can see.'

'What have you done? Have you reported this to the Andorran police?'

'I thought you might like to do that, then get the fuck up here. You must have a helicopter at your disposal, yes?'

He did. By the time he arrived, we had been joined by a sizeable chunk of the local constabulary, but not by the top man himself, who was, as it transpired, a Barcelona follower and en route at that time to an away game in San Sebastian.

The local detectives took statements from Hector and Xavi, in which they told the same story I had fed to Valencia. They took nothing from me, since there wasn't an English speaker among them and once again I'd conveniently forgotten all the Spanish and Catalan I've ever known.

It didn't take their dogs long to find the body in the forest. It had been stripped almost naked by the trees, so there were no questions raised by its being dressed in a maid's uniform. The face had been smashed beyond recognition and beyond dental identification . . . even supposing that Valentina Barsukova's records had been available for comparison.

However it didn't come to that; the body was taken to the morgue tagged as 'Barsukova V, Russian national. Suicide.' I heard later that the honorary Russian consul in Andorra arranged for it to be cremated, and attended the ceremony as a mark of respect.

He didn't have much choice in the matter, for something else had happened before Julien Valencia's arrival. Using Hector's laptop, Xavi had written his first story in years, and filed it as an exclusive on every digital newspaper in the InterMedia group.

It was a detailed account of how and why Valentina had been hunted and hounded to her death, and of the collateral murders of Bernicia Battaglia and Jacob Ireland.

He named the killer as Ana Kuzmina, a reasonable guess since that was the name on the driving licence that we'd found in a bag in the chalet supplies building, and handed to the police. He added the assertion that she had been sent on her mission by 'powerful interests in Moscow', stopping just short of saying 'the Russian government'.

The message got through regardless. Twenty-four hours

later, the Russian Embassy in Madrid issued a statement condemning the death of one of its nationals, and promising all assistance in the hunt for Kuzmina.

And the real, live, Valentina; what about her? By the time the police arrived she had crossed the border, heading south in her Skoda Yeti, registered in her new name . . . which I will not share with you . . . back to her new life and her new job as a bookkeeper in the city of Segovia, just north of Madrid.

In a few months' time she will be admiring *Guernica* in the Reina Sofia gallery when her eye will be caught be a charming man in his early thirties.

They will get talking, do the things that new couples do, a drink, a quiet dinner in a nice restaurant . . . but definitely not Fatigas del Querer . . . and will go on to live happily ever after, I hope most sincerely.

Hector went back to Barcelona with Julien Valencia, in his helicopter. Since the Battaglia murder investigation had a 'success' tick against it, his interview was a brief formality, and he was able to visit his recuperating father and his mother in hospital, before taking a taxi north, as we had done twenty-four hours earlier, to be reunited with his ostentatious Porsche Boxster.

As for me, I did, as you can imagine, brood for a time over my duel with Ana Kuzmina, and its outcome. Heading away from the snowline in the passenger seat of the Range Rover, I searched within myself for a scrap of guilt over the fact that I'd tossed her off the balcony, accidentally or otherwise, instead of knocking her unconscious, tying her up and handing her over to the Mossos d' Esquadra.

I couldn't find any. She was a murderer and a torturer. She could also handle herself pretty well, so trying to restrain her could have gone fatally wrong. And if I had been compassionate, the world would have had to discover that Valentina was still alive, and another hit man would probably have been set on her trail.

I can live with the way it ended, and so, happily, will everyone else . . . apart from Ana Kuzmina.

Xavi was preoccupied too on the way south. He said very little for most of the way, and it wasn't until we reached Vic that he started to open up. I'd assumed he was brooding over what he'd seen me do, but I was entirely wrong.

'Am I a dinosaur, Bob?' he asked me, out of the blue.

'You're bigger than quite a few of them,' I chipped back.

'You know what I mean.'

'Are you hidebound in your business thinking?' I said. He nodded.

'I don't know enough about it to be definitive,' I told him, 'but I do know that what Hector said, about people other than its owners having an interest in a company, that's spot on. When I was a kid in Lanarkshire I saw the steel industry disappear up its own arse; a great deal of the blame for that could be laid on its management's lack of foresight.'

'How do you think I should have handled Battaglia when I met her?'

'Come on,' I laughed. 'I'm a simple plod.'

'Then give me your simple view.'

'If you insist.' I paused. 'First off, I'd have asked her to put it all in writing, before giving any sort of response. While she was doing that, I'd have done a lot of research. Some of it would have been on her, to find out how strong her business really was. The rest would have been on my own position. Then when a formal offer came in I'd have put it to the board and to the senior staff.'

'That's all very good, but what would you have done when she threatened to take your life?'

'You saw that a few hours ago.' I frowned. 'In circumstances like those I'd have gone to her major shareholders and sounded them out about a reverse bid. What I wouldn't have done was stay sat in my comfy chair and laugh her off.'

'Mmm,' he murmured, his brows forming a single thick black line.

'My profession has never been dynastic,' I continued. 'Yours could be. What do you want for Paloma, down the road, or for Ben?'

'Between you and me,' Xavi growled, 'I don't like Ben very much, so I don't dwell too long on his future. I'll do anything for him that his mother asks me to, but that's all. My daughter, however, yes, you're right. I'd like to pass something on to her.'

'Then listen to Hector, and to his father, because they see the future a lot more clearly than you do.'

He promised that he would, and then we carried on, to Girona and back to the park where I'd left my car.

He asked me if I'd like to come back to the *masia* for dinner and one more night. I thanked him, for the prospect was attractive, but I felt that I'd been out of contact with my life and family for too long, and being under my own roof was part of that.

Then he asked me, awkwardly, to send him an invoice for the time I'd spent on the hunt for Hector.

I told him, without a hint of awkwardness, that I don't have a private investigator's licence, and that even if I did, he could fuck off, that friends were friends and that we'd been out of each other's lives for too long.

We parted with a handshake and a promise to keep in touch, and I drove back to L'Escala.

I got there at eight fifteen on that Saturday evening, travel-soiled and hungry. I stuck my used clothes in the washing machine, then had a shower and dressed decently, for I didn't fancy freezer food and had decided to eat out. Finally I was able to put my phone on charge, and so I did that too, before reaching for the landline to call Sarah.

All the adrenaline had gone from my system. I felt drained, lonely, and I wanted to be at home with my kids, the surest way of banishing an image I knew I'd see very soon in the night, a replay of the look in a woman's eyes as she realised that she had indeed chanced upon the wrong bloke to threaten with a knife.

I picked up the handset and as I did, I saw the 'message waiting' symbol in the LCD window. Hoping that Sarah hadn't been worrying about me, I hit the button and listened.

But it wasn't her. No, it was Alex, and she sounded as close to frantic as I'd ever heard her.

'Pops, how long are you staying in bloody Madrid? Your mobile's on permanent voicemail. I need you to get in touch with me, for something bad's happened here. Like they used to say on telly . . . there's been a murder.'

Twenty-Six

I ran for it.

I backed away from the body in the chair, my foot slipping on the rodent-like thing that turned out to be Coyle's dislodged hairpiece, then turned on my heel and legged it out of there.

I didn't stop until I was back in my car, in Slateford Road. I sat there, wide-eyed, working to control my breathing and waiting for my heart to stop trying to pound its way out of my chest.

As soon as I was steady, and back in control, I called my father . . . what else would I do? . . . but his mobile came up as unavailable. It sent me to voicemail, but there are some messages that can't be left.

What I should have done next, indeed what I should have done first, was dial the three nines.

I should have, but I didn't. I'd gone there to find out about Linton Baillie, thinking of myself as a tough lady who was ready for anything, only to bolt like a startled rabbit when I found that I wasn't.

'Come on, girl,' I said to myself. 'You're better than that.'

I eased myself back out of my car, and headed back to

Portland Street. I looked around as I walked for anyone and anything that didn't seem right, but nothing was moving and no shadows lurked in doorways.

When I returned to Baillie's front door, I realised that I'd shut it behind me as I fled. That might have stopped me in my tracks, but when I tried the handle, using the sleeve of my Afghan to keep from messing up the forensics, I found that it was off the latch.

I went back inside. I didn't believe that anyone else would be there, but on the off chance I kept my hand on my pepper spray, while my other rested on a thin high-intensity torch that doubles as a baton. (A present from my father. He'd have given me an extending baton, but they're illegal . . . he'd point out that most weapons used in the commission of crimes are illegal, but criminals don't mind that.)

Coyle was still in the big chair when I went back into the living room, and he was still just as dead. *Twelfth Night* was still unfolding on the Bose radio, but it was wasted on him. However, I noticed something I'd missed before: a bottle of white wine, opened, on a low table, with two glasses, one half full, the other empty.

I've seen enough stuff not to be squeamish, so without standing too near, I leaned towards him and took a closer look.

I hadn't imagined the mark around his neck, it was red and it was vivid. He'd been garrotted, by a wire, or something else fine and strong enough for the job.

Dad never gave me blow-by-blow accounts of crime scenes when I was growing up, but I know enough to realise that the complete absence of marks on his fingers meant that he'd been taken by surprise by the strangler. He must have been wholly wrapped up in his Shakespeare, or what-ever else he'd been listening to when he'd met his end.

But what the hell was he doing there? There were only two possibilities. One was that Tommy had fancied his chances of getting into gullible, ever-so-grateful Lexie's quick-release knickers and had made up the meeting with Baillie, inviting me to his place rather than his own.

The other was that Tommy Coyle actually was Linton Baillie.

Beyond doubt, I should have called the police at once, as soon as I found the body, or, allowing for my panicky exit, as soon as I'd recovered my composure in my car. I knew that I couldn't delay it for much longer, but I decided to take a couple more minutes to look around, to see if I could nail down those answers.

Before I started, I went into the kitchen and found a pair of disposable gloves; no need to leave evidence of my curiosity.

The first thing to strike me was the impersonal look of the place. There was nothing on view to give any clue to the person who lived there; not a single family photograph, no pictures on the wall, none of the favourite things that we all collect and keep around us.

Whoever lived there didn't seem to want to be known.

I went back into the kitchen and opened the fridge. There was nothing in it but some eggs, a tub of butter substitute, half a dozen bottles of Miller Draft, and one of the same Tesco white wine that stood opened on the coffee table next door. Nothing short-term. No vegetables, no fruit, no milk. I looked in the cupboards; I saw plenty of tins, but no bread.

I touched the second wine bottle; it was nowhere near

refrigerator cold, so it couldn't have been there long.

If it was indeed Tommy Coyle's place, and Linton Baillie was an alter ego, it didn't look as if he'd been living there lately; neither had anyone else, for a while.

I rummaged through the kitchen drawers, and through a sideboard unit in the living room, looking for utility bills, or anything else bearing the occupant's name.

There were none to be found, but that wasn't completely surprising; I don't have any either since all my household business is done online, with paperless billing. The fact is, it's entirely possible to live these days without leaving a paper trail behind you.

There were two bedrooms. One was pristine; the bed was made up, but didn't look as if it had ever been used, and the wardrobe was empty, save for a man's light raincoat and a black tuxedo.

The other was much more lived-in. There was a clock radio by the side of the bed, and a couple of books. One caught my eye: a true crime story about a Glasgow hoodlum, not by Linton Baillie, by another writer whose name I did recognise from bookshop browsing.

I thought of my own putative synopsis. *Had Mr B been picking other people's brains?* I wondered.

I moved into the bathroom, and that's where it started to get interesting. It was a man's place for sure, with Gillette blades and Nivea toiletries in a cupboard below the wash-basin.

The toothbrush was electric, on a stand with a container. I flipped the lid open and looked inside; there was only one head and it looked almost new.

And something else: a tube of hair gel for a man. I know

guys get up to some funny stuff, but I've never heard of anyone putting Brylcreem on a toupee.

I went back into the bedroom and looked into the wardrobe. It was full; I took out a suit and held it up for inspection. It was M&S but at the top end of their range, a modern cut that did not look like Tommy Coyle's style. I checked the waistband on the trousers: thirty-two inch. The dead guy next door had been high thirties, minimum.

No doubt about it: poor little Lexie had been set up. I wondered whether, if I searched Tommy's pockets, I'd find a tab of Rohypnol, or a similar date rape drug.

I was tempted to take a look, but I didn't. Instead I contented myself with a quick peek into the bedroom drawers. Shirts, socks, underwear filled all six.

Making a mental note to bin the stuff that Andy had left in my bedroom as soon as I got home, finally I took out my phone and called the police. To speed the process, I asked the communications centre to put me through to the divisional CID office in Torphichen Place. I was in their territory and knew they'd be attending.

'DI Singh,' a deep voice announced as my call was answered. As I'd hoped, someone I knew.

'Tarvil,' I said. 'This is Alex Skinner. Remember me?'

His chuckle made me think of molasses. 'Who could ever forget you? What can I do for you?'

'I'm in a bit of a predicament,' I began.

'Locked yourself out your car?' he asked, cheeky sod.

'Not exactly.'

Twenty-Seven

The uniforms beat CID to the scene but not by much, which was just as well, because an over-enthusiastic rookie constable was about to do her career prospects no good by putting my wrists into plastic restraints.

She'd ordered me to leave the apartment. I'd told her that the detectives would bring me back in as soon as they arrived, but she'd decided to use force.

'Stop that!' Acting Detective Inspector Jack McGurk bellowed as he stepped into the living room. He was followed by Tarvil Singh, and by two crime scene officers, all four wearing disposable tunics.

The PC ignored him and looked at her sergeant for guidance; he'd been in the kitchen and had missed our confrontation.

'For fuck's sake, Annie!' he shouted. 'D'ye no' ken who that is? Get the fuck down the stairs and secure the entrance. Let nobody in except folk that live here and let nobody out, nobody at all.'

Annie shot me a look that said, 'I'll remember you,' and left the scene.

'Go and join her, Bill,' McGurk told the sergeant. 'We're

going to need room in here and, besides, you're not sterile.'

The veteran looked up at him. 'I wish your faither had been,' he said, affably, then did as he was told.

I'd finished my search while I waited for their arrival. Linton Baillie was still a mystery, but he existed, that I'd established to my own satisfaction.

There was a roll-top bureau in the sitting room, alongside the window, with a high-backed typist chair tucked into the kneehole. I'd expected it to be locked, but it wasn't; inside I'd found a stack of receipts and credit card slips against the First National Mutual Visa that Sauce had told me about.

One of the slips was clipped to a receipt for a laptop computer, an expensive piece of kit that he'd bought a year and a half earlier. Of the computer itself, there was no sign.

'Question time, Alex,' McGurk said, as he approached me. I was standing in the corner of the room that was furthest from the body, since I was the only person there who wasn't in a tunic.

'Before we go any further,' he added, 'do you want me to get word about this to the chief?'

'Which one?' I replied.

He must have detected a trace of bitterness in my voice, for he raised an eyebrow, and murmured, 'Oh yes? Trouble?'

'Let's not complicate this situation further, Jack,' I retorted, 'by bringing my private life into it. I've already tried and failed to contact my father, but I'm not going to make life difficult for you by bringing Andy into this.'

'Appreciated, but if I don't tell him, he might go ballistic when he finds out. I'm only acting DI, remember, while Becky Stallings is on maternity leave. I don't fancy torpedoing my chances of confirmation.'

'You won't,' I assured him, 'but if you have to, tell him I asked you specifically not to because I didn't think it appropriate. Andy's above and beyond this level of incident, so you've no reason to report it to anyone other than your line manager. Who is that, incidentally, under the new set-up?'

'It's still Mary Chambers, although the word is she's going to Lothians and Borders and Sammy Pye's taking over. Big changes all round,' he added. 'Maggie Steele's the chief's designated deputy and Mario McGuire's the DCC in charge of all crime. Any word,' he added, 'on what your dad might do?'

'When he decides,' I said wryly, 'I'll be the first to hear.'

'Mmm,' Jack murmured, then he snapped into professional mode.

Singh had drawn the curtains and was standing beside the body as the DI joined him. 'Cause of death's pretty obvious,' he observed.

'Yes.' Jack glanced back in my direction. 'Was he dead when you arrived, Alex?' he called out.

For all that I've known him for years, since his spell as my father's exec, that made me shiver. He's a good detective and he has to deal with what's before him, regardless of the personalities involved. At that moment all he had to deal with was a dead body, and me in the same room.

'Obviously,' I retorted.

'Not to us,' he countered. 'The pathologist will give us a time of death, but for the record, what time did you get here?

'Just after eight.'

'Your call was timed in at eight twenty-three?'

'I know.' I told him most of the truth; that I'd found the body, bolted in blind panic, then recovered my courage. I left out the part about searching the place.

'Okay. Now tell me . . . who the fuck is this guy and what were you doing here?' He grinned. 'He doesn't look your type.'

I've been around cops all my life, so I'm used to graveside humour. I can even play the game.

'To be honest,' I said, 'he doesn't look any worse dead than he did alive; maybe even better, because he wore a really bad hairpiece. His name was Thomas Coyle, but I didn't think I was coming here to meet him.'

'Explain?'

'It's a long and complicated story, but I'll do my best. My father's just discovered that he's been stalked for the last few months by a private investigator. He didn't know until he went to Spain, at short notice, and found her there ahead of him.'

'Where's she from?'

'Edinburgh, as far as I know.'

'What's her name? I know some of the licensed PIs around here. If she isn't accredited, we'll have her.'

'Carrie McDaniels.'

He nodded. 'I've come across her. She's ex Military Police, and she does have a permit. She's not great, but she's dumber than I thought if she's taken on a contract to snoop on the gaffer. Who's her client?'

'His name is Linton Baillie, and he's an author. Coyle's his agent. I thought I was coming here to meet Baillie.'

'Why?'

'To find out what he's playing at, and put a stop to it,

322

whatever it is. My fear is that he's writing some sort of sleazy biography of my father. He's already approached someone who was once close to Dad, trying to coerce her into meeting him.' I hesitated, and he picked up on it.

'And?' he said.

I decided that I knew him well enough to confide. 'He may have uncovered some very personal stuff, Jack.'

'Are you going to tell me about it?' he asked, gently.

'I wouldn't hesitate if I thought it was relevant to your investigation, but for now I'd rather not.'

'It's that personal?' I nodded. 'Okay, leave it for now. But Alex, this I must ask. If you were coming here for a serious talk with this Baillie man, why the hell are you dressed like a student?'

I explained how I'd introduced myself to Tommy Coyle, and his invitation to meet Baillie.

He considered my story, then voiced the question that I'd put to myself earlier. 'Does this so-called writer really exist, or is he only a pen-name for Coyle?'

'I'm pretty sure that he does, but I'll grant you that Coyle could have created a second identity. You'll have to decide that for yourself.'

'What does he write, this guy?'

'True crime stuff.' I told him about my talk with Clarissa Orpin, and the story about the angry namesake of a deceased London gangster. 'His bestseller is a so-called exposé about MI5; from what his editor said it's done pretty well.'

'Well enough for MI5 to want him silenced?'

'Come on, Jack, I hardly think so, do you?'

'Maybe not,' he conceded, then he smiled. 'I hope you took precautions.'

I stared at him.

'I hope you wore gloves when you looked around this place.'

'I . . .'

'Come on, Alex, you're a Skinner. You could never resist playing detective.'

'No comment.' I grinned back at him. 'But I'll bet you find that the clothes in the wardrobe wouldn't fit Coyle, suppose you boiled him for a week in a sauna.'

'So what was he doing here?'

'There's no fresh food in the kitchen, so it looks as if Baillie's away, and Coyle had the run of the place. If that's so, my assumption is that he had ambitions of doing me.'

'From the sound of it, that's a reasonable explanation. Does the gaffer know about this, Alex?' he asked. 'Does he know you were coming here?'

I nodded. 'Yes, and I got the "Be careful" lecture. I came prepared.' I showed him the contents of my bag.

'You didn't bring a length of cheese wire as well, did you?'

'Don't be funny.'

'What makes you think I am?' he countered. 'If I was another officer, one who didn't know you from Adam, I'd be thinking that on the basis of what I've been told so far, and what I've seen here, you've got a potential motive for this murder, and here you are standing over the body.'

'Standing here, because I found him. I reported it. Would I have done that if I'd topped the bloke?'

'It's been known,' Jack pointed out. 'In fact, it's pretty common; domestic homicides, arguments between friends that go too far, it's often the perp who calls it in.'

Then he grinned again. 'But this man is definitely not your

type, so I'll cross you off the suspect list . . . for now.' He winked. 'In this new set-up I might come under pressure for a quick result, in which case you'll be a handy backstop. They say that our new chief constable's turning into a megalo-maniac.'

'He can turn into a fucking frog, for all I care,' I snapped.

'Ouch!' He winced. 'I don't want to know that.' He paused, then went all cop. 'Is there any other help you can give us? Did you see anyone when you arrived here?'

'No, I'm afraid not. I saw nobody, and heard nothing, apart from the radio. I have to say, though, that in the short time I spent with him this morning, the late Mr Coyle didn't strike me as a Shakespeare buff.' The Bose was still playing; no one had bothered to turn it off.

'You mean he might have switched on to listen to something else, and been killed before that started?'

'Yes. If so it might help establish time of death.'

'True. Good thinking.'

'One other thing, Jack,' I added. 'I didn't turn the place over completely, but I did find a receipt for a laptop in that desk over there. There's no sign of any computer, though.'

He nodded. 'Okay, thanks for that, Alex. Maybe it's hidden somewhere. We'll be doing a full search, obviously, as soon as you're gone. We'll need a formal statement from you for the murder book, but it needn't be tonight.'

'Do you want me to call into Torphichen Place?'

'No, it's okay. We can come to your office.'

'I'm working from home just now,' I explained.

'Fine, we'll come there, Err,' he hesitated, 'will there be any problem if it's Karen Neville that does it?'

Detective Sergeant Neville is Andy's ex-wife, back in CID

and on Jack's team. 'You should ask her,' I replied. 'I'm fine with it. To make it easier for her I'll draft something out. If she's happy with it I'll print it and sign it.'

'Fine,' he agreed. 'I'll tell her to call first to agree a time. Off you go, then, and let us get on with things. The first thing we have to do is establish the victim.'

'I've told you who he is.'

'Yes, but that's not what I mean. I walk in here and I see a man sitting in a comfy chair, my first thought is that he must be the householder. But if what you're saying about the clothes is right, he's not; he's someone else. So I have to ask, and answer a question. Did the killer make the same mistake?'

'Whatever,' I said, 'I hope you catch him. Tommy might have been a sleaze bucket, but that shouldn't get you killed.'

I hoisted my bag on my shoulder, ready to head for the door. 'One last thing, Jack,' I added. 'If you do find Baillie's laptop hidden somewhere, my father and I wouldn't mind knowing what's on it.'

'I can imagine,' he agreed. 'But do you want me to know?'

Twenty-Eight

In the aftermath, I was glad that I didn't sleep a wink that night. Only a seriously maladjusted person could have enjoyed an untroubled night after an experience like the one I'd had.

By the time I made it home, my composure had more or less worn off. If there was ever a time I needed Andy, that was it. I came close to calling him, asking him to come round; I even thought about landing on his doorstep.

But in the end I was strong enough not to; I'd never have forgiven myself if I'd gone limping back to him at the first moment of crisis. Jack McGurk might never have forgiven me either, if the chief constable had taken a personal interest in his murder investigation.

Instead of all that I put on some calming music, and poured myself a calming glass of Rioja. As I sipped it I thought of Dad, in Spain. I'd called him first, of course, as soon as I was back in my car, but his goddamn mobile went straight to voicemail, as before.

What would he have done? I thought. As a private citizen, probably much the same as I had. Then I changed the question. *As a cop, what would he be doing now?*

He'd be trying to trace Mr Baillie through that address, I decided.

It's very difficult to live a completely secret life in a modern state, even one that's fairly liberal and doesn't go in for routine monitoring of its citizens. Just for fun, I switched on my computer and logged on to a website where you can trace registered electors.

I entered Baillie's name and address: it came up blank. I tried another that checks the whole public record. There were plenty of the clan in Edinburgh, but not a single forename that matched.

That avenue was closed off; I tried another. Baillie had a credit card and it was active; that meant he had to be servicing it through a bank account. On my first search I messed up the name, but second time around I found the First National Mutual site. Yes, it did have a banking division. I tried to log on to it under the user name 'Lbaillie', with a made-up password. It was rejected, but only as 'password incorrect'.

A small step, but if I could take it, Jack McGurk could go a lot further.

I was pouring my second glass of Rioja when I realised that there was someone I could call. If I couldn't sleep, why the hell should Mia?

I hadn't deleted her message from my voicemail, so I was able to retrieve her number. When I called it, I got her answering service. She'd left her mobile number on it; I noted it then dialled it on my own.

She wasn't alone when I called; I could hear music in the background but other sounds as well, the clunk of glasses, other people's voices. 'Who's this?' she asked suspiciously, before I'd had a chance to speak.

'It's Alex. Sorry to interrupt your party.'

'It's not. I'm at a club.' Suspicion turned to anxiety. 'What's wrong? Has something happened to Ignacio?'

'No, he's safe and sound. But Linton Baillie may not be.' I explained what had happened.

'And the police think whoever did this got the wrong man?' she asked, when I was finished.

'I don't know what they think, not yet, but that's the way it seems to me.'

'Isn't that a pity,' she murmured. Her apparent indifference surprised me.

'It is for Thomas Coyle, although . . .'

I paused to gather my thoughts, and to play back what I had seen in the flat, a detail that had seemed insignificant at first, yet which fitted with other pieces of the puzzle.

'There was a hall table, and I noticed a few days' worth of junk mail, addressed to "The Occupier", lying there. Now, I reckon that Coyle picked them up on his way in, which would mean that Baillie hasn't been at home for a while.'

'So what?' Mia asked.

'The calls you had, the one to the radio show and the one to your home, were both traced to an Edinburgh number. I'm wondering whether Coyle made them. In fact I'm sure he did.'

'Which means that Baillie could be anywhere; is that what you're saying?'

'More than that,' I replied. 'It means that he really doesn't want to be found.'

'That would be very wise on his part. I don't care where he is, as long as he stays there and doesn't bother me again. Here,' she exclaimed, 'you don't suppose he killed this man Coyle, do you?'

The notion hadn't occurred to me. I doubted that Jack McGurk would fancy it either. Even if they had fallen out, or Coyle had become an embarrassment, to do someone in in one's own front room did not seem like the act of a sensible man . . . or even a sane one.

I left Mia to her clubbing and tried to get some sleep, but as I've said, I didn't get close. I gave up around 1 a.m. and spent the waking hours studying, then listening to music after my eyes ceased to focus properly, but my brain couldn't shed the image of a dead man staring up at me from an armchair.

I've never felt as lonely as I did that night, and yet somehow, once it was over, I felt stronger too, and more independent.

As the day started to make its presence felt, I could see that it was pissing down outside, so a run wasn't an attractive prospect. Instead, I took the car up to the Royal Commonwealth Pool, and swam for a good thirty minutes. I felt more awake after that, and a cold shower.

Back home, I put a pot of coffee on the stove, then fixed myself a couple of bacon rolls. When they were done, I settled down in front of the telly to catch up with current affairs on the BBC news channel.

I nodded off halfway through the second roll, and with the coffee untouched. I have no idea of how long I slept, but it must have been less than an hour, for I was wakened by the ringing telephone at five past ten.

My head was mush as I answered, but I did my best to sound alert. After all, it could have been a client . . . Easson Middleton has many friends.

It wasn't. Instead it was a cool, measured female voice.

'Alex, this is Karen, DS Neville for the purposes of this call. Jack McGurk's asked me to call on you to take your statement about the suspicious death in Portland Street.'

She sounded very formal, I wondered whether she wasn't too keen about having to pay a house call. 'I'll come to you,' I offered. 'I don't mind.'

'No, we'll do it as the DI wants it. What time would suit you?'

God, I'd promised to draft something before she arrived, but it had slipped my mind in the course of the night.

'How about eleven thirty? Would that be too late?'

'I'll see you then.'

All of the renewed energy I'd found in the pool seemed to have disappeared. I felt drained and crotchety. Indeed I was so narked that when my dad's mobile still showed up unavailable, I rang the house number in L'Escala and left a terse message for him to await his return from his mystery trip to Madrid . . . whenever the hell that might be.

That done, I booted up my computer and keyed in an account of the previous day: my hunt for Linton Baillie, without elaborating on the reason for it, my 'undercover' visit to his agent, and the appointment that had led to me finding Coyle.

I finished it at five to eleven, leaving time to brew some more coffee ahead of time for my visitor's arrival. I can't deny that I was a wee bit nervous. The relationships between Karen, Andy and me have been complicated, but in the eyes of most people, mine among them, she has never been in the wrong in any sense. She was sinned against and he and I were the sinners.

However, in my defence, Andy and I sinned just the once.

He was in Edinburgh, he visited me in my flat in Stockbridge, and what happened took both of us by surprise. If it had stayed between the two of us, then probably I wouldn't be talking about it now, but it didn't, thanks to some nasty snooping bastard who found out and spread the story, with pictures.

The marriage hung together for a while after that, and it was only after it had ended, on the ground of mutual indifference, I was assured, that Andy and I began a new relationship. As far as I knew, or rather as far as he told me, Karen held no grudges, but I'd never heard that directly from her.

She arrived bang on time. I buzzed her in, told her where the lifts were, then went to the landing to greet her.

She was dressed pretty much as I do for work: dark suit, skirt rather than trousers, high heels but not precipitous. I was dressed like a slob, in tracksuit bottoms, my Yes for Scotland sweatshirt, and sheepskin-lined slippers. Her hair was immaculate, mine was a mess, just combed through and pulled back in a ponytail. If she'd ever seen me as a femme fatale, that illusion was shattered.

I didn't know how to play it as I showed her into my home. If she'd been planning on keeping it strictly professional, she cracked after a couple of seconds.

She looked round the place, nodding. 'Very nice, Alex.' She walked across to the doors that lead on to my tiny balcony and peered through the glass. 'Lovely view, too.'

She turned and looked me in the eye, properly, for the first time since she'd stepped out of the lift. 'Do my kids come here?' she asked.

'They have done,' I admitted. 'Before you ask,' I added, 'when they have been, those doors were locked . . . always.'

I frowned, slightly. 'It's not something you need worry about from now on,' I said, as I walked towards the tray where I'd put the coffee pot and two mugs.

'Does that mean . . .' she began, as I poured, but stopped short. 'Sorry, none of my business what it means.'

'Of course it is, Karen,' I told her. 'I've seen a lot of Danielle and Robert at the weekends, since you've been back in Edinburgh, and back in the job. You have a right to know about it. So go ahead, ask.'

She did. 'Are you moving too?'

'No, I'm not. I'm going nowhere. I was asked . . . in fact it was implied that I should.' I felt an involuntary half-smile as I added milk to the mugs and handed one to her. 'I didn't react well to the lack of consultation, I'm afraid. We've had a bust-up.'

I thought I might see a little triumph in her eyes, but I didn't, just genuine concern. 'You'll patch it up, surely.'

'No, we won't . . . at least I won't. We should never have got back together.'

I paused, then added, 'And here and now I apologise to your face for what happened between us when you and Andy were married. That was not planned, I promise you; I'm ashamed of it.'

'It's okay,' she said, as we seated ourselves. 'I got over that a long time ago. There was history between you two, I know that; unresolved issues. Plus, Andy, for all his faults, was never a serial adulterer, and I don't think you are either. The kids like you, and they tend to be good judges. They'll miss you.'

'And I'll miss them.' As I spoke the words, I realised the truth of them. 'However, Andy is right; we're two career-driven people. That was the problem first time around, and it's happened again.'

'That's a pity.' She grinned. 'How did he take it?'

'Not well,' I admitted.

'He wants me to move too.'

That took me by surprise. 'But you've only just come down here from Perth,' I exclaimed.

'That doesn't matter to Andy. He's buying a house in Glasgow and he wants me to do the same.'

'Just like that?'

She nodded. 'Just like that. He's even pointed me at a DI post I should apply for. The damnable thing is I probably will. There's nothing to keep me here, and it will make things easier for the children.'

'No new relationship?' I ventured.

Karen laughed. 'Hell, no. I did think I might have had something going, last summer. I was seeing a guy, but it ended in disaster. He was a widower, so we took it gently. Not gently enough, as it happened; the first time we got naked, he burst into tears. He just sat there on the edge of the bed and said he couldn't do it. That was bloody obvious too, from what he had on show. I beat a hasty retreat. So much for Internet dating.'

'I'll make a note to avoid it,' I promised. 'Good luck, whatever you decide.'

'Thanks,' she said. 'Now to business, yes?'

'Sure.' I went to my desk and retrieved the draft statement that I'd printed. 'I've put that together for you. If you've got any additional questions, fire away.'

She read it through, carefully, then looked up at me. 'Everything?' she asked.

'Everything . . . including the part where I admit to having a look around the place while I was waiting for the police to arrive.'

'In that case it's fine. Print out another copy, we'll sign both, and I'll leave one with you.'

'Okay,' I agreed, then took her by surprise by asking if she had a business card on her. She did, and handed it over.

I went back to my computer and ran off the second copy. While I was there, I did something else.

As I returned to my seat, Karen looked up at me. 'Jack says I can share some things with you,' she announced. 'He told me your father has an interest in what this man Linton Baillie's been up to.'

'That's good of him. Dad's in Spain just now, and out of touch, but when he does contact me again, it's the first thing he'll ask me. What have you got?'

'We've established that the council tax on the property is paid by direct debit, drawn on an account with the First National Mutual bank, the holder being Linton Baillie. The same's the case with the utilities bills, gas, leccy and phone. They're all settled through the same account. Everything's done online.'

None of that surprised me, but I didn't tell Karen.

'We're looking elsewhere,' she added. 'Passport Agency, DSS and so on, but those buggers take their own time.'

'You didn't find a computer?'

'No, but you didn't expect us to, did you?'

'Not unless he'd hidden it in the toilet cistern, like they did with the gun in *The Godfather*. It does confirm something, though, doesn't it? Or rather its absence does.'

She frowned. 'What?'

'It knocks on the head the outside chance of Coyle and Baillie being one and the same. Coyle was in the flat, but the laptop wasn't. I've been in his office; he has a computer there, an old Windows thing. Baillie's laptop, the one described in the receipt I found, is an Apple; hardly compatible, so I doubt you'll find it there.'

'Wherever the laptop is, so is Baillie?'

I nodded.

'I have something I can share with you,' I told her. 'My father sent me a couple of images that he took off the silly woman who was paid to trail him. They include one of a man; we don't know who he is for sure, but he might just be Mr Baillie. I've just emailed it to you; you might want to show it to the neighbours.'

She nodded. 'Thanks, Alex. I'll discuss that with Jack, as well as your thought about the missing laptop. Speaking of the acting DI . . .' she finished her coffee and rose to her feet, 'he's expecting me back before lunch. If anything else occurs to you,' she said, as I showed her to the lift, 'let us know.'

Actually something else had, but I planned to check that out for myself.

As soon as Karen had gone, I went into my bedroom and smartened myself up. I could have done so earlier but I'd chosen to let her see the other Alex, the one behind the quality clothes, the expensive hair and the make-up.

I didn't go the whole hog in changing, but chose jeans, a plaid shirt and a long waxed raincoat, with a matching hat, and my beloved Panama Jack boots.

The rain had gone, but not too far away, as I set out. I walked through Holyrood Park, heading east, sticking to the grass rather than the roadway, as I didn't want to be splashed by passing traffic. On another day I might have stopped to count the swans in the loch, but I had business in hand.

I'd been to Meadowbank House before. It's an ugly seventies office block, on London Road near the Jock's Lodge junction, but it's screened off by greenery and the only thing that most people notice is the entrance. Its looks belie its purpose, for it houses one of our most valuable public resources, the Land Register of Scotland.

I walked in off the street, found the customer service centre and put a request to the desk officer. Ten minutes later I walked out of there with a history of the ownership of twenty-seven slash two slash c Portland Street, from its construction in the first year of the new millennium to the present day. It didn't answer all my questions, indeed it begged a couple, but it told me one thing. Linton Baillie might pay the council tax on the property, but it wasn't his.

I took the bus to my next port of call; while Meadowbank House will tell you all you want to know about Scotland's property, Register House is the place to go for answers about its people.

I spent half an hour in there; when I came out I knew quite a bit more; although it didn't relate to anything else in the inquiry, it did leave me feeling pleased with myself.

Back home, there was a message showing on my phone. I'd hoped it was from Dad, but no, it was Roger McGrane, telling me he'd booked a table for a pre-show dinner in a restaurant near the Festival Theatre, and offering to pick me up.

When I called him back, Mrs Harris told me he was busy, so I left a message with her saying simply that I'd see him there. I wasn't ready for him to know where I lived. It would take another couple of dates for us to get there, if we ever did.

I'd planned to go to Torphichen Place with what I'd found, so I was surprised when it came to me, just after three thirty, in the person of Jack McGurk.

'I thought I'd drop by to say thanks,' he explained, as I let him in. 'I had that image shown to as many neighbours as we could raise, three to be exact. Two of them identified him as Linton Baillie.' He sighed. 'Mind you, it's the only bloody positive we've had today. Baillie doesn't have a UK passport or a UK driving licence; he doesn't even have a National Insurance number. It looks like he isn't a UK citizen. I've spoken to his publisher, but she was no help. She told me that when a writer sells as many books as Baillie for a small house like hers, he can be as mysterious as he fucking likes.'

'Then add this to the mix,' I said. 'He might live at Portland Street, but he doesn't own it.'

'You sure?' he exclaimed.

'I'm certain,' I replied, handing him a foolscap envelope with all the information I'd dug up on my midday safari. 'You can't find Baillie, but that will give you someone else to look for.'

He beamed at me. 'In that case, Alex, you've earned this bonus. We didn't find Baillie's laptop, either in the flat or at Coyle's place . . . which was definitely his residence, by the way. However, we did find, in Baillie's bureau, in a drawer that you must have missed, an external storage device, the kind you plug into a computer to make a back-up of the hard disk.'

He reached into a pocket and produced a memory stick. 'There's lots of stuff on it that'll be of interest to the gaffer, so,' he handed it over, 'I made a copy and it's yours, with my compliments.'

I'd have plugged the thing in as soon as he left, but he hung around for a while, and screwed up my timetable.

Out of politeness I offered him a drink, not thinking he'd accept, but he did, a bottle of Coors light, one of a few that I'd put in the fridge for Andy. I poured myself some of the previous night's red and we chatted for a while.

I asked him about his fairly new second marriage, and he sympathised with me over my relationship; I'd dropped a big enough hint to him the night before that it was in the crapper, so it hadn't come as a surprise when Karen confirmed it when she got back to the office.

'Thanks,' I said, 'but worry not. I'm fine about it, and so is he.' I checked my watch. 'As a matter of fact, I have a date tonight.'

He chuckled. 'Same old Alex. I didn't think you'd be lonely for too long, but twenty-four hours, that's pretty quick off the mark.'

'Just dinner and the theatre,' I insisted.

'What are you going to see?'

'I have no idea,' I admitted. 'Whatever's on at the Festival Theatre.'

Jack managed to grin and shake his head at the same time. 'Like I said, same old Alex. Is this one a cop?'

'No fucking way,' I snorted.

Twenty-Nine

I dressed conservatively for the theatre, not too much glam; this was in part because I knew it would have been over the top in the restaurant Roger had booked, and also because I didn't want to lead the guy on.

Before calling a taxi to take me there, I checked on the entertainment ahead: a musical based on sixties Californian pop. I'd have preferred *Jersey Boys*, but it was okay. I was definitely not in the mood for Wagner.

The taxi took longer than promised to pick me up so I arrived a few minutes late. My date was there; I could see him through the glass wall, studying his watch with a frown that I can only describe as impatient. The street light nearest to me was out and so he couldn't have seen me, even if he'd looked straight at me. I paused, feeling suddenly uncomfortable.

I was brought up to believe that the eyes are windows to the soul. In some people the face is an open doorway.

Have you ever caught a person off guard and seen something that you hadn't suspected was there? That's what happened to me, right there on that cold pavement in Nicolson Street.

I looked at Roger McGrane and I didn't see the urbane,

charming, attractive man that I'd seen in his own environment. I saw someone else; someone cold, calculating and predatory. I knew for certain that if I went to his car wherever he'd parked it, I'd find a bag, with a change of clothes for at least one day.

If he'd caught sight of me what would he have seen? I've no idea but it wouldn't have been the Alex he'd met. She was, as I'd told him, in a comfortable long-term relationship. She'd also been in denial, unwilling to admit that said relationship was constraining and ultimately pointless, and possibly, no certainly, she'd been throwing out signals.

Hadn't he said I was 'wonderfully direct'?

A lot can happen in a couple of days, as it had to me. Andy and I had stopped pretending; in the process I'd re-established my identity, and asserted my ambition. I didn't need to flirt with a superficially attractive man, who was, when seen off guard, distinctly unattractive on the inside.

And something else had happened.

Twenty-four hours before I'd dressed in another fashion to meet a man. I'd kept that appointment and been faced by a sleazy sexual predator, even though he was dead. (Jack had told me that afternoon that when they'd emptied Coyle's pockets at the mortuary, they'd found a packet of condoms, and a till receipt from SemiChem.)

As I looked at Roger McGrane through that glass wall, from my position of invisibility, his impatient, bored face was replaced by two visions of Tommy Coyle, leering at my tits in his office, and then lolling dead in Linton Baillie's chair.

I backed away until my date was out of my line of vision, then turned and waved at the first taxi I saw. 'He's all yours, Mrs Harris,' I murmured, as I climbed in.

341

On the way home, I called Sarah. She had brought the kids to her house in the Grange for the weekend, so I asked the driver to take me there instead. We had almost arrived when my phone sounded. The screen showed a number I didn't recognise, but I guessed who it was: I bottled it and rejected the call.

Sarah . . . I call her my sometime stepmother . . . does the best corned beef hash in the world, and she never under-estimates, so there was enough for me when I got there. I didn't say much; I just played with Seonaid and let James and Andrew do the talking, until it was time for them all to go upstairs.

As soon as the field was clear, Sarah fetched two beers from the fridge, handed one to me and settled down beside me on the sofa. 'Shitty day?' she murmured. 'Sorry, kid, but you look whacked.'

'Shitty week. Completely fucking crazy. Even by your adventurous standards I'll bet you've never had one like it.'

There are very few people I'll allow to see me cry, but she's one of them. I let myself go for a couple of minutes then when I was composed again, I took her through it, right to the end. By that time I was feeling a little guilt about Roger.

'I left the poor guy sitting there like a lemon,' I said, 'after he'd come all the way through from Glasgow. He'll be angry and I won't blame him.'

I took my phone from my pocket and saw that I had one voicemail message. I played it back, on speaker. It was Roger, of course, but 'angry' had been an understatement. Pure, foul, threatening vitriol spewed out, until I couldn't listen to any more and cut it off.

Sarah's eyes were on fire. 'Gimme,' she growled, taking the mobile from my hand. She found recent calls and hit the number. She'd left it on broadcast, so I heard Roger when he picked up. 'Yes?' he crackled. He was on the road.

'Dr McGrane,' she began. 'My name is Sarah Grace, associate professor of Pathology at Edinburgh University. I'm calling to tell you that after the message you've just left for my troubled stepdaughter, I am really looking forward to performing your autopsy, the sooner the better.'

'Maybe I over-re—' he began.

She cut him off in mid-word. 'Too late, mister. Think on this as you drive home. The pathology work your lab gets comes directly from me, and people like me. There aren't too many of us, and I know them all. You can start to plan for a life without that income stream.'

She hit the 'End' button and dropped the phone on the sofa.

'Christ, Sarah,' I exclaimed. 'Now I really feel sorry for the man.'

'Then don't. There are two sorts of guy in this world. Them that are gentlemen, and them that are not.'

She took a swig of her beer. 'I knew about Mr Coyle,' she told me. 'I opened him up this morning. Jack McGurk was there to witness, and he told me you'd found him.'

I nodded, dumbly.

'This thing you're doing for Bob,' she continued. 'Is it a threat to him?'

'I dunno,' I confessed. 'There was a threat to Ignacio, potentially, but I dealt with that at the prison. I won't be able to see the broader picture until I've looked at the contents of Baillie's computer. I'll do that when I go home.'

'You'll do it tomorrow,' she countered, firmly. 'You're going to stay here tonight. You've got the weight of the world on your shoulders. A major career change would be enough to carry on its own, without all the shit that's been thrown at you this week. You need a good night's sleep and I don't trust you to get it at your place, so you are going to hit the pillows upstairs.'

I did, and I hit them hard. I turned in not long after ten, and was still sound when Seonaid wakened me next morning at eight fifteen. Sarah was taking her to meet Santa Claus that morning, and she couldn't wait any longer to tell me about it.

After breakfast we tried to call Dad, but with no more success than the day before.

'What do you think he's up to?' Sarah asked.

'I have no idea,' I told her truthfully, then laughed. 'My only worry is whether this McDaniels girl, the one I told you about last night, might have pushed him too far and he might be in jail.'

She shook her head. 'Nah, I don't see that. Bob's too fond of women to kill one of us. No, it'll be something mundane that's keeping him out of touch. You know how he is. He has a brilliant mind, but don't ask him to pack his own suitcase.'

I went home from Sarah's feeling a hell of a lot better. When I got in, there was a new message on my landline. It was from Roger, contrite and apologetic. I wasn't surprised after the way Sarah had sunk the boot into him.

Rather than call him back, I wrote to him . . . yes, a real letter . . . saying that I was sorry for my no show, but explaining that it just hadn't felt right, and that experience had taught me not to start anything I wasn't prepared to finish. I found a stamp in a kitchen drawer, went out and dumped the missive in a postbox in the Canongate, then went back home to attend to the business I'd postponed from the previous evening.

I put the memory stick Jack had given me in a USB slot in my computer, powered it up then clicked the icon that appeared on the screen.

Whoever Linton Baillie was, he was organised. His computer management was clear, with his life set down in a series of folders, in alphabetical order.

They began with 'Bank'. I'm sure that on his laptop it would have been password protected, but he hadn't done that with his back-up disk. I clicked on it and got straight in, expecting to find account details, credit card statements and so on . . . but all I found was email correspondence, mostly incoming from First National Mutual and none of it meaningful.

I scrolled down the list; there was one called 'House', and another labelled 'Travel', but the others all appeared to relate to projects. A couple meant nothing to me, but 'Glasgow' and 'MI5' were in line with his list of publications.

The one that caught my eye, though, the one that hit me was headed 'Skinner'.

I clicked on it and went straight in.

It was arranged in a series of sub-folders, headed 'Carrie invoices', 'Carrie reports', 'pics', 'research' and 'manuscript'.

I opened the first. When my father called me, almost eight hours later, I hadn't taken a break, and I was still reading.

Thirty

I left the message programme and dialled Alex's number. As it began to ring, it occurred to me that she might not be in; then she picked it up and I was filled with a feeling of sadness that my daughter should be home alone on a Saturday night.

'What's happening, love?' I asked, anxiously.

'Pops,' she exclaimed, 'where have you been? I've been trying to raise you for ages. Why were you in Madrid anyway? Did it have to do with the McDaniels woman?'

It wasn't the time to go into detail. 'No,' I assured her, 'nothing at all. I had some business there and forgot to take my phone charger. I'm sorry if you've been worrying and sorry I wasn't there when you needed me. Now what the hell is this about a homicide?'

'It's Linton Baillie's agent,' she blurted out. 'I thought I was going to meet Baillie, but when I got there Tommy Coyle was waiting for me, and he was dead.'

My heart jumped into my mouth. 'You found him?' *Talk about running in the family*, I thought. *Like father, like daughter.*

'Yes. And I ran for it, Pops. I did a complete girlie thing and got out of there as fast as my legs could carry me.'

'That was exactly the right thing to do.'

'Then I felt like a childish fool,' she continued, 'so I went back.'

'You did what!' I shouted.

'I went back in there,' she repeated, 'and I made sure that he really was dead and then I called the police, and waited for CID.'

'Who took the call? Who's the SIO in the investigation?'

'Jack McGurk. It was his territory: Slateford.'

That calmed me down, immediately. McGurk had a spell as my executive officer; he's a good detective, calm, methodical, efficient. (As a manager and a mentor, I've always tried to excise my own weaknesses from the people under my command and guidance.)

'How did he die?' I hoped Alex hadn't been exposed to the things I'd seen that week.

'He was strangled, with a leather thong, but it wasn't left there. Sarah did the post-mortem; she told me she found fibres in the mark round his neck. Jack came to see me yesterday. He said that the Yale was unlatched . . . although I knew that . . . and that Coyle was probably taken completely by surprise. That was certainly how it looked to me,' she added. 'Very professional.'

'Jesus, Alex,' I sighed. 'How close did you get?'

'Close enough.'

'I hope you didn't screw things up for the CSI team.'

'I was careful, Pops.' She sounded hurt by the mere suggestion that she might have.

'Do they have a result yet?'

'Not a sniff, as of yesterday.'

'Mmm.' I couldn't help it; satisfied that my daughter was okay, I was in full detective mode. 'You went there expecting to find somebody else,' I said. 'I wonder if the Slateford Strangler did as well.'

'That notion's occurred to Jack and the team,' she told me. 'But it's pure supposition as yet. However,' she continued, 'we are closer to Linton Baillie. Our friendly DI gave me a copy of a computer storage disk they found; I've been going through it all day, and Pops, it's very interesting. You're right; you've been under the spotlight.'

'That I knew,' I replied. 'I've had a long talk with Ms McDaniels.'

'Who's been well paid for her time,' she retorted. 'I have copies of all the bills she submitted to her client. Better than that, I know what he looks like. Those images you sent me, the man on the beach: it's him, identified by the neighbours.'

That didn't surprise me too much, but what she said next came from out of nowhere and rocked me back on my heels.

'Baillie lives in Portland Street all right, but the strange thing is, he doesn't own it. I've been to the Land Register Office, and to Register House. The property belongs to a man named Ben McNeish; he appears to have inherited it four years ago, from his late father; his name was Gavin McNeish.'

That hit me harder than anything I'd experienced all week. I'd been emotionally detached from Battaglia and Jacob Ireland, but what Alex had told me was like a grenade being lobbed into my own front room.

'I want to see all this stuff,' I told her, 'everything.'

'It'll be ready for you when you come home.'

'No, love, I want to see it now: tonight. Email it to me, everything you've got, including your detective work on McNeish.'

'I will do, Pops. But when are you coming home? I could use you being around right now.'

'That's understood, kid,' I assured her, 'and I promise you I'll be back as soon as I can. I've done what I came here to do . . . and a hell of a lot more besides. Just send me that stuff now. Once I've dealt with it, I'll be able to book a flight.'

I left her to do as I asked. While I was waiting, I opened my computer and opened the image files from Carrie's SD card. I scrolled through them until I found the ones that had been taken on Gullane beach, in which the man had been captured.

As I'd expected from my earlier study, there was no full-face image; I chose the one that came closest to it, and set to work. Using an edit programme I cropped the face, eliminating the background, then enlarged it as much as I could without losing quality.

Putting on my reading glasses and leaning close to the screen, I studied it, trying to remember as many of Ben McNeish's features as I could. Then I closed my eyes and tried mentally to strip away the beard from the man that I'd met on only one brief occasion.

When I opened them again, I wasn't certain that they were one and the same, but eighty per cent was good enough for me to be confident that Xavi's stepson was Linton Baillie.

A tone from the speakers told me that Alex's email had arrived; in fact there were three of them, as the attachments were too big for a single transmission. I opened the first and saw a message that said, 'Concentrate on this one. It's the most relevant.' I could see why she'd said that; the folder that it carried had my name as a label.

I downloaded it then clicked it open, to find four sub-folders. I ignored the first; Carrie McDaniels' hourly rate wasn't of interest to me, even if, as she'd boasted, it was higher than police officers' pay. But her reports were: I opened that folder and saw that they were listed in date order.

As she said, she'd been on my case since early summer, and following me sporadically for seven months. The early reports were pretty bland; if I'd been keeping a daily journal myself, its entries would have looked much like they did, with a little more colour.

I couldn't be arsed reading them all, and so I went straight to the date that was of most interest to me, that on which Ignacio had made his appearance in the High Court to plead guilty to culpable homicide. I opened it and read:

Significant development: as you instructed today I went to the High Court to photograph people going in and out. To my surprise, the subject arrived. He was hailed by a woman who was unknown to me. They spoke briefly on the pavement with no outward sign of affection.

They went into the court building and I did likewise. They went into the first courtroom and again I followed; it was busy but the woman took a seat on the bench reserved for family members, and the target found a place in the row behind. The accused was a teenage Spanish boy named Ignacio Centelleos, who pleaded guilty to the manslaughter (*Should that be womanslaughter? <g>*) of his grandmother.

It was revealed in court that Centelleos was arrested in L'Escala, Spain. You will be aware that the subject has a holiday home there. Monitoring reveals that he was likely to have been there at the time of the arrest, although not under our observation. Although she was not identified in court, I am certain that the woman is the boy's mother, who was named in the proceedings as Mia Watson by the advocate depute.

*** Moreover, having been able to observe them both in the same room, it is beyond doubt that there is a strong physical resemblance between Centelleos and the subject. This may explain the subject's unexpected private visit to the Forest Gate Laboratory in Glasgow, which I observed and photographed. Certainly I recommend a search of birth records in Spain. ***

When the hearing was over, Centelleos waved to the woman as he was taken out and called out something in Spanish which may have been '*Adios, madre*'. The woman and the subject left the courtroom separately, but met up again outside where I was able to photograph them. They went into Cafe Saint Giles and stayed for twenty minutes. As per your telephone instruction, when they left I followed the woman, rather than the subject. She went to a large house below Blackford Hill, where she used a keypad to open the security gate.

Relevant photographs are attached with this report.

I closed the file, admitting to myself that just maybe Carrie was better at her job than I thought. If she hadn't been a bit unlucky in revealing herself to me in L'Escala, I might never have known she was tagging me.

I frowned. One thing still puzzled me. Carrie had assured me that she had never met her client, and I'd believed her. Was I wrong about the man in the photograph, or had she been lying?

I put that consideration to one side and opened the folder headed 'pics'. I expected a show of thumbnails, but instead I found more sub-folders, headed 'Associates', 'Career', 'Domestic', and finally, 'Women'. I chose the last, and clicked on it.

This time, the thumbnail images did appear. I sat bolt upright in my chair. Every woman in my life was there, Sarah, Alex, Myra, Aileen . . . even my mother. She was wearing evening dress, in a grainy black and white shot that must have come from the archives of *The Motherwell Times*, my local paper when I was a kid. As I looked at it, I remembered it, taken at a civic dinner she'd attended with my father, on one of their rare public outings together. Myra's image was taken from a newspaper too; I had given it to a journalist when she was killed, to get him off my doorstep.

There were more: Maggie Steele featured, in her chief constable's uniform.

Paula Viareggio McGuire, Mario's wife, in a designer frock.

Alison Higgins; dead all these years, it still tugged at my heart to see her, in an informal shot that I remembered appearing in the *Daily Record* after her death.

Leona McGrath: Sarah and I adopted her son Mark after her death. I hoped that was the only connection between us that had been made.

Mia, of course; from the background I knew that it had been taken outside the High Court.

There was one other and she set the hair prickling at the back of my neck: Pamela Masters, my biggest ever mistake, of whom the least said the better.

I felt my face twist into a scowl as I closed the picture folder and opened 'Research'. That proved to be a series of links to newspaper websites, and scanned images of stories in which I was involved, from the early stages of my career.

One of those was from the *Courier*, the Dundee-based daily; it dealt with the discovery of the body of my brother, Michael, in a house in Perth. It wasn't my case to investigate, since it was in Tayside territory, but I was quoted, accurately. I said that Michael's life had been troubled, and that he and I were estranged. I added that I was shocked and saddened by his death. The first might have been true; the second certainly wasn't.

Along with the press stuff here were several documents titled 'Questionnaire interview transcript', each with a different set of initials as a suffix. I clicked on one with the letters 'JC'; it was a record of a conversation with a man called Jackie Charles, courtesy of the Governor of Shotts Prison, which had been his home for several years.

I knew Jackie well; it took me years to put him away. For a short while he and I were near neighbours in Gullane. Myra and I were in our twenties; we socialised with them, because Myra was somewhat smitten by their car dealer lifestyle, and because I didn't know any better at the time. She was killed not long after that, the Charleses left the village and before I knew where I was I was investigating his other businesses, which involved bank-rolling armed robberies and the like.

Jackie had a lot to say about me, and my wife, including the claim that he had shagged her at a party. That would have shocked me too, if I hadn't known that it was true, from Myra's secret and comprehensive diary, which I only got round to reading years after her death.

Making a mental note to visit him when he got out of jail, I moved on to a transcript subtitled 'AD'. At first sight, I'd wondered who that might be, but when I saw the name Alafair Drysalter, I wasn't surprised. I checked the date; the interview had taken place three days after Carrie had followed Mia to the house beside Blackford Hill, where Alafair lived with her ex-footballer husband Derek.

In stark contrast to Jackie Charles, she had said very little about me . . . probably because she didn't know much. She'd been guarded about Mia too, but she had revealed that her father . . . *'His name was Perry Holmes; he was a business-man'* . . . had brought her into the family when she was fifteen, to rescue her from a background in which she was being exploited and sexually abused.

The transcript showed her being unable to link Mia with me, beyond saying that I had investigated the murder of her brother, when Mia had been working as a radio presenter on an Edinburgh station. She did say that Mia had told her that she fancied me, but she had left Edinburgh abruptly, and nothing had come of it, as far as she knew.

I glanced through the other transcripts. One was from a name I didn't recognise, even when I'd got past the initials, 'WM'. It was only when I got into the substance of the interview that I remembered: William Macken had been a detective constable in the Serious Crimes Unit that I'd taken over on promotion to detective superintendent.

He was a lazy, insolent boozer, and I'd got rid of him so fast that I'd never even got to know his first name. He'd volunteered the information that I was 'screwing yon lassie Higgins, at the time' and that I'd kept the interview with Mia Sparkles – her radio name – for myself and 'his gopher, yon Martin that's the chief constable now'.

All the time I was looking for the initials 'PM', but since not even I know where Pamela Masters is – and believe me, I check for her every so often – no amateur snooper was likely to find her.

But one set of initials did catch my eye: 'CM' set me wondering, and I could only come up with one name to match. I confirmed it by opening the transcript. Cameron McCullough is a Dundee businessman known universally as Grandpa, on account of having become a grandfather at the age of thirty-six. As I told you earlier, that granddaughter, who bears his name, is now Sauce Haddock's partner.

Since he operated off my patch, he and I don't know each other very well, and so I wondered what had made him an interview subject. I was none the wiser after I'd read the transcript. Neither could Linton Baillie have been, for McCullough had no information about me to offer, and he told the truth when he said that we'd only ever met once.

I set that folder aside and moved on to the main course, 'Manuscript'. It contained only one file, a document in Word format, entitled 'The Secret Policeman'. I opened it and began to read the preface.

Throughout a thirty-year career, Chief Constable Robert Morgan Skinner has forged a reputation as Scotland's toughest cop, and as one of its most successful detectives. This book will show that these two qualities are linked as it looks behind the scenes at Chief Constable Skinner's career and life, and will highlight a third, a ruthlessness that has made him feared by colleagues, friends and foes alike, and saw him banish his only brother to a life of hopeless alcoholism in a hostel for the homeless.

'Will it indeed?' I growled as I read. 'If all that's true . . . how fucking stupid have you been to do this?'

The narrative began in my childhood. The author had done

his research well, to have found Charles Donnachie, a month before he died last summer, aged ninety-six. Mr Donnachie was a lawyer in Motherwell, senior partner in what was the largest practice in town until my father's firm challenged its supremacy and eventually supplanted it. The old man had never forgotten that, it seemed, or forgiven it.

William Skinner was a cold man [he was quoted as saying]. He had no friends, only clients, rivals and acquaintances. The commercial side of the law and his own enrichment were his only interests, and he crushed anyone who stood in his path with the cold power of a steamroller.

I remember both of his sons. Michael was a colourful character, a popular boy about the town, and a natural leader, as he showed when he joined the army straight from school and won a commission. Robert, on the other hand, was a withdrawn, sullen child, with a coldness about him that was the equal of his father.

I met him a few times, when I had occasion to visit William Skinner's office. It was his eyes that I recall most clearly. Even as a child they made me a little afraid. As a teenager he showed me why, when he drove Michael away from the family, and the town. One day the poor lad was there, the next he was gone.

'And I remember you, old Charles,' I whispered. 'You were one of the few men my father ever spoke badly of. "A *drunk, a danger to your clients' funds and a waste of a law degree*," was what he called you. For all the disparity in your ages, you and Michael drank together in the Ex-servicemen's Club . . . drank a lot.'

I steeled myself and read on. As I read, it seemed to me that the book was looking at my police career through a window of distorted glass that bent it out of shape. The implication was that I intimidated colleagues, witnesses and criminals in equal measure. It quoted men like Macken, and others, among them Greg Jay, the sleaziest man I ever worked with, who took payment in kind from prostitutes for allowing them to work with only token interference from his officers.

Jay alleged that I'd forced him out of a key investigation, that I'd shopped him to Alf Stein, our boss, and that I'd covered up an improper relationship (I hadn't, and it wasn't) with a fellow officer, Alison Higgins. It was vicious stuff, yet it was close enough to the truth to make it hard to challenge legally. Yes, we did clash over a case, and Alf did give him a rocket. As it happened, I'd been in the right but in fact I had made no complaint; Alf hadn't needed one, not after he discovered that Jay had spied on Alison and me, at my home.

The Jackie Charles view came through loud and clear too. My interest in him was personal, the book claimed. I'd discovered his affair with Myra, and I hadn't stopped in my persecution of him until he was in prison. He'd lain in fear of me for years, he said, and when his car showroom was torched and his wife was killed in the blaze, he'd suspected that I was behind it.

I'd caught Charles and was being blamed for it in the book. I'd failed to catch Tony Manson and that was held against me too. The text suggested that I was a regular visitor to Manson's house in Cramond . . . I was, but always with a fellow officer, and my visits were always related to some blag I knew, but couldn't prove, that Tony was behind.

And then there was Pamela Masters.

I'd been steeling myself for her appearance in my life story, but when it came, the narrative missed the mark completely; it wrote her off as a piece of heartless philandering on my part, exposed, to my embarrassment, by a journalist called Noel Salmon, described, inaccurately, as 'fearless'. I noticed that particular piece of shit hadn't contributed to the research for the book; he was as long gone as Pamela, and if he knew what was good for him, as far away.

There was other stuff, lots of it; the book was comprehensive, and I have to admit that it asked some pretty good questions.

For example, it focused on a political assassination in Edinburgh, just after I'd become an ACC. It had ended in gunfire, I'd shot a gunman, two other people had died and Mario McGuire had taken a chest wound that might have killed anyone but him.

Despite all that, no one ever came to court and there was never any form of public inquiry into the massacre. The Baillie text asked, Why not?

More than that, it asked another good question. The official account, released to the press, said that I'd been shot in the leg in the incident. In that case, the book wondered, why had I been pictured walking away from the scene in a newspaper photograph?

Then there was the murder of the wife of the Secretary of State for Scotland and the kidnap of their child. Andy Martin and I had recovered the wee girl, but again, no one had ever come to court charged with the crimes. That was true, and it was another box that nobody wanted to see reopened.

I read into the night, until I reached the end of the manuscript . . . but not the finished work, I reckoned. The book ended abruptly, with Ignacio's arrest in Spain, his extradition, and his court appearance. As I'd expected, there was the suggestion, based on circumstances and facial resemblance, that he might be my son.

'*One more question for Bob Skinner to answer,*' it ended.

I closed the file, and leaned back in my chair, considering everything that I'd learned that evening, and putting all the events in order. It was well after midnight and I was much in need of sleep. However, I knew what I was going to do, first thing in the morning.

Thirty-One

'First thing' turned out to be ten thirty, by reason of me having to go out for breakfast, since I was starving and had no food in the house.

Instead of going to the old town I drove down to the suburb of Riells. It was much busier than I'd anticipated, having forgotten that it was Sunday and that the street market would be in full swing, but I was lucky, and found a pavement table in the sun. The weather had changed and it was warm enough to sit outside.

A tortilla baguette and a coffee later, I dug out my mobile from my trouser pocket and called Xavi. I'd picked up a copy of *GironaDia* on the way there; it lay on the table in front of me.

'Hello, Bob.' He sounded just a little anxious. 'Is everything okay?' Meaning I guessed, *Have there been any awkward questions from Andorra?*

'Sure,' I said. 'Everything's put to bed. That's a cracking front page in your paper today,' I added. 'I wish I could read all of it.' The Valentina story had blown everything else away.

'Isn't it just,' he agreed. 'It'll run for days, too. There are police all over Europe looking for Ana Kuzmina. Good luck to them.'

An unfortunate waste of resources, I thought, *but there's nothing I can do about it.*

'Yes indeed. Where do you go from here?'

'Upward,' he replied. 'I've just had a long talk with Joe.' He chuckled. 'Actually it was more of a lecture, from him to me. As a result we're going to make a move to acquire the BeBe group; he says it's been in a state of chaos since Battaglia's death, and its backers are open to any offer that'll secure the future of the business.'

'With you as CEO?'

'I'll have to be initially, but I've promised Sheila that it'll be short-term, until Hector's ready to take over the reins. He's right; digital's the future, Bob, and that's his world. I'm an inky-fingered guy.'

'Maybe I can be your crime correspondent,' I said.

'Are you serious? I'd have you in a heartbeat.'

I laughed. 'Language would be a problem.'

'Bugger that, I'll give you assistants who can handle that.'

'Thanks, Xavi, but a million times no, it's not what I do.'

'So what will you do? Become part of Police Scotland?'

'Never!' I retorted, vehemently. 'I'll campaign against its existence until the politicians realise they've made a mistake, and put it right.'

'In that case, I'll give you a platform. Come on the board of InterMedia.'

'What?' I gasped. 'What the hell could I possibly contribute to a media group?'

'Independent oversight of all our investigative activity, right across the group. We're a news business, Bob. Investigation's our heartbeat. You're a natural fit.'

'Yeah, sure.'

'I'm serious; I've talked this over with Joe and he's all for it. I was going to call you tomorrow to float the idea. Please, think about it. We're not talking full-time or anything like it; one day a week, maximum. We'll pay you three grand a day, sterling, net of tax, and we'll give you an office in the *Saltire* building; one in Girona as well if you need it.'

'For fuck's sake, Xavi!'

'Think about it.'

'Okay, I'll consider it,' I conceded, knowing even then that I'd accept, if Sarah agreed to it.

'Now,' I continued, 'to the reason for my call. Is Ben with you?'

'Ben?'

'Yes, I'd like to talk to him about something. It's book-related,' I added. 'That was his trade, wasn't it?'

'Yes, it was, but no, Bob, he's not here. He hasn't been for a few days, in fact. He's still off with that woman. We don't know who she is, either. I was wrong about the girl in the office, by the way. I checked, quietly. It's not her.'

'The secret world of Ben McNeish,' I murmured.

'Seems like it.'

'Maybe I'll investigate.'

'You do that, and if you find the little bastard, let me know. Cheers, my friend, and think very seriously about our proposition. The money's negotiable, by the way; that was just an opening offer.'

I ordered a sparkling water and a Magdalena, then picked up my newspaper, looking at it with a renewed interest that was almost proprietorial. Xavi's proposal had taken me by surprise. It wasn't the first offer of a directorship that had come my way in the previous few weeks, but it was the most attractive, and not just financially. It was a job that I could do, and give value for money, rather than being simply a name on the letterhead.

Eventually I pushed it to the back of my mind to get on with what I'd intended to do. Carrie McDaniels had never given me a business card, but she hadn't been hard to find. Before leaving the house I'd tracked her down on the Internet, finding her on a list of registered private investigators, with mobile number supplied. I keyed it in and called her.

'This is Carrie,' she answered, sounding assured and professional even on a Sunday morning.

'And this is Bob,' I replied, 'as in Skinner.'

'Uh?' A crack appeared in the façade. 'What do you want?'

'I need to see you. We've got unfinished business, Carrie, and I know you're not in Scotland. This can't wait; it has to be today. Tell me where you are. Don't piss me about, please; I'm not in the mood for it.'

'Why should I do that?' she demanded. 'You've given me a hard time ever since we met. I'm not tailing you any more. Even if Baillie asks me, I'm going to tell him I've had enough.'

'It isn't only you I want to see. It's Ben as well, but I don't want him to know I'm coming.'

'Ben? How did you . . .'

'I'm a fucking detective,' I laughed. 'Now, where are you?'

She sighed, and gave in. 'We're in the Parador de Aiguablava. Do you know it?'

'Yes, I can be there inside an hour. Don't think about running for it. The Mossos owe me all sorts of favours; they'd trace you for me, if I asked them.'

'We won't; we'll wait for you. But what's this about, Mr Skinner?'

'I'll tell you when I get there,' I replied. 'This isn't really about you; it's about Ben. Remember, say nothing to him, but his life could be in danger.'

I left her wondering, paid my bill and headed for my car.

In the summer the road to Aiguablava would have been busy, but in December it's quiet, even on Sunday. I'd said that I'd be there in an hour, but I wanted to make it faster than that, against the outside possibility that they'd do a runner, so I ignored the twisty coastal trail, heading instead for Palafrugell. I turned off north of there, at a place called Regencos, joining a road that skirted Begur and hit the coast north of my destination.

The Parador hotels are a Spanish institution that goes back over eighty years. They were founded in the pre-Franco days and have survived all the upheavals since, still state-owned and still providing luxury accommodation and dining in landmark buildings. I've thought for a while that if our royal family did a similar thing with all its property, there would be no need for the Civil List.

The Aiguablava Parador stands on a headland looking down on to the bay below. It isn't an historic building, as many are, but a squat three-storey structure, functional rather than pretty.

The sun was still casting light on to the terrace, but only just, as I strode towards the couple seated in the furthest corner. It was still short of noon but the cocktail hour seemed to have begun, if the tall glasses on their table were any indicator. Beside them I saw a silver laptop, closed.

Carrie saw me first; Ben's eyes followed hers. They were interesting, as they caught sight of me; they widened in the instant, then narrowed with suspicion, all in the space of a second, before a forced smile appeared.

'Mr Skinner,' he exclaimed. 'This is quite a surprise. Did my stepfather hire you to find me?'

I shook my head. 'No, Ben,' I replied. 'The truth is, I didn't find you. My daughter did.'

'I don't understand,' he murmured, but I could see reality beginning to dawn.

I smiled. 'Sure you do. She was looking for a man called Linton Baillie, who's been taking an unhealthy interest in me for the last few months. She didn't find him because he doesn't really exist; instead she found you.'

He stared at me. 'You've been drinking Xavi's Sangria,' he murmured. 'So has she, by the sound of it.'

I glared back. 'Imagine a man walking a greasy tightrope,' I shot back at him, 'in a high wind, over a lake of shit. You are that man, Ben, and I'm ready to shake the rope. You thought you were on a real winner, didn't you? I'm a public figure in Scotland and beyond, a controversial cop with a bit of a past, and you thought you could cash in on me.'

I took half a step towards him, and he flinched. 'The bugger of it is, you almost did. You came very close to pulling it off; indeed you probably would have, but for me turning up here, and finally running into your snooper. Very close, but the cigar humidor stays closed. The Secret Policeman's going to stay secret.'

'Do you think you can stop it now?' he asked, with a show of truculence.

'Oh yes,' I said. 'But I won't have to. You're going to abandon the project yourself, Linton, Ben, whoever you'd like to be.'

Carrie's face was a picture. If I'd ever doubted her claim that she'd never met her client in the flesh, it ended then. She stared at him. 'You're Linton Baillie?' she shouted.

Ben sat there, trapped, and in that moment silent.

I nodded. 'He is. Now ask him why he never told you.'

He sighed. 'I didn't see the need, Carrie,' he said, quietly. 'I sourced you on the net and hired you by email to do the surveillance job on Mr Skinner. Then I got curious about you, so I followed you.'

She looked ready to thump him. 'Does that mean that when we first met, in the Bank Hotel bar, that was a set-up, was it?'

'Not exactly. Yes, I'd followed you in, but you made the first approach, remember? It was you who asked me if I was waiting for someone.'

'So bloody what?'

'So you did,' he exclaimed, 'and I discovered I liked you. I could have said so long and left it at that, but I didn't want to. Then when we started dating, I thought it was kind of cool, since I was doing as much of the Skinner surveillance as you were. We could work closely together without you realising it.'

'And that way,' I chipped in, 'you could judge how accurate her reports were when she submitted them, since you'd been there for some of them.'

'No!' Ben protested. 'That wasn't it, not at all. I love you, Carrie, honest. It wasn't meant to happen but it did.'

'Then why keep secrets from me?' she countered.

'Linton was a secret from everybody. Not even Tommy Coyle knew who he really was.'

'Who the hell is Tommy Coyle?'

'Linton's agent: my agent.'

I didn't want to drop my bombshell just then. Instead I said, 'Let's start from scratch, Ben. How did Linton Baillie begin?'

'Casually, really. It goes back to when I was working in the bookshop. I was an assistant manager and that gave me access to detailed turnover figures. I could see which genres were doing best, and which were turkeys. Crime in general has always been good, but when I saw how many true crime books go off the shelves, it blew my mind. You must know that, surely, Mr Skinner.'

'Why should I?' I challenged him. 'I've spent my life immersed in true crime. The last thing I want to do when I get home is read about it.'

'Then you're in the minority,' Ben declared. 'When I saw those sales figures I decided to have a go myself. I started in London: I did some research on the old East End villains, then found one whose son had become a priest. I traced him and wrote a book from his perspective. Donside bought it. They only gave me an advance of two grand, but it earned out inside a month.

'They were hot to trot for another, but set in Scotland. I looked at the cast list of our organised crime, at who'd had a biography done and who hadn't. I decided to pick one who was dead, as I'd done with the London book.'

'To avoid the risk of your car blowing up when you switch on the ignition?' I suggested.

'More or less. Anyway, I chose James McGarrity, known as Jim the Cobbler, because he liked torturing people who upset him by crushing their feet with a device that he copied from one he'd seen in a museum.'

'How did you do your research?'

'Most of it I did online; the rest was through a questionnaire that I sent by post or email to retired cops who'd known him. They were only too keen to tell me stories, so it didn't take me long. Writing the thing wasn't hard. We're not talking Booker Prize here, you understand.'

I nodded my agreement. 'How did you find Coyle?' I asked.

'Through the *Writers' and Artists' Yearbook*. He was listed there.'

'Did he know who you were? Did you meet him?'

'I met him as Linton Baillie. I'd decided on that as a pen-name; I came up with it by blending the names of two pubs I know, simple as that. My London manuscript was finished by then; I showed it to him and he took me on. He did the deal with Donside very quickly, and the royalty money began to roll in, much more than I'd expected. To maintain my anonymity, I put it in an online bank account that I'd opened in Linton's name, minus Coyle's commission, of course.' He showed a flicker of a smile. 'Tommy's a real shyster. He wanted twenty per cent, but I'd researched that too so I knew that fifteen is tops. We settled on twelve and a half.'

'What about the flat?'

He peered at me, his eyes narrowing. 'How do you know about that?'

'Never mind. When did that happen?'

'I inherited it from my father, just before I finished the London manuscript. He and I had been in touch for years, but my mother never knew.

'Dad wanted it that way; he said she was better off thinking he was dead. He reckoned she'd been in love with Xavi since they met as teenagers. He was happy that it had worked out for her after he left, and that she should forget all about him.'

'What happened to him?'

'He died at work. He'd a stroke at the wheel, in his cab, in Italy. He left everything he had to me: the flat, his lorry, an insurance policy, and some invested cash. That's all in my own bank account,' he added, 'not in Linton's.'

'Coyle knew about the flat?' The question was rhetorical, but Ben didn't realise that.

'I had to give him a correspondence address. He's looking after it for me while I'm here.'

'So where do you actually live, Ben?' Carrie demanded.

'You know,' he protested. 'In my stepfather's place in Queensferry Street; you've been there. You've even got a toothbrush there, remember? That really is my home.'

'Leave your domestic till later, the pair of you,' I said, 'and get on with it. The McGarrity book was a success, yes?'

'Sure was. It was a bestseller in the genre, and Donside, my publisher, wanted another. I thought about it and came up with a synopsis about people who've died mysterious deaths that could have been linked to the security services: the man behind the Profumo affair, a couple of MPs whose deaths have never been properly explained, and so on. It was all supposition really; I was asking questions that I knew would never be answered.'

'Did it ever occur to you that winding up MI5 might not be a good move? Did you never imagine yourself becoming one of those questions?'

He frowned. 'No, not at all. Look, it's just a bit of fun.'

'And me,' I murmured, 'am I just a bit of fun? Are my children there for the amusement of your readers? Is my career to be trivialised, and damned by innuendo?'

His eyes hardened, as he showed me, for the first time, the real Linton Baillie, and the real Ben McNeish, the one that Xavi doesn't like. 'You're a commodity, Mr Skinner,' he said. 'That's all, a public figure, as you said yourself, for public consumption.'

'Not when you put my son in danger,' I retorted, matching his stare with one of my own, letting my anger come to the surface. 'Not when your agent calls his mother and threatens to out him to the media.'

Ben's mouth dropped open. 'Tommy did that?'

'Yes he did.'

'The stupid bastard!' he exclaimed. 'What the fuck did he think . . .'

'He thought he could extort another few quid out of us, I guess. You should have given him his twenty per cent.'

'Bloody hell!' He was rattled. 'I had no knowledge of this, Mr Skinner, I promise.'

'I believe you. I don't see you being so stupid. But it doesn't matter. He did it, Carrie got unlucky and I clocked her, and soon after that Mr Coyle got unlucky too. Now I know the whole story, I have a copy of your book on me, and I'm here to tell you that it will never see the light of day.'

'That's what you think!' Ben retorted, angrily. 'That book's worth a small fortune; you're a national name, Mr Skinner.'

Carrie had been studying me, looking and listening; her anger towards her partner seemed to have dissipated. 'Hold on a minute,' she murmured. 'How did this man Coyle get unlucky, like you said he did?'

'He was sitting in Linton's chair, in Linton's apartment, on Thursday night, pretending to be your man here, in the hope of getting his leg over an aspiring young writer, when somebody slipped a ligature round his neck and throttled the life out of him.'

Ben's expressive face sagged, and went white, his pallor in contrast with his black beard.

'You're blown,' I told him. 'Coyle was killed, but in your place. You know what that means.'

'Who killed him?' he croaked.

I spread my hands in a 'search me' gesture. 'How the fuck would I know? Anyway, that's the wrong question. You should be asking whether whoever it was meant to kill him, or did they mean to kill you?'

I let him think about that for a while, vindictively enjoying his pain, his fear, and his confusion.

'Looks as if you've really wakened the wrong bear,' I continued. 'It's not like the security service to make a mistake like that, but as your book suggests, it's not perfect. That said, it never gets it wrong second time around.'

'Mr Skinner,' Carrie whispered. 'They wouldn't . . . would they?'

I pointed in the general direction of her boyfriend. 'Ask him, he's the fucking expert . . . or he thinks he is.' I paused for a second. 'But this is gospel,' I went on. 'I know these people. I'm practically one of them. Now I also know who Linton Baillie is, what he looks like, and where he really lives.'

'No!' Ben yelled.

'No,' I repeated. 'I'll keep you safe, if only for your mother's sake. But here's the deal. Whoever killed Coyle got Linton as well, effectively. He no longer exists. He's closed for business.

'Ben McNeish can go away from here and do something useful with his life; for example, he can grow up, develop a conscience and marry this nice lady, having promised never to lie to her again.

'Your book would never have been published anyway,' I added. 'I'd have stopped it, without even having to go to court.' I smiled. 'But as added insurance, this is going in the sea.'

I took his computer from the table, walked to the edge of the terrace and tossed it.

The aerodynamic qualities of a lightweight laptop are quite remarkable. There was no outcrop of rock to break its fall as it floated outwards, then curved in a gentle arc before disappearing into the waters of the Mediterranean, with barely a splash.

'The police recovered your back-up device from Portland

Street,' I told him. 'They also found a copy of *The Secret Policeman* on Coyle's computer. They've both been wiped, accidentally, of course. If you have another, I want it, now.'

He looked up at me and shook his head. 'I haven't, honest.'

'In that case, we're done. One way or another, Linton Baillie is dead. Long live Ben McNeish . . . for as long as he's careful.'

'Do you want me to thank you?' he whispered, bitterly.

'Not for a second,' I answered. 'You should thank your mother. It's only for her sake that I haven't shaken you right off that fucking tightrope. Think about that book of yours, then look at me. Do you really think I'd have taken that without coming back at you as hard as I could?'

I turned to leave. 'If you'd like one last piece of advice,' I said, 'it's this. Take this nice lady back home, and introduce her to your mother and Xavi. She's gullible, but she's okay.'

Thirty-Two

I left them there and drove back to L'Escala, then went online, looking for the first flight available. I found one that left that same day out of Barcelona to Prestwick Airport, and booked it on the spot.

Alex picked me up, and drove me back to Edinburgh, to her place since I didn't want to rouse my own household at one in the morning.

We didn't talk much on the road, because I slept most of the way . . . and until almost noon the next morning. The only thing of import she did tell me was that Jack McGurk had no leads to Tommy Coyle's killer; that didn't surprise me.

She didn't ask me why I'd gone rushing off to Madrid, nor has she since. That was fine by me, for it wasn't something I was keen to discuss with anyone, especially not her. I couldn't lie to her, and if she'd asked me the wrong question . . . well, it would have been tough to explain.

Next day, when the kids came home from school, I was there for them. By the time Sarah came in from work, they were all fed and I had our dinner under way.

I'd done several other things by then. For example, I'd spoken to Mitchell Laidlaw and asked him to expedite my redundancy package from the police service. I didn't call Andy Martin. Instead, I allowed him to learn of my decision through formal channels. I knew it was for the best, and so would he.

If I'd phoned him, one of two things would have happened. Either he'd have tried to persuade me to change my mind and I'd have dented his ego by turning him down, or he wouldn't have, and made a big hole in mine.

Worst case for both of us would have been if I had decided to stay on in a manufactured capacity . . . having an éminence gris in the background doesn't work in football, and I'm sure it would be a disaster in the police service.

I'd also got in touch with Amanda Dennis, to thank her for her back channel help with Battaglia, and to decline her informal offer of a job in Scotland with the security service. However I did tell her that I was prepared to accept consultancy assignments, on an occasional basis, and that since I'd already been vetted from here to hell and back, she could consider me an available resource.

'That sounds like an even better option than having you officially on the strength,' she said. 'We all need our secrets, even me, and you'll be a good one to keep.'

I shared all this with Sarah, after dinner.

'I'm glad,' she confessed. 'I know how tough it's been to get to this decision, but it's the right one. If you'd stayed you'd have been going against your own principles, and that's not you. If your friend in Five keeps you busy, that's good too, as long as she never gives you a gun.'

She leaned against me, on the sofa. 'I'm not a psychiatrist,' she murmured. 'I'm even better than that; I'm your best friend. So I can tell you now what I should probably have told you a few years ago, before we broke up. The police service has been killing you, Bob, slowly and steadily over the years. Every case you've tackled, every burden you've borne, has eaten away a piece of you, body and soul. You've taken everything personally, your responsibility to victims and their families, and to the people you've had under your command.

'When you went to Spain you were in a state of emotional and physical exhaustion. I don't know what you did over there apart from think, but whatever it was, it's cured you. You look more relaxed than you have in years, and happier.'

'You know what?' I said. 'I feel it, too.'

'What did you do over there?' Finally, she did get round to asking.

'I helped some people to find a way forward. There was a trade-off, but it's all worked out for the best.' I smiled. 'Oh yes, and one other thing.' I told her about Xavi's offer of a seat on the board.

'That's great,' she exclaimed. 'You've put your life on the line for a salary. It's time you picked up some money for old rope. Accept,' she insisted, 'but hold out for five thousand a day. You're worth it.'

PS

So there I was, plucked from the depths of depression and confusion by spending a few days away from the pressure cooker in which I'd confined myself. In that time I'd been able to practise my true vocation in a private capacity, with no paperwork, no reporting chain, no nothing; just me and an intellectual challenge . . . with a little of the physical thrown in.

I'd loved it, and as Sarah said, it has restored me and made me whole again.

I have a new perspective on life, and my priorities are clear and unfettered by the responsibility of public service. They are, in no particular order, my family, my family and my family.

My older daughter's new career will take up my time, in an amount equal to that of my younger daughter's growing interest in the works of A. A. Milne, the Reverend Wilbert Awdry, and Roald Dahl, and her eagerness to be able to read them for herself.

I can observe and assist my younger sons' growth in age, size, and personality, and I will engage myself with their half-brother by visiting him, very privately, courtesy of Kemp, in the institution, and helping him plan what he'll do when he's released. On the day that happens, it'll be me who's waiting outside the gate.

I've already started work with InterMedia. (Xavi upped the day rate to four thousand without me having to ask.) The work is interesting, and I find that I'm contributing more than I thought I could, not only to the crime reportage of the group, but also to the training of young journalists in basic investigation techniques.

Amanda Dennis hasn't called me yet, but she will, of that I'm certain.

But . . .

But what?

Who did kill Tommy Coyle?

I still don't know, in that I can't put a name or a face to the person who strangled him, but I'm pretty damn close.

I'd been prepared to let the whole thing lie. I hadn't forgotten about Coyle, but far be it for me to butt into an official police investigation. The man had been killed, okay; so had Princess Diana, St Thomas à Becket, half a dozen prostitutes in Whitechapel, and JFK, but I couldn't do a hell of a lot about them.

Whatever I'd allowed Ben McNeish and Carrie to believe, I'd never accepted the notion that the security service was behind Coyle's death. Such things look good on telly, but they don't actually happen.

Nor had I bought into an alternative theory, that an associate of the late James 'Cobbler' McGarrity might have done it. Nearly all of those guys are either as dead as he is, or they're in care homes. Even if there is one still out there, he wouldn't have the guile to pull off such a murder without being caught.

Just for the fun of it, I did some thinking in one of my newly idle moments. As always, unless I'd caught the killer standing over the body with the murder weapon still in hand, I started with one word. Why?

There are motiveless crimes, but Coyle's wasn't one of them. Just as Ana Kuzmina had done with Hector Sureda, he'd been tailed, or just as Carrie had done with me, twice. The flat in Portland Street had been kept under observation. When Coyle showed up there, he was followed inside, as Battaglia and Hector had been, with the same fatal outcome.

Having read *The Secret Policeman*, I knew that it was a sound piece of work, a little suggestive, a little titillating, but even if advance copies of the text had wound up trending on the Internet, it wouldn't have triggered a series of death threats to the author.

No, the only thing that was dangerous about it lay at the very end. It was the part about Ignacio and his parentage, and over that, I could see only two people who might be moved to silence the author, taking out Coyle by mistake.

I had an alibi, so that left only one.

The mystery was one I wasn't sure that I wanted to solve, but my curiosity has always been insatiable. I cleared a day in my diary, then drove to Edinburgh, to a big, posh art deco house at the foot of Blackford Hill.

I'd been there before, almost twenty years in the past. Back then, Alafair Drysalter wouldn't have let me in without her lawyer being present, but my retirement from the police service had been pretty well publicised, so she was more amused than alarmed when I turned up at her gate. She let me in without a moment's hesitation.

'What a . . . surprise,' she exclaimed as she met me at the door. 'I was going to say "pleasant",' she added, as we walked into a living room the size of an airport VIP lounge, 'but let's wait to see if it is. I haven't got long; I'm playing bridge with the girls at lunchtime, so, what can I do for you? Are you selling double glazing to supplement the pension?'

'Not yet, Alafair,' I chuckled, 'not yet. No, I was wondering about Mia.'

'What about her? She doesn't live here any more.' She frowned, as a memory reasserted itself. 'Wait a minute. This doesn't have to do with that questionnaire, does it?'

'What questionnaire?' I asked, all innocence.

'A thing that came through the post. There was a covering letter from a guy called Baillie. He said he was an author, researching a book, and wondered if I could help him with some information. The questions were all about you and those murders you investigated, when my brother was arrested. They asked about you, and they asked about Mia and they asked if you ever saw each other, away from her radio station.'

'How were you supposed to get the answers to him?'

'Stamped addressed envelope.'

'Did you answer the questions?'

'Yes,' she admitted, with a trace of guilt showing. 'Out of mischief, I confess. I hope it hasn't caused any bother.'

'Don't worry about it,' I told her.

'There wasn't a hell of a lot I could tell them anyway. I had no idea whether you and Mia were seeing each other back then. I was distant from all that.'

I winked at her. 'So you were.' I knew why; she'd been having an affair with a business rival of her father, and it had started a very unfortunate chain of events. 'But let's not go there.'

'No, let's not,' she chuckled.

'Did you tell Mia about this?' I continued.

'Eventually. I never had a chance until the middle of last month . . . the last time I saw her, in fact.'

'Where was that?'

'It was at a dinner she invited Derek and me to; a big charity fundraiser at a hotel up in Perthshire. Her radio station had a table. Very swish, the place was; real five star. The owner came across at one point; I got the impression that he and Mia knew each other quite well.

'I told her that night; I took the questions and the covering letter and showed them to her. In fact I left them with her; she said she might write to the guy herself.'

'Mmm,' I murmured. There are a few swish hotels in Perthshire, but my antennae were picking up signs of an impending coincidence. 'What was the place called?'

'Black Shield Lodge.'

A palpable hit. 'I've been there,' I told her. 'I've even met the owner.'

'That's a coincidence,' she remarked, without guile.

'Isn't it just.'

I left her to her lunchtime bridge with the girls. Back in the car I called Trish, our children's carer, to say that I'd be out for the rest of the day and into the evening. Then I drove to Dundee.

Black Shield Lodge is every bit as posh as Alafair had said. It's in the heart of the Perthshire countryside, it has its own golf course, its own spa and it doesn't advertise because it has no need. People gravitate to it, and through it, to its owner, for a range of reasons.

Some go because he's a very successful businessman, a multimillionaire, and because, as a result, it's necessary to be seen and known by him.

Some go because they're summoned; when he calls, they always go, because he has the reputation of being a man who doesn't take refusal kindly.

Some go because they're groupies; not the run-of-the-mill sort who follow actors, talent show survivors, and footballers, but groupies nonetheless.

I go when I choose to. That's only ever happened twice.

'This is a very unexpected invitation,' Mia said as she approached my table in the middle of the great baronial hall that is its main dining room.

'Come on,' I replied, 'we have a common interest. You kept my son from me for eighteen years, but now that I know about him, I plan to be a proper dad. If that means a civilised relationship with his mother, so be it.'

'If only you'd felt that way when he was made.'

'Hey,' I retorted. 'You never gave me a chance; you left the bloody country. You could have come back when you knew you were pregnant, but you didn't.'

'To what kind of welcome? I was running for my life, remember . . . at your suggestion.'

'With Ignacio inside you, you'd have been safe back in Edinburgh.' I held up a hand. 'Enough, though; it's history, all of it. We look forward now, agreed?'

'Agreed.' She glanced around the room. 'What made you choose the Lodge?' she asked.

'I've been here before,' I said, 'and I know the owner. In fact, he's joining us for lunch.' I glanced over her shoulder. 'Here he comes now.'

Her eyes narrowed as they followed mine, and fell upon a tanned, silver-haired man, dressed in a blue suit with silk in the fabric.

'Cameron,' I called out as he reached us, stretching out a hand. 'You know Mia Watson, I believe,' I added as we shook.

'We have met,' Grandpa McCullough admitted. 'This is a

surprise, Mr Skinner. It's unusual for me to be invited to lunch in my own restaurant.'

'My pleasure, and let's not be so formal.'

'Whatever you say, Bob,' he replied, cheerfully. 'You're a gentleman of leisure these days, I hear. Is fine dining going to be your pastime from now on?'

'It might be,' I conceded. 'I'm a director of the InterMedia group now, the owner of the *Saltire*. I could make myself its food critic.' I smiled. 'The only problem with that could be that I upset a lot of people in my former career, and you never know who's working in the kitchen.'

McCullough laughed. 'In that case, can I suggest that we all choose the same things today. The chef's Cullen Skink is superb, and he tells me that the venison casserole comes from a deer that was shot on the estate, and hung to the point of perfection.'

The head waiter was hovering, ready to be summoned. He took our orders, and then sent the sommelier across. I was driving, Mia was working later and McCullough said that he never drank alcohol before six in the evening, so he left disappointed, with 'mineral water' scribbled in his pad.

'How's my granddaughter?' McCullough asked, out of the blue, halfway through the first course. Until then we'd been talking about the weather, radio and the parlous state of Scottish rugby.

'The last I heard, she was fine,' I answered. 'She and young Haddock are very happy together. But why are you asking me?'

'I don't see her as much as I used to. As you know, I have a wildly exaggerated reputation, and she's had to distance herself from me, because of the boy's career. I've never met him, you know,' he added, as if he was trying to assure me. 'We've spoken on the phone a few times, but we've never been in the same room. Cheeky says he's doing very well in the force.'

'He is,' I confirmed, 'although we call it the service these days. Give him fifteen years and he'll be an assistant chief constable, minimum.'

'Do you still have that much influence?' Mia's quiet question cut in.

'No, I don't,' I admitted, 'but I know that once you've lit the blue touchpaper on a rocket, the rest is pretty much inevitable. That's how it is with young Sauce Haddock.'

The chef hadn't been kidding about Bambi's mother. The casserole was perfect, as he'd promised; we paid it proper respect by enjoying it in silence. It wasn't until the cheeseboard that Mia's patience gave out.

'How did you find out that we knew each other?' she asked. 'Have you been spying on me?'

I said nothing; instead I looked across the table, at McCullough. He caught on and leaned towards her. 'The police could probably tell you what brand of toilet paper I use,' he said, speaking quietly even though the next occupied table was almost ten feet away. 'Let's have coffee somewhere else.'

He rose from the table, nodded a signal to the maître d' and led the way out of the dining room along a corridor and into a small lounge that overlooked one of the greens on the golf course. He dropped into a Chesterfield chair, and seemed to expand, to loosen off as if his real personality had been corseted until then.

'You're the mother of Bob's son,' he continued, as if he'd only paused for breath. 'And you've been a very bad girl in your time. You haven't exactly brought the kid up on the straight and narrow, otherwise he wouldn't be in fucking Polmont right now. Of course he's been checking up on you.'

She turned on me. 'You've been following me?'

'He didn't have to,' McCullough laughed, amused by her indignation. 'He might not have influence any more, but he still has friends. All he has to do is reach out . . . that's the buzz phrase these days isn't it, "reach out" – and he can find things out.' He looked at me, eyebrows raised. 'Isn't that true, Bob?'

I nodded, grateful to him for sparing me the need to admit that indeed I had followed her, a week before, from his house, where I'd seen her car parked in the driveway, to her radio studio for her evening show, and then back again when it was over.

'How did you meet?' I asked.

'I own the station,' McCullough explained. 'Actually, my granddaughter does, although she doesn't know it; with hind-sight, naming her after me was a very smart thing to do, although I didn't appreciate it at the time. But I'm the Cameron McCullough they pay attention to; I don't appoint all the staff, but I like to know about the people who're our public face. I interview all our potential presenters and if they're not on my wavelength, they're not on my airwaves.'

He smiled. 'Mia was a natural. I could tell the moment I cast an eye on her. She got the job, and I got to know her. Now we're a couple. We don't flaunt it . . . especially not around the station . . . but it's no secret.'

'I see,' I murmured; actually I'd seen for a while. I don't like to go into a room with people like them without knowing the whole story in advance.

'Tell me then, Mia,' I continued, 'when you had that first call from Tommy Coyle on your programme, why did you call me and Alex, and not Cameron?'

'She did call me,' he said. 'I told her to ring you. The threat was against Ignacio; there was nothing I could do to protect him in Polmont, but you could sort it, no problem, and you did.'

'You didn't tell me about the third call, though,' I countered, my eyes still on Mia.

'What third call?'

'The one you made to Tommy Coyle, arranging to meet him in the Sheraton.'

'How did . . .' she gasped.

'Because I'm some sort of fucking genius at what I do,' I replied, blandly. 'My daughter found out who and what Coyle was; she went to see him pretending to be an author. He bought her line, but he had to cut their meeting short because he had to rush off to see a client in the Sheraton Hotel.'

I saw her flinch. 'Every time I see that place,' I went on, 'every time it's mentioned to me I have a memory flash. I go back to the nineties, to when we met, and to the first time we had coffee together, when I started to be attracted to you. The venue was your choice, and you chose the lobby in the Sheraton. It was your hangout, you explained, the place you could go where nobody would know you.

'When I got home from Spain and started to think about the Coyle murder . . . I had a motive for doing that, because it was Alex who found him, otherwise I might not have been bothered . . . the Sheraton link was like a bell in a fire station.

'So I retraced my daughter's route to Coyle, and I discovered that Linton Baillie's editor, a woman named Orpin, had another inquiry about him, just before Alex, from a Scottish-sounding woman who claimed to be a programme researcher. She said she wanted to set up a radio interview. Ms Orpin did what she did with Alex; she gave the caller Coyle's number.'

'So what?' Mia snapped defiantly. I glanced at McCullough. He was leaning forward, frowning for the first time since we'd all met up.

'When I was chief constable,' I told her, 'there was a very short chain between me and Special Branch. A lot of its job is keeping a lookout, and not only around mosques and ethnic restaurants, but at the other end of the scale, big and busy venues where people like you think they'll blend in with the crowd, and where the security isn't intrusive. Do I need to go on?'

She nodded.

'Okay, if you insist. I've been to see an old colleague, a man I put in his chair. I've seen the CCTV footage from the Sheraton and I've seen you, Mia, meeting with Tommy Coyle. Clearly it isn't a friendly conversation. What did he want?'

She looked at me, with dead eyes, and then she hissed, 'What else? Money. Twenty thousand to keep the secret about Ignacio being your son.'

'What did you tell him?'

'That I didn't have that sort of cash. He said that he was sure you did, and that he'd call me in two days to arrange a handover.'

'And the very same evening he was conveniently dead.'

'Yes, and good riddance to him, but I didn't do it.'

I stared at her and took a deep breath before going on. 'I know that,' I exclaimed, dismissively. 'You're not capable.' I turned my attention to Cameron McCullough. 'But you know a man who knows plenty of men who are. I looked at some more CCTV footage,' I went on. 'This lot was from a very obvious camera in the square outside the Sheraton. It shows Coyle leaving, on foot; then a man comes into shot, out of nowhere. He's much too cute to show his face to the camera. He's wearing a big heavy coat because it was a cold day, but,' I smiled, 'he should have worn a hat as well, for he has a very distinctive head of silver hair. He follows Coyle down Lothian Road, as far as a bus stop, and then they both get on the same bus, Coyle first.'

'I thought you were retired,' McCullough said. His tone gave no hint of what he was thinking.

'I am,' I replied, 'otherwise I'd have gone to Lothian Buses and asked to see their CCTV. They have it on their vehicles, and it's very difficult to hide from.'

I leaned back in my chair. 'But even if I could identify you, Cameron, it would prove nothing. You didn't kill Coyle either; no way would you take a risk like that.' I shook my head. 'No, this is what I think happened. Late that evening someone went to Coyle's place. He won't be on any CCTV either.

'Before he could do anything, Coyle came out. It could have been mission aborted at that point, if Tommy had got into a car, but he lost his licence nine months ago, so he took the bus, and once again he was followed. He got off in Slateford, and so did the man who was following him, but there will be no record of it, because the bus company's system isn't that good.

'He went into Portland Street, where Linton Baillie had his flat. His pursuer watched him go into a stairway, and then he probably saw the lights go on in a first-floor flat and saw Coyle, drawing the curtains. The street was very quiet that night, so nobody saw the pursuer go into the building.

'Coyle never heard him open the door, because he had the radio on by then and he was sitting in Linton Baillie's comfy chair, waiting for his date to arrive, the would-be author that he thought would be an easy touch. No, he never heard a thing, ever again.'

It was McCullough's time to hold my gaze, as he whispered, 'You really do believe you're a fucking genius, don't you?'

'I know it,' I said.

His eyes hardened. 'But you're not a cop any more.'

I relaxed in my chair and grinned at him. 'That's very true; now ask yourself this, Cameron. Is that a reassuring thought or might it be just a wee bit scary?'

I didn't give him time to answer; instead I leaned forward. 'So here's the situation,' I continued. 'I could take this to the SIO in the Coyle investigation. If I could steer my old protégé Jack McGurk in the right direction, that might be no bad thing for him. I have a hunch that in Andy Martin's new Police Utopia, everything will be measured and judged by statistics, even though we know what they say about those.

'However, even if I did that, it's long odds against Jack ever catching the bloke, and suppose he did, it's absolutely fucking impossible that he could link him to you, because any instruction will have been given at second, third or fourth hand, and your name would be nowhere near it.

'Because of all that, and because Ignacio's going to have enough to deal with when he's released, it stays where it is. Now, please, call your head waiter and let me pay for our excellent lunch.'

McCullough nodded, and reached across to a buzzer on the wall. 'You can have the staff discount,' he said.

'I couldn't accept that. Full price, please.'

'Bob,' Mia exclaimed, 'if you're not going to do anything with this theory of yours, what's all this been about? Is it just a big ego trip for you?'

'It probably is, in part,' I admitted freely, 'but there is a serious side to it. I want you both to know, just in case anyone is worried about Linton Baillie trying the same stunt, that when Tommy Coyle died, so did he. All his stuff, all his research material, that's gone too. I propose that his whole business, it ends here and now. In the absence of any counter-proposal, I'll take that as agreed.'

A door behind me opened. I gave the head waiter a credit card, without looking at the bill.

As the man left to fetch his card reader, I saw that McCullough was smiling. 'Here's something for you to think on,' he said, 'while you're heading back home. Mia and I are getting married. That means that your son will be my stepson as well. Some fucking irony, eh?'

I nodded agreement. 'In which case,' I countered, 'we'd both better steer him in the same direction.'

It occurred to me to add that if Cameron looked at Ignacio's history, he should take care to be good to his mother, but I left that unsaid. Instead I paid up, and headed down the road, back to my new, unconstrained, happy family life.

That night after a very light supper, I told Sarah all about my day, to the last detail.

'Did Mia think that Coyle and Baillie were one and the same?' she wondered.

'I didn't ask her,' I confessed. 'However, if she thought that paying him off would have stopped publication, it suggests she did. I couldn't leave it to chance, though.'

'Hence your warning to the pair of them. To protect Ben McNeish, I take it?'

'Yes, although he's no threat to our boy any more. He's safe in Polmont, and the secret won't be a secret for long. I'm going to give June Crampsey a *Saltire* exclusive on the day he's released.'

'Will there be problems, with Ignacio being under McCullough's influence?' she asked.

'It'll always be less than mine,' I said. 'I'll make sure of that.'

'Good luck with that one,' she replied. 'You've only known the kid for a few months. You're both starting from scratch.

'By the way,' she added as I pondered the truth of her observation, 'that came for you in the mail, when you were on the golf course.' She pointed to a letter in a pale blue envelope, lying on the coffee table.

I picked it up. As I opened it a card fell out, but I let it lie as I took out a single sheet, unfolded it, and saw a clear, handwritten script. There was no heading, only the date. I began to read, murmuring the words aloud:

Dear Bob

This is a blast from the past. I hesitate to contact you on the basis of a brief acquaintanceship; indeed I hope you remember me. However, a certain problem has arisen in my life and I need advice in dealing with it. I wonder if you might be available, in your new status, for consultation on a professional basis.

If you are interested, please call me on the number enclosed.

I laughed out loud. 'My God, not another,' I exclaimed.

Then I saw the signature: a tide of memories flowed into my mind, and swept me away.

One

I've never felt more positive than I did when I left home that day for the start of my working week; I was the new Bob Skinner, new career, new attitude, new life; I'd turned a corner.

A couple of months before, I'd been in a proper mess, in such a confused state of mind that I'd taken myself off to Spain to sort myself out, and to try to shape a new life plan.

One exciting road trip with a friend was all it had taken. A different environment, a new challenge, and a satisfactory solution to a seemingly insoluble problem, and I felt that I was back in shape. When our journey was over, I had made a clear decision to walk away from the police service, for good. I even had a new job, part-time, one that was ideally suited to a man of my talents and experience.

Best of all, for the first time in years I had a secure and happy home life. I was reunited with my ex-wife Sarah, the mother of two of my five kids. Although she still had her own house in Edinburgh, we were spending more and more time *en famille* in Gullane.

Okay, my oldest son was a few months into a prison sentence, and his mother was about to marry a gangster, but isn't it true that perfection can lead too easily to complacency?

I had set out that morning to spend some time in my office. The new employment? I am a director of a Spanish company, InterMedia, of which my friend Xavi Aislado is chief executive. It owns the *Saltire* newspaper in Edinburgh, but that's only a small piece of its portfolio of online and printed newspaper titles, plus radio and TV stations, across Spain and Italy. It's a real job; I have independent oversight of all group investigative activity, and I instruct young journalists on developing relationships with police that do not rely on brown envelopes changing hands.

Contractually it's on a one day a week basis, but in practice I contribute more than that. I have a base in the *Saltire* building in Fountainbridge, and I share a secretary with June Crampsey, the managing editor.

That's where I was headed on the Monday it all kicked off. I planned to spend the morning finalising a training manual I'd written, preparing it for translation into Spanish, Catalan and Italian, before moving on to a working lunch with an old acquaintance.

He had contacted me a couple of weeks earlier, asking for my help with what he had described only as 'a certain situation'. It had taken that long for him to find time to meet me, so I assumed that whatever it was, it couldn't be too pressing.

Before she left for work that morning, Sarah asked me to do her a favour. 'Honey, I have a sudden, uncontrollable craving,' she confessed, 'for Marks and Spencer lemon drizzle cake. I woke up with it this morning; it must be the effect of reading Mary Clark's book. I don't have time to pick one up on the way in, and I'm not sure when I'll be finished, so . . . would you be a love and call in there on the way to the office?'

What Sarah wants Sarah gets . . . it wasn't always that way, I confess . . . although I was still wondering about 'uncontrollable cravings' as I cruised into the Fort Kinnaird shopping mall, and parked as close as I could to M&S.

Its food store is always busy, even at nine fifteen on a Monday morning: when I reached in and grabbed the last lemon drizzle cake from the rack, I beat a blue-rinse matron to the punch by less than a second. She glared at me, as if she expected me to hand it over. I smiled and shook my head.

'Sorry,' I said, 'but my future happiness may depend on this.'

She sniffed, and gave me another long look. It told me wordlessly that if I died in utter misery she wouldn't give a damn, and allowed me to go to the quick checkout without a single fragment of guilt.

I paid and went back to my car, laying the precious confection, in its five-penny bag, on the front passenger seat. Before starting the engine, I called Sarah via Bluetooth.

'Got it,' I told her, 'although I had to fight for it.'

'I'll bet,' she chuckled. 'Those cakes go like crazy.'

'So, this craving of yours . . .' I ventured. 'Should I read anything into that?'

'No, you should not,' she replied, still with a smile in her voice. 'As if . . .'

'Why not?' I said. 'We have an extra room in Gullane.'

'Which we could need this year,' she countered, 'when Ignacio comes out of the young offenders place.'

She had a point. Ignacio is the teenage son I never knew about until we met last year in Spain, by which time his reckless mother, Mia, had allowed his life to become seriously fucked up; he was going to need a secure roof over his head, and I did not want it to be hers. She was about to marry a man named Cameron 'Grandpa' McCullough, a millionaire Dundee businessman, whose legitimate enterprises had been built with cash laundered from serious organised crime. Better coppers than I had tried to put Grandpa in jail, but none had ever succeeded.

Initially, I had decided not to visit Ignacio in prison; my reasoning was that he'd be endangered if he was revealed as the offspring of a very senior cop. However, a few months into his sentence, I realised that we could waste no more time bonding, and a cooperative governor had allowed us private meetings, away from the open hall where routine visits took place.

'He and I will discuss that next week,' I told Sarah, 'but you have a point. See you tonight.'

I ended the call, and turned on the engine, letting it warm up for a few seconds. With my foot on the brake, I slipped the lever from P for Park, into R for Reverse, then checked my mirrors, all three of them, and the screen that shows the view from my car's reversing camera.

Satisfied that all was clear I began to reverse out of my space, slowly. I had travelled no more than a yard when, on the edge of my vision, I saw it coming, a red car travelling towards me at a speed that was way too high for a shopping mall park.

I braked, instantly, but it was too late; the idiot, a man in a hoodie, I registered, caught the nearside corner of my rear bumper, bounced off it sideways, into the middle of the narrow carriageway and stopped, just in time to avoid hitting a Grand Cherokee that was coming in the other direction.

The law is imperfect; whatever the constitution may declare, there are occasions where there is indeed an assumption of guilt, and that situation was one of them. I'd driven with due care and attention, yet I was well aware that insurance companies, and all too often the courts, take the view that the reversing driver is in the wrong, automatically. When I was a chief constable, I instructed my traffic officers that every incident should be approached with an open mind, but those damn insurers paid no attention.

My car, a nice silver Mercedes, was less than six weeks old, yet there it was with damage to its rear end, thanks to some clown who didn't know the difference between a shopping centre car park and Brands fucking Hatch . . . and chances were, the bloody insurers were going to pin the blame on me!

Worst of all, the bag on the passenger seat had hit the gear lever, bursting it open and smashing Sarah's precious lemon drizzle cake. That lit my fuse; I'd been a happy family man, joking with the love of my life, only to become, in the space of a few seconds, an explosion waiting to happen.

I popped my seat belt and stepped out, ready to do battle with the stock car driver in the red car; it was a BMW, I noticed, with a few years on the clock. I was ready for whatever story the bloke came up with, ready for a confrontation, ready to blow him out.

I waited for him to climb out and face me. To my surprise, he didn't; instead he began to move forward, blasting his horn at the Grand Cherokee that was blocking the roadway, as if the sound could push it backwards. The big jeep didn't move. Its lady owner sat behind her steering wheel, looking bewildered and a little frightened.

Giving her a wave and a sign that I hoped she would read as 'Stay where you are', I moved towards the Beamer. Its driver, seeing no way forward, started to reverse, but got no further than a couple of yards before slamming hard into a Mini that had come to a halt behind him. He was trapped; no escape route.

We made eye contact as I advanced on him. I saw a thin, sharp, youngish Caucasian face within the hood, eyes narrowed.

I guess he saw a tall, angry, grey-haired bloke in a dark suit, white shirt and blue tie.

My view of him lasted for only a couple of seconds, for as long as it took a cloud that had obscured the low winter sun to pass by, and for a ray of light to hit the red car's windscreen, reflecting into my eyes and blinding me momentarily.

I took a couple of steps to my left to escape it; by the time my vision had cleared the man was out of his car and legging it across the park. I gave a moment's thought to chasing him, but abandoned the idea, for he was moving like a bat out of hell. I still go out running along the coastline in front of my house, but I never was a sprinter. I knew that he had too big a start, plus he had at least twenty-five years on me.

Instead I walked round to the Mini. Its bonnet had been crunched, and its engine had stopped, probably stalled on impact. The driver was also a lady, but older than the Grand Cherokee's pilot. She was white haired and in her seventies, I guessed.

She was shocked. She stared straight ahead, heavily veined hands grasping her wheel, so tightly that her knuckles showed bony white.

'What the hell was that all about?' a voice demanded. Grand Cherokee woman, a striking redhead in her thirties who could have been modelling her M&S clothes, had overcome her initial scare and stood behind me.

'You know as much as I do,' I replied. 'This thing,' I nodded towards the BMW, 'hit me, and the driver legged it.'

'Why would he do that?' she asked.

'My best guess,' I told her, 'is that this is stolen, probably from this car park. Look, do me a favour,' I added. 'Will you take care of the old lady? She's had a hell of a fright and might need medical assistance. If you do that I'll call for help and alert site security.'

She nodded and stepped up to the Mini's driver door, while I dug out my phone. I have the police communications centre number stored. I retrieved it and pressed the onscreen button.

'This is Bob Skinner, formerly chief constable,' I told the civilian operator who answered. 'I'm in the Fort Kinnaird car park, close to T K Maxx and M&S. There's been a traffic incident involving my car and two others. The driver of one of them, registration,' I glanced at the plate, 'Charlie Oscar Sierra One Echo, has fled the scene on foot. White male, twenties, slim, medium height, wearing a grey hoodie and blue jeans. I suspect vehicle theft; either that or he's uninsured, and just panicked. I need police attendance, and paramedics for a third driver, an elderly lady who looks to be in shock, after the so-and-so drove into her vehicle.'

'Officers and an ambulance will be with you as soon as possible, Mr Skinner,' the man replied. 'You'll need to remain at the scene yourself.'

'I know that, pal,' I snapped: my temper was still on a hair trigger. In fact, I couldn't have gone anywhere even if I'd wanted to, for our little section of roadway was blocked at either end by the redhead's off-roader and the old dear's damaged car.

Pocketing my phone, I turned to the BMW once again. The driver's door was open and the engine was still running. I walked round, leaned inside and turned it off, using a handkerchief to twist the key and touching nothing else. As I did so I could see my own car through the windscreen. As I had expected there was a dent in the corner, but it looked drivable.

Backing out, I took a longer look at the red saloon. The personalised number gave no clue to its age, but from the dullness of its paintwork and its boxy lines, I judged that it had to be at least ten years old. For sure, 'COSIE', its personalised plate, was worth more than the car itself.

'So why steal it?' I murmured to nobody in particular. 'Not just for the number surely . . . unless the guy's a total idiot, for that only has value to the registered owner.'

I moved slowly around the vehicle, inspecting its damage. The collision impact on the front nearside wing was less than that on my Merc: old steel versus modern plastic, I imagined. There was a scratch along the side, the kind a vandal might leave with a key or a nail, but it was the rear end that had been most affected by the shunt. A light cluster was smashed, and the boot was distorted, its catch shaken loose.

I took out my handkerchief again, wrapping it round my fingers before giving the metal a firm push. But the lock didn't take; instead the lid swung slowly upwards, opening fully and revealing what was inside.

In the moment that I saw it, I jumped backwards, my reactive scream muffling itself in my throat.

A child stared up at me, a little girl. She looked to be around the same age as my younger daughter, Seonaid. Her eyes were wide, and her mouth was open too, as if she was as startled by me as I was by the sight of her. She was dressed in a tartan skirt and a blue quilted jacket. Beneath, she wore a sweatshirt with a cartoon penguin on the front, the type of garment that has taken the place of a blazer in many schools.

I reached into her place of containment and touched her cheek, as gently as I touch Seonaid's sometimes, when she's asleep, but I didn't need to feel the coldness against my fingertips to know that the poor little innocent was dead.

I couldn't put a number to the crime scenes I've visited over a thirty-year police career, or to the number of victims of violence I've stood over.

Latterly, I was involved in a couple of really bad ones; they got to me in a way that others hadn't, and made me vow to walk away, to leave the bloody aftermath to others while I could still feel some compassion for the dead, before I became as dehumanised as they were.

I never quite managed that as a serving officer, not even as a chief constable, but as a civilian, that day in that car park, I did something I'd never done before. I buried my face in my hands, so that nobody could see my tears.

That's how I was standing when the cops arrived.

Two

I suppose that an objective observer looking at my career might say I did all right for myself, but I see it differently. I was okay until a few years ago, and then it all went south.

My problem was that I found myself in a job for which I was totally unprepared, and temperamentally unsuited. Most of my police service, from detective sergeant up, was spent in major criminal investigation. I was a specialist, not an all-rounder.

In my final years I was in a position to take myself out of that; as chief constable of my force, and before that as deputy chief, I could have positioned myself well away from CID.

Sir James Proud, my predecessor in the top office in Edinburgh, was a career administrator. I could have followed in his footsteps and played it his way; if I'd been any good at the job, I would have done that very thing.

But I'm not Jimmy, nor could I ever have been like him. I had no background in the things that he did well, nor any aptitude for them, and that was a problem, for those were the skills that had made him such an outstanding chief police officer.

In my heart, I'd known this. I had resisted, until the very last minute, the pressure that was put upon me to follow in Sir

James's footsteps, pressure applied subtly by the man himself, more overtly by friends and colleagues, and most forcefully of all by she who was my wife at the time.

They meant well, all but one of them. I didn't know it then, but out of all my boosters only one person had her own interests at heart, rather than mine. That's one of a few reasons why Aileen de Marco and I aren't married any more.

My ego won over my common sense; in truth that was never a contest. When Jimmy announced his impending retirement, I put my name forward and I was anointed, as Chief Constable Robert Morgan Skinner, QPM.

So there I was, sat in the big chair, I had all that silvery braid on the uniform that I'd always hated wearing, and I had all the power in my hands, with a few thousand people, cops and civilians, under my command. And most of it bored me bloody rigid.

I was lousy at the job. Nobody said so then, and nobody's said so since, but I know it. As soon as I was properly away from it and could look back objectively I could see that I'd got almost everything wrong.

I made appointments on instinct, without proper consideration, decisions that my head of human resources would have advised me against had I bothered to consult her, as Jimmy Proud always did.

I allowed myself to get sucked into a battle with the politicians, my wife among them, over the creation of a single Scottish police service. It was a proposal by government that I was dead against, and the argument was public and divisive. Inevitably, with little or no political support I lost the fight and, with it, my marriage . . . not that the latter was worth saving.

My old mentor, Sir James, was as opposed to a single force as me, but he would never have tackled it as I did. He would have played its proponents quietly, identifying any divisions in their approach and exploiting them until they fell into line with his thinking without ever realising that they'd been steered in that direction.

But all that said, it wasn't really the battle for the future of the service that derailed me as a chief constable. I'm a pragmatist; let others create the framework and I can work within it. No, my biggest problem was that when it came to the parts of the job that I loved, I could not delegate to save my life; I could not look at a major criminal investigation and stand aloof from it.

Don't get me wrong when I say this, for Jimmy Proud, an Edinburgh toff by upbringing, made a point of getting to know every square yard of his territory, down to the very roughest, but he was always content to leave the messiest part of the job to those of us who were good at it. He had no CID background and he would only ever appear at the scene of a homicide if one of our own had fallen.

Me? I couldn't keep away. When I became chief I had the best head of CID in the country and some of its best detectives, and yet I was all over them, looking over their shoulder in everything they did. I was rarely called to the scene of a major incident and yet I hardly missed one, not even the open-and-shut domestic homicide cases.

I should have known that my constant presence was undermining the people who were supposed to be in charge, but it didn't occur to me. I'm sure they felt it, but they were my friends, not mere subordinates. If they found the situation difficult, they'd have been reluctant to say so.

All the same it might have come to that, if a sudden act of violence hadn't catapulted me from Edinburgh to the place I'd said I'd never go, Glasgow, and into the chief constable's office in the massive Strathclyde force. Unification was on the way, but Scotland's largest constabulary needed a chief to see it out of existence. Sure, I could have turned that job down too, but the Skinner ego really was out of control by then.

It all came to an end when I found out about Ignacio, the Spanish-born teenage son I never knew I had. He's the product of a one-night stand back in the nineties, with a woman named Mia Watson, who had a very shady family background. She had to leave Scotland in a hurry shortly after our encounter, and she didn't come back until she was in even more trouble than she'd run away from. Unfortunately she landed Ignacio right in the middle of it, and that's why he's in prison now.

Ironically, his predicament was my salvation. I decided that it made my position as a chief constable untenable, and so I withdrew my name from candidacy for the leadership of the unified Scottish Police Service. I'd opposed its creation, but career-wise, it was the only show in town, and I wasn't ready at that point to chuck it.

But for Ignacio I'd have gone through with my application and I'd have been appointed. I would have taken the post and been a disaster. It would have finished me.

There has been darkness in me from my earliest days, since my childhood, when I was abused and terrorised by my beast of an older brother. I survived that, and when I was ready I overcame him, but he left his mark upon me.

Myra, my first love, shone some light into my life and gave me my precious daughter Alexis, but she had her own demons. Even if she had not been killed at the wheel of her speeding car, I doubt that our marriage would have endured.

Raising my child alone gave me no time to dwell on my past;

when the job was done Sarah came into my life and, with her, what I call my second family.

I might have put those earlier years behind me, and become a normal human being, but that's not how it worked out. I was stabbed, and almost died; in recovery I unearthed some secrets that would have been better left untouched. Subsequently I was involved in some very serious work incidents, and they took their cumulative toll.

Sarah had her troubles too, and we were heading for the rocks, when Michael, the brother I thought I'd put away forever, came back into my life through his death, reminding me of all my childhood horrors.

I was never the same after that. My humanity started to erode, I grew harder, became less kind, and behaved in all the wrong ways. I cast Sarah aside for a woman who was always wrong for me. I became difficult to work with, testing the loyalty of my colleagues. Even worse, I found it more and more difficult to live with myself, and I found myself hating the man I'd become, yet I was driven onwards by my obsession with the work that had supplanted even my children as the focus of my existence.

Then Sarah came back, and almost simultaneously I learned that I had a teenage son who'd been kept from me all of his life, and who needed me very badly at that time.

Between them, the two events forced me to look at myself, and to own up to my failures, my imperfections, my selfishness. Most of all they made me realise that I had been drowning in a well of loneliness. The greatest blessings this life can give are the people who love us, warts and all, yet for years I'd been keeping them at a distance, and in Sarah's case, I'd been pushing her away from me.

And so I put it all behind me, I set a different course, and through that I felt reborn.

It was a different Bob Skinner who stood in that car park, that morning, shocked and weeping over a dead child.

I didn't hear the officers arrive. I wasn't aware of them at all until someone grabbed my right arm and tried to put me in a restraining hold.

Shaken back into the moment, I reacted instinctively, without thinking, wrenching myself free and planting a hand in my assailant's chest, then shoving violently, sending him sprawling backwards across the roadway. It was only when I turned to face him that I saw he was a cop, a youngster, one of the new breed, probably fresh from college, and from one of those stop-and-search courses that they say don't exist.

He was scrambling to his feet and reaching for his extendable baton when a voice called out, 'Jules, hold up! Do ye no' ken who that is?'

I looked beyond him, and saw a sergeant whom I recognised from past encounters. He was called Jack Lemmon, which used to be worth a few laughs, until his old actor namesake died.

'But Sarge,' the PC protested, 'do you know what's in that car?' The boy was rattled; I doubted that he'd ever been near a body in his brief service.

Discover the highly acclaimed Bob Skinner series by

Quintin
Jardine

Find out more about Edinburgh's toughest cop at
www.quintinjardine.com